THE LONG WAY HOME

As the only daughter of a wealthy and indulgent father, Lydia Middleton faces a bright future, secure in the knowledge that her childhood sweetheart, David Drayton, will one day be her husband. When Mr Middleton loses his fortune and then his life, the Draytons swiftly reconsider and Lydia's uncle repossesses the family home. Lydia decides to accompany her brother to Middlesbrough but she promises herself that, one day, she will return to exact a fitting revenge on her uncle. Lydia prospers but risks losing David, who has stayed faithful to her. Vengeance or the path of true love – which will Lydia choose?

THE LONG WAY HOME

THE LONG WAY HOME

by

Jessica Blair

Magna Large Print Books
Long Preston, North Yorkshire,
BD23 4ND, England.

British Library Cataloguing in Publication Data.

Blair, Jessica
    The long way home.

    A catalogue record of this book is
    available from the British Library

    ISBN   0-7505-1782-4

First published in Great Britain in 2001
by Judy Piatkus (Publishers) Ltd.

Copyright © 2001 by Jessica Blair

Cover illustration © Gary Day-Ellison by arrangement with Piatkus
Books

The moral right of the author has been asserted

Published in Large Print 2002 by arrangement with
Piatkus Books Ltd.

Magna Large Print is an imprint of Library Magna Books Ltd.

Printed and bound in Great Britain by
T.J. (International) Ltd., Cornwall, PL28 8RW

29356547

JOAN

for you departed

I reach out,
But you aren't there.
I hear a whisper,
I turn,
But you aren't there.
You are gone,
I am lost.
Wait for me.
Wait.

'I will wait.
I am here
But you are there.
You will come,
I will be here.
We will touch.
Together,
Beyond the end of time.
Our love
For eternity.'

Chapter One

Lydia put down the fourth monthly part of *David Copperfield* with regret that she had finished it. The publishers had planned that this novel by the popular author, Charles Dickens, would continue through the remaining four months of 1849 and into 1850, so she looked forward eagerly to the next instalment, trying to anticipate its developments.

As she rose from her chair and walked to the window her mind was full of sympathy for Copperfield and the tragedies life had dealt him. But when she reached the window the story was cast to the back of her mind for from her room among the new houses high on Whitby's West Cliff she had a view which always moved her, or had these last three years at least since she was seventeen, the age when an appreciation of her surroundings had begun to play a part in her young life.

The sun this late-August afternoon flamed the red-tiled roofs of Whitby's east side where the houses, crowded one on top of the other, climbed the cliff. She could see the gaunt outline of the ruined Norman abbey on the cliff top where tomorrow afternoon she would ride with David Drayton. It had become a regular Friday activity for them since Easter, as it had done last year.

Their respective families approved of the

friendship, seeing a future marriage between them as forging a closer alliance between two mercantile businesses in Whitby's thriving port. Lydia knew this but kept her own counsel. She liked David a great deal and enjoyed his company, but did she love him? He had become a handsome twenty-one year old, standing just over six foot tall. His angular jaw gave him the appearance of a man who loved a challenge, and in Lydia he'd found a tempting one, for she always rebuffed his more amorous advances, desiring for now at least to keep their relationship to one of close friendship only.

David respected her wishes but went on telling himself that one day he would marry this pretty girl with hazel eyes and silky hair which shimmered like the peat-brown waters of a bubbling moorland stream. He knew that behind the pleasant, vivacious exterior there was a stubborn streak to Lydia, and this conflict in her nature he found unusual and appealing.

So he went on being attentive, escorting her to parties with friends, to the plays occasionally held in the Freemasons' Tavern, to lectures held by the Literary and Philosophical Society, and to other functions in the town, making no secret of his admiration and affection for her.

As she stared thoughtfully from the window Lydia acknowledged to herself that life with David Drayton would be comfortable, she'd want for nothing, since one day he would inherit his father's company. And the time would come when she, in her own right, would inherit a share in her own father's business together with her brother, Luke.

She pursed her lips. Should she agree to what both families saw as an ideal match, hold back no longer? Maybe tomorrow when they rode along the cliff top she would speak to David and embark upon a new stage in her life...

Lydia's reverie was interrupted by a loud rapping on the front door which resounded through the house. The sound alarmed her with its urgency and persistence. She ran out on to the landing and heard a maid's footsteps scurry across the hall below. Stepping close to the banister rail she looked down and saw the alarmed girl open the front door wide.

'Mr Middleton, is he at home?' The words were spoken with such compelling force that the maid could only splutter something unintelligible. 'Quick, girl, is he?' The man stepped past her as if he would find out for himself, but she outmanoeuvred him and scampered towards the drawing-room door. He followed, paused while she knocked and opened it, then was into the room before the maid could make any announcement.

Lydia started for the stairs. She had recognised the man as Julian Briggs whom her father employed as clerk in the small office near the harbour from which he conducted his business. Briggs was usually calm and steady in even the most exacting circumstances. This unusual agitation must presage a major catastrophe.

She started down the stairs then stopped. In her haste to retreat, the maid had failed to close the door properly and Lydia overheard Briggs's shattering announcement.

'Sir, the *Mary Anne* has been lost!'

'What?' Tristram Middleton gasped in disbelief.

'Merchantman, the *Aurora*, bound for Newcastle, put in with the news. *Mary Anne* went down in a storm off the French coast. The *Aurora* tried to help but couldn't get near.' Briggs's voice broke as he added, 'I'm sorry, sir.'

There was total silence, the house filled with the stillness of tragedy. Earlier today her father had spoken of his high hopes for a successful trading voyage. Now disaster had blighted those hopes.

'Total number of lives lost?' Tristram asked weakly as he anticipated the worst.

'All hands, sir.'

There was a heavy silence again then Lydia heard her father's muttered words of dejection. Though the loss of the *Mary Anne* and its cargo of Spanish wine and lace would hit him hard financially, she knew that the fact there were no survivors counted far more with him. Each member of the crew was personally known to him, he'd seen to that, believing that friendly and sympathetic relations with his crew members made for loyalty and good work. She realised that he would suffer anew with each meeting with the men's families, the wives, mothers, fathers, brothers, sisters and sweethearts of each sailor who had perished and now lay in a watery grave.

The men's voices became more distinct and Lydia could follow their conversation.

'Is there anything I can do, sir?'

12

'Thank you.' Her father's voice was firmer now. She pictured him squaring his shoulders, subduing his own sense of shock so as not to appear weak in the eyes of his employee. 'I'd like a list of the crew and the addresses of their nearest relatives. I'll have to visit them.'

'Yes, sir. I'll get that ready for you.'

'Thank you. I'll be at the office shortly.'

'Very good, sir.'

Lydia watched her father accompany Briggs to the front door.

'I'm sorry you had to be the bearer of such bad news.'

'So am I, sir.' The clerk tightened his mouth to a grim line. He gave his employer a deferential nod and left the house.

Tristram closed the door. When he turned, Lydia saw his shoulders slump. His face was grave and his footsteps dragged as he started across the hall.

It hurt her to see her father like this. She wished she was able to reassure him that things were not as bad as they seemed, but she couldn't. All she could do was offer comfort and sympathy and give him her unstinting support in the difficult days ahead.

Her footsteps, tripping quickly down the stairs, drew Tristram's attention. Seeing his daughter, he tried to disguise the despair which had settled on him, but realised it was too late. He could not fool Lydia, he knew from her expression that she had heard everything.

His heart filled with sorrow to think that even she, the daughter he loved so much, would feel

13

the harsh effects of what happened so far from Whitby. He held out his arms as if to shield her from the harsh realities of the world, rather than to seek comfort from her.

'I'm so sorry, Father,' she said, her voice full of sympathy.

She was in his arms. They hugged each other, finding reassurance in their closeness. He held her for a few moments, controlling his feelings while he struggled to find a way of breaking even more catastrophic news to her.

Slowly he released her, placed his arm round her shoulders and led her gently to the drawing room.

'Father, I know it will be hard for you to visit the families of the missing men, but if it will help I'll come with you,' Lydia offered.

He smiled wanly. 'That is kind of you. You will be a great support and comfort to me, I'm sure.'

'I know Luke would do the same if he were here.'

'I'm sure he would.'

'He will be devastated when he hears the news.'

Tristram nodded. 'No doubt word will reach the iron workings before he leaves.' He changed his mind about revealing the extent of the tragedy now. It would be better to break the news when both his children were home. 'I think we should go and get this unpleasant task over.'

As they made their way to the older parts of the town, they sensed that Whitby had already taken on the mantle of mourning. The usual bustle of a busy working port was absent. Orders were toned down; people going about their daily lives spoke in hushed tones when they could not stay silent. Even the children, usually raucous in their play, were muted, their enthusiasm curbed by watchful mothers or stifled by an inbred understanding of the tragedy that can strike any port that sends its men to face danger on the sea.

Well known in the town as the owner of the *Mary Anne*, Tristram Middleton received sympathetic glances from those who knew him by sight, brief words from those who were more familiar with him.

The Middletons had become a respected family in Whitby after moving there from Pickering, a market town sixteen miles inland across the wild North Yorkshire Moors. Tristram's father, John, had built up a successful merchant's business in the market town but had seen better opportunities in the growing port and moved his wife and two sons there when Tristram was five and his brother Nathan seven. Through perspicacity, good judgement and a little luck linked with a likeable personality, John had prospered. When his wife died the firm and his two sons became the be all and end all of his life. He found it trying at times to be both father and mother to two growing boys and many times wished he had his wife's help still to tame the harsh, sometimes vicious streak in Nathan which frequently brought him into conflict with his gentle younger brother. Nathan had an adventurous streak, was daring to the point of irresponsibility, and would cruelly mock the more cautious Tristram.

15

John found in his eldest son a sharp brain and an eager desire to shoulder responsibility within the family firm when he came of age. He had a flair for trading and, because of the adventurous side of his nature, sometimes secured business which even his father would have thought twice about soliciting.

Tristram, on the other hand, liked to play safe, which cast him always in the shadow of his brother.

It therefore came as a shock to both of them, though for different reasons, when their father's will was read to them by Whitby's leading attorney, Abraham Marsh, after John's funeral had taken place at the old parish church high on the East Cliff close to the ruined abbey.

Mourners eager to resume their normal routine and escape the chill wind which brought with it the threat of rain briefly commiserated with Nathan and Tristram and their families, and hastened from the cliff top. Closer friends came to the house on the west side where John had lived his brief married life and afterwards in his widower's state. His many virtues were mentioned in hushed tones by those who had known him well. Nathan and Tristram graciously accepted their comments, comforted by the knowledge that their father had clearly possessed considerable standing in the eyes of many in Whitby.

Once the mourners had left, the two brothers and their wives settled themselves with the attorney in what had been John's study. He had conducted most of his business from this room, leaving his clerk to handle the finer details from the harbourside office.

Nathan smiled in satisfaction as he settled himself in a comfortable armchair. He could see himself continuing to run the firm from this very room. Though he had little time for his brother, whom he personally considered weak, he would no doubt have to continue to employ Tristram. Well, he would tolerate his continued presence so long as his brother did not interfere in the new schemes Nathan was already hatching.

As Abraham Marsh intoned praises for the way John had clearly formulated his assets, making it easy to draw up a will respecting all his wishes, Nathan had a hard job curbing a desire to tell the attorney to get on with it. Tristram comforted himself with the knowledge that their father had obviously been well liked; he barely speculated about what might be coming his way. He was sure his father would have left him provided for while leaving the future control of the business in Nathan's hands. The prospect did not dismay Tristram.

'And so I come to the will itself,' the attorney continued. 'It is fairly simple and straight-forward.' He cleared his throat, casting a quick glance over the four people before him, dressed in deepest black, who waited to hear the bequests which would shape their futures. '"I leave to my grandchildren, Nathan's daughter Isobel and his son Christopher, the sum of two hundred pounds apiece. I leave the same amount to Tristram's children, Lydia and Luke. I thank them dearly for the joy they have brought me."'

There were murmurs of satisfaction that John had seen fit to acknowledge his love for his grandchildren. "'I also thank my two daughters-in-law for being kind to me, especially in my loneliness after Martha died. To each of them I leave the sum of three hundred pounds.

"'I deliberated for some time as to how I should disperse the rest of my assets and after considerable thought have decided what would be most beneficial to Nathan and Tristram, both of whom, in their different ways, have been good and dutiful sons to me.

"'I leave all my properties, a list of which is appended, to my son Nathan, provided he and his family shall agree to reside in number sixteen Bagdale.'"

This announcement brought a sharp gasp from Nathan for he had expected to take over this house, his father's residence. He exchanged a sharp glance with his wife who raised her eyebrows in surprise.

"'My son Tristram shall be allowed to live rent-free in my own residence, number twenty-one St Hilda's Terrace, for the duration of his life. Upon his death the property shall revert to his brother Nathan or his heirs. I also bequeath to Nathan the sum of three thousand pounds.

"'To Tristram I leave two thousand pounds plus all the assets of the business known as John Middleton, Merchant.'"

This information brought an even louder gasp from Nathan. All his expectations of assuming his father's mantle in the business were destroyed with those few words. 'It can't be true,' he pro-

18

tested. A quick glance at his brother showed that Tristram too was surprised and he knew without a doubt there had been no conniving with his father which he could use to invalidate the will.

The attorney gave Nathan a disapproving look. 'I assure you it is quite true, Mr Middleton. I did not come here to read false statements.' Nathan smarted under the rebuke, mouth set grimly. 'May I go on?' Abraham Marsh turned to the will again.

'"I do this against the probable expectations of both my sons and feel it is only right I should furnish an explanation as to why I divide my assets in this way. Tristram does not possess the business acumen of his brother, but I believe, given the chance, and based upon the solid foundation I have laid, he can continue the success of John Middleton, Merchant."' The attorney ignored a contemptuous grunt from Nathan. '"I am sure that with the money I have left him my eldest son will be able to establish his own concern. I hope the two businesses will be run in a spirit of friendly competition rather than rivalry. Signed, John Middleton, and witnessed by Abe Dickinson and Tom Heathcote this day 12th August 1843."'

In an atmosphere that was heavy with surprise and disbelief the attorney saw Nathan's face darken with anger. He knew the eldest son had expected to take control after his father's death, and not without reason given his own hard work and the custom of favouring the eldest son. But such practices were not always followed in wills. Abraham had seen many similar situations and often they had led to family rifts. He could see John's thinking. Tristram was the more likeable person, but easygoing, someone who needed responsibility thrust upon him to develop a latent talent. That would never have happened with Nathan in control; he would not have allowed it but kept his brother strictly in his own shadow.

'Well, gentlemen, that is all.' Abraham broke the stunned silence, and provoked an angry outburst.

'The bloody sod!'

Abraham started, frowned and glared at Nathan. 'Do not speak ill of your father.' The words were heavy with reproof but Nathan was impervious to that.

'He must have been out of his mind to expect this nitwit to keep the business thriving!' His mouth tightened in disgust. 'After all I've put into it, *this* is how I'm repaid.' He turned a contemptuous gaze on his brother. 'You played your cards right!'

'This is as much of a surprise to me as it obviously is to you,' returned Tristram quietly.

'So you say,' sneered Nathan. He rose from his chair and looked hard at Abraham. 'Get the funds sorted out quickly and lodge my share with my bank.' He looked back at Tristram, his eyes narrowed. 'Don't expect any future favours from me, and don't come crawling to me for help when you start to make a mess of things, as you certainly will.' Then, without so much as a 'good day', he headed for the door, flinging over his shoulder as he did so, 'And remember, this house reverts to me and mine so your family needn't get too comfortable in it.' He slammed the door behind him.

Tristram watched him go with no sense of triumph. In fact, he felt pity. He knew how badly disappointed his brother was, and inwardly wondered at the wisdom of his father's decision.

Little passed between the brothers during the next six years. Tristram had seen Nathan prosper quickly, using his inheritance to good effect to create a business which would have elicited their father's admiration.

Now, as Tristram walked through Whitby with a heavy heart, he wondered what his father would have thought of his handling of the family firm.

The next two hours were agony for him. He was lost for words to comfort the families who had lost someone on the *Mary Anne* and faced a future without a husband, son or father, the breadwinner snatched from them by the angry sea. He was thankful for Lydia's support. She was able to express their heartfelt sorrow even without speaking, for her eyes could speak volumes. The mourners appreciated a look or a gesture of sympathy from the owner's daughter whom they all knew, some having seen her grow from a gangling schoolgirl into the pretty, vivacious young woman she was today. The younger ones, while 'knowing their place', saw her as a friendly lass with a ready sense of fun when she accompanied her father on sailing days or watched his ship return to the safety of her home port.

As they trudged homeward with steps as heavy as their hearts, duty done, Tristram realised that a little money would ease the immediate burden of those who had lost someone. How he wished he could help but the future looked equally grim for him.

When they reached home an anxious Luke was waiting for them. 'Father, I'm so sorry.' His eyes and voice betrayed how shocked he felt. 'I came straight home when I heard.'

'Thanks, son. We've been to see the families who...' Tristram's voice faltered.

'I wish I had been here to go with you.'

'I know, but you had your work.'

'I'll get Maggie to make us some tea,' said Lydia. She headed for the kitchen while Tristram and Luke went into the drawing room. A few minutes later she helped Maggie bring in the heavy silver service and fine bone china.

As Lydia poured she was aware that something was seriously amiss with her father. He wasn't just sad over the loss of the men, he was in despair. Something was weighing heavily on his mind. She made no comment for she sensed that he would tell them what it was in his own good time.

Tristram stirred his tea and then, still staring into his cup, replaced the spoon carefully in the saucer. He looked up slowly. 'I have something to tell you both, and then we must decide what best to do for the future.' His voice was quiet, each word spoken as if it had been the subject of careful deliberation beforehand. 'Four investments I made shortly after the *Mary Anne* sailed turned out to be bad ones. I lost heavily – in fact every penny I had invested. I did not tell you because a successful voyage by the *Mary Anne* would have meant I would just about break even.' He paused to let the full significance of their situation sink in.

'The insurance will help,' suggested Luke.

Tristram shook his head and looked frankly at his son. 'The *Mary Anne* wasn't insured.'

'What?' Luke was astounded. That his father, usually the most careful of men, should have overlooked this was unbelievable. A sharp glance at his sister showed him that she too had grasped the enormity of the statement. 'You forgot?'

'No. I did it so that I could put the insurance money into those investments. I was assured they were sound and would bring a good quick return.'

'Oh, Father!' cried Lydia.

'Please don't condemn me,' he pleaded with tears in his eyes. The last thing he wanted was to lose the trust of his children. He needed their unwavering support and loyalty in this terrible crisis. 'I did what I thought was best.'

'We don't blame you, Father.' Lydia was quick to reassure him and offer comfort.

'How can we?' said Luke. 'How many times has the *Mary Anne* sailed without anything bad happening to her? You couldn't foresee this tragedy.'

'You weren't to know what was to happen.' Lydia was quick to lend weight to her brother's view. 'We'll work something out.'

'We won't be able to.' Both Lydia and Luke sensed doom in his tone, and tensed to receive more bad news as they waited for him to continue. 'You see, I borrowed heavily to add more money to those investments. I'm afraid I will be bankrupt.'

They stared at him in horror. This could not be true, yet there was no other reason for him to make this shattering statement.

Tristram read their shocked expressions. 'I'm afraid it's true,' he sighed. 'My creditors will take all the assets I have: the office, the warehouse, all the furnishings and contents of this house.'

'They can't!' cried Lydia. 'Not my beloved piano! It's a family heirloom.'

Tristram looked sadly at his daughter. 'I'm so sorry, but I'm afraid they will. They'll take everything to regain as much money as possible, and even that will be nowhere near what I owe.'

'But they can't take the house, it belongs to Uncle Nathan so we'll still have somewhere to live,' said Lydia, seeking some small crumb of comfort.

That was crushed by her father's next statement. 'I could go to prison.'

'Oh, no!' she gasped. 'Surely no one would seek retribution that way?'

'They wouldn't.' Though Luke made the remark as a statement it carried a note of query which he tried to dismiss as he went on, 'Your creditors will know you as an honourable man who will repay them in the future. If they put you in jail you would not be able to set about recouping their money.'

Tristram gave a little grunt of doubt. 'You never know which way people will turn.'

'There must be something we can do to help

ourselves,' said Lydia, deeply disturbed by the thought of her father in prison for debt.

'What? Who will help?' he said with a sad shake of his head. 'If I tried to borrow more, and I doubt if there is anyone who would lend me money to pay off my debts, it will only worsen the situation. I'd face an exorbitant interest rate with no assets or possible source of income.'

Lydia saw there were other thoughts disturbing him. His lips tightened as he went on. 'What I regret most is what I have done to you, my children. I'd hoped, nay, dreamed of leaving you a thriving business which you both could run. Luke was already gaining a wide experience. And you, Lydia,' he glanced at his daughter, 'I know how interested you were in it, and you showed a willingness to learn. Together you'd have made a successful team of whom I and your grandfather would have been proud. But, now...' His voice faltered. 'I've brought you nothing but poverty.' He sank on to a chair, covering his face with his hands. His whole body seemed to fold in on itself, oppressed by the collapse of his world.

Lydia was quickly on her knees beside him, taking his hands in hers and drawing them down so she could look into his eyes with an expression of love to combat the guilt he was feeling.

'Father, you've given us your love and that is more important than anything.' She glanced at Luke who had also come to kneel beside him. 'We love you and nothing that has happened can destroy that.'

'We'll be here for you,' added her brother. 'Whatever we can do to help, we will. I earn only a little but it can go towards necessities.'

Tristram nodded. 'Thank you, Luke, but I must find a way to pay...' His voice faltered as the enormity of his situation bore down upon him with unrelenting force.

It troubled Lydia to see her father like this. She knew that behind the easygoing exterior there was a proud man who would take this reversal hard. But worse even than the loss he had suffered, he would have an overwhelming feeling of having let people down: the victims of the tragedy, their families, his employees, herself and Luke. He believed he had failed his own father and betrayed John's trust. She had to show him he was wrong.

Her eyes brightened as an idea occurred to her. 'Uncle Nathan!' she cried. 'He'll help!' Why she had thought of their rarely seen uncle, why he had sprung to mind when they had never directly communicated since her grandfather died, she did not know, but his name was on her lips almost before she had thought it.

Tristram gaped at his daughter in astonishment. 'What on earth gave you that idea? You know we haven't spoken in six years, ever since Father left the business to me.'

'That may be,' said Lydia, 'but he's still family. He wouldn't see his own brother go to prison for debt.' She stopped then added a little cautiously, 'Surely?'

Tristram gave a wry smile. 'You don't know your Uncle Nathan. He never had any love for me even when we were boys. He'll probably delight in my predicament.'

'But you've never been in a situation like this before,' said Luke, seeing a possible way out of their dilemma in Lydia's suggestion. 'Why not go to see him? He may say no, but he may agree.'

Tristram raised his eyebrows as if to say it was a preposterous idea.

Irritated by this attitude, Lydia spoke sharply. 'If you won't go, then I will.'

He recognised the stubborn streak in her, rising to the surface. He must stop her before she took matters completely out of his hands. He would not have her or Luke suffer the humiliation of asking Nathan for help.

'No,' he protested. 'You will do no such thing!' He glanced at his son. 'Nor you, Luke. I forbid it!'

'But why, Father?' asked Lydia.

'Because I know my brother.'

'He may have changed in six years,' Luke suggested.

'Not he.' Tristram straightened. 'Now, no more of this. Forget your Uncle Nathan and let us concentrate on more practical measures which will help us to a solution. First, we will list our assets.'

They got down to practicalities but their conclusions were not encouraging and when Tristram went to bed he was a very worried man.

For a long time sleep eluded him. His mind was too preoccupied with his problems. The future was a blank. When some sort of sleep eventually came it was broken by visions of his father, openly disappointed in a son who had brought a once thriving business to the point of bankruptcy. The disgust on John's face and the accusing finger he pointed sent Tristram cowering into a dark corner in an attempt to escape. There he found his brother laughing loudly, delighted at his downfall. The noise grew louder and louder until he woke up, shouting, arms lashing out to ward off the condemnation of his father and the mockery of his brother.

It was a weary man who dressed the following morning, but by the time he walked downstairs his mind was made up. In spite of the hostile ghosts that had haunted his night, he realised in the chill of the morning that maybe they were adding their strength to Lydia's suggestion and that, for the sake of the firm and his father's memory, he should approach Nathan who surely would not want to see the family business ruined.

Lydia and Luke were already in the dining room and tried to make their morning greetings as bright and near-normal as possible. Tristram did not respond with his usual enthusiasm, meeting each day as a new adventure. Today there was a sober note in his voice. He poured himself some tea and sat down.

'Can I get you some bacon, Father?' asked Lydia.

'No, thank you,' he replied quietly, staring at his cup.

'Mrs Harrington has fried it just how you like it,' she tried to tempt him.

He shook his head. 'I'm not hungry.' He looked up and decided that the only thing to do was to inform them of his decision. 'It goes very much against the grain but I'm going to see if Nathan will help.'

'Good,' said Luke brightly. 'I believe it's the right decision. Uncle Nathan won't want to see the business Grandfather founded pass out of existence.'

'That is good news.' Lydia agreed her father was doing the right thing. 'I'm sure he'll help.'

'We'll see,' Tristram replied in a tone which showed he still had doubts. He rose from his chair, his tea untouched.

'Would you like me to come with you?' asked Luke.

'You have your work.'

'Mr Martin will understand.'

Tristram shook his head. 'Maybe, but it's important you make sure you don't jeopardise your job. No, you go to work.'

Lydia was about to suggest that she accompany her father but held back when she realised that he did not want either of his children to see him in the embarrassing role of begging his brother for help. She watched him walk from the room, his step lacking the usual briskness, his shoulders slumped under the weight of the situation. There was no final word for them as he left.

Chapter Two

'And what would it be you're dreaming of, Sean Casey?' Eileen Nolan twisted over on to her stomach so that she could lean on her elbows to catch his reaction. The sheet slipped from her

29

shoulders and her brown hair, shot with a touch of gleaming copper, fell forward over her naked breasts. Her blue eyes searched the daydreamer's face for an answer.

Sean continued to stare past her at the ceiling where he saw beckoning horizons instead of flaking distemper marked with Dublin soot and grime.

She poked him in the ribs to remind him that she had asked a question.

Slowly brown eyes, soft as suede, met hers. 'Ah, sure, your beautiful self, Eileen.' The Irish brogue rolled off his tongue softly and caressingly, trying to lull any doubts she might have about his answer. But he did not succeed.

'Away with you, Casey,' she replied, eyes sparkling with delight that she had seen through his ploy and he knew it. 'I wasn't in those thoughts. You wouldn't have held that faraway look if I had been, they'd have lingered on closer pleasures. Tell me and tell me now, what's that idle brain of yours thinking?'

'Nothing that can't be set aside for more tempting matters.' His fingers pushed aside her falling strands of hair and ran provocatively over the smooth skin of her firm breasts. His eyes danced with teasing laughter as he looked deep into hers, tempting her to forget her question.

'That's what you think, Sean Casey, but don't you believe it. You can't tempt me with anything until I know what's hatching in that brain of yours.' She saw protests spring to his lips but cut them short, eyes narrowing with suspicion. 'I hope it's not another of those wild ideas you had in the past?'

'Like emigrating to America?'

'Like emigrating to America,' she agreed.

Sean had met Eileen four years ago when they were both twenty-one. Their eyes had met across a crowded dance floor in Saint Patrick's Church Hall and from that moment their lives had come together. They could not live without each other. Being apart held no joy and within three weeks they had both left home in what was a respectable but poor part of the city, north of the Liffey. They had not gone far, having found rooms to rent in an area of similar reputation, though it was on the borders of a far worse district with rundown buildings and brawling tenants. They would have liked better but realised that in their circumstances they could not be choosey.

Their two rooms comprised one floor of what had once been an elegant eighteenth-century town house, one of a terrace built, among many others, for the elite of Dublin society by Luke Gardiner, a banker who had married well and seized his opportunity to buy land cheaply on the north side. Now the properties were of little interest to their owners, who saw them only as a source of income and did not care if they moved down the social scale to house the poorest poor like those in the near neighbourhood. There the dregs of Dublin lived, many of them driven to the towns and cities for reasons of sheer survival during the famine and now remaining there with nothing to entice them back to the land.

31

Sean's and Eileen's move was disapproved of by both families, the local priest and the tongue-wagging neighbourhood. But they considered only their passionate love for each other and were the envy of others their own age who had not the courage to go against convention.

They were ostracised by many, longer by some than others, but with their friendly, easygoing natures they soon laid the ghost of their mode of living, though the priest and some of his close supporters in the parish continued to look down their noses at them for 'living in sin'.

Sean had been in and out of jobs since he was fourteen. Born restless, he was always looking for the pot of gold at the end of the rainbow. When love hit him he regretted that he could not take Eileen to: 'The type of house you deserve, away from the impoverished side of Dublin, in one of the fashionable seaside places like Donnybrook, Blackrock or Kingstown.'

She laughed off his concern, saying, 'Houses don't matter, Sean, as long as I'm with you.' But she looked no further than Ireland. She rode the condemning looks, the snide remarks and the derogatory names she was called until they mostly ceased though there were still those, even among her one-time friends, who would have nothing to do with her.

She had quickly recognised that Sean cherished his freedom and had no desire to be tied down by marriage, at least not yet. She knew that if she wanted him she would have to 'live in sin' for the time being. He had charm, charisma, the gift of a flattering tongue that would tempt any girl. But she knew he would charm others but go no further, for without marriage ties she could walk away from any unfaithfulness and he would not want that. He loved her deeply, as much as she did him.

She did what she could to make their rundown home more comfortable though that was not easy with little money to spend except on necessities and sometimes it was hard even to get those. Jobs were not easy to come by and Sean took work here and there whenever it was available. There were too many unskilled men like him chasing too few vacancies. But they managed and lived on love, determined that their circumstances would never detract from their powerful feelings for each other.

Now his fingers ran enticingly down her spine. Eileen shivered. Sean's lips twitched in amusement, he winked, and with one arm threw the bedclothes to one side.

'No, Sean!' She eased the prohibition by adding, 'Not yet. Not until I know what's in that brain of yours.'

He was a dreamer, always coming up with ideas to make their fortune. 'Some day, my love,' he would say, 'I'll dress you in the finest clothes and parade you before the gentry of Europe. They'll envy me your beauty and flock to meet you.'

At first she'd treated his words with a frivolous response, laughter on her lips, until she'd realised there was something deadly serious behind them. She loved a man who, though a dreamer, believed that one day he would do exactly what he promised. When he changed 'the gentry of

33

Europe' for 'American society' she started to treat his ideas seriously. The prospect of travelling three thousand miles over water and then goodness knows how many on land was daunting. She was not going to go that far from home and she had told him so.

'Ah, Eileen, don't be so hasty. We'd escape this poverty and all the wagging tongues. There'd be no more disapproving glares and headshakes from Father O'Connell. We'd be far away where no one would know us.'

'Too far,' she had responded.

He had ignored this. 'And there'd be a fortune to be made. Think of it, me bonny – money. Rings on your fingers...'

'Bells on your toes to trip us up,' she had cynically interrupted.

'Now, Eileen, me love...'

She had tossed her head and snorted contemptuously. 'Don't be "loving" me, Casey.' She'd set her chin defiantly at him and fixed him with an uncompromising stare. 'No! Not America!'

He recognised the signs, and, though he dwelt on the idea for many a day, had allowed it to fade gradually from his mind.

She knew she had won – but now? What scheme was hatching in the mind of the man who lay naked beside her? His mind was filled with but two things at the moment. One she would withhold until she knew the other. She inclined her head provocatively, promising much if he answered the quizzical light in her eyes.

'Well?'

His eyes sparkled in anticipation of what would follow after he had answered her question. 'England, me love, England.'

Her look of disdain was meant to dampen his eagerness. 'You've been listening to the likes of Seamus O'Leary and Kevin Harper.'

'No, no,' Sean put in almost too hastily.

'You have and I know it,' she insisted. 'They've filled your head with...'

'...real prospects,' he finished her sentence before she could complete it. 'They say there's a fortune to be made if you're not afraid of work. And I'm not frightened of that.'

'Bend your back with a shovel in your hand?' Her voice held disbelief. 'Is that for the likes of Sean Casey?'

'If needs be.'

Eileen looked doubtful, ignoring the soft touch of his fingers as they ran persuasively up and down her spine. 'And for how long? You've never been keen to pick up a shovel here in Ireland.'

'That's as maybe. But there's more money to be made over there than there is here. And the shovel is only a means to an end.'

'I might have known.' She raised her eyebrows heavenwards as if entreating the Lord to wipe the ideas, whatever they were, from Casey's mind. 'Dreams, dreams!'

'Now don't be hasty, me love. The shovel will get me to England and I'll be able to see what other prospects there are for me there. Sean Casey won't be slow in spotting them, believe me.' He gripped her shoulders and looked hard into her eyes. 'Don't you see? This is our chance to find a new life away from here, to better ourselves. Industry's expanding on the other side of the Irish Sea, it needs workers. Seamus and Kevin have money in their pockets now, money to spare. That's more than we have. I realise America is too far from home for you. I know you didn't like the idea of leaving Ireland forever. But this is on our doorstep.'

'It isn't Ireland,' said Eileen wistfully.

'I know, but what has Ireland to offer us? Me in and out of jobs, with no chance of anything permanent, no chance to move out of this trap. Think what there might be in England.' He saw he was making no headway. There was no spark in her eyes, no current of excited anticipation in her body. 'Let's compromise,' he suggested. 'Let me go first, see what the prospects are. If there's nothing for us, I'll come home. But if I think there is a chance for us, I'll come back to fetch you, let you see for yourself and then you can decide.' He put emphasis on the role she'd have to play, using his most persuasive lilt. 'Let me give it a chance?' he urged.

Eileen hesitated. Though she was reluctant to leave Ireland she knew there was some truth in what he'd said. There were opportunities in England. She had seen evidence of it in friends who had returned on brief visits home. Had she the right to put obstacles in Sean's way, to deny him his chance? Sean was a dreamer, which was part of his attraction, and dreamers sometimes fulfilled their dreams. Might not he do the same? Who was she to stand in his way? If she did, might she not wonder, for the rest of her life, what could have been?

'Please?'

Her mind spun under the soft caress of his voice. But she was not ready to commit herself for another doubt had sprung to her mind.

'I might lose you,' she said quietly, looking down at him with troubled eyes.

His arms came round her bare shoulders. 'Never!' he cried as he pulled her to him and his lips met hers with a passion which said his love for her was unbreakable.

She returned his kiss with equal ardour, vowing her love for him would prove stronger than any temptation that came his way.

Afterwards they lay entwined in silence for a few minutes, each wrapped in the wondrous love they had shared.

'Eileen Nolan, your loving tempts me to stay,' he said quietly as he stared at the ceiling.

She did not move but replied in a hushed tone, 'It'll be even better when you return for me.'

Sean twisted over to look down at her with eyes which danced with delight at her permission to embark on a quest to change their lives for the better.

'You'll let me go?'

She nodded.

He kissed her hard. Her arms came around his neck and held him there with a kiss he would long remember.

'When will you go?' she asked quietly.

'The day after tomorrow, with Seamus and Kevin. They know the ropes when we dock in Liverpool.'

Startled, she pushed herself away from him so that she could examine his reaction the better. 'Sean Casey, you've had this planned all along,' she said sharply.

'Ah, now, mavourneen,' he said lightly as if to brush aside her objection, 'maybe I did and maybe I didn't.'

'Maybe you did is more likely.' Her eyes flashed with annoyance. 'Did you figure on leaving without telling me?'

'Maybe I did and maybe I didn't,' he repeated teasingly, his eyes twinkling with amusement at her reaction. He saw anger clouding her face then. 'Ah, come here, my sweet.' He grabbed her arm as he saw her move to slip out of bed and pulled her back towards him. 'Sure, would I be doing such a despicable thing as to leave without telling you? Would I jeopardise my chances with you forever by doing that? Of course not. But Casey likes it when you flare up, there's passion there.'

He brought her the final few inches until his lips met hers. For a moment she did not respond, but as his hands slid down her spine and round her waist she succumbed, and in their mutual giving they left each other with much to remember during their parting.

'There they are!' Sean's voice rose with excitement as, holding Eileen's hand so that they did not become separated in the crowd milling on the quay, he weaved his way towards Seamus O'Leary and Kevin Harper.

'Ah, sure, the little lady's coming with us.

38

Couldn't bear to leave her behind?' queried Seamus with a teasing grin and an added insinuating wink.

'Away wi' ye, Seamus O'Leary, I wouldn't walk the same road as you, let alone get on board the same ship,' Eileen retorted.

'Oh, she's a mite touchy,' said Seamus, cocking his head on one side. 'Annoyed that what you have to offer won't keep Sean here?'

'Why? Are you jealous you've not had it offered to you?' she snapped.

'Ah, what would I want with that when there's a host of willing lasses the other side of the water?' Seamus's eyes twinkled as he added, 'Want us to keep an eye on Sean for ye?'

'A right bollox you'd make of that.'

'She'll be telling us next she trusts ye, Casey,' put in Kevin.

'And she can,' rasped Sean.

The two men laughed in disbelief. 'Wait 'til you see what we've seen.'

'You two's all mouth,' Eileen shot at them. 'I'll bet you wouldn't know what to do if it was offered you on a plate.'

They let out a great guffaw. 'If you won't test us we'll let Sean be the judge when he gets to the other side,' teased Seamus.

Sean put his arm round Eileen's waist. 'Take no notice of these two, me darlin'. I'll have no time for their antics when I'm setting about making a fortune for us.'

'Promising ye gold, is he?' asked Kevin. 'More likely all he'll get is blisters and a thick head.'

'I thought you told him there was money to be

39

made in England?' said Eileen.

'Oh, they did,' put in Sean quickly, 'but I'll not spend it on drink and colleens, and there won't be any blisters.'

'There will from the shovels and picks, and you'll be so homesick ye'll find comfort in drink and ... you know what soon enough,' predicted Seamus.

Sean flexed his shoulders. 'Not Sean Casey. Better things await him.'

Kevin and Seamus looked at each other and raised their eyebrows. 'The great Sean Casey, still out to make his fortune,' they both said in unison.

'And he will one day,' said Eileen, wanting to spike their doubt.

Seamus and Kevin had no opportunity to respond with their glib teasing tongues. Sean cut in to change the subject as he saw Eileen beginning to seethe beneath her cool exterior. Looking around at the milling crowd, pressing towards the two steam packets lying alongside the quay awaiting passengers bound for Liverpool, he asked, 'Are all these people seeking work in England, and taking the whole family with them?'

'Good grief, no. Most of the families here will be bound for America,' explained Seamus.

'Why go via Liverpool? Why not direct to America?'

'The Coffin Ships, Sean, the Coffin Ships, remember?' said Kevin. 'There were once cheap passages direct from these shores to America but the ships they used often weren't seaworthy and were manned by inexperienced hands. Many

40

ships never reached America. Passages from Liverpool have a better reputation. They cost more but there are many willing to pay for a better chance of reaching America.'

'Most of the men on their own will be seeking work in England,' added Seamus. 'Some with the idea of making enough to take them across the Atlantic to a better life – they hope.'

'Haven't you two thought of doing that?' asked Eileen.

Seamus gave a laugh. 'Like to be rid of us, would you?' He gave a little shake of his head. 'Sorry to disappoint you, sweetheart, we're happy as we are.'

'Got your ticket?' asked Kevin, raising a querying eyebrow at Sean.

'Ticket?' He looked puzzled.

'Aye, to get aboard ship.'

'No one told me.' Sean looked around in panic.

Planks were being run out from the ships and the crowd surged forward. Passengers eager to make sure they got on board bustled each other. Angry voices rose in protest at being jostled or knocked unceremoniously by luggage. Mothers firming their grip on their children's hands screamed at them to hold tight as the crush bore down on them. Wives yelled at their husbands to do something to ease their burdens or take the strain of the bodies pressing around them.

'Where do I get one?' Sean's voice was full of anxiety as he envisaged being refused passage and having to watch the ship sail without him. That would be a tragedy after winning Eileen's approval.

'At the office,' said Kevin.

'Where's that?' yelled Sean, annoyed at Kevin's nonchalant attitude.

'Other end of the quay.' Kevin inclined his head in the direction of some buildings way beyond the crowd.

'Hell, will I ever make it?' Sean thrust the bundle, which he had been holding over his shoulder, to Eileen. 'Here, hold this.' As he turned Seamus stepped into his path. Sean made to go past him but Seamus once more blocked him. 'Out of the way, man,' snapped Sean. 'What the bloody hell are you playing at? Do you want me to miss the ship?'

Seamus spread his hands as if he had done nothing. 'Not I, man.'

Sean felt a tap on his shoulder and heard Kevin say, 'Nor I.' He swung round to see his friend grinning at him and holding up a boarding ticket. 'Yours,' he said, and then cast a mischievous glance at Eileen. 'We told you we'd look after him.'

'You pair o' eejits,' Sean snapped, and grabbed the ticket. He relieved Eileen of the bundle and glanced in the direction of the ships. 'Which one?' he asked.

'Take your pick,' replied Seamus, still grinning at Sean's irritation over the trick they had played.

Sean eyed him suspiciously but Seamus just shrugged his shoulders to indicate, 'I couldn't care which one.'

'The ticket isn't for a particular ship?'

'No. Now get on with it.'

'Right. The *Nimrod*.' Apart from the fact that

A sudden unexpected shrilling from the ship's steam whistle, which burst with piercing abruptness across the dock, shattered his dreams and brought him back to reality. Cries rose from those still trying to get on board as officials barred their way, yelling that the full complement of passengers had been taken aboard the *Nimrod*. Those refusing to believe it scuffled with the authorities. Others tried to step on the gangplank to prevent it being hauled from the quay.

'Try the *Sea Horse!*' the cry went up among those still without a passage. Most of the crowd took the advice and surged towards the other ship. A few hoped that, relieved of the crush, the officials would take kindly to them and order the plank to be run out again. But it was not to be and curses were heaped on their heads as orders came to cast off from the captain on his bridge who would not be delayed any longer.

He wanted to be clear of the harbour before the *Sea Horse*, for he knew her captain would show him no consideration, and would use all the power he could muster to reach Liverpool first.

Smoke which had been rising from the *Nimrod*'s solitary funnel now thickened as the boilers below were stoked in readiness for departure. Noise ground from the depths of the vessel. Slowly, the large encased paddles began to turn. Orders were shouted, sailors hurried about their urgent tasks, ropes were cast off, and the *Nimrod* began to ease gently away from the quay.

People shouted their final farewells, yelled good wishes, offered last-minute advice, urged their loved ones to write, waved, dabbed their eyes or

45

wept openly. Tears streamed down Eileen's cheeks. She felt shattered, as if a part of her life was being torn from her. And yet, she reminded herself, this parting was nothing compared to that of some of the people around her. She would see Sean again before long, whereas for others this parting could be forever. She waved, trying to make her gesture one of approval of what he was doing, but she hated, with all her heart, the gulf widening between them as the steamer moved further and further from the quay.

Sean waved back silently, oblivious to the noise around him, his thoughts all on the girl he loved, the one who had brought meaning to his life when it had seemed to be going nowhere. She had instilled a purpose to his dreams, and now this ship was taking him on his first step towards achieving them. As he watched her growing smaller, he vowed he would never let her down.

When she was no longer in sight, Kevin broke the silence between them. 'Well, me boy, a new life for you.'

Sean, still looking downcast, nodded.

Seamus slapped him on the back. 'We'll soon have you a pretty girl to take yer mind off Eileen.'

'Don't want my mind taking off her, thanks. You go your way and I'll go mine.' His voice carried a warning that he wanted no meddling from them. He knew their ways, trusted them only so far. They could get up to all sorts of tricks and he knew that in Ireland they had had several brushes with the law but always managed to talk themselves out of trouble with their glib tongues. That wasn't Sean's idea of achieving his ambitions. Nevertheless, knowing that Seamus and Kevin had experience of life in England, he realised they would offer him useful advice.

Kevin held up his hands in acknowledgement. 'All right, Sean, we understand. But allow us to give you a few tips when we reach Liverpool. We don't want you being done over by the runners or the dock dollies.'

'The latter hold no interest for me.'

'Maybe, but they'll try to lure you on, manoeuvre you for pickpockets and thugs to do their thieving and robbing.'

'And what about the runners?'

'Well, they work chiefly on emigrants to America who are most vulnerable to their game. There's a gang of men known as the "Forty Thieves". They hang about the docks when the ships come in. They are well organised, pretend to be porters to help the emigrants.'

'Help?' put in Seamus with a laugh of derision. 'They have a vicious system worked out to deprive the emigrants of all the cash they have. They'll spin them a yarn of looking after their interests, telling them they know just the man to book them a passage to the New World. If they already have a passage, then they'll suggest they can arrange accommodation until the ship sails. The travellers'll want food, too, so these rogues will tell them they know just the man to direct them to the cheapest good-quality shops.'

'So they pass the gullible emigrant on to the runners who take them on their rounds, each time working with a passenger-broker, a shop-keeper and a proprietor of a boarding house.

47

Needless to say the emigrants are overcharged, cheated and left in a parlous state.'

'Can't anything be done about it?' asked Sean, amazed at the unsavoury sound of Liverpool.

Kevin shrugged his shoulders. 'There's a token display of concern by the authorities but who cares about an Irishman and his family? Liverpool folk are against us, don't like us flooding into their city even though it's on a temporary basis, so the emigrants get the poorest dwellings in the city to house them until they move on. Nobody seems to care.'

'But surely not everyone in Liverpool can be against them?'

'True. There are the do-gooders who try to help and continually press the authorities to do more, especially about the overcrowded conditions which bring health hazards.'

Sean shook his head. 'I don't look forward to seeing Liverpool.'

'Oh, it's not all bad. And we are lucky we can pass through quickly, knowing where we're going.'

'There'll be men on the quay when we arrive, recruiting. They'll have placards offering work. You'll have to sign up but we won't as we have our old jobs to go to, digging out docks at Grimsby on the east coast. Stick by us, we'll have a word with Joe Sanders who'll be doing the recruiting for Grimsby. He signed us on when we first came and will probably hurry you through if you're with us. Bottle of Irish whiskey usually does the trick.'

'Thanks,' replied Sean. Before leaving Ireland

he had made up his mind that once they reached England he would go his own way, but now he was weakening. If his companions were to be believed they could ease his way considerably once they were ashore. 'Seems I chose the wrong steamer,' he added, indicating the *Sea Horse* which was steadily gaining on the *Nimrod*. Thick black smoke belched from her funnel; her paddles churned the water with a regular thunderous pounding as if to show the *Nimrod* how it should be done.

'Well, if you want to get there first, yes, you have, but it doesn't matter in our case,' said Kevin, leaning casually against the rail. 'Relax, Sean, enjoy the sea air.'

Sean did just that, his mind dwelling on the girl he had left behind. It roused his determination anew that this 'adventure' to England should bear the fruit he wanted and that Eileen should enjoy it to the fullest.

The sea was calm, causing only the slightest rolling of the deck which did nothing to upset Sean and allowed him to enjoy his first voyage.

'Land ahoy!' The cry from the lookout sent a wave of excitement through the ship. Passengers strained to get their first glimpse of new horizons.

Sean saw the distant change of colour, a smudge 'twixt sea and sky, but his attention was drawn to the *Sea Horse* which had not out-distanced the *Nimrod* as much as he had expected though nevertheless she would be first into Liverpool. He cast his eyes towards land, eager to see it grow clearer, his first sight of shores beyond his native Ireland. Excitement coursed through his veins. It couldn't be dampened by the sight of his two companions in casual conversation with an attitude of 'we've seen it all before'.

As the shore grew more distinct he looked to the progress of the *Sea Horse*. 'She's heading straight for that island,' he cried, drawing Kevin's and Seamus's attention to the ship whose wake had cut across the *Nimrod*'s course.

Both men give a short laugh. 'Not her,' replied Kevin. 'Looks like it but the captain will soon alter course to sail wide round what's known as the Rock.'

They watched, waiting for the manoeuvre to take place, but the *Sea Horse* ploughed on. The *Nimrod* shuddered as her captain altered course to give the Rock a wide berth.

'Captain of the *Sea Horse* is leaving it late,' observed Seamus.

'Aye, he is that,' agreed Kevin, his voice filled with concern.

Tension sparked as they concentrated on the progress of the other ship.

'My God, he's going to cut it fine,' cried Seamus. 'He'll be running very close to the Rock.'

Water churned more vigorously from the steamer's paddles, sending white foam streaming behind them.

'He's putting her under more speed,' cried Kevin, astonished at this latest change of pace with the vessel nearing the Rock. 'What the hell's he up to?'

'All to gain a few minutes,' observed Seamus in disgust.

The Rock was off the *Sea Horse*'s port side now.

'Good grief!' There was alarm and disbelief in Seamus's cry.

Another steamer had appeared, sailing in the opposite direction around the Rock. The two ships were closing fast. Alarm ran through the *Nimrod* as passengers and crew saw that a collision was unavoidable. The names *Sea Horse* and *Eagle* would be emblazoned on their minds forever.

'There's no room for the *Eagle* to swing to starboard. If the captain tries it, he'll be on the Rock!'

The captain of the *Sea Horse* had ordered the helm to be thrown hard over but it was too late. There was a grinding crash, a rending of timber as the *Eagle* cut sharply into the port bow of the *Sea Horse*. She tore open under the force.

It seemed as if the collision would never stop. Her topgallant forecastle was carried away, the deck split halfway across. There was pandemonium on her crowded deck. Passengers were tossed about by the force of the impact. Screams rent the air. Families were scattered. Panic-stricken mothers looked around frantically for children who only a few moments before were standing beside them, not knowing whether they had been tossed into the sea. Men and women clung desperately to whatever they could seize hold of as the vessel lurched, shuddered and juddered, throwing the *Eagle* aside before it

51

finally stopped, to be left wallowing in a sea churned into tumult by the impact.

The captain of the *Eagle* did the only thing he could to save his vessel and those on board. Grasping the situation quickly, he assessed that the watertight compartment had held and headed for the nearest shore to beach his craft.

As soon as the captain of the *Nimrod* saw that a collision was unavoidable, he brought his steamer round to head for the stricken vessel which was taking in water quickly. Orders flew, clear and precise, boomed with an authority that demanded instant obedience. His crew were already moving with that instinctive calm born of an emergency at sea. His calls rose above the clamour of the passengers who had never witnessed a tragedy of this proportion. They felt the helplessness of people driven into shock, wanting to help, wanting to eliminate further horrors, but could only stand and stare or move in hopeless confusion.

The *Nimrod* came round on to a course which would take her close to the doomed ship. The captain, his eyes alert, took in the ever-changing scene. More people were thrown into the water or jumped, with the hope of surviving, taking their destiny into their own hands rather than allowing the *Sea Horse* to yield them to the mercy of the sea.

Passengers at the *Nimrod*'s side, numbed by the sight of men, women and children trying to cling to life in the heaving cauldron, were jerked out of their bemusement by the crew yelling at them to clear the rail and supplementing their orders with

52

physical persuasion. Realising that the sailors were desperate to facilitate a rescue, several male passengers, including Sean, Seamus and Kevin, helped them in their task.

A mother cried out that she had lost her child. Sean, aware of what had happened in the crush and confusion, whisked a little girl off her feet and shoved her into her mother's arms. He gave the woman a broad smile and a wink in acknowledgement of the relief in her face and tears which streamed down her cheeks. Kevin persuaded an old man that he was too helpless to give aid in a physical way and suggested to the man's son that he would be better employed looking after his father.

The Captain concentrated on bringing the *Nimrod* as close as he dare to the people in the water without endangering their lives further. The ship's paddles could exact a vicious toll if he did not hold back. The crew were fastening ropes to the rail and dropping them overboard to dangle in the sea and provide support to any victim who managed to reach the *Nimrod*.

Sean grabbed a rope from one of the crew.

'Know how to tie that?' asked a sailor doubtfully. He did not want anyone's chance of rescue snatched away through incompetence.

'Sure, I can fix it as good as you.' With the dexterity of long practice Sean fastened the rope securely. He looked up, saw approval in the sailor's eyes, and grinned.

The man thrust three more ropes at him. 'Fix these. I'll get more.'

The *Nimrod* slowed, her engines quietening.

The paddles turned just enough to keep the vessel under control. Boats were lowered, and as soon as they hit the water were cast off. Backs were bent at the oars to power the rescue vessels towards the sinking ship.

The air throbbed with the screech of the *Eagle's* engines as she pounded her way to the beach. Heart-rending pleas for help came from those in the water and cut through the awful sound of the sea gulping at the *Sea Horse* as it sucked the vessel towards its doom.

There was tumult everywhere. Water foamed and boats swayed as sailors heaved victims over the gunwales into the sodden safety of the life-saving craft. People struggled for life. Heads bobbed, arms flailed as if trying to pluck support from the air, while others grabbed at any floating debris.

'Come on! Come on! Swim for it! Swim!' There was pleading in Sean's urgent cajoling when his eyes fixed on a man struggling to support a young woman who was floundering in the heaving sea. He realised that the man was only a weak swimmer and would never make it to the *Nimrod* unless he released his grip on the woman.

Seamus and Kevin hauled another man over the rail when he reached the top of one of the ropes, then followed Sean's gaze and joined him in his encouragement.

He straightened up from the rail, urgency in his movements as he threw off his jacket and tore off his boots. Before Seamus and Kevin were aware of what he intended he was on the rail and diving into the sea.

He went down and down, slowed, then kicked for the surface. He burst into daylight, water streaming from his hair. He trod water, brushed it from his eyes and took his bearings quickly. He found the man and relief swept over him when he saw that the woman was still supported. Sean struck out towards them, his strokes strong. As he neared, he saw the man was weakening but his determination to keep the woman afloat super- seded everything else.

Sean reached them. He trod water again and shouted, 'I'll take her!'

The man, breathing hard, was thankful to be relieved of the responsibility.

Sean took the weight of the woman on his left arm, holding her close to reassure her. 'Relax! Don't struggle, I've got you.' His words did noth- ing to banish the fear from her eyes, but she recognised that he might be her saviour and allowed him to take control.

'You all right?' Sean eyed the man.

He nodded, and when Sean started towards the *Nimrod*, followed.

Sean saw that their best chance of survival was to make for the narrow metal platform fixed to the paddle housing, just above the waterline. His stroke with his free arm was strong but, having to support the woman, his progress was slow. He appeared to be making no headway.

Sean's stroke faltered. The movement trans- mitted itself to the woman and he felt her tighten her grip on his arm and stiffen her body in alarm.

'It's all right,' he called encouragingly. 'Relax.' He felt her grip slacken in response. He knew how much she depended on him and hardened his resolve that the sea should not have them.

Slowly, ever so slowly, he drew nearer the *Nimrod*. He heard shouts from above and realised they came from Seamus and Kevin.

They had watched his actions, willing him to succeed. When they realised his intention, they hurried along the deck and clambered over the rail to drop on to the narrow platform. Gripping the paddle-casing, they shouted encouragement to their friend. Holding on one-handed they knelt down and reached out with their free hands when Sean began to tread water.

Realising that safety was within her grasp the young woman made her own effort to aid the rescue. She slipped her right hand free from Sean and stretched it towards her would-be rescuers, but help was tantalisingly just out of reach. Her face contorted with the strain. One more push. Fingers touched and then she felt a strong grip. She freed her other hand from Sean and grabbed the fingers reaching out to her. Seamus and Kevin took her weight, paused, and then together pulled her out of the water as Sean gave a helping push.

Oblivious to the hard edge of the iron platform, she lay sprawled beside the two Irishmen, gulping air into her aching lungs, ignoring the sodden weight of her clothes and the lank hair clinging to her head. She was safe. Then she realised she was alone. 'Father!' Her scream reverberated with her worst fear. She sat up, twisting round to search the waves. 'Where is he?' Her eyes pleaded with the Irishmen to give her the reassurance she sought.

She felt a comforting arm around her shoulder, heard a rich Irish brogue close to her ear, and saw a finger point across the water. 'He's there. He'll be all right. Sean will rescue him.'

She saw her father battling to keep swimming, saw Sean strike out from the *Nimrod*, and was gripped by the scene unfolding before her which could end in tragedy or joy.

The older man was weakening, his face creased with strain. His body sapped of energy, still he tried to drive onwards until, overwhelmed by the effort, he threw up his arms as if making one last grab at some invisible support. An agonised cry for help was lost as he disappeared beneath the waves.

His daughter screamed and would have jumped into the sea had not Kevin and Seamus restrained her.

Sean dived, took three strong strokes. He saw the man underneath him, grasped his clothes and kicked for the light. Water streamed from their heads as they broke the surface. Their lungs gulped greedily at the air. Sean got a better grip under the man's arms.

'Relax,' he shouted. 'Soon have you out.'

A few minutes later the strong hands of Kevin and Seamus hauled the man out of the water. Sean held on to the *Nimrod's* side, thankful that his effort had not been in vain. His chest was still heaving as Seamus and Kevin pulled him from the sea to lie beside the man.

'Father! Father!' The young woman crawled the few feet to him.

'Sarah...' Her father's voice was weak but it strengthened as he added, 'Thank God you're safe.' He felt the reassuring pressure of her hand on his shoulder and fear for her safety drained from him.

She looked round at Sean who was struggling to his feet. 'Thank you for saving us. We'll be ever in your debt.'

Sean gave her a heartening smile. 'Ah, now don't go on so, miss. It was nothing.' In spite of her dishevelled and sodden appearance, with face drawn by the ordeal and eyes lacking sparkle, he realised he was looking at an attractive young woman. Before his thoughts ran away with him he added, 'Come, I think we had better get you both back on deck and find you something warm to wear.' He held out his hand and, as Sarah took it, she felt uplifted. His touch was gentle but firm, imparting the feeling that she would be safe with this young man. She felt an empathy with him as their eyes locked for a moment before she turned them, and her concern, to her father.

Seamus and Kevin were helping him to his feet and giving him the support he needed after his battle with the sea. He caught his daughter's eye and nodded to confirm that, apart from his loss of strength, he was no worse for their ordeal.

The deck was packed with people and noisy with the cries of passengers struggling to be reunited with loved ones. Small boats crowded with survivors dragged from the edge of a watery grave scraped the side of the *Nimrod* as they rode the swell. Eager hands dragged women and children on board before turning to the men.

58

Hysterics, anger, thankfulness and shock were apparent on every side.

Nimrod's crew and passengers did what they could to ease the suffering. Blankets were brought from cabins and from the crew's quarters. Male passengers took off their overcoats and jackets and women wrapped their shawls around the shoulders of the rescued to bring warmth and comfort.

Sean, who had retrieved his jacket and shoes, held the jacket out to Sarah.

She shook her head. 'No, you need it as much as I.' Her voice was soft yet firm with refusal.

Sean started to protest but at that moment a sailor hurried to them cradling some blankets in his arms. Sean whisked one from the pile and swung it around Sarah's shoulders. Kevin grabbed one for her father.

'Thanks,' he said, a grateful light in his eyes, and turned to Sean. 'And you, young man, Sarah and I will never forget what you did today, risking your life the way you did.' He held out his hand. 'James Langton, and this is my daughter, Sarah.'

Sean smiled and returned the handshake. 'Sean Casey,' he replied. 'And my friends, Seamus O'Leary and Kevin Harper.'

Any further exchanges were muted for the time being as a shout went up around the ship. 'There she goes!'

The *Sea Horse*, stern in the air, slid beneath the waves leaving a trail of heaving water in which debris and bodies were tossed around like corks.

Sarah was numbed by the sight. Only a short time ago the *Sea Horse* had been a proud ship, filled with passengers and crew facing a future full of hope. Now it had disappeared forever, leaving shattered lives in its wake.

No one spoke. A mantle of silent tribute hung over the *Nimrod* until it was broken by the captain who realised that there might still be survivors in the water. His orders rang clear across the waves for the *Nimrod*'s boats to continue the search.

When all the boats had done what they could and had reported back to their parent ship and been brought on board, the Captain ordered the *Nimrod* to get under way so that she could reach her dock with all possible speed.

News of the tragedy had already reached Liverpool and by the time the *Nimrod* docked every assistance for those struck by the catastrophe was already on the quay. Doctors and their assistants were ready with medical support as soon as the first victim was ashore, despatching the more seriously injured to hospital in ambulances. The less serious cases were shepherded into two warehouses where they received the necessary attention for shock and injuries such as broken limbs, minor cuts and bruises. They were helped into dry clothing which had been hastily assembled. Volunteers had also organised warm drinks which were welcomed by victims eager to drive the cold from their bodies.

In the warehouse set aside for male passengers Sean put on his own change of clothing which he had brought from Ireland. James, pleased to be out of his wet clothing, was thankful for anything, ill-fitting though it might be. When they were satisfied that he needed no further attention the three Irishmen accompanied him outside to await Sarah.

Five minutes later she emerged from the warehouse used by the female passengers. As she walked towards them, in spite of their efforts to stifle their laughter the four men could not do so.

Sarah's anger started to rise. She knew she must cut an amusing figure in the ill-fitting clothes she had been given. Her plain brown dress was about four inches shorter than it should be and the waist sat oddly high. Her auburn hair, which could cascade like a mountain stream, was drawn severely straight back and tied in a tight bun at the nape of her neck.

Indignant at their laughter, she drew herself up only to stumble because of the ill-fitting shoes she had been given. Annoyed that her attempt at dignity in the face of adversity had been thwarted, her lips set in a hard line. She cursed beneath her breath, kicked off her shoes in a flare of temper and, setting her hands on her hips in a gesture of defiance, faced the four men.

'Laugh, would you? Well, it does you no credit. Laugh indeed! You should be showing compassion for a poor girl dressed in such clothes – all they could give me. It was take them or leave them, I had no choice. And what are you going to do about it?' The sharp tone was accompanied by flashing eyes which boded ill for anyone who continued to be amused by her plight.

'Oh, come now, daughter,' put in James quickly.

He knew the signs and a major outburst of temper was imminent. It very rarely happened but, when it did, the tantrum could be fiery. He only hoped the three Irishmen read the warning in what he was about to say. 'We were not making fun of you.' He had stifled his laughter and replaced it with a more serious demeanour. 'We were just amused at the sight. My dear, we are concerned for you and you can be sure that I will lose no time in finding you more suitable clothing. We will delay our onward journey until tomorrow and stay overnight at the Imperial. That will give you time to choose yourself a complete new outfit and have the evening to recuperate.'

Sarah felt her anger subsiding with each additional suggestion he made. 'Thank you,' she said stiffly.

'Sorry, miss. We meant no disrespect with our laughter.' Sean had read James's intentions and made his own apology gracefully.

'Ah, sure now, miss, we meant no harm.' Seamus took his lead from Sean.

'They're right, miss, we did not intend to insult you. Besides, how could we? You'd look elegant in whatever you wore.' Though there was still a twitch of amusement at the corners of Kevin's lips and a twinkle in his eyes, Sarah could not ignore his expression which not only begged forgiveness but contained real admiration.

She tossed her head. 'You've all got glib tongues. I suppose I'd better forgive you, though thousands wouldn't.' Her temper was under control now. Her eyes lit up with mischief as she added, 'But, Father, it will cost you two dresses.'

'Two?' James spluttered. 'Now, see here, young lady...'

'Two!' There was a sharp, no-nonsense tone in her voice again. She knew she had the upper hand and would brook no refusal. 'And, it goes without saying, the best suite in the hotel.'

James raised his eyes heavenwards, as if pleading for someone to rescue him from this extravagance. He knew Sarah to be a determined young woman who would extract full payment for their mocking laughter. He glanced at the Irishmen. 'What can I do?' he pleaded.

'Nothing, I suppose,' said Sean, 'except agree.'

James grunted his assent. 'Young men, if ever you marry, don't have daughters. But if you do, make sure they can't twist you round their little fingers.'

'Now, Father, what kind of advice is that to give? You know you don't mean it. You enjoy our friendly disputes.' Laughing, Sarah came and linked arms with him in a loving gesture. 'Which always work in my favour.'

He pouted thoughtfully for a moment. 'I suppose I do,' he admitted, giving her a look of devotion. 'Now, we had better be on our way, but first we must acknowledge our debt to these three gentlemen, especially Sean who risked his life.' He started to protest at the praise but James halted him with one upraised hand. 'It's true,' he said. 'I want to repay you in some way. I suppose all of you are coming to England seeking work?'

'Yes, sir,' replied Seamus. 'Well, that is, Sean is. Kevin and I have been coming over for two years already. We've been working at Grimsby, helping dig out the new docks.'

'And you are contracted for this year?'

'No, sir, not contracted, but we have an understanding that if we do return, after visiting our relatives in Ireland, there's a job for us if we want it.'

James showed a little surprise. 'Unusual terms. You must be good workers if they take you on that footing.'

'Ah, well, though I say it meself there's no slacking by Seamus O'Leary and Kevin Harper, and we don't care what we do,' put in Kevin brightly.

'And you, Sean, had you planned to go with your friends?' asked James.

'Well, sir, it's my first visit to England so as these two know the ropes, and I realised they could put in a good word for me, I was prepared to go with them.'

'Well, Sean, I can assure you of a job elsewhere.'

'You can?' Surprised, he added almost without thinking, 'Doing what? Where?'

'I'm managing the Bolckow and Vaughan bar iron manufactory at Middlesbrough, a new town on the south bank of the River Tees.'

'And as such you can guarantee me a job?'

'Oh, yes. I can hire and fire if necessary. I normally leave hiring the men to my overseer but if I make a recommendation he'll follow it.' He turned to Kevin and Seamus. 'If you're interested, the offer's open to you as well.'

'Thank you, sir,' said Kevin. 'A change will do

64

us good.' He knew Seamus would agree whatever he decided.

'So you've three new employees,' said Sean. He had noted Sarah's rapt attention during this exchange. Had he really seen relief and approval cross her face or was he letting his imagination run wild?

'Good.' James nodded. 'Come to Middlesbrough. Anyone will direct you to the Bolckow and Vaughan rolling mill. Ask for me.'

'Thank you, sir,' echoed Sean and Kevin.

James turned to his daughter. 'Come, Sarah, let's get you out of those clothes.' His eyes twinkled as he spoke.

'Father!' Her sharp tone reminded him that he should not overstep the mark.

He held up his hands in mock surrender.

Sarah accepted it with an inclination of her head then turned to the three Irishmen. 'Thank you for what you did. Maybe we'll meet again in Middlesbrough.'

'Sure and that would be my pleasure, miss,' Sean replied with a warm smile.

Kevin pressed agreement with his eyes.

As she accompanied her father from the dock, Sean stood watching until Seamus gave him a dig in the ribs.

'Getting ideas?' he said with mocking amusement. 'Sure, you can't have designs on a manager's daughter – she's far above the likes of us.'

'Oh, I don't know about that,' replied Sean.

'Ah, now, don't you go forgetting Eileen,' admonished Kevin.

Chapter Three

Tristram had lost his customary briskness and usual happy demeanour with its accompanying smile which brought pleasure to friends, acquaintances and even strangers. Instead there were leaden feet, a worried frown and a sombre expression which gave no acknowledgement of the respectful greetings given to him by those who knew the tragedy that had befallen him.

The course on which he was now embarked caused his stomach to knot and brought a chill to his heart. To have to beg from his brother was bad enough, but to hear the mockery, which he knew would come, and be accused of letting their father down by destroying the firm he had so painstakingly built up, would inflict deep wounds on Tristram's mind and heart.

He made his way to the east bank of the river, hardly aware of the people around him or of the ships which usually drew his attention. The *Mary Anne* should have been one of them but now she lay with all hands at the bottom of the English Channel, victim of the storm that had brought him ruin and now humiliation.

He had chosen to visit his brother's office rather than his house, for he wanted privacy. His sister-in-law would not be around to nose out the reason for his visit after all these years. There would be no servants within earshot to snap up a

never seen such a wild expression on his employer's face as he had witnessed when he had announced Mr Tristram by name. Whatever had divided the brothers it must have been serious.

'Well?' snapped Nathan, leaning back in his chair. His dark eyes bored into Tristram with menace and contempt. They were cold, without any shred of comfort or brotherly love. 'If you've come looking for sympathy here because you've lost a ship, you'll get none.' His eyes narrowed, matching a voice that was filled with suspicion. 'But I wonder if it's more than that?'

These last words upset Tristram's plan of approach for they made him wonder if his brother already knew of the deep dilemma he was in. As he hesitated he glanced at the unoccupied chair on the opposite side of the desk from his brother.

'Oh, sit down if you must,' snapped Nathan. 'It can't be for long. I've work to do, if you haven't.'

Tristram sat down, trying to assume a firmness he did not feel. 'The ... er ... loss of the *Mary Anne* has hit me hard. I...'

'It will have done. All hands, I hear. That's bad enough but think of the cargo, the profits that now lie at the bottom of the sea. You'll miss them, I'm sure, but the insurance money will go a long way to easing your burden.'

Tristram was shocked by his brother's callous attitude towards the loss of the crew. All he had focused on was the money. But this was no less than Tristram had secretly expected. However, it seemed his brother knew only of the loss of the ship.

'Well, you see, there is more to it than that,' said Tristram, shuffling on his chair.

'Must be for you to come here. Though how it can concern me, I have no idea.' Nathan riveted his eyes on Tristram. His curiosity had been aroused and he was enjoying his brother's unease. A slightly mocking tone came into his voice. 'Embarrassing, is it?' He pursed his lips, enjoying the taunt.

'I need your help.'

The bald statement made Nathan throw back his head in a laugh. 'You need *my* help?' He swung forward on his chair and slammed his fist down hard on the desk. 'You have the gall to come to me for help after you got what was rightfully mine?'

Tristram flinched, but the thought of Lydia and Luke strengthened his resolve. 'It was no fault of mine that I inherited Father's business,' he pointed out. 'He made the will, not me.'

'No doubt you played up to him.'

Tristram's eyes sharpened at the suggestion. 'I did no such thing.'

'So you say.'

'I didn't,' he said firmly. The accusation had had the effect of hardening his attitude.

Nathan gave a grunt of disbelief. 'You still haven't told me why you need help,' he pointed out in a uninterested voice. But beneath the bland exterior he was curious. Tristram wouldn't have come here if the situation didn't go beyond even the loss of a ship with all hands. 'So tell me and then get out.' The last two words were spat with such venom that Tristram felt himself weakening. All his resolve to be strong was disappearing. He dreaded the attitude his brother would take when he learned the full truth. He was beginning to wish he had not come but he must put his case, for Lydia's and Luke's sake.

He drew himself up and squared his shoulders. His voice was hardly above a whisper when he said, 'I need money to survive.' The tremor in it made the words hard to distinguish, but Nathan caught them.

'You what? Your ship and cargo would be insured, surely?'

Tristram shook his head slowly.

For a moment Nathan stared at Tristram in disbelief. Then realisation of what his brother had done, or rather had not done, dawned on him. 'You weren't insured?' His face contorted with renewed scorn as he leaned forward over his desk, his expression full of incredulity. 'Why the hell not?'

Tristram started his sorry tale. Nathan did not interrupt but was not averse to shaking his head in disbelief or grunting with disgust at each further revelation. 'What a mess,' he commented when Tristram had finished. He paused for a moment then, with mouth set hard, poured scorn on his brother. 'You're a damned fool! How could you allow the business Father built up so meticulously to be destroyed in this way? He must be turning in his grave at such carelessness. Didn't you damn' well think of what might happen?'

'Can you foresee an act of God?' said Tristram weakly.

71

'No,' snapped Nathan, 'but I can be cautious enough to safeguard myself should one arise.' He stared hard at his brother. 'And I suppose you've come snivelling here to me expecting me to save you? Well, you'll not get a penny from me. You'll have to sink in the mess of your own making.'

Tristram shuddered under this scathing onslaught. 'Please, for Father's sake? To save his business?'

'Don't try to get round me by using him. It's no longer his firm. He left it to you. It's *your* business, and I couldn't care a damn what happens to it.'

'I'll have to sell everything and even that won't be enough. I'll be brought to court as a debtor and go to gaol. Surely you wouldn't see that happen to your own brother?'

'I could and I would,' snapped Nathan, revelling in the sight of Tristram squirming as each word of condemnation and denial hit home. 'You're an incompetent fool and should pay for it.'

'But the family name?' Tristram made what he felt must be his last appeal. Was there no way he could soften his brother's heart, change his outlook? 'Surely you don't want to see the name of Middleton dragged through court, see stigma attached to it?'

Nathan's pitiless eyes bored into him. 'It's the name of Tristram Middleton that will be bantered around the court, no other. It's you who'll be paraded for all to see, no one else. The dirt will be stuck to *you*. Folk know I don't own you, that I don't even regard you as family.'

He saw that his brother realised it was useless to pursue the matter further. He saw Tristram's eyes dull, his expression become forlorn, his shoulders droop. A defeated man sat before him and Nathan liked what he saw. He delighted in deepening the wound.

'You're a weakling. Couldn't even maintain what was handed to you as a successful business. There's not a drop of common sense in you. If there was you wouldn't be in this dilemma.' He gave a little laugh of derision and triumph. 'All that's left for you is the debtors' prison.'

Nathan savoured the pronouncement, delivered with slow deliberation, for he saw each word pierce his brother's mind, filling it with dread of the consequences of his folly.

Tristram flinched. He was utterly deflated, all energy drained from him. He hadn't the will to protest, nor to fight back. His brother had sapped the last of his resolve. The future was as bleak as it could be. He faced the horrors of prison, of being branded a debtor and failure. He would never be able to hold his head up again. Friends would shun him, others would point the finger at him, but worse than anything he had failed his daughter and son. How could he face them again? The thought of them made him turn to his brother with one last appeal. 'Please...' But that was as far as he got.

Nathan cut in sharply. 'No! Get out of here, you whining good-for-nothing. I want nothing more to do with you or your family. Tell those two brats of yours not to come pleading with me either, as well they might. If they do they'll get

73

short shrift from me.' Nathan's lips curled, his eyes blazed with fiery contempt. 'Now get out of here, destroyer of what should have been mine. I don't want to see you again – ever!'

Tristram reached the door a broken man.

Nathan leaned back in his chair and watched with satisfaction. Revenge for what he saw as the injustice perpetrated six years ago had come, but in an unexpected way. Nevertheless the spectacle was sweet. He chuckled to himself as he listened to Tristram's footsteps shuffling away along the corridor.

He was unaware of reaching the outside door and stepping out into Church Street. Nathan's scathing words still swam in his head, the condemnation burned deep. His brain was awash with self-accusation too. He walked unsteadily, unaware where he was, ignorant of normal life going on around him until the sounds began to penetrate his thoughts. Something of reality came back to him then but with it a greater horror. Lydia and Luke would be tainted by what was to happen to him. He didn't want that. He didn't want folk nodding in their direction saying they were a debtor's offspring. And there would be poverty, for there would be nothing left after all his possessions had been sold. Oh, why had he listened to those promises of a good investment?

Poverty – everything gone. His children destitute. Oh, Luke had a job but with that as their only source of income the outlook looked bleak. The comfortable lifestyle they had been used to would disappear. Oh, why had he been so stupid as not to take care of the insurance of his

74

ship and its cargo before he had been tempted to make a quick profit? Insurance... Something stirred in his thoughts.

Oblivious to the people passing around him, his thoughts became more and more fixed on the future of his children. His mind was blank to everything else. It was as if he had become spellbound by a possible solution. It filled his mind to the exclusion of everything else and blotted out any consideration of the terrible deed it would entail. Those thoughts had a compelling effect on him, seeming to direct his very steps. His children must not know poverty, must not share the disgrace which faced him.

He was insensible to the wind strengthening as he moved along the west pier, away from the protection of the cliffs. He stopped at the end and stood for a few moments gazing out to sea, across the grey waves. They seemed to call to him, offering comfort in their undulating depths.

The solution was there. He turned as if to walk back. A fishing boat slid from the sea to the calm of the river. Along the pier two men watched it. He saw them move in his direction. His step faltered, he tottered. His hand came up to his chest. He doubled up and staggered sideways. His hands came up as if he was trying to save himself. Then he was falling. Falling. Down. Down. He hit the water and allowed it to take him.

'I would have expected Father to be back by now.' Worry was clearly visible on Lydia's face.

'Well, you don't know Uncle Nathan's views. He may have wanted a lot more detail about the business and Father's assets before he committed himself, and that would take time.' Luke tried to offer comfort but secretly he too was worried.

'But two hours?'

'I know. It does seem a long time but...' He shrugged.

'I wish we'd gone with him.'

'Father didn't want that and we had to respect his wishes.'

'Yes.' Lydia bit her lip. 'Do you think Uncle Nathan will be more amiable?'

'Who knows? Maybe the years have mellowed him, though what I hear of his usual attitudes doesn't augur well.'

'And he's never attempted to get in touch.'

'Well, nor has Father.'

Lydia fidgeted. She couldn't settle to anything. She had sat down, paced the room, stared from the window, always with her thoughts on what might be happening between her father and uncle. Her uneasiness had permeated her brother and he became more and more anxious to know the result of the interview as each minute passed.

A loud rapping resounded throughout the house. Its suddenness and urgency startled them. For a brief moment they shared a glance of fear and doubt. There was something about that urgent knocking which spelt trouble. They started for the door together. Luke flung it open to see the maid hurrying across the hall.

She opened the front door and was met by a request. 'Are Mr Middleton's son and daughter here?'

Before she could reply Luke stepped across the

hall. 'Yes.' He saw a solemn-faced member of the Watch standing there. 'What can I do for you?'

'May I come in, sir? I need to have a word with you.'

'Yes, yes.' Luke was a little flustered by this unexpected visit.

'Constable Isaac Smurthwaite, sir,' said the big, bulky man as he stepped into the hall.

'Come this way,' said Luke. As he started towards the drawing room, the maid closed the door and at a signal from him, hurried away to the servants' quarters at the back of the house.

Lydia was standing in the doorway. Though she realised her brother knew no more than she did she looked askance at him.

He pursed his lips and gave a slight shake of his head. After ushering the constable into the room, he closed the door and said, 'I'm Luke Middleton, and this is my sister, Lydia.'

The constable nodded. 'I know you both by sight but have had no cause to speak to you. I'm sorry that this first time must be the occasion of bad news.'

Alarm gripped Lydia. Her stomach felt hollow as if all sensation had been drained from her. Solemnity marked the constable's expression and the corresponding sadness in his eyes caused her face to drain of colour.

Luke shivered as a chill ran through his body. His mind was racing, trying to fathom the reason for this visit. He almost missed the man's words.

'Sir, miss, I'm sorry to bring bad news about your father. I'm afraid he's dead.'

Disbelief filled them. Luke stared at the man.

Lydia wanted to cry out in denial. Her father had walked out of the house a little over two hours ago. He had been alive and well, weighed down by the problems he faced but healthy. He couldn't be dead. But the weakness of shock creeping over her told her this was true. Why should this man be here if it weren't?

'Oh, no!' She sank on to a chair.

Luke refused to accept the announcement. 'He can't be. There must be some mistake.' He was willing the constable to contradict himself, urging him to admit that what he had said was untrue. But it was no good. Breaking news such as this was part of the man's job, though not something he enjoyed doing.

'There is no mistake, sir. I'm afraid your father is dead.'

'How? What happened?'

'He fell from the west pier.'

'Fell from the pier?' Luke was incredulous. 'What was he doing there?'

'Well, sir, I was hoping you might be able to answer that. Had he gone for a walk?'

Before Luke could answer, Lydia broke in quickly, shooting her brother a look which she hoped he would interpret correctly. 'Yes, he went out just after breakfast.' She was relieved when Luke confirmed her statement. He had realised that if the visit to Uncle Nathan was mentioned the whole sad story of their father's losses might come out.

'Did he seem in good health?'

'Yes.'

'I know that he had lost a ship with all hands

78

recently, might that have been preying on his mind?'

'It worried him as it would any man who had lost a ship, and he felt for the families of the crew. However, he had matters in hand.'

The constable pursed his lips thoughtfully as he nodded. He glanced at Luke. 'Would you agree with your sister?'

'Most certainly.'

'And would you say that Mr Middleton's health was good?'

'As far as we know.'

'But this loss had been a real shock to him?'

'He felt it deeply because of the crew.' Luke cocked his head suspiciously. 'What are you implying, constable?'

'Well, sir, your father fell from the pier and with what had happened to his ship...'

'Are you implying he committed suicide?' Lydia's voice was full of indignation.

The constable raised his hands in a gesture of apology. 'I'm sorry, miss. No, I'm not saying that, I'm only wanting to verify certain facts to tie in with our observations.'

'And what might those be?' she asked.

'Well, miss, he was seen at the end of the pier by members of a fishing boat returning to harbour, and also by two men walking there. He turned as if to walk back, staggered, seemed to grasp his chest and fell. It would seem from what these men say, and knowing of his recent loss, that your father had a heart attack. The boat manoeuvred quickly but it took some time to find him for he had been swept back out to sea.'

79

Luke and Lydia were silent, assessing the implications behind these words while still in shock at the news.

'I'm sorry to be the bearer of such sad tidings.' The constable broke into their thoughts. 'This is a tragic time for you both. I hope that you approve of what I have done and that it will relieve you of some of the pain of dealing with the situation.' He glanced at them both and then continued, 'I contacted Reuben Mason, the undertaker, and he has taken care of the body. He will call on you to make the funeral arrangements. I hope I did right?'

Luke nodded. 'Yes, thank you, constable.' The words were almost dismissive. After what the man had said he wanted time to consider the nature of his father's death and saw from the thoughtful look on her face that Lydia shared his feelings. 'Is there anything else we should know?'

'I don't think so, sir. I must thank you both for your frank statements. I am most grateful. They clear up any doubt about your father's death. I'm sorry I had to ask them but it is my duty. May I say before taking my leave that I often had a few words with your father whenever I met him in the street, on his way to work or whatever. He always seemed a pleasant, straightforward sort of man, one who valued his family and would do nothing to upset them.'

Lydia rose from her chair. She clasped her hands tightly together, keeping a grip on herself to hold her emotions in check until he had gone. 'Thank you for those kind words, constable. We are most grateful for them and for your thoughtfulness in trying to spare us the worst of this tragedy.'

Luke made his thanks too and escorted the man to the front door.

Lydia sat down slowly, hardly aware of the voices in the hall as the official made his departure. Part of her was still in a state of shock, but another part conjured up vivid mental pictures of Tristram's death. The numbness which gripped her body did not subdue them. It was as if she had witnessed them in the clear knowledge of what was happening. She sat perfectly still, fingers entwined on her lap, her fixed gaze unseeing.

Luke's footsteps approached the room. She did not move. The door opened and closed. Still she stared straight ahead.

As he turned from the door, he was saying, 'I can't believe this nightmare is true. Father gone? He was...' His voice faded. Alarmed by the trance-like figure, he looked with concern at his sister. 'Lydia, are you all right?'

Her gaze remained fixed but she spoke. Her voice was low though it embraced the strong conviction that what she said was the truth. 'Father committed suicide.' The statement filled the room with tension.

'Lydia!' he gasped, astonished by his sister's bald statement.

'It's true.' Her voice never faltered. Her gaze remained fixed, as if she was witnessing her father's actions here and now.

Shocked, Luke stepped forward and sank on to his knees in front of her. He took her hands in his and looked into her face with sympathy and a desire to relieve her of such terrible thoughts. 'You can't say that, love. You don't know.'

Her eyes slowly met his. 'I do. I'm right.'

'No, Lydia. The constable said that witnesses saw Father grasp his chest and stagger before falling off the pier.'

She shook her head. 'That's not right. Oh, they related what they saw, and I don't question the truth of it, but Father was healthy, you know that.'

Luke had to concede the fact but added, 'But who can tell what the shock of the loss of the *Mary Anne* did to him?'

'I don't believe it gave him a heart attack.'

'Well then, what happened?'

'I've already said. He committed suicide.'

'Lydia, you must be careful what you say. You'll sully Father's name. The constable believes the witnesses. The verdict will be that Father had a heart attack, so let's leave it at that.'

A fierce light had come into her eyes. 'I won't leave it at that!' She raised a hand quickly to stem Luke's protest. 'I'll not make my views public but I will accuse one man to his face.'

While he was relieved by the first part of Lydia's statement, he was puzzled by the second. 'What are you getting at?'

'I believe that Father's interview with Uncle Nathan was a waste of time. He spurned Father's request for help. Imagine Father in that situation, desperate for money, facing ruin, disgrace and probable imprisonment.'

'You're saying that's what caused him to commit suicide?'

'No. Father wasn't the type. He loved life too much. What I'm saying is that in that situation he saw a way in which his debts would be cleared.' She paused a moment to let the meaning of her words sink in.

Puzzled, Luke prompted, 'Go on.'

'We know that Father had comprehensive life insurance – remember, he told us when he took it out three years ago?' She paused for verification. Luke nodded and she continued, 'Realising this, he saw that death was the only way he could clear his debt.'

Luke's words came out thoughtfully. 'So you're saying he faked an accident so we'd receive the insurance?'

'Yes, and by so doing saved us the stigma of having a bankrupt father, and ensured we would not be left completely impoverished as we would have been if he had stayed alive. Don't you see, Luke, he did it for us!'

He was battling to accept this. Harder still to take in that his father was dead. It was such a terrible thing. And to do it deliberately... 'But suicide?' He shuddered.

Lydia reached out and touched his cheek lightly. 'I know it's hard to take, but don't look at it as such. Look at it as an act born of love for us.'

Luke gave a little nod and pressed his cheek more firmly against her fingers, drawing strength to cope with their loss.

Lydia said nothing for a few moments, knowing that her brother needed time to accept her theory. She recognised that that was all it was but, nevertheless, she felt strongly that she was right. She would test out her ideas. She knew she could never receive definite proof that she was right but she needed to know for her own peace of mind if she was near the truth. And that meant finding out what had happened between her father and Uncle Nathan.

She stirred. Luke glanced up at her. 'I'm going to see Uncle Nathan.'

'He's the one man you said you would accuse to his face?'

'Yes. If Uncle Nathan refused to help then he is the cause of Father's suicide!'

Luke scrambled to his feet in alarm. 'Be careful, Lydia. Even if what you say is true, what can you do about it?'

'That remains to be seen,' she replied quietly. She stood up, smoothed her dress and started for the door.

'You're going now?'

'Yes.'

'Then I'll come with you. You're not facing Uncle Nathan alone.'

'Thank you.'

'Besides, I want to hear what he has to say.'

Within half an hour they were being shown into Nathan Middleton's office, having accepted the commiserations of the clerk when they'd announced who they were. Lydia was pleased to receive them for it meant that news of her father's death must have reached Nathan.

When they entered his office, he stood up and hastened from behind his desk to greet them cordially. 'My dear young people, this is truly a tragedy. I am deeply sorry. My commiserations to you both.' He took Lydia's hands in his and kissed her quickly on the cheek then shook hands with Luke. He fussed as he showed each of them to a chair and then returned to his where he leaned back and clasped his hands across his chest.

Lydia plunged in, wanting to get straight to the point and avoid the crocodile tears. 'I believe my father came to see you earlier this morning?'

'He did indeed.'

'About the loss of the *Mary Anne?*'

'Yes.' Nathan was becoming concerned. He really did not care for his niece's tone of voice.

'He sought your help financially?'

'I think you know that's why he was here.'

'What was the outcome of his appeal to you?'

Nathan leaned forward. His eyes were cold. 'I don't think that is any concern of yours, young woman.'

Lydia straightened. Her eyes met her uncle's unflinchingly. 'I think it is. Luke and I will now have to deal with our father's affairs and if you and he had any sort of arrangement, then we should know of it.'

'My sister is perfectly right,' put in Luke to lend support to her statement. 'We need to know just where he stood, and especially if you had agreed to make him a loan.'

Nathan was beginning to seethe at this line of questioning. 'I had done no such thing!' The words came out before he could check himself.

'You refused to help your brother?' Lydia feigned shock. It was as she had expected all along.

'Brother? He was no brother of mine.'

'Of course he was,' said Luke. 'You can't escape that fact.'

'In fact, yes,' conceded Nathan irritably. 'But in every other way he was not.'

'You still bore him a grudge over Grandfather's will?' queried Lydia.

'He took what was rightly mine,' snapped her uncle.

'And you refused him help because of that?'

'He made a mess of the business, he got what he rightly deserved. Nincompoop! Had no idea about trading. Destroyed the firm carefully built up by your grandfather... Gone, just like that.' Nathan's face had grown red and flustered-looking. 'I told him straight what I thought of him. A failure, a weakling, a...'

'Uncle Nathan,' cut in Luke sharply. 'We don't wish to hear any more of this. Father was none of those things. In fact, in compassion and love he far outshone you. The loss of the *Mary Anne* was unfortunate – not Father's fault.'

'But it was his fault he hadn't insured her,' exclaimed Nathan triumphantly.

'Don't tell me you've never taken risks,' insisted Lydia, quietly implying that she knew of some deals of his which had sailed close to the wind. Before he could react to this she went on, 'I believe his death was a direct result of your refusal to help him.'

Nathan threw up his arms in horror. 'How on earth can you jump to that conclusion?'

'The shock of being rejected.'

'A heart attack could have come at any time.'

'Father was extremely healthy.'

Suspicion had started to mount in Nathan's mind. 'What are you getting at, young lady?'

'We hold you responsible.' Her voice was cold.

He gave a harsh laugh of derision. 'Me? How could I be responsible?'

'Your refusal to help Father must have put a great strain on him.'

'It's not my fault he couldn't take my refusal like a man.' He gave a scornful grunt. 'Tristram was a weakling all his life.'

'By not helping, you condemned him. You drove him to his death.'

'What are you implying, young lady? Are you suggesting that your father committed suicide?'

'Interpret it how you will, and live with your own conscience.'

Nathan got to his feet. His eyes were wary. 'If this should come out...'

'Your reputation would be severely harmed,' Luke finished for him. 'How would people view you, a man who refused to help his brother and drove him to take his own life?' Nathan looked startled, so Luke pressed home his point. 'Besides, the stigma of a suicide in the family wouldn't go down too well in this town.'

'But I heard there were witnesses to what happened?'

'True, but I think you realise now there could be a different interpretation of why Father fell from the pier. I don't think you will voice it, though, because of the possible repercussions. For it to be passed off as a heart attack will suit us all. Father's name will not be stained.'

87

A look of relief that his niece and nephew were adopting this attitude was wiped from Nathan's face as Lydia went on. 'But nevertheless, Uncle, we three will always have good reason to believe it was no accident. Though you are beyond any retribution from the law you will not escape ours. An offer of help could have saved Father but you refused him. It will have serious consequences for you.'

'Don't you threaten me, young lady.' He could not conceal the fury mounting within him.

'Feeling threatened, Uncle? Suffering from a guilty conscience?' Lydia gave a little smile of satisfaction.

Nathan stiffened and slammed his fist down hard on the desk. 'Damn you, coming here with your veiled accusations that I drove Tristram to his death!'

'Didn't you?' put in Luke quietly.

'Don't think we'll let you get away with it,' added Lydia in an equally meaningful tone.

Nathan looked from one to the other, wondering just what they had in mind. His eyes narrowed. 'You can do nothing to harm me. You won't voice your suspicions because you'd only sully your father's name. As his death is being passed off as a heart attack it will suit you to remain quiet. I emerge from this unscathed.'

Luke gave a knowing grin. 'Oh, there'll be ways of paying you back, you'll see.'

'Your business,' suggested Lydia.

Nathan read the meaning behind the words and gave a harsh laugh of amusement. Then his lips tightened. 'I've heard enough. Now get out!'

88

Lydia and Luke rose slowly from their chairs.

'We've said all we have to say. We've seen all we need to see,' said Lydia. As she stood there looking down at him the light from the window highlighted one side of her face, driving the other into a shadow. It added a touch of menace to her last words.

Nathan felt compelled to resist their attempt at intimidation. 'Under the terms of my father's will I now have legal title to your house. I will soon be moving in where I should rightfully have been since he died. I give you two weeks to settle your affairs and move out.'

'You can't mean it?' gasped Luke.

Nathan leaned back in his chair, a grin on his face. 'I can and I do. Two weeks. If you're not out then I'll have you evicted.'

Luke started to speak again but was silenced by Lydia's hand on his arm.

'Leave it, Luke. This is typical of our uncle. This is how he treated Father. We'll leave you,' she continued, her gaze fixed on Nathan, then she moved it slightly to one side as if she was seeing beyond him into the future. 'Retribution will come and it will be sweet.' She pronounced the words slowly, letting them assume an ominous tone. She turned with head held high and walked from the room followed by a silent and dignified Luke. They had to show him that, his threat to dispossess them notwithstanding, he could not intimidate them.

Once outside, tension drained from them in spite of the cloud of uncertainty which hung over them. They started along Church Street in the direction of the bridge across the Esk.

'Well?' said Lydia after a few moments during which both of them turned over in their mind the confrontation with their uncle. 'Do you think as I do – he drove Father to commit suicide?'

'We could never prove it,' replied her brother cautiously.

'I know, but what do you think?'

'Weighing everything up, I believe it is the likeliest solution.'

Lydia's eyes gleamed with excitement. 'Good. I'm glad you share my opinion.' Her tone was virulent.

'Steady on, Lydia. We could be wrong. Besides it may not have been any deliberate intention on Uncle's part.'

'Maybe not, but it happened. He was responsible and in my view deserves to be punished.'

'You'd never get him into court.'

'I know, but there are more ways than one of avenging Father's death.'

Chapter Four

There was so much for Luke and Lydia to think about over the next three days that life crowded in on them, but Luke could not eliminate from his mind the vow of revenge his sister had made as they had left his uncle's office.

He knew her as a determined young woman

who, in spite of being younger than he, always took the lead when they were together with decisions to make. Not that he sat back; he always made his opinion known but it was hers which generally prevailed. Now he determined to see that she made no rash moves which might bring devastating consequences. He sympathised with her attitude, for he felt the same animosity to their uncle. He too wanted revenge and agreed that there were more ways than one to achieve it. They must be subtle in their approach.

During the three days after their father's death they had to face enquiries from the authorities. But their tone was sympathetic and, having no doubt that Tristram had suffered a heart attack, they probed no further. There was also a stream of visitors to the house in St Hilda's Terrace offering sympathy and condolences.

With her world turned upside down, Lydia was pleased to see them. She was shattered by the loss of a man whom she'd loved dearly and to whom she had drawn close after the death of her mother. She found she needed support. She received this from Luke but knew that he too was suffering.

One of the first to visit was an anxious David Drayton, eager to be of assistance to the girl he admired and whom his family expected him to marry. Though he knew that his mother and father held a businesslike approach to the match, seeing it as of benefit to their own trading pursuits, he chose to ignore this motive, for Lydia had touched his heart.

She was grateful for his sympathy and for the

steady and practical way he helped Luke to deal with the funeral arrangements.

That took place in the old parish church high on the East Cliff. The minister extolled Tristram's virtues to a church packed with people, there to pay their last respects to a man who was well liked in Whitby.

As Lydia followed the coffin to the burial site she marvelled that the weather had been kind to them, in keeping with her father's character. Even the wind, which could lash viciously across this exposed cliff top, was today but a gentle breeze. As it caressed her cheeks she could almost feel her father's soothing touch comforting her in her woes. There was comfort too in Luke's firm grip on her hand as they watched the coffin lowered into the ground. Though her mind was torn, her body aching with grief, she fought the tears. Two escaped and trickled down her cheek. The rest welled inside her and were shed there.

As they turned away from the grave people offered their sympathies in low, respectful tones or in silent looks. Once that ordeal was over Lydia and Luke set off down the one hundred and ninety-nine steps to Church Street.

Lydia broke the silence when they were halfway down. 'Uncle Nathan didn't even come to the funeral.' There was bitterness in her voice.

Luke expressed his disgust and added, 'I thought Cousins Isobel and Christopher would have come. They were always friendly whenever I came across them. They never forgot the childhood days we shared before Grandfather died and caused the rift between our parents.'

'No doubt Uncle Nathan forbade them to come and they daren't go against his authority.'

'I expect so,' agreed Luke. He grimaced at the thought of the disunity in a family which could have enjoyed a close and loving relationship, for he too liked their cousins. 'Thank goodness Father wasn't cast in the same mould as Uncle Nathan. We will always have happy memories of him in spite of what has happened.' He paused then added, 'We have a problem, Lydia, and we have to face it quickly.'

She sighed. 'I know, but it will have to wait until we've received our visitors. There are sure to be some mourners who will come to the house. I wish it was all over.'

'So do I, but we must go through with it, for Father's sake. I'm sure his last thoughts were of us. Our suspicions about how he died must stay our secret.'

The preparations for the funeral tea had been made earlier in the day so that Mrs Harrington, their housekeeper-cook, and three maids could fulfil their wishes to attend the service. They had not gone to the graveside, deeming it better to return to the house and make the final arrangements there before anyone arrived.

Lydia and Luke were most appreciative. They had nothing to do but to prepare themselves to receive callers.

David Drayton was the first to arrive. He gave his heartfelt condolences again without being over-effusive. He made them simple and left them at that. He was more concerned about Lydia and wanted to ease the ordeal for her as much as he could. She appreciated his consideration and felt reassured by his physical presence. He saw that she was never monopolised by any one person and insisted she should take some refreshments. Lydia was thankful that he steered his father Jonas away from making any direct enquiries about the future of the business. Its demise would become clear to the people of Whitby soon enough.

Guests were taking their leave when two more arrived. When they entered the room Lydia's face broke into a smile of pleasure. She rose from her chair to greet her cousins.

'Isobel, Christopher, I'm so pleased to see you.' She hugged Isobel, remembering happier times they had been free to share until six years ago. Her arm still round Isobel, she held out her other hand. 'Christopher.' He took it and she felt in his touch the warmth of a friendship he still treasured deeply.

Isobel kept hold of Lydia's hand but stood back to look more closely at her cousin. She was pleased to see that Lydia, though a little pale, seemed in good health and appeared to be standing up to the ordeal well. 'We just had to come, had to let you know we do sympathise. We're only sorry we could not be at the church – Father forbade us.' Her regret at this ban and the one which had kept the cousins from close association was evident in Isobel's expression.

'Knowing approximately what time the funeral would be over, we made an excuse to leave the

94

house and here we are,' explained Christopher.

'I'm grateful to you for coming,' said Lydia, a tremor in her voice. 'Luke will be pleased as well. Come, sit down. We must catch up on the news.'

They had been seated only a few moments when Luke and David came into the room. Surprised at seeing his cousins, Luke hurried forward and expressed his pleasure. David greeted them and then turned to Lydia. 'You will be more than occupied now so I'll take my leave.'

She held out her hand to him. 'Thank you for your kindness and support today.'

David made his farewells and the cousins settled down for a long chat. Over the past six years contact between them had been accidental and brief. In his bitterness Nathan had commanded his family to have no association with his brother's. Though hurt by the loss of a formerly deep friendship with their cousins, Isobel and Christopher dare not flaunt the iron rule of their father. But now, in adulthood, they judged that they could no longer abide by that rule on an occasion when Lydia and Luke were in mourning.

All four of them enjoyed the exchanges and reminiscences. Isobel and Christopher were pleased that they had brought smiles to their cousins' faces to counteract the sombre atmosphere which had reigned in the house before their arrival.

Inevitably the question of the future came up. 'Will you continue to run the business?' Christopher asked.

95

'Won't be able to,' replied Luke. 'The loss of the ship and its cargo is a great blow and, after paying some debts, there will be nothing left on which to rebuild. But we have a great deal still to sort out before we know the exact position.'

'But you'll continue to live here?' queried Isobel.

Lydia smiled wanly. 'We have to be out by the end of next week.'

'What?' Both Isobel and Christopher stared at her in amazement.

'Under the terms of Grandfather's will all his properties went to your father with the proviso that our father had a life interest in this house. Beyond that there was no provision made for his family.'

'I don't believe it!' gasped Christopher, though he knew his cousin had no reason to lie.

'It's true,' Luke confirmed.

'Then we must speak to Father,' said Isobel firmly, receiving a nod of agreement from her brother.

'No! Please don't.' Lydia was quick with her request.

'But we must.'

'We don't want you to,' she insisted. 'Please, don't let us fall out over this.'

'You've seen Father?'

'Yes, at his office.'

'And he said he wanted you out?'

'Most certainly.'

'I know there was trouble between him and your father, but surely he couldn't see you out on the street?'

'He can and he has. Please don't ask any more. One day you may know the full story.'

Isobel glanced at her brother and received a signal that she should comply with Lydia's wishes.

'Very well.' Isobel squeezed her cousin's hand in an assurance that she would do nothing to upset her. 'But where will you go?'

'Father's death and the funeral have occupied all our time. We really haven't given it a great deal of thought, but now we must.'

'If there is anything we can do to help, please contact us,' said Christopher.

'Oh, do,' Isobel added. 'And if you change your mind and want us to speak to Father, we will.'

'Don't think about it. You'll only bring his wrath down on your heads because he'll know then you've seen us. We wouldn't want to be the cause of any friction between you. After all, he is your father and we know from our early years how much he dotes on both of you.'

Isobel and Christopher recognised she was right and they agreed to keep their own counsel but made their cousins promise that if there was anything they needed in the future, they would not hesitate to ask.

'I'm so glad they came,' said Lydia as she and Luke returned to the drawing room after saying goodbye to their cousins. 'They made me recall the happy times we used to share. Father would have been pleased.' She paused halfway across the hall, drawn by the sounds coming from the dining room where refreshments had been laid out for any visitors. 'We must thank Mrs Harrington and the maids for taking care of everything today.'

When they entered the dining room they found the three young maids clearing the tables, supervised by Mrs Harrington. The girls hesitated on seeing their employer, uncertain whether to continue their work or not. They bobbed a curtsy and stood where they were.

Mrs Harrington came over to Lydia, smoothing her apron as she did so. Her round red face broke into an understanding smile. Lydia drew immediate comfort from the presence of this kindly, motherly person who had been with the family for ten years. At that time she had been recently widowed and had appreciated the kindness she was shown by the Middleton family. Mrs Middleton was seeking a cook and a house-keeper, as live-in employees, along with two maids. During the interview Mrs Harrington had shrewdly weighed up the position. Realising that Mrs Middleton was the type of person who would like to do a certain amount of supervision in her own household, she had suggested that she could combine both positions if Mrs Middleton employed a third maid. Mrs Middleton saw the wisdom in this suggestion and agreed to a trial period. Mrs Harrington's gentle but firm authority, her thoughtfulness for the welfare of the family and happy working relationship with Mrs Middleton, left her employer with no cause for anxiety and the trial period was quickly forgotten.

Two years after she had come to the

Middletons' she was shaken by her mistress's sudden death. Without ever overstepping her position, she'd adopted the role of surrogate mother to Lydia and Luke. Her observance of the rapport between Mrs Middleton and her children enabled her to continue in the same manner, a fact much appreciated by Tristram.

She had seen the young Lydia blossom from a gangling, rather plain schoolgirl into a pretty, likeable young lady, and Luke into a handsome young man. She always had their interests close to her heart.

Now, knowing the ordeal they had been through, she came forward to offer succour. 'I hope it has not been too much for you, Miss Lydia?'

'No, it hasn't, thank you, Mrs Harrington.'

'You're sure you are all right?'

'Yes.'

'Good. Go to the drawing room then and have a nice quiet sit. I'll bring you both some tea. I'm sure you had very little when everyone was here. It's always the same.'

'Thank you, that would be welcome. But first I came to thank you all for the way you have managed everything today. We're sorry for all the extra work, but both Mr Luke and I appreciate what you have done.'

'All in the line of duty, Miss Lydia,' replied Mrs Harrington. 'Now, off with you, and I'll see to that tea.'

When she and Luke were settled in the drawing room, Lydia voiced her apprehension at one of the tasks they would now have to face. 'It's going to be dreadful having to tell Mrs Harrington and the maids that we can no longer employ them and that we must all leave.'

'It will be a blow to her and we're going to miss her terribly,' said Luke, a catch in his voice.

'I wish there was something we could do. She's been like a mother to us. I think I'll get it over with as soon as we've had tea. She and the maids must have time to adjust.'

Luke nodded. He tightened his lips and then said, 'I suppose so, but it's going to hurt.'

As they drank their tea and enjoyed Mrs Harrington's home-made cake, he brought Lydia up to date on developments with the business.

'When I was out yesterday I went to see the agent with whom Father took out his life insurance. Everything there will be straightforward. I also found out who advised Father about his unsound investment and went to see them – Mr Sleightholme and Mr Wear.'

Lydia raised her eyebrows in surprise. 'I would have thought their advice was genuine?'

'Oh, it was. There was no intention to deceive Father for their own ends. They thought the investment to be sound and they too have made losses though it hasn't affected them as deeply as Father. They kept within their means. They merely passed on the information to Father – it was up to him to judge it and decide what he should do. He acted on the information and, like Mr Sleightholme and Mr Wear, made his investment through Chapman's Bank. I saw Mr Chapman and explained what money would be forthcoming to meet the debt. He agreed to waive any further interest on the loan.'

'That's good of him. I hope he will be discreet about the debt?'

'He will be, and I got Mr Sleightholme and Mr Wear to promise to say nothing about Father's difficulty. They readily agreed, don't want it known that they too made a bad investment.'

'That is some comfort,' said Lydia. 'Will the insurance money meet what Father owes?'

Luke shook his head. 'I'm afraid not. When I came home I made a quick assessment of our assets as far as I could. I did not want to trouble you with it the day before the funeral.'

'And?' she prompted anxiously.

'Father was right, we'll have to sell everything.'

'Not my beloved piano!'

'I'm afraid so, love,' replied Luke sadly.

'But it's a family heirloom.'

'I know.' He wished he could give her better news and wipe the anguish from her face. 'It's a wonderful instrument and should fetch a tidy sum. That and what we get for the rest of the furniture plus the insurance money should cover Father's debt.'

The thought of losing her piano had brought tears to her eyes but she felt some relief at Luke's final words. Then, almost immediately, despondency returned. 'We'll have nothing?'

'Not a thing, except a few pounds saved from my wages.'

The enormity of their dilemma hit her then. The loss of her father, dealing with sympathisers, the funeral arrangements and then the funeral itself had all taken precedence in her mind. Now, in the aftermath, their own predicament came to the fore.

'Luke, what are we going to do?' She was on the verge of tears.

He saw that he had better word his observations carefully or his sister, who had coped extremely well up to now, would succumb to feelings she had bravely kept suppressed.

'Lydia, love, we must take things one step at a time. If we do that thoughtfully and without panic I am sure we will cope.' He gave his advice steadily and assured her that he was in control of their affairs. 'Our first priority is to find somewhere to live. I'm sure Uncle Nathan will exact his legal right immediately our notice is up.'

Lydia gained strength from her brother. She dried her tears, straightened her back and smoothed her dress. Running her hands across the soft material gave her comfort. 'But first, we had better break the news to Mrs Harrington.'

Luke expressed his agreement by rising from his chair and pulling the long cord beside the fireplace.

A few moment later one of the maids appeared.

'Liza, please ask Mrs Harrington to come to see me,' Lydia instructed.

'Yes, miss.' Liza scurried away to do as she was told.

When the housekeeper arrived Lydia indicated a chair and said, 'Please sit down.'

Mrs Harrington said nothing, sensing the unease her young employers felt.

'We are in a dilemma, Mrs Harrington. We have something to tell you which we regret very much.'

Lydia paused as if searching for the necessary words. Mrs Harrington could see that her young mistress was both embarrassed and upset.

'We would ask you, first, that you keep strictly to yourself some of the things we have to tell you.' Lydia's words were accompanied by a steady gaze which required a pledge.

'Miss, you know my tongue will be silent as it always has been about the private affairs of this family, ever since the day your dear mother engaged me.'

'We know that, Mrs Harrington. And we do trust you, as we always have, but I had to mention it so that you would appreciate the gravity of our situation.' Mrs Harrington nodded but made no comment and Lydia continued, coming straight to the point. 'Because of the loss of the *Mary Anne*, we are penniless. Father had certain debts which must be met. There is no need for me to go into detail, but please believe me when I say our situation is serious.'

'I wouldn't want you to elaborate, miss.'

'When the obligations are met, we will have nothing. We will have to sell everything.'

'Even the house?'

Lydia gave a wan smile of regret. 'The house doesn't belong to us.' She saw the amazement in Mrs Harrington's eyes and explained. 'When my grandfather died he left all his properties to our uncle with the proviso that Father had a life interest in this house. Now that he is dead, Uncle Nathan has told us he wants the house.'

'Oh, miss, surely he couldn't turn you out?'

'He could and he has,' injected Luke bitterly.

'We have until the end of next week to sort things out,' added Lydia.

'But, miss, what does this mean for me and the maids? Will you no longer want us?' There was a catch in Mrs Harrington's voice as she contemplated the happiness she had experienced with the Middletons.

'I'm afraid we just can't afford to employ any of you any more.'

'Oh, miss.' Tears came to Mrs Harrington's eyes but she fought to keep them back. She did not want to impose her own woes on these two young people who had become so much a part of her life. She dreaded having to face a future in which this family did not feature.

'We are sorry about this,' put in Luke, 'but there is nothing we can do about it. We would dearly like to keep you all in our employment but there just isn't the money. I'll have my wage but it is small at the moment. I was hoping to progress in the iron trade out of Whitby. Maybe I shall, but that won't solve our immediate problems.'

'I understand, Mr Luke. You both have enough to cope with without our predicament being thrust upon you. Do you want me to tell the maids?'

'No,' said Lydia. 'It would not be fair to put what is our responsibility upon you. Besides I'd rather the bad news came from me.'

'Very well, miss. When will you want us to leave?'

'We would be grateful if all of you would stay for the remainder of our time here.'

'You'll be paid, of course. We have made sure we can manage that,' said Luke.

'We'd willingly forego...' Mrs Harrington began.

'No,' Lydia interrupted, 'you must have your dues.'

The housekeeper knew better than to object any further. Miss Lydia was a strong-minded, independent young woman whom she knew would not want anything that smacked of charity.

'Very well, miss.' Mrs Harrington put her hand before her mouth as if plucking up the courage to voice a question which had just occurred to her. 'Miss, may I ask where you and Mr Luke are going to live?'

'You may ask, Mrs Harrington, but I can't give you an answer. We do not know ourselves.'

'With the last of the money we have, it will probably be a hovel on the east side,' put in Luke in a dispirited tone.

'Oh, Mr Luke, you can't go to one of those! They aren't fit for a beggar, let alone respectable people like yourselves. The squalor could be enough to finish you, but the degradation of living among the neighbours you'd find there would certainly destroy you.'

'Mrs Harrington, it can't be as bad as that.' Lydia gave a shaky laugh.

'Miss, you cannot go there.' The firmness of this statement reminded Lydia of the days when she and Luke were children and had been forced to obey Mrs Harrington.

'We might have to if nothing better turns up, and there isn't long to go.'

'But something *has* turned up,' said Mrs Harrington. She gave a knowing little smile as if she was pleased with the idea she was about to impart.

'What do you mean?' asked Luke. Lydia was as mystified as he.

'You know that when my husband died I kept our little house, anticipating there might come a day when I would retire? I haven't seen fit to do that yet. It's there still, just big enough for two, so I suggest you young people use it.'

'You mean, move in there?'

'Yes, it's furnished so it won't matter that you'll have to sell everything here.'

'But won't you want to go there?'

'It's only big enough for two. I needn't go there until you leave, and that must be whenever it suits you.'

'But what will you do?'

'I'll go to my sister. She's on her own and is ailing a bit so she'll be pleased of the company. I'll find work as a cook locally without having to live in, so you use my cottage for as long as you want.'

'What can we say, Mrs Harrington?' Lydia's eyes were damp with gratitude. 'This has taken one problem off our minds and will give us time to work out where our future lies.'

There were more tears when Lydia broke the news to the maids. They were sorry to have to leave a kindly, understanding employer and feared they would not find such a post again. They were only too willing to stay for the remainder of the allotted time.

106

The following Monday morning when David Drayton turned into St Hilda's Terrace he received a shock to see activity around the Middletons' house and furniture being taken out of it and loaded on to carts. His step quickened and, finding the front door open, he hurried straight in. Lydia, with tears running down her cheeks, was standing at the bottom of the stairs watching the removal of her piano.

'Lydia, what's happening?' he gasped.

'We are having to sell everything,' she said wearily. 'Most is going today, the rest on Saturday.'

'But you love that piano.'

'I know, but it's got to go.' She started to sob.

He put a comforting arm around her shoulders and led her to the drawing room.

'Now tell my why?' he said as he closed the door.

She swallowed hard and dabbed her eyes with her handkerchief. 'We have to move out and can't take all this with us,' she answered cautiously. She wanted to keep her father's debts a secret if she could.

'But why do you have to move out? This house is yours now. Well, yours and Luke's.'

'I'm afraid it isn't.'

'Your father would naturally leave it to you. There's no one else.'

'But it was never his.'

David frowned in disbelief. Lydia explained the situation.

'And now your uncle wants it!'

She nodded.

'Surely he hasn't turned you out?'

'Yes. He wants to move in at the end of the week.'

'I knew he and your father had differences but I didn't know they ran so deep that he would evict his own niece and nephew.'

Lydia gave a little sigh. 'Then you don't know Uncle Nathan.'

'What are you going to do? Where are you going?'

'Mrs Harrington has kindly offered us her house in Wellington Square. We'll go there when we leave here.'

'Wellington Square?' David looked shocked. 'But that's not what you're used to.'

'Maybe not, but we'll have to get used to it for the time being.'

'It's a crowded area and just off Baxtergate. Goodness knows who you'll get snooping around.'

'I know it's not St Hilda's Terrace nor Cliff Street where you live, but being Mrs Harrington's it will be respectable and clean, and it's good of her to offer it to us until we can decide our future,' Lydia answered a little testily. 'Goodness knows where we'd have ended up if it hadn't been for her.'

'I'm not disparaging Mrs Harrington. I know how much she has meant to your family, and it's extremely kind of her to help in this way.' David changed the subject. 'Lydia, I haven't seen you since the day of the funeral. I've kept away thinking you might prefer some time to yourself but I could keep away no longer. I want to know how you are?'

Pleased with his concern, she smiled her appreciation. 'You are very kind. Physically I'm quite well. There's much to occupy my mind at the moment, but it's still hard to believe I will not see Father again.' A catch came into her voice.

He reached out and took her hand. She felt comforted by his touch and he thrilled to the contact. Desire surged in him. The girl he loved was in trouble and there flashed through his mind a way to solve her problems.

'Lydia, I know so soon after your father's death may not be the best time to say this, but I'm going to.' She heard the intensity in his voice. His eyes had come alive. 'Marry me and it will solve all your problems.'

For a moment she was taken aback by the suddenness of this proposal. She stared at him, speechless. Her mind whirled as difficulties and solutions occurred to her, threatening to stifle her reason. There was an almost overwhelming desire to say yes, for this would indeed solve everything. There would be comfort, riches even, she would never want again. Luke had his job. But even as she made this quick appraisal, caution raised its head. Was this what she wanted? She loved David but would it appear as if she was taking an easy way out to solve her immediate problems? She did not want that. Then the facts of her father's death thrust their way to the fore and her mind churned with the desire to avenge him. If she married David, she dare not pursue that course. He would not want the cordial relationship which existed between his father's firm and her uncle's to be affected by her theories and accusations.

'Marry me,' he said again.

She hesitated. She could see that he was hanging on her answer, wanting her to say yes. She reached out and touched his cheek. 'That is sweet of you but I can't give you an answer now. With so much happening I must have time to think.'

He did not look disappointed but said in a tone of meek acceptance, 'If that is what you want then so be it. I'll await your answer eagerly.'

When Lydia broke this news to Luke he was surprised. He knew Lydia and David had felt a great admiration for each other since childhood but he had not realised that this had blossomed into true love. He knew David's parents had seen a link between the families as advantageous to the businesses, but what would their views be when they learned that Tristram Middleton's firm no longer existed?

'And what will your answer be?' he asked.

Lydia gave a shrug of her shoulders. 'I don't know. It would solve one of our problems. I would have a husband to look after me. You have your job and could pursue your ambition without the worry of providing for me.'

'Lydia,' Luke took on an extremely serious tone, 'I must not come into your calculations. It is your happiness that must count. I want that, and I know Father and Mother would have wanted it too. So it must be uppermost in your mind. The real question is not how to solve your problems or ease our situation, but whether you love him or not.'

Lydia shook her head. 'Oh, I don't know. I like him. We've always got on well together. He's kind and considerate. He's asked me before but I was always evasive. He swore that one day he would get me to say yes. I've always thought I probably would, but is now the time? He doesn't know that we have lost everything, but has he maybe taken advantage of our homelessness, thinking it will make me grasp at any opportunity to escape it?'

'You must not marry for convenience. If you do you will never be happy.' Luke paused, but seeing that she had listened to his words carefully didn't press his opinions further. She would decide in her own good time.

David could not concentrate on his work. In mid-afternoon he left his office on the east side overlooking the harbour and crossed the swivel bridge, an improvement on the drawbridge it had replaced fifteen years ago. He walked along St Anne's Staith, through Haggersgate and on to Pier Lane. The afternoon had turned grey and the wind had freshened but David was well cloaked against its chill. He rather liked this sort of weather; it brought briskness to his walk along the west pier, drove sharp air into his lungs and stung his cheeks with a refreshing tang. It gave him a feeling of well-being which would be all the more enjoyable if Lydia would only say yes.

He breathed deeply of the salt air and strode

towards the fluted Doric column of the stone lighthouse, an important addition to the harbour facilities in 1831. He approved of the continued employment of Francis Pickernell as resident Harbour Engineer, for it meant continual supervision and development which in turn meant improved amenities for the ships in which his father had invested. There were now better methods of handling goods and facilities for storage. Lydia would benefit from all this if she married him.

The sea was running high, driven by the wind. From the pier he could see it pounding the cliffs below the ruined abbey and beyond. In the other direction waves rolled their white caps towards the long stretch of sand running to Sandsend. They broke in a whirl of foam, sending their whiteness streaming up the beach. The water then ran back to meet the next white cap which was flung its way. Spray rose on the wind and lay across the scene as if cloaking a mystery. David revelled in the atmosphere and anticipated sharing the experience and his enthusiasm for it with Lydia.

The more she occupied his mind, the more sure he was she would say yes. Tonight over dinner he would break the news of his proposal to his mother and father. He reckoned they would be pleased for they had never disguised their hope that this would happen.

He knew that they saw such a marriage as bringing an alliance between the Drayton and Middleton firms, and thus strengthening their position within the trading fraternity of Whitby.

They had never doubted that Tristram would approve of this equally. Lydia was the apple of his eye and would bring her share of his business with her when she married. But that situation had changed. With Tristram's death Lydia would surely get her share of the business sooner?

Thoughts of his son occupied Jonas Drayton's mind when he left the office. He was surprised to find that David had already gone and offered no explanation to the staff as to why he too was leaving early. He was a law unto himself and did not let them forget it. He ruled his firm with strict discipline and an iron resolve, being only marginally more tolerant to his son during working hours than he was to the rest of his employees. Jonas deemed this rigidity was good for him, breeding character which would manifest itself when David assumed full control.

With Jonas's departure the atmosphere in the office eased and the staff relaxed in the knowledge that there was no need now to keep their noses inside their ledgers, manifest papers and invoices.

Today Jonas's stride was measured but slow. He was satisfied with life. He ran a successful merchant's business with investments in ships which brought a good income. But it had not come about without the hard work of his early trading years and an astute mind for seeing and seizing an opportunity. He saw such an opportunity in his son's marriage to Lydia Middleton. Tristram Middleton's business was sound but it had lacked a man with flair to expand and

113

develop it, something Jonas was certain he could do. His chance had come sooner than he had expected. Yes, life was good. Maybe a little celebration was called for. A call at the Angel Inn was merited.

Coaches had been running from the Angel in Baxtergate since 1795 and, as the route grew busier, the inn became a hive of activity, a meeting place, the site of social functions both public and private. With its good food and congenial atmosphere, businessmen of the town met here, either by appointment or casually to exchange notes and gossip. Jonas called in maybe once or twice a week, finding it advisable to keep up with local news and what was happening in the town.

He passed the time of day with the landlord when he entered the inn, called for his usual glass of brandy and made his way down some stairs to a snug. It was cosy and quiet, a place which seemed to call for hushed voices, a room with an atmosphere which encouraged the exchange of gossip and rumours.

Four tradesmen, well known to Jonas and he to them, were already enjoying their tankards of ale or glasses of spirits. They greeted him amiably as he lowered his tall, lean body into a chair at their table, and took him into their flow of conversation about proposed developments to the quays on the east side of the river.

'It's a pity Tristram can't give us his views, he was keen on certain aspects,' said a rotund man who leaned back in his chair as he made the observation.

'His loss is a tragedy,' commented another. 'And if what I hear is true his son and daughter are left almost penniless.'

Jonas started. His dark eyes, which had grown somnolent in this convivial atmosphere, now became sharp and searching as he glanced around the men seated at the table. 'Penniless?' His word was clipped. 'They can't be.'

The man who had offered this information spread his hands in a gesture of deference. 'Only rumours. I cannot vouch for their truth.'

'What have you heard?' asked the rotund man, anticipating a story to take home to his wife.

'Maybe Jonas knows more than I,' came the answer. He glanced at the new arrival. 'Your son and Miss Lydia Middleton see something of each other, I believe.'

'They do,' Jonas admitted. 'But I have heard nothing of what you imply.'

'As I say, they're only rumours.' The man added with a wise-owl look, 'But often truth will out after rumours are heard.' He continued when pressed by his companions, 'Well, I've heard tell that Tristram left debts which Mr Luke and Miss Lydia are having difficulty in meeting.'

'Debts?' Jonas put the query cautiously.

'Yes.' The man nodded. 'True or not, I've heard that he made some unwise investments and now there's nothing left. His children are having to sell everything.'

'If the rumour is true this is terrible news,' commented Jonas, hiding the real reason for his concern. 'Where did you hear it?'

'Sam Charters. Where he'd got it, I don't know,

115

but a hint had been dropped somewhere, picked up and passed on to him because he had had dealings with Tristram in the past. He wondered if I had heard anything. I hadn't, so couldn't confirm or deny.'

'So it's just a rumour,' said one of the others dismissively as he placed his tankard on the table.

With that the conversation drifted to other matters, like the vessels being built in the thriving shipyards, the shipment of iron ore out of Whitby, the state of the jet trade, the economies of the Peak alum industry, and the possibilities of further links with the Whitby-Pickering railway which would ameliorate the port's isolated position on the Yorkshire coast. All these nuggets of information were useful to the minds of men who saw in the development of the town a boost to their own fortunes.

But today Jonas had only half his mind on what was being said. The other was still trying to decide whether the earlier information was just unsubstantiated rumour or not. Maybe David knew something. Well, if he did, his father would have it out of him and chastise him for not imparting his knowledge sooner.

David was not at home when Jonas arrived and he took the opportunity to inform his wife, Eugenia, of what he had heard.

'Surely this can't be true?' she queried.

Jonas shrugged his shoulders. 'Who knows? But one thing is certain: if it is, David had better look elsewhere for a bride. I'm not having him marrying Miss Lydia without her bringing something

116

to the marriage.'

'I should think not,' agreed Eugenia. 'You need her interest in the Middleton business to help us expand.' Eugenia had never gone against her husband. Meek and humble, some folks said with a sneer behind her back, but she was also shrewd. Agreeing with her husband bolstered his ego and that produced renewed confidence in his own ability to make deals which were profitable. And she liked profits. They gave her an extremely comfortable and leisurely lifestyle with all the assets that money could buy. And she liked the idea of these increasing further. Her hopes of a favourable development soon had now received a setback. But then her mind latched on to an idea.

'Jonas, there is another Middleton other than Miss Lydia,' she announced with a note of satisfaction.

'What do you mean?' asked Jonas.

'There's Miss Isobel.'

'Nathan's daughter?'

'Of course.'

Jonas greeted his wife's ability to see an alternative so quickly with pursed lips, bright eyes and a chuckle.

Eugenia smiled, content in the knowledge that her hint had struck home.

He nodded. 'That could well be better. Isobel is a good catch. It would make Nathan less of a rival, more of a friendly enemy, for he would have to drop his animosity to us and be more willing to exchange ideas. We would not gain the same overall influence we would have with Tristram, but Nathan is a shrewd judge of opportunities

117

and he would want his daughter to benefit through us. I have no doubt he would see that we learned of anything worthwhile. Yes, if this rumour is true then David will have to set his sights on Isobel.'

'Don't rush in as soon as he comes home. Do it quietly towards the end of our meal. Let's have some special wine. Work him into a good receptive mood.'

'You're a crafty witch.' He laughed quietly, drawing her into his euphoria. Maybe there would be other ways to celebrate.

'And a tempting one?' There was suggestion in her eyes as she came towards him.

He laughed and spanned her waist with long thin fingers to draw her into his kiss.

She knew she had him under her spell and that he would handle their son in the way she had suggested.

By the time he reached home David had decided that he would choose the right moment to inform his parents of his proposal to Lydia. It would need subtlety to make them see that he did not want to marry to advance his father's business but wanted to do so for love. If the business was helped by that then it was all to the good, but if it wasn't then so be it.

Dinner was a congenial affair. The cook's special vegetable soup was followed by a succulent roast duck with an exquisite orange sauce, potatoes and green vegetables. There followed an apple pie and syllabub. Wine flowed freely, putting them all in a good mood.

David wondered why his parents were so exuberant but did not question it when he saw it working to his advantage. Relaxed in this way they would be more receptive to his news. At the start of the meal, preoccupied with what he wanted to tell them, he had felt a little strained but the good food and wine had banished his apprehension.

'Let's take coffee in the drawing room,' said Eugenia, rising from her chair. She indicated to the maid to bring it and received a nod of understanding from the girl.

Once they had settled, Jonas leaned back contentedly in his favourite chair. 'David, there is...'

At the same moment he started, 'Father, Mother, there is something I want...'

Father and son pulled up short with nervous laughs.

'What is it?' asked Jonas.

'No, sir, you shall have the first say,' replied David quickly, seizing on the chance to take a few more minutes to collect his thoughts about the approach he should make. Start gently in a roundabout manner or plunge straight in? But the answer to that question was speedily apparent.

'On my way home today I called in at the Angel and there I heard some very distressing news. I've already told your mother and she's just as shocked as I was.' Jonas paused. He saw he had David's concentrated attention. 'It was more a rumour that Tristram Middleton's firm is no longer operating because of debts he had

119

incurred. Everything, even his personal possessions, furniture, the lot, is having to be sold to meet them apparently. You are close to Miss Lydia, I wondered if you can confirm or deny this rumour?'

David had not expected this and his hesitation in replying gave him away.

'You do know something?' pressed his father.

David nodded. 'Earlier today I visited Lydia, a courtesy call to see how she was. I was surprised when I reached the house to see all the furniture was being taken away to be sold.'

'And did you hear any reason for this?' his mother asked.

'Yes. Apparently the house was left to Mr Nathan when his father died but his brother had a life interest in it. Now Mr Nathan wants it for himself.'

'He's turning Lydia and Luke out?'

'Yes.'

'Have they bought somewhere else?'

'No. Mrs Harrington has given them the use of her house until they decide what they are going to do.'

'Did Lydia mention what will happen to the firm?'

David shook his head. 'No.'

Jonas looked thoughtful. 'If Miss Lydia and Luke are selling everything, then what I heard could be true.'

'But Lydia said it was because there was no room for their things at Mrs Harrington's,' David pointed out.

'That may be the reason she gave you, but tie it

120

up with what I was told. If they were going to carry on the business they would have stored the furniture until such time as they were able to get another house. They would not be selling it. I reckon it's right it is being sold to meet part of the debts Tristram is said to have left. And no doubt the business is either being sold quietly for the same reason, or there'll be no money left to operate it and it will cease to exist.'

'If that is true Lydia will be penniless, so all the more reason for her to say yes to my proposal.' David spoke almost to himself but his words were audible enough for his mother to pick up.

'Proposal? What do you mean?' she asked sharply.

'I asked Lydia to marry me. I love her. I would have asked her sometime in any case.'

'What? You proposed marriage to a girl who will bring nothing?' Jonas spat.

'Yes, now seemed as good a time as any. Marriage would solve the predicament she is in, though she did not indicate it was as serious as you've heard.'

'And I expect she said yes! She'd grasp the chance to get your money behind her.' Jonas's tone was scathing.

'She's not like that,' David protested. 'You should know, you like her. You've always approved of our relationship.'

Eugenia gave a dismissive wave of her hand. 'People can change, especially when they face possible poverty. Lydia has never given you the same encouragement you have given her.'

'Mother, you don't know how close we are, and

121

I'm sure she'll say yes.'

'Then she hasn't yet done so?'

'No.'

Jonas and Eugenia showed relief in their exchange of glances, but that was dashed as David continued.

'Not there and then. She said she wanted time to think as there was so much happening.'

Jonas seized on his words. 'So much happening. What was she implying by that? She told you they were selling the furniture because they couldn't take it with them, yet she talks about so *much* happening. What else? Seems like there's something to these rumours after all.'

'And when do you expect her answer?' asked Eugenia.

'When she is ready to give it. But I'll press her for it. The sooner she realises she needn't face poverty, the better.'

'You'll tell her no such thing,' said Jonas coldly. 'In fact, you'll forget any idea of marrying Lydia Middleton as from now.'

David was so taken aback by his father's blunt words that he was speechless.

'You heard your father,' said Eugenia, enforcing his command.

David nodded. 'I heard. But you can't forbid this. I love Lydia.'

'Love has nothing to do with it,' snorted Jonas.

'It has everything to do with it. I love her and I believe she loves me. There's no better reason than that to get married.'

'And what about advancement?' asked Eugenia quietly.

'Advancement?' he queried.

'You can't be blind to the fact that in our social circle marriages are made so that families may prosper by them. If love is there as well, then so be it,' Jonas pontificated.

'It's true, David. Don't look so surprised,' said his mother with a faint smile at his bewilderment.

He was shocked at their cynical view. 'Then it will be different in my case. If Lydia brings nothing to the marriage in the way of worldly wealth and goods, it doesn't matter. I love her for what she is, not what she has.'

'She would once have had a share of Tristram Middleton's business, and her share coupled with what you will inherit would have given you more power among the Whitby merchants.'

'I'm not bothered about power. I don't want...' He paused. Behind the mask of disapproval on his father's face he saw a deeper meaning. 'Ah, I see it all now. You aren't concerned about my feelings in all of this. It once suited you very well that I had feelings for her, but only because it accorded with your plans for the business. Well, I'm sorry to disappoint you but you can forget them. I'm sticking to Lydia.'

Jonas's lips tightened. 'There are other girls who would enhance your prospects.'

'You mean yours,' snapped David.

'Ultimately benefitting you.'

'I'll marry Lydia and you'll have to like it.'

'I won't like it and you won't marry her!' Jonas's face reddened with anger.

'I will!'

'Very well, but from the moment you do your allowance will be cut off.' His father's voice was rapier-like, making each thrust at his son painful. 'You will no longer be employed by me and the firm will go to your cousin in Scarborough on my death.'

There was no mistaking that his father meant it. The signs were there in the deadly seriousness of his eyes which never wavered as he stared at his son. There was no reaction from his mother, no gasp of horror at the pronouncement, no plea on her lips, so David knew she was in full agreement with his father.

He was beaten but he was still defiant. He sprang to his feet and glared at Jonas, wanting to wipe the look of anticipated triumph off his face. 'Then you'd better get used to not having a son.' There was no reaction from his parents and he started for the door.

When he reached it he hesitated as a voice spoke in cold, considered tones.

'Think again, son. Look elsewhere. Lydia's cousin Isobel would make a good catch and would be a joy to bed.'

Chapter Five

Still seething with anger, his body taut with defiance, David stormed up the stairs. The light from the candelabra in the hall sent his shadow swinging round the curved wall as it matched him step for step. It flirted with him momentarily when he reached the landing and then was gone as he moved towards his room.

He flung open the door and slammed it shut behind him. The oil lamp, which had been lit by one of the servants half an hour earlier, juddered as the table shook with the crash of the door. He sank his back against it, trying to control the rage heaving within him. His face was twisted with anger and exasperation. He cried out to the heavens to guide him from the corner into which he had been driven. Choose! The word clamoured in his brain. Choose! Gradually his breathing, heavy after his exertions, eased back to normal. He pushed himself from the door and sat in a chair.

He gave a sigh, rested his elbows on the table and held his head in his hands. He tried to assess his situation with a clear mind. As he did so, Lydia became more and more prominent in his thoughts. There was no doubt that he loved her but he was confused as to what form that love should take. Should he defy his father for the girl he loved and condemn the two of them to a life of poverty? He would go to her penniless whereas he had expected to be able to keep her in the style to which she had been accustomed. No doubt she was thinking he would be able to do that. But, in view of his father's stipulation, what would life hold for them if he did defy Jonas? Could David face seeing her scratching and scraping, day after day, to save a penny here, to save one there? Could he face the anguish that would bring him? He had never wanted for

125

anything so could he cope with poverty and the continual struggle of trying to overcome it?

But if he bowed to his father's wishes he would have to face Lydia with a decision which could tear her heart in two. If only he hadn't mentioned marriage at this stage. Maybe if he explained the situation carefully she would consent to wait until he could persuade his parents that he loved her and would not give her up. They must be made to see that there could be an amicable solution which would negate the drastic step his father had proposed.

Tomorrow would be a day of decisions when the destiny of many lives would be forged.

That same night when Lydia went to bed she was still undecided about David's proposal. The easiest path would be to say yes and accept whatever the future brought. But she did not want a marriage born on the horns of a dilemma. When she made her vows in front of a priest it had to be alongside a man who loved her for herself, one who wanted to be there because his professed love came from the heart and not out of sympathy and a desire to help her in her troubles.

She fell into a fitful sleep, hoping that by the time David came for her answer she would have made the right decision.

That moment came sooner than she'd expected.

The following morning David waited in his room until he knew his father had left for the office. He did not want another confrontation on top of the deliberations he had subjected himself to during the night. He also avoided his mother by forgoing breakfast and leaving the house immediately he came downstairs.

The morning was sharp with a fresh breeze but pleasant enough as there were few clouds to hide the sun. The port had come alive with all the activities the day's trading brought. Ships were being loaded with foodstuffs for London, alum for Newcastle and London, and iron ore for the works on Tyneside and the more recent developments on the banks of the River Tees. Even though there were now more men working on merchantmen than at fishing there were still a number of cobles with lines ready to leave the safety of their moorings for the hazardous North Sea. The clash of hammers rose from the shipbuilding yards renowned throughout the shipping world for the reliability and soundness of their work.

But David was oblivious to all this as he hurried to St Hilda's Terrace, nodding only curtly to any friends and acquaintances he passed.

He jerked the bell-pull at number twenty-one and impatiently rattled the brass doorknocker shaped like a fish. When the door was opened anxiety about Lydia's reaction brought unwonted sharpness to his query. 'Is Miss Middleton at home?'

'Yes, sir,' replied the maid nervously. Although she had opened the door to him on many occasions, she had never seen him in such an agitated mood. She stepped to one side and closed the door after he had entered the hall.

'Well, where is she?' David snapped.

'In the dining room, sir.'

He strode across the hall, hoping Luke was not with his sister. What he had to say was for her ears alone. The maid scurried across the tiles trying to circumvent him but before she could announce him he was into the room.

Lydia, taken aback by the intrusion, looked up from her cup of tea. 'David, what a surprise so early. After yesterday I thought it might be a few days before you came for my answer.'

'You have one so soon? But I...'

'Let me give it to you,' she interrupted quickly, and he could do nothing but allow her to go on. 'I'm sorry, David, I cannot marry you now.' She hurried on with her explanation before he could react. 'Due to our change of circumstances there are certain things I need to do. If I married you and still did them it would not be fair on you.'

David felt an unmistakable pang of relief but at the same time sharp disappointment.

'What have you to do?' he asked automatically. 'Can I help?'

'No, you can't.'

'Tell me and let me decide?'

'No.'

He knew he should not pursue the matter. 'Very well, but if ever...' He shrugged his shoulders. 'Maybe this has turned out for the best. Your decision eases mine, and you said "now" so there is hope for the future?'

She nodded but said, 'That sounds as though you've had second thoughts about the proposal?

Is there something you're not happy about? If so then we'll just forget you ever made it.'

'No, I don't want that. But waiting until I am in a position to give you the life you have been used to and deserve might be no bad thing.'

'Can't you give me that now?'

He shook his head dejectedly. 'No.'

Lydia was astonished at his answer. 'What are you implying?'

He went on to tell her of his confrontation with his parents and the ultimatum made by his father, but did not mention Isobel.

Lydia listened without comment until he had finished and then said quietly but tellingly, 'So you wouldn't give up your kind of life for one in poverty shared with me?'

'It isn't that, Lydia!' he cried. 'I want to be able to provide for you as I should. I can only do that if we wait until I persuade my parents that it is no good expecting me to marry where they decree.'

'They're so calculating,' said Lydia in disgust. 'I knew them to be snobs but was always pleased it hadn't rubbed off on you. They're thinking only of themselves and not of your happiness.'

'It's not like that,' David protested though inwardly sharing her opinion. 'We just need to be patient. We need to give them time to...'

'They'll never give in, but you will. You'll find someone more to their liking and that will be that.'

'No!' His voice rose. 'It's you I love. It's you I want to marry. We're both of the same mind so let's just wait.'

'But even then, won't it depend on your

parents' attitude? I'll never be able to bring to the marriage what they want.'

'Waiting will give me time to change their minds.'

'You're sure you can do that?'

'Yes. I'll show them you would bring more to our marriage than mere money, more than the assets of a thriving company.'

Lydia extended her hand to shake his. 'Then we have an amicable arrangement to see how things turn out.' But secretly she wondered if David would still feel the same once Nathan had finally exacted his right of ownership and turned his nephew and niece out of their home.

When David had gone Lydia went to the kitchen and sat down wearily on a chair beside the table. She tightened her lips in exasperation. How her life had changed! From being comfortably off, living happily with her father in the expectation of a marriage which would see her want for nothing, she now faced life without parents and with little money, and having to wait for an eventual marriage to David Drayton if he could ever persuade his parents to allow it.

Her thoughts turned to David and his attitude. If he really loved her, wouldn't he have defied his father, forsaken the life he knew, married her and faced life's trials in partnership with her? He had said his decision was made because of her but was it rather because of himself? Could he really bear to give up his comfortable way of life?

If she had married him and continued to move in the same social circles, her desire to avenge her

130

father's death could have had dire repercussions for a husband. If David had come to her on the other hand, ostracised by his father, shunned by society because of their poverty, her revenge could have been pursued relentlessly. But as he had chosen not to, best to set thoughts of him aside and concentrate on paying back her uncle, she decided.

When Lydia told her brother of David's visit his first concern was for her. 'Are you sure you have done the right thing?'

'Yes,' she replied firmly. 'But I am a little disgusted he did not defy his father and call Jonas's bluff.'

'Don't be too hard on him. You've always liked David and you know how demanding his father can be. Jonas wields an iron fist.'

'You really believe he'd cut David off completely?'

'Undoubtedly, if it came to it, but David has one thing in his favour. Jonas makes no secret of the fact that he hopes some day David's son will take over the business. At some point therefore David has to marry. If he can only hold out long enough Jonas will be forced to welcome you eventually. But if David walks away from his family now he'll lose everything.' Luke was careful to check that his sister fully understood her best course of action. 'Don't condemn David, I think he has done this because of his love for you. He wants the life for you that you deserve.'

Lydia looked thoughtful as she took his words

131

to heart. 'Maybe you're right, but Jonas might bring pressure to bear on David to find someone else. We'll just have to wait and see.' Her eyes narrowed as her thoughts turned elsewhere. 'Unencumbered by marriage, at least I can concentrate on our plans for Uncle Nathan.'

'And just what do you propose?' asked her brother cautiously.

Lydia eyed him closely. 'Does that tone of voice indicate you are having second thoughts?'

'No, no.' He was quick to alleviate her suspicions. 'But it will be a hard task and could lead us into all sorts of trouble.'

Lydia recognised the side of her brother's character which at times made him over-cautious. It was then that he would let things slide. This could not be allowed to happen now. She must take the initiative and keep their objective constantly to the fore.

On Saturday morning the last items of furniture had gone from St Hilda's Terrace by ten o'clock. All that was left were Lydia's and Luke's remaining personal possessions.

They had just finished their breakfast and were having a final word with the maids in the kitchen when they heard the front door burst open. Footsteps stormed along the bare boards of the hall. Doors were flung open and then crashed shut. Surprised and curious at the intrusion, they hastily left the kitchen.

'Ah, there you are.' Nathan's voice boomed out, seeming to fill the denuded rooms and echo throughout the house. 'Time's up, so get out.

This is *my* house now. I'm moving in today. The carpets will be here soon and the furniture later in the day. So out with you!' Smug with the satisfaction of having at last attained something he had always regarded as rightfully his, he gesticulated towards the front door.

'You've no right to come bursting in here,' protested Luke.

Nathan laughed. 'I have every right. This house is mine. It's you who have no right here.'

'You had a key?' Lydia was stunned by what this might imply.

'Yes.' He held it up triumphantly. 'Ever since I lived here.' He saw the look of distrust on her face. 'Oh, no, my dear, don't give me that. I have never used it until today, I'd swear to that on the Bible. Now stop shilly-shallying. Leave!'

Lydia drew herself up. 'We will. I would not want to stay in this house another minute. You've tainted it by your presence. It no longer feels like home.' She turned and hurried back to the kitchen.

A few minutes later the maids had departed by the back door after a brief but tearful goodbye. With their few possessions in two bags, sister and brother, accompanied by Mrs Harrington, left without another word to their uncle.

When they reached her small house in Wellington Square, off the thoroughfare of Baxtergate, she started to apologise for its state.

'Mrs Harrington,' Lydia halted her excuses, 'this is simply delightful.'

'But it's so small and not at all what you have been used to.'

'It's cosy, comfortable, and I know we will like it here.' Lydia raised an eyebrow and gave a little smile. 'I suspect you have been coming here every day to get things to your liking.'

'And, I hope, to *your* liking?'

'Of course,' put in Luke, to add weight to Lydia's assurances.

Though they had only been in the house a few minutes they felt comfortable in its welcoming atmosphere. That feeling persisted as Mrs Harrington showed them round. From the front room, which gave immediately on to the street, they stepped into the back parlour which served as a kitchen with its black range of fire, oven and a boiler for water.

Noting the fire burning brightly, Luke said, 'How thoughtful of you to come here early this morning and light a fire, Mrs Harrington.'

'I thought it would look more welcoming,' she replied.

'It's so cheery, it seems to lighten our troubles,' said Lydia, her eyes damp.

'And such a nice table and chairs,' observed Luke, wanting to direct his sister's mind from the thoughts he knew still bothered her. These items of furniture occupied the centre of the room. A matching cupboard stood in a recess between the chimney breast and the outside wall.

'My husband made them.'

'A skilled man.'

'Woodwork was his spare-time occupation when he was not away fishing. He liked to keep busy between sailings.'

A window looked on to a yard, part of which

was occupied by a scullery with access from the back room. Upstairs were two small bedrooms lively with brightly coloured crocheted bedspreads, the work of Mrs Harrington's never-idle hands.

'This is a lovely little home,' said Lydia appreciatively. 'We cannot thank you enough for being so generous in allowing us to occupy it until we settle our problems and can find somewhere we can afford.'

'Take as long as you like. My sister will be pleased to have me around.' She filled a kettle and hung it on the reckon over the fire. 'I think a cup of tea is the first thing you should have in your new home.'

The next half hour would be forever marked on Lydia's mind. They sat at the table together over a cup of tea, a fire dancing in the grate. A conversation which revolved round Mrs Harrington's childhood and marriage brought some sort of peace to Lydia.

But once Mrs Harrington had gone and they had chosen their bedrooms, Lydia taking the front and Luke the back, the changes she was forced to undergo almost overwhelmed Lydia.

She sank wearily on to a chair. 'Oh, Luke, what are we going to do?'

The girl who had generally taken the lead, making most of the decisions for them with a firm resolve, now seemed to be bordering on despair. Luke knew he must be the rock she could lean on.

'We'll manage,' he said firmly, kneeling in front of her and taking her hands in his. 'At least I have work and we are lucky to have this house, thanks to Mrs Harrington.'

'I know, but it's all going to be so different.' Her voice choked with emotion.

'It will be, but we are strong enough to adapt to a new way of life.'

'Oh, Luke, are we?' Uncertainty rang in her words.

'Of course we are.'

'Without Father?' Her voice broke for a moment then strengthened with a resounding cry to heaven. 'Why, oh, why, did that ship have to go down?'

'Oh, love, I don't know. Who can see the reason in God's ways?'

'God? There can't be a God to let that happen.'

'Father wouldn't have liked you to talk like that,' Luke pointed out quietly. 'And he wouldn't...'

Lydia's eyes flared. She finished what he was going to say. 'Want me to take revenge?'

Luke nodded. 'He wouldn't.'

'What about you?' Her eyes were fixed on him unflinchingly.

'Like you, I believe that Uncle Nathan's refusal to help caused Father's death...'

'Then he will not go unpunished.' His sister's voice was cold and remorseless.

Lydia had never been used to household work but, capable as she was, having inherited her mother's qualities, she quickly adapted to it and established a smooth routine.

Once that work was done she had time on her

hands. She had her own books and could borrow more from the subscription library which had been established on the quay as an important asset to the town. She now had to do her own household shopping, and made sure that she kept to the daily walk she had been used to. When she attempted to make contact with old friends she soon found out who were the true ones. Some offered sympathy and encouraged a continued relationship in spite of her changed circumstances. But there were those who made no such offer, who got rid of her quickly and made it plain that she was no longer welcome – snobs who wanted nothing more to do with her now she no longer had the same standing in Whitby society.

She stored these experiences in her mind, noting who might innocently impart information about her uncle when she wanted it.

Much of the time her thoughts were fixed on the desire to see Nathan ruined. She had pangs of conscience about her cousins but forced herself to ignore the fact that other people too would suffer. She narrowed her mind along the tunnel of revenge.

But the more she explored her possible courses of action, the more frustrated she became. She realised she needed assets to put her into a position strong enough to challenge her uncle's business interests. She needed secretly to establish a firm to compete for trade with him. To outbid him in negotiations, financial strength was essential, while to outsmart him she needed to know his intentions and for that she must have inside information.

Time and again she and Luke discussed the matter for she made sure his desire for revenge was kept alive. But they always found themselves at a disadvantage through the lack of money. Luke's discreet enquiries to try to raise capital were met with polite refusal. As Tristram had run into debt no one would trust Luke not to do the same. He was regarded as unsound.

Lydia was tempted to seek David's help but after carefully considering what that might involve and what she would have to reveal, suppositions she was not prepared to voice to anyone but Luke, she decided against it. So David's visits to the house in Wellington Square remained social calls only and were carried out discreetly for fear his father should get to know.

Throughout the next two weeks Lydia felt constantly frustrated at having to curb her desire for revenge. She tried to draw some comfort from the fact that she was still in Whitby where she could keep a check on her uncle's trading activities, storing the knowledge for future reference when she would initiate her vengeance. Then, one day, when Luke arrived home from work, she received what seemed at first like a setback.

As Luke came into the kitchen where she was preparing a meal Lydia could sense his excitement. She looked up from the table which she was setting and saw the light of enthusiasm in his eyes. His face was alive.

'Lydia, I've been promoted!' he cried.

Her eyes lit up with joy for her brother. 'Oh, Luke, I'm so pleased for you.'

'It means more money and a better chance of advancement.'

She came to him and hugged him affectionately. 'You deserve it.'

'There's only one snag,' he added on a cautionary note, as if he expected her to disapprove of what he was about to say. 'I ... well, we ... must move to Middlesbrough.'

Lydia's joy turned to bewilderment and her expression was puzzled. 'Middlesbrough? But why?'

'Well, Mr Martin is so pleased with my supervision of the loading of iron ore and the way I handle the men that he wants me to take over at the wharves on the River Tees. The manager there appears to be losing his grip and the men are taking advantage of his weaknesses and not working to capacity. The result is a slower turnaround of Mr Martin's vessels which means loss of revenue and could even lead to his losing the contract.'

Lydia nodded. 'And you feel capable of putting things right?'

'Yes.'

'If these men have become used to an easier time under an overseer they can manipulate, you could make enemies,' she warned. 'Wouldn't you be better here among friends?'

'It's a challenge and one I want to face. Father sent me to Mr Martin to gain experience. He intended to move me on to other merchants in the town so that I gained knowledge of many

139

sides of Whitby's trading before we took over from him. But now, with those prospects gone, Mr Martin's offer presents a fresh opportunity.'

'I can understand why you want to do this, but to leave Whitby...'

Lydia saw what a vast change it would make to them. They had lived all their lives in this York-shire port. She loved it and knew that Luke did too. It was in their blood. To move away to a new town would be a wrench, and living away from Whitby would make it more difficult to pursue her dream of revenge. Would that desire fade with distance?

'It's a new life, a new challenge. We can make a fresh start, forget all our troubles,' pressed Luke.

'Forget? How can we forget what Uncle Nathan did?'

'I'm not suggesting we do that. But a move from Whitby may make us see things differently.'

'You mean forget our revenge? Never!'

Luke realised that recent events were still too painful for his sister to tone down her attitude. He had had work to occupy his mind. While he still ached to teach their uncle a lesson, the chance of ever doing so seemed to be remote and had become even more distant as he had thrown himself vigorously into his task of supervising the ore ships. But Lydia had had time to brood and keep alive the grudge she harboured. So Luke toned down his attitude in a way which he hoped would placate his sister and make her see that this move might be used to their advantage.

'At present no one will finance an enterprise for us here, but who knows what opportunities might arise if we move away from Whitby? This offer could be just what we want.' He emphasised the words and saw they were having an effect on Lydia.

She began to look upon the idea more enthusiastically. 'You think we might find someone to back a venture with which we could challenge Uncle Nathan?'

'Who knows? Middlesbrough is a new town, not yet twenty years old. There could be a boom time coming with the growth of the iron industry.'

'Do you think that's possible?'

'Well, Mr Martin's shipment of ore is steadily rising. He wants no unrest among the men, either here or on Teesside, and that's why he has offered me this job. Who knows what it might lead to?'

Lydia's nimble mind began to see that a move from Whitby might give her the chance to work secretly towards her objective. 'When would we go?'

'A week today.'

'All right, Luke, I'll come with you.'

'Good!' He grabbed his sister, swung her off her feet and twirled her round, laughing with relief. 'We'll make good,' he cried. 'You can be sure of it.'

She laughed with him, pleased that he was happy with her decision. As he lowered her to the ground she looked at him with a deadly serious expression. 'But, Luke, we must never forget Whitby and what it means to us.'

Behind those words he read the implied threat to their uncle.

141

Chapter Six

'Sure now, if you two aren't coming to Middles-brough, I'm off tomorrow. I didn't come over here to skylark in Liverpool.' Sean spat the words angrily at Seamus and Kevin.

'What's y' rush?' Seamus slurred his words as he flopped down on to his bed after an evening spent exploring some of Liverpool's ale houses. 'Sure, an' haven't we given y' a good time, haven't we shown y' the sights?'

'Sights? Aye, and what sights!' retorted Sean.

Seamus struggled to sit up. His eyes narrowed drunkenly and he shook his head slowly. 'Sure y' should have stuck with me every minute and then ye'd have seen better entertainment than y' ever did see.' He licked his lips lasciviously. 'Or were y' frightened Eileen might find out?'

'She had nothing to do with it,' snapped Sean. 'I didn't want to visit a brothel and nor did Kevin.'

Seamus snorted with disgust. 'Y' both sissies. Neither of y' knows what a good time is.' He pointed a finger at Sean. 'I'll tell y' what ... yes ... I'll tell y' this an' I'll tell y' no more – that little lady of yours won't be giving a damned thought to y'. She'll be bedding all and sundry.'

Sean's temper flared. He struck out at Seamus but Kevin, knowing his friend's talent for goading people, was ready for this reaction. He grabbed Sean's arm as it swung forward.

'Don't,' he hissed. 'Seamus doesn't mean it.'

Sean swung round on him. 'Then tell that bugger to curb his tongue.'

'Sean's right, Seamus,' interposed Kevin. 'We should be getting to Middlesbrough now we know that Mr Langton and his daughter have left Liverpool.' He turned to Sean. 'You must admit it was a good job we decided to stay here until Mr Langton left, and that I sweet-talked the hotel receptionist into letting me know when he and his daughter had checked out. We'd have been high and dry if we'd reached Middlesbrough first. Now our contact will already be there.'

'So you're coming with me tomorrow, Kevin?' Receiving a nod of agreement Sean added, 'What that disgusting excuse for a man decides is up to him.'

'Y' right, Sean, right. What I decide, I decide, whether you like it or not.'

'I won't like it, whatever it is.'

'Well, then, y'll have to lump it.' He collapsed backwards on the bed, his arms wide, muttering, 'That little lady Sarah Langton'll see a lot of dear old Seamus. A lot!' He chuckled.

'She's a respectable young lady who'll have nothing to do with the likes of you,' warned Sean.

'Think so?' Seamus went on chuckling, amused by his own lewd thoughts.

'Watch your step,' warned Kevin. 'We don't want you messing up our chances after what Sean did for Mr Langton.'

Seamus made no reply. He was already snoring.

The following morning, still nursing an aching head which seemed frequently to go into a spin, Seamus was bad-tempered as the other two cajoled him into getting ready to leave.

'Shut your nattering. Yous two are like a couple of aud washerwomen,' he snapped as he tucked his shirt into his trousers.

'If we didn't natter you'd miss this train,' pointed out Kevin. 'You've missed breakfast as it is.'

'Ugh! Don't mention food.' Seamus gulped and clasped one hand to his forehead.

'Get a move on or I will,' threatened Kevin.

Ten minutes later, having paid for their lodgings, they headed for the station.

'Not so fast,' called Seamus who bumbled along behind Sean and Kevin.

They took no notice. There was a train to catch and catch it they would. A few minutes later, seeing Seamus dropping further behind, they glanced at each other and turned as one to head back to him. Without a word they stood close, one on either side of him, and took hold of him under the armpits, lifting him off his feet. They strode out. Seamus's feet moved in a running motion but without purchase on the paving. He protested at their rough handling but, when he saw that they were taking no notice, resigned himself to the ride.

At the station they dumped him, purchased the tickets, grabbed him by the arms again and bustled him on to the train. As they shoved him into a carriage he lost his footing and sprawled on the floor, bringing sharp protests and glances of disgust from the two females who occupied corner seats and had been looking forward to a carriage to themselves.

Sean and Kevin clambered in, yanked Seamus to his feet and shoved him into one of the vacant corners before stowing their bags. All the time they muttered apologies to the two ladies for the state of their friend.

The two men's rich Irish brogue and smiles which would have melted any female heart soon won the forgiveness of their two travelling companions who, they learnt, were going as far as Manchester. Seamus knew nothing of the conversation or the journey, however, for he fell fast asleep as soon as he was settled.

He slept most of the way for which Sean and Kevin were thankful. Once they emerged from the station in Middlesbrough, Seamus was all for finding the nearest pub.

'Sure, and isn't that the bright idea?' said Kevin, seemingly with an air of approval. 'But not to drink.'

Seamus, who by now had his wits about him, eyed his friend in amazement. 'Sure now, an' what would you be doing going to a pub and not drinking?'

Kevin leaned towards him, bringing his face close. He raised a forefinger and tapped Seamus on the head. 'Seeking information, wise one, information.'

'On what?' Seamus's voice rose and his face twisted in disgust.

'We have to sleep tonight. For that we want a boarding house. The landlord of a pub is likely to 'know of one.'

Sean had been looking around him. 'We'll go this way,' he suggested.

He received no objection and the three of them set off to find a pub. They had not gone far when they entered the Iron Smelter. They found themselves in a room with a mahogany counter running along one wall and small tables set beside the other three, leaving a space in the middle for customers to crowd towards the bar. Though it was still daylight the room was dreary. Light barely filtered through the coloured glass at the window or from the clouded gas mantles.

The bar was busy but had not reached the point where the three barmen would be kept continuously filling glasses. That would come about shortly as workers anxious to slake the dust and heat of work from their throats packed in demanding beer after their shift.

Only cursory glances were cast at the three Irishmen as they crossed the sawdust-strewn floor to the counter. A burly red-faced barman with a long white apron tied at his waist came over to them as they dropped their bags on the floor and lined themselves up along the bar.

'Evening,' he said curtly, eyeing the newcomers with an assessing look. 'Beer?'

Seamus's face broke into a smile. 'Ah, sure now, here's a man after m' own heart. Three tankards of your best.' He glanced at his companions. 'You two aren't going to say no?'

'Just the one,' said Kevin firmly.

The barman looked up from the glass he had already started to fill. 'Just in from Ireland?'

146

'Aye, we are that,' returned Kevin.

'First time in Middlesbrough?' His gaze swept quickly over the three of them. He'd had trouble with some Irishmen but these three were reasonably dressed and had not swaggered into the pub as if they were kings of the world.

'Yes.'

'Looking for work?' The barman started on the second glass.

'We think we're fixed up,' replied Sean, 'but we are looking for lodgings. Can you help us?'

The barman did not reply immediately but watched the beer foam at the top of the glass, allowed it to run over and then carefully topped it up. He placed the glass in front of Sean. In those few seconds he had confirmed to himself his first assessment of the newcomers.

'Aye, lad, I might be able to do just that.'

'Good, we'd be obliged.'

The barman had picked up a third glass and now he started to fill it. Seamus had already drunk half of his in anticipation of ordering another but slowed when he received Kevin's warning look – no more. He knew his friend was recalling one time when they had arrived in Grimsby and he had escaped Kevin's clutches. Turning up at their respectable boarding house drunk had not been a good idea. Kevin did not want it happening again.

The barman waited until he had filled the glass. He had held back from imparting the required information and unobtrusively observed Seamus's consumption of his beer. He noted him slow up now and decided that the man had just

147

been keen to quench his thirst.

He put the third glass in front of Kevin who pushed some pennies over. The barman took the money and then added, 'Try Mrs Hartley in West Street. She's my sister. Just lost three of your compatriots. Decided they'd had enough and moved up north.'

'Thanks,' all three of them said at once.

'Where's West Street?' asked Sean.

'Turn right out of here. The way you were heading when you came in – I'm supposing you'd just come from the station?' They nodded their confirmation. 'Keep right on into the Square – the Market Place. To the left is West Street. Number ten. Tell Nell Jim sent you.'

'Thanks,' they chorused as he moved away to serve some arrivals with whom he was familiar.

'Come on, drink up,' urged Sean as he picked up his glass. 'Let's find West Street. I reckon our luck's in.'

There were no protests from Seamus and in a few minutes they called their thanks again to Jim and left the Iron Smelter.

They took little notice of the busy shoppers as they headed up South Street. The Market Place was dominated by the tall-spired tower at the west end of St Hilda's church.

'Imposing,' commented Kevin. 'Better-looking than that.' He nodded towards the northwest corner of the Square.

'Can't be anything else but a chapel,' said Seamus in a tone which showed he agreed with Kevin's assessment of the building.

'West Street.' Sean brought their attention back

to their purpose by pointing across the open space.

Within a few minutes they were knocking at the door of number ten. It was opened by a short, plump lady dressed in black with a white apron tied at her waist. Her brown hair was taken back and tied in a bun. Her cheeks were rosy, her eyes bright but filled with curiosity on finding three strangers on her doorstep.

'Good day, ma'am,' said Sean. 'Mrs Hartley?'

'Aye.'

'Jim sent us. Said y' might be able to give us lodgings.'

'I might. Seen our Jim, have you? Well, he doesn't let the grass grow under his feet, nor mine by the sound of it.' Nell Hartley knew her brother well. Older than her, he had looked after her interests when they were kids and was still doing so. 'Well, if he's vetted you, you'd better come away in and have a chat.' She turned back into the house, leaving the last of the Irishmen to close the door.

The passage led to a room at the back. They followed her and found themselves in a square room with a door leading off it to a scullery in which there was another door giving access to a yard with a high brick wall. The room they were in felt cosy. A bright fire burned in the grate of a kitchen range which was no doubt Nell's pride and joy for it was as bright as a new pin. A kettle puffed gently away on a reckon above the fire.

'Sit you down.' She indicated a sofa let into an alcove formed by the stairs rising from the passage. A pinewood table and four matching

149

chairs were placed in the centre of the room. A mahogany press was set against one wall and a cupboard occupied a space beside the fireplace.

'A cup of tea?' suggested Nell, wanting to create a friendly atmosphere. She had summed these men up quickly and in her own mind confirmed her brother's judgement. 'Though if you've seen our Jim you'll already have had something a bit stronger.'

'A cup of tea would be welcome,' replied Kevin, sensing that acceptance of the offer would strike an agreeable chord.

Over that cup of tea Nell promised them lodgings, but first they had to agree to certain conditions and she warned that if they were broken their agreement would be terminated immediately.

'No drink will be brought into the house. That would threaten Jim's trade and I won't be party to that. I have no objection to your partaking of whatever liquid you like but – and this is a big but – you never enter this house the worse for it. No female will be entertained here either unless there is serious courting with whoever she be and I am first introduced to her.'

'You'll approve or disapprove our choice if it arises,' commented Seamus with an amused twitch of his lips.

'I will that,' replied Nell firmly. She eyed him seriously, having judged him to be the one who would cause trouble if trouble were to be caused, but she had already decided she liked the rogue in him. 'Now if you are agreeable to that and to my charge of ten shillings a week each for

150

lodgings, board and washing, then I'll show you your rooms.'

'That seems highly satisfactory,' replied Kevin, 'and we thank you for your kindness and hospitality.'

Nell nodded. She liked the look of these three and felt there was something different about the one who had just spoken, but she kept her thoughts to herself. She opened the door into the passage and turned up the stairs. At the top she went into a room to the right. 'Two of you will have to sleep in here.'

A brass bedstead, a chest of drawers, a wash stand on which there stood a large basin and ewer with clean white towels laid beside them, were all the furnishings apart from two chairs, one on either side of the bed.

'You two in here,' said Sean quickly, wanting to be on his own and having no desire to come between two friends.

'Very well. You'll be just across the landing.' She showed Sean a room which was similarly furnished.

He had noted there were only two bedrooms. 'What about you and Mr Hartley?' he asked.

'Oh, there's no Mr Hartley,' she replied. 'He was killed in those newfangled ironworks. I hate 'em for that but I suppose they're progress. At least that's what we're told, and I must admit Middlesbrough wouldn't be here without them.' She cocked her head and looked wryly at him. 'I suppose you're wondering where I sleep?' She saw he was embarrassed and went on quickly, 'I know you only mean well by that thought. When

151

I have lodgers I sleep on the sofa in the kitchen. But don't worry, I'm used to it. I'm comfortable enough and it's warm there.'

When she had returned downstairs the three men emptied their bags then joined her in the kitchen. She was already making a meat pie.

'This will be ready for six o'clock. I suppose now you're going to try and find work?'

'We've been promised something,' replied Kevin. 'We need to find the Bolckow and Vaughan works.'

'Ah, then you'll be wanting those towards the river. You wouldn't be wanting their Witton Park works – they're way north of the river near Auckland.'

'We were told to come to Middlesbrough and contact a Mr Langton.'

Nell raised her eyebrows in surprise. 'My, you will be riding high. Important man is Mr Langton. Firm but fair. And kind to me when my husband was killed. Go back into the Market Place, go down North Street to Commercial Street then turn right. You can't miss the works.'

'Thanks, Mrs Hartley,' said Sean.

As they were leaving the kitchen she stopped them, saying, 'Being Irish, I expect you'll want a Catholic church on Sunday?'

The three men cast sharp glances at each other. True they had all been baptised Catholics and brought up in that faith as youngsters but all three would have to admit they had become less particular about their religion as they had escaped the influence of their families. But they were caught out now and wanted to keep on the

152

right side of their landlady.

'We will that, ma'am,' replied Kevin quickly in case his companions made any adverse comment.

'Well, you needn't go looking. I'm a Catholic myself and you can come with me on Sunday.'

'That's very kind of you,' replied Sean.

'Sure, we've landed in good hands, Mrs Hartley,' commented Seamus in his smoothest Irish lilt. 'It's a comfort for three young men far from home to have someone to look after us bodily,' he nodded in the direction of the pie she was preparing so that there was no misunderstanding his meaning, 'and spiritually.'

'Off with you and take your smart talk with you. You don't fool Nell Hartley but I'm sure we'll get on well if we understand each other.'

The three men bustled out of the house without another word until they were outside with the door shut tight behind them.

'Sunday Mass!' Seamus raised his eyes heavenwards as if to plead exemption from a higher authority.

'I'll tell you this and I'll tell you no more,' said Sean, 'it won't do us any harm.'

'Ah, listen who's talking – the man living in sin with Eileen Nolan,' commented Kevin.

'Who casts the first stone?' Sean returned knowingly.

'Ah, well, maybe we're all tarred with the same brush,' said Seamus. 'None of us can preach.'

'So, don't let's any of us cross Mrs Hartley,' Kevin insisted. 'We've got good lodgings there. We've been lucky so far. Let's find these works

153

and hope our luck holds good.'

They hardly needed Mrs Hartley's directions for once they had started along South Street the rising smoke from several chimneys was a guide in itself. The hum of industrial power and the bustle of its accompanying activity was a new world to the three men and by the time the works were in sight they felt caught up in the energy of this place, heralding a future as yet unknown.

They paused as they turned into the open space beyond the railway where pig iron was being unloaded and then taken to the long row of buildings above which rose the rolling mill's chimneys.

As a man came hurrying past, Sean grabbed him by the arm. 'Where will we find Mr Langton?'

'Yonder,' came his curt reply. He pointed in the direction of a door close to the east end of the buildings.

'Thanks.'

He was gone and the Irishmen, avoiding the bustle of men intent on their work, crossed the open space in the direction of the buildings.

As they reached the door a man came out. Unlike the other workers he wore a suit of brown serge. His jacket was unfastened to reveal a matching waistcoat spanned by a watchchain slung between two pockets. He was slapping a bowler hat on to his head as if it was a symbol of authority.

'Mr Langton?' queried Sean, who had taken on the role of enquirer.

'Second door on the right.' He cast an eye over

them as he spoke but made no further comment and went on his way.

They entered the building to find themselves in a passage with several doors leading off it. They stopped outside the designated door and all automatically straightened their jackets and firmed their shoulders. Seamus and Kevin glanced at Sean and he took their silent inference that he should continue to take the lead. He rapped on the door and after the call of 'Come in', opened it.

James Langton looked up from the maps he was studying. His face broke into a broad smile and he pushed himself quickly from his chair.

'Sean Casey!' He came from behind his desk, his hand held out in greeting.

As Sean took it he felt a strong friendly grip.

'Good to see you, young man.'

'And you, sir,' returned Sean with a smile, responding to the kindly greeting he had been given.

James looked beyond him to see Seamus and Kevin stepping into the room. 'So you two decided to come after all?'

'We did that, sir,' replied Kevin.

'Couldn't let him go off into the big wide world alone,' chuckled Seamus.

'When did you get to Middlesbrough?' James asked.

'Just today,' replied Sean.

'You've wasted no time in looking me up then.'

'No, sir. We want jobs and you said you could probably help.'

'I did and I'm a man who keeps his promises.

155

First, have you found lodgings?'

'Yes, sir.'

'Good. Then it's just the jobs that have to be arranged. You can have employment here at the rolling mill or at our blast furnace at Witton Park.'

'Where's Witton Park?' queried Kevin.

'About twenty miles west of here.'

'That would mean moving, and leaving the excellent lodgings we've found in West Street.'

'Not far away.'

'No. So we'll take any work you have here,' decided Sean.

'Right. It'll be mundane work, I'm afraid. You aren't frightened of physical labour, I hope?' James queried.

'Kevin and I have had it physical at Grimsby docks,' said Seamus, 'but I can't answer for this fella here.' He nodded at Sean with a teasing twinkle in his eye.

'Away wi' ye,' rapped Sean. 'I'll match ye any time.'

'I'm sure you will,' replied James with a smile. 'Come, I'll take you to my supervisor. He directs the workers as necessary. We're currently shipping iron ore in from Whitby. That's got to be unloaded from the ships for transportation by rail to the blast furnaces at Witton. There it's turned into pig iron and brought back here by rail to the rolling mills, so there's a lot of humping and grafting to be done. Maybe one day after you've seen how things are done here we'll find you a job in the rolling mill.'

He took them outside, pausing a moment to

156

cast his glance around the activity taking place between the railway and the mill but did not see the man for whom he was looking.

'With that train just arrived, Eric Gilmore, the supervisor, won't be far away. He has five foremen under him, each of whom oversees a team of men in the loading and unloading of the trains.'

'How many in a team, sir?' asked Sean, determined to show interest.

'Varies depending on the work. We maintain a pool of men whom we can move around as required. Numbers are down at the moment and we've had to lay off a few.'

'How's that, sir? I thought the iron trade would be experiencing good times.'

'It has but we're suffering a bit of a setback at the moment.' James was impressed by this young man's curiosity which he judged to stem from a genuine interest in anything new. He was minded, therefore, to expand a little further. 'Two reasons. The deposits of iron ore close by the Witton blast furnaces haven't produced the quantity we expected, so we are having to ship in ore from Whitby which is adding to the cost. And there's trouble with the men unloading the ships. The Whitby firm insisted that their own workers be employed for this but at the moment those men are slow, only making a pretence at work. A weak overseer's the trouble. The men take advantage of him.'

'Can't you do anything about it, sir?'

'Not personally, but I have contacted the shipowner in Whitby and he has promised to replace the overseer. Because of the trouble Mr Bolckow and Mr Vaughan have been forced to cut back on production. If the new man from Whitby fares no better, they'll have to reconsider the situation.'

'Any danger of closure?' asked Sean.

James shook his head. 'I shouldn't think so. I'm sure Mr Bolckow and Mr Vaughan see a future in iron so long as they can overcome the present setback and keep supplies of ore coming.' He changed his tone. 'Ah, there's Mr Gilmore.' He indicated a man who had come out of the rolling mill, and raised his arm in a gesture which brought Gilmore in their direction.

They saw that this was the man in the bowler hat they had encountered previously.

'This is Mr Gilmore, our supervisor. Eric, I want you to employ these three men.'

He raised an eyebrow. 'I thought we weren't taking on any more hands for the time being?'

'In this case we'll make an exception.'

Sean noticed Gilmore's expression darken and was sure that where the employment of men was concerned he did not like to be told who should be given work and who shouldn't. His burliness brought a belligerent attitude with it and his stern, unsmiling features did nothing to foster a friendly feeling. Sean sensed that Gilmore revelled in wielding authority over his fellow human beings and in their capacity of labourers looked down on them. They wore flat caps, he wore a bowler.

'These are the men I told you about who saved my life and my daughter's. I promised to help them,' explained James. 'I'll leave them in your hands.' He turned to the three Irishmen. 'Mr Gilmore will look after you.' He gave them a friendly smile and headed for his office.

Gilmore ran his gaze over them. 'Who's who?' he asked curtly.

'I'm Sean Casey. This is Seamus O'Leary and Kevin Harper.'

Gilmore grunted and ignored Sean's proffered hand. He glanced across at the office and saw James disappearing inside. 'Don't come here thinking you'll get privileges for what you did for Mr Langton. You're just another three pairs of hands to me, and don't you forget it. Here you'll work as you've never worked before – if not you're out. And don't go whingeing to Mr Langton. He'll listen to me before you.'

Sean read jealousy of their personal tie with James Langton.

'You start work tomorrow morning at six o'clock.' The supervisor gave a little chuckle to accompany his knowing grin. 'Gus Arnold will be there with his team to move another load of pig iron from Witton.' Without waiting for acknowledgement he hurried away towards the train, leaving the three Irishmen staring after him.

'Nice fella,' commented Seamus, deep sarcasm in his voice.

'A new friend,' Kevin joined in with Seamus's assessment.

'We shan't have to step the wrong side of that bastard,' agreed Sean. He glanced at his two friends. 'Wishing you'd gone to Grimsby?'

'No.' But there was a note of doubt in their

159

answer. 'We'll see a different life here, then we'll decide.'

Sean's eyes narrowed knowingly as if he was seeing the future. 'There's one thing for sure, Sean Casey isn't going to spend much time heaving iron ore. There have to be better ways of making a crust than that.'

Chapter Seven

'Now, my boys, nine o'clock Mass tomorrow,' Nell laid it down as if she would brook no objection, and they knew better than to make one. In the few days they had been with her they had come to respect and like her, and, knowing that they were fortunate to have found such good lodgings, were determined not to upset her.

Dressed in their best clothes, clean-shaven, boots highly polished, they duly awaited her in the front room, hardly daring to move on their seats for fear of upsetting the precise placing of the furniture: 'Just as Mr Hartley liked it.'

When she appeared they stood up as one.

Nell looked them over with a quick glance. 'My, we are looking smart,' she commented approvingly.

'Ah, sure, we are no better than y'self, ma'am.' Seamus made a bow. 'Indeed you're a picture.'

'Flatterer,' she replied with a dismissive wave of her hand, but inwardly she was pleased.

'It's true,' confirmed Sean and Kevin.

Nell drew herself up that little bit taller. It was a while since she had been paid endearing compliments by three young men.

In fact she had taken pains with her appearance as she always did for Sunday Mass. She wore black and it suited her. The woollen dress was plain, nipped in slightly at the waist and flaring to a bell shape. A grey ribbon drew the neckline close to her throat and fell away in a long streamer across her full bosom. A silk bonnet was shaped close to her head, its narrow brim trimmed with grey lace. She wore a waist-length shot silk shawl, patterned in grey, and black gloves.

'Shall we go?' she said.

'Yes, ma'am,' they chorused.

As Mrs Hartley locked the door, Seamus and Kevin donned their bowler hats but Sean bucked convention and went without any headgear. He noticed Mrs Hartley had observed this but the expected comment did not come.

Nell was amused. She knew Sean had seen her reaction and that he had expected a rebuke but she refrained. After all, hats would be taken off in church and did it really matter outside? Besides, she had taken to Sean more so than to the other two. Not that she didn't like them, she did. Maybe it was because he had that extra charm, that Irish twinkle in his eye and a way with words that would charm a woman of any age, and she was not above being charmed in a friendly way.

'No rushing away after Mass,' she ordered. 'I want you to meet Father O'Flaherty, the parish priest. He always says this Mass on a Sunday. His

161

curates officiate at the others.'

Seamus raised his eyes heavenwards. He had been anticipating a dash to the nearest pub. He'd make his escape as soon as he could.

Crowds of people were converging on the dull exterior of the church, hemmed in by taller buildings on three sides. In spite of this, long lancet windows let in sufficient light to make the nave and chancel with their white-painted walls seem bright.

Knowing that the church would be full, Nell had left home early so that they would all be able to sit together.

They had been there about three minutes when she nudged Sean with her elbow. She leaned closer to him and whispered, 'I didn't tell you they were Catholics.'

He followed her gaze and saw Mr Langton and his daughter taking their seats nearer the chancel on the other side of the aisle.

As he waited for Mass to begin Sean's eyes kept straying to Sarah. He had a three-quarter view of her and was thankful that she wore the smallest of bonnets so that her face was not hidden.

He remembered that even amidst the chaos of the tragedy off Liverpool he had seen that she was an attractive young woman. Her soaked and bedraggled condition had not been able to disguise that. He smiled to himself as he recalled the laughter she had invoked when she came to join them on the quay, and the defiant stance she had taken then. Now, sitting beside her father, she looked so demure and calm. Her auburn hair was tied neatly at the nape of her neck below a

162

bonnet made of the same material as her white muslin dress and patterned in small mauve motifs. The bodice was plain, coming into a point at the waist to offset the flounces of the skirt and the wide, bell-shaped sleeves.

Throughout the service Sean found his thoughts and eyes constantly straying to Sarah. With the service over he saw father and daughter leave their pew. Anxious to try to make contact with her, he itched to follow them but knew it would be bad manners to rush out before Mrs Hartley was ready, and her head was still bowed in prayer.

The few minutes that passed before she gave a little nod to her three lodgers to indicate that she was ready to leave seemed interminable to him.

Emerging from the church, Sean felt a surge of relief. Sarah and her father were talking to the priest who, in the midst of his conversation, acknowledged other parishioners as they were leaving. Nell hesitated, then held back.

But Sarah glanced up and saw the three Irishmen. Her face immediately broke into a broad smile as she saw them. With a quick, 'Excuse me,' she broke away from the priest and her father. 'Sean! Seamus! Kevin!' She was so friendly and natural in her greeting they might have been the oldest of friends. 'Father told me you had come to Middlesbrough and I hoped I might see you all again. How are you? Getting settled?' She glanced at their landlady. 'Don't tell me they're staying with you, Mrs Hartley?'

'Yes, miss.' Nell was mystified as to how Miss Sarah knew her lodgers.

163

'Then you know what they did?' Sarah saw the woman's puzzled look and added, 'You don't? They've never told you?'

Nell shook her head.

'They saved my life and Father's.'

Nell looked even more astonished as if she did not comprehend the meaning of Sarah's words.

'That shipwreck off Liverpool – oh, maybe you didn't know about it? Well, we were thrown into the sea and would have perished but for Sean.'

The group had now been joined by Mr Langton and the priest.

'These three young men were on board another ship,' explained James. 'Sean dived overboard and saved us. And, thank goodness, there were another two pairs of hands to haul us out of the water.'

'Well, I never,' gasped Nell. 'To think I have heroes staying with me. What do you think of that, Father?'

The priest smiled. 'You're in good company, Nell, as are they.' He held out his hand to each of the Irishmen in turn, introducing himself as Father O'Flaherty.

As they all fell into conversation, Seamus gradually edged himself away until he could leave without anyone noticing.

Five minutes later the priest said his goodbyes and returned to his house near the church. It was then that Kevin missed Seamus. Knowing full well why his friend had disappeared, his mouth tightened in annoyance. Seamus's habit of a drink after Sunday Mass was not to be forgone even though he was in new territory. Recalling some Sundays in the past when his friend might have ended up in the Liffey if Kevin hadn't been around, he hoped Seamus would not be upsetting Mrs Hartley later in the day.

As they left the church grounds, Sarah managed a quick quiet word with her father.

'A good idea,' he whispered. Then he stopped and addressed the men. 'Sarah and I would like to say a proper thank you for saving our lives, though what we propose is not really adequate. Please would you all come home with us and join us for Sunday dinner? We'll introduce you to Yorkshire pudding, made as it can only be made in Yorkshire.'

'Sir, there's no need. You owe us nothing for what we did. Besides you have already helped us by finding us work,' said Kevin.

'That's beside the point,' returned James with a dismissive shake of his head. 'We'd like to do it.' He turned his gaze on Nell. 'Of course, you're invited too, Mrs Hartley.'

'That is very kind of you, Mr Langton.' She was embarrassed by this invitation from a man she regarded as of a different station in life. Though social attitudes were changing, she felt they still had not gone far enough to permit such familiarity between the classes. From her experience when her husband was killed, she knew there was no snobbery in the Langtons but wondered if he would have made this offer if he had not felt beholden to the Irishmen. 'But I'm afraid I have an appointment with Mrs Stuart about the cleaning of the church and the arrangement of flowers for the coming week.'

'Oh, dear. I am sorry, Mrs Hartley,' said Sarah.

'That's all right, miss. I'll expect my boys when I see them. Thank you for the invitation.' Nell felt a little relieved as she walked away.

As they fell into step, Sean found himself walking with Mr Langton, and Kevin, to his delight, escorted Sarah.

'Not far to walk,' said James. 'We live on Queen's Terrace, close to the Head Office of the Owners of the Middlesbrough Estate, an energetic body set up in 1830 to develop Middlesbrough. So, do you think you'll like it here?'

'Yes.' Sean's reply was firm. 'But I look beyond humping ore and pig iron.'

James gave a little smile. 'I thought so. Well, see how you get on. And if in the future I can be of any help, come to see me.'

'That's very kind of you, sir.'

'I found a kindly man in Mr Vaughan when I first met him. He was the manager of a small ironworks in Carlisle then, with a special gift for handling men. For some reason he took to me, gave me a helping hand, instilled the confidence in me to tackle a job which was new. And he persuaded me to come to Middlesbrough with him. I've never forgotten the lessons he taught me and I never shall. I see something of myself as I was in you, though of course I was older and had held responsible positions before I came here. Nevertheless there are lessons to be learned at all ages and I certainly learned from him.'

'He sounds to be a fine man.'

'Indeed he is. And so is Mr Bolckow, for that

166

matter, but in an entirely different way. They are just right as business partners. Bolckow has the capital – a very rich man – and Vaughan has the more practical knowledge. We can learn from them both.'

'And I think from you, too, sir.'

'Well, I saw opportunities for promotion and took them. I don't regret being here. You know, I can see this town expanding fast. Maybe there's a setback for the company at the moment but I'm sure that will pass and then there'll be expansion on a scale never seen before. And, Sean, that means plenty of opportunities for young men with flair who are not afraid of work.'

'I'll be on the lookout for them, sir.'

'That's the right attitude.'

Kevin, who was enjoying Sarah's company, nevertheless, caught those words and stored them in his mind. If Sean could do it, so could he.

'You'll be well looked after by Mrs Hartley?' Sarah observed.

'Oh, indeed.' He concentrated again on the girl beside him.

'A kindly person. Such a tragedy that she lost her husband.'

'She mentioned an accident at the rolling mill. What happened?'

'A boiler exploded, ripped the roof off and brought some walls down. A number of workmen were hit and some trapped. Mr Hartley was killed by a falling beam.'

'Was he the only one?'

'No. Two others died. One suffered a horrible

167

death – he was thrown under a burning furnace.' Sarah grimaced at the recollection.

Kevin noticed her distress. 'I'm sorry. I shouldn't have asked.'

She gave a wan smile in appreciation of his concern. 'That's all right. It's as well to know of the dangers. The whole town was upset by the tragedy. Mr Bolckow and Mr Vaughan were very troubled by it. They felt the loss almost as much as the families.' She switched the conversation to a pleasanter tack. 'Let's talk of brighter things. I can tell that young man in front is ambitious.'

Kevin smiled. 'Sean? Sure now, he has big ideas.'

'And you?'

'Not in the same way. But I can see my life here being different from digging docks in Grimsby. There was nothing to do there but watch them fill with water.'

Sarah laughed. 'Nothing beyond that?'

'Little.'

'And here there is?'

Kevin had a beautiful girl beside him and was not going to give her the impression he was a mere labourer with no higher ambitions. This girl seemed interested in him. Dare he hope...? He had seen Sean eyeing her in church and somehow that had riled him. Sean had his Eileen, couldn't he keep his mind on her? He knew Sean had had a reputation for liking all the girls when he was younger and would flit from one to the other like a moth flirting with the flickering flames of a candelabra. Was that trait still there, dormant in him, even though he had established a steady relationship with Eileen Nolan? Was it surfacing again at the sight of a pretty girl now there was distance between him and his lover? Well, maybe Kevin Harper would have something to say about that.

'Oh, yes, Miss Langton. I can see this town growing and growth means new opportunities for those sharp and quick enough to exploit them.'

'You sound just like Father. He believes this will be a boom area, especially if more ironstone deposits can be found.'

'Then I'll find them for you, Miss Langton, and name the mines after you,' said Kevin with a lighthearted laugh.

'Miss Langton? Please don't be so formal. I'm Sarah. After what you saw on the quay at Liverpool, I should say formality was rather misplaced.'

They both chuckled at the memory.

'Then I'll have to call them the Sarah mines.'

She inclined her head gracefully and said, 'And Seamus? What of him? I'm sorry he disappeared after church.'

'A man with a big heart but his own worst enemy. He's so generous money runs through his hands like the beer he drinks. As long as he has the money for that he's a happy man.'

'And has a friend like you to look after him.'

Kevin shrugged his shoulders but made no comment.

Kevin studied the three-storey dwelling in Queen's Terrace as they approached it. Its red bricks exuded an air of solidity and seemed to lend the house a safe, welcoming atmosphere.

Ahead of him, Sean, still beside Mr Langton, was promising himself that one day he would own such a house. It spoke of a world in which Sarah walked with ease. He wanted to do the same, to be part of it, but that would only come about if he threw off the mantle of labourer. He would have to show some special talents, but first he would have to discover them. Maybe with Sarah's encouragement... He started. A voice within him reminded him of promises made to a girl in Ireland. They had not been idle ones. He had believed in his own ability and had won her belief too. Eileen, who had shared so much with him, who had defied convention because she loved him, deserved better than to be cast aside.

Had he really entertained such a thought? Ruthless ambition had temporarily blinded him. He'd made promises before he came here and Eileen Nolan was relying on him to keep those promises. He had sworn to take her out of the life they knew into the sort of life she deserved, with the world at her feet. Could his path to riches start here among the ironworks of Middlesbrough? Could Sarah Langton be a stepping stone on that path?

From now on he would be on the lookout for any opportunity to achieve his goal. He would listen and absorb, see and remember, talk and elicit useful information. He would prise open a world of possibilities and choose the best of them to turn that world into his oyster.

He was even more determined to achieve his objective when he stepped inside the house. Here was elegance and richness such as he had never seen before. Everything was of the best, yet he knew from Mr Langton's conversation on the way home from church that these things had not been gained easily. This life, with its trappings of luxury, had been achieved by Langton's hard work and determination to become a man of responsibility – a manager trusted implicitly by his employers. If this was the home of a manager, how must those above him live? They must inhabit a different world. Let there be a place in it for Sean Casey and Eileen Nolan!

Unused to this way of life, he was keenly observant of everything he saw here. In Dublin he had not been used to maids to take visitors' hats and coats, and to wait on table. Here the cutlery and tableware baffled him but he avoided any embarrassment by hesitating until Mr Langton had made his choice.

James, an astute judge of men, was aware that Sean had moved out of his class but saw in him something different from the usual Irish labourer who sought work in what was regarded as the booming economy of England. The difference was visible in Sean's bearing. James had been conscious of it on the quay at Liverpool and again when the Irishman had faced him in his office. If Sean had talent and ambition it would out and his present occupation would soon be a thing of the past.

Kevin was different. He was more at ease here, not obviously overawed as Sean was. Kevin could progress easily but he could equally well be held back by his friend Seamus. There was a loyalty in him which might force him to put his friend before his own interests, and Seamus would play on that as he probably had done ever since they had met. His contentment lay in a glass of beer. He could stare into the golden liquid, not caring for the world around him. That attitude led nowhere except possibly to trouble, but did he care as long as Kevin was there to help?

James knew his daughter was making her own assessments and thought it would be interesting to hear them later. He thrust his own speculations from his mind and became the attentive host.

The roast beef and Yorkshire pudding brought praises from the Irishmen. The apple pie, served in the Yorkshire tradition with Wensleydale cheese, increased their accolades for the cook.

It was mid-afternoon when Sean and Kevin left the house after offering profuse thanks for what had been a splendid meal and a pleasant occasion.

As he closed the front door, James took hold of his daughter's hand and started towards the drawing room.

'Now, Sarah, come and tell me what you thought of them. No, don't tell me you weren't closely observing our two guests.'

His voice carried a tone that said he would brook no denials.

Sarah smiled. 'There's no fooling you. But what does my opinion matter anyway when you have made your own?'

172

'Ah, come now, you know I value your thoughts.' He smiled at her. Father and daughter loved these moments of banter.

They reached the drawing room and sat down opposite each other beside the fire.

'Well?' he prompted.

'Setting aside the fact that they saved our lives, I like them both. Their Irish charm could win over anyone.'

'You're not suspicious of it?'

'No. I believe they're genuine. And Sean has a twinkle in his eye that could entice any female.'

'A man for the ladies? Could get him into trouble.'

'He's in control.'

'And, as a young woman, you would know?'

'He flirted with those eyes of his but he knew when to stop.'

James raised one eyebrow. His daughter was more worldly-wise than he had thought.

'From what he said I believe he has ambitions to better himself, but you probably know more about that than I. You had his company from church.'

'And you had Kevin's.'

'More dependable, more cautious, but there's something about him... Whatever it is it makes me surprised that he's a labourer.'

'My sentiments exactly.'

'Maybe there's loyalty owed to Seamus for some reason.'

'From what we've seen of him, he's a typical Irish labourer. Which Kevin isn't.'

'Yes, did you notice his comments about the

173

wine? I feel sure that knowledge was derived from a better background. I mean to solve the mystery.'

James made no comment but thought, I'm sure you will.

The week before they were due to leave Whitby for Middlesbrough was a hectic rush for Lydia and Luke. He had several interviews with his employer and was pleased with the authority he had been given.

'Keep your eye on what is happening in Middlesbrough,' Mr Martin instructed. 'If the iron industry is set to expand then we must try to find new sources of ore, and hope that they are near enough Whitby for us to take advantage of them.'

'I'll do that,' Luke reassured him. 'And I'll see that nothing holds up the unloading of the iron-stone.'

'Good. I have every faith in you. I have a letter here introducing you to Mr James Langton who is manager of the Bolckow and Vaughan works. It was he who asked me to look into the reason for slow deliveries and hinted that the trouble might lie with our overseer, Jos Sigsworth. There is another letter authorising you to take over if necessary, and one recalling him to Whitby if you deem that a wise move.'

'Thank you, sir. They will make things easier for me.'

'But they won't ease the unrest among the men which Mr Langton has indicated. That will be up to you when you assess the situation and decide what remedies are needed.'

'I'll soon have things sorted out, sir, and get the movement of ironstone back to the capacity expected.'

'I'm counting on you, Luke.'

'And I'll not let you down, sir.'

'Now, I don't want to pry into your private affairs but you've had a trying time recently. If it's not too nosy of me, may I ask if your sister is going with you?'

'Yes. There is nothing and no one for her in Whitby so it makes sense for her to come with me and make a new life away from here.'

'That's sensible thinking,' agreed Mr Martin. 'You can always return, as I'm sure you will. After all, you're both Whitby born and bred and Whitby gets into the blood. A break will do you both good, though. I've naturally agreed to pay your fare to Middlesbrough, but as a gesture of goodwill I'll pay your sister's as well.'

'That's very generous of you, Mr Martin.' Luke was surprised at his employer's offer even though he had always got on well with him.

Mr Martin smiled. 'Just see you do a good job for me.'

Lydia was adjusting to the prospect of leaving Whitby when David called on her unexpectedly.

He was astounded when she broke the news and stared at her in amazement. 'Leave Whitby? You can't!'

Anger rose in her at the way he had worded this. It was as if her decision was seen purely as an affront to him. 'I can and I am,' she snapped.

175

'Why should I stay when there's no one here for me?'

'There's me.'

'But you won't marry me now.'

'You know why I can't. You know it's because I love you and care about our future together.' His voice was firm; there could be no compromise in what he thought was the right way for them to tackle their future.

'I've said I'll wait but I'm not prepared to sit around here while you try to persuade your father to be more reasonable. It may never happen.'

David stepped closer and reached for her hands. He took heart from the fact that she did not draw away. 'I love you, Lydia. It's going to be painful without you here. Do you have to go?' There was pleading in his voice.

'There's Luke to think of.'

'He can take care of himself.'

'There are things I have to do.'

'Can't you do them here and let me help you?'

She shook her head. 'No, I can't.'

'Are you sure you can do them in Middlesbrough?'

'No.'

David raised his eyes heavenwards as if he despaired of her.

'But I can try.'

'Try? What do you have to try to do?'

'I can't explain, and if I could I wouldn't expect you to understand all the whys and wherefores. But unless I try I will never be able to live with myself, believe me. Please don't ask

176

me any more.'

His hesitation was only momentary. 'All right, I respect your wish. But don't forget me. And don't find anyone else.'

She touched his cheek and looked into his eyes, sorrowful at the thought of parting. 'Dear David, I promise you this. If what I want comes to be, I'll be back in Whitby that very instant.'

'That's a definite promise?'

'Yes.' She kissed him, confirming what she desired.

She would have broken away but he held her and his lips sought hers again. She yielded, and as she was swept up in his love regretted the circumstances which had forced their parting.

Later she offered him tea which he graciously accepted. Their talk was of friends but Lydia gradually eased the conversation on to the subject of Whitby's trading fraternity and the future prospects of those involved. She stored this information away and realised that in David's knowledge of mercantile activities in the port she could find vital assistance in any future campaign against her uncle.

'When will you leave?' he asked.

'A week today, by the morning coach.'

'Did you not think of the railway?'

'It would have been a long and tedious journey, having to go via Pickering and York. The sooner the talk of constructing a line between here and Middlesbrough becomes a reality the better.'

'I'll try to be there when you leave.'

'If your father will let you.' Irritated by the words 'I'll try', Lydia spoke before she realised

177

what she was saying and in what tone. As soon as she did she wished she could unsay the words. She saw anger and hurt in David's face.

He held back the cruel words which came to his own lips and said instead, 'I'm here, aren't I? And Father does not know.' But there was annoyance at her attitude in his expression.

Lydia and Mrs Harrington were in tears when the time came for the coach to leave, but the parting had to be made and, as the four horses bent to the reins, Mrs Harrington extracted a promise from Lydia and Luke that they would visit her whenever possible.

Through the tears in her eyes, Lydia searched in vain for David, hoping that he would make an appearance even if it was at the last minute. The final words they had exchanged had haunted her and now thrust themselves more prominently into her mind. Had he taken them too much to heart? Had she hurt him so deeply that their relationship had been affected? None of this would have happened but for the loss of the *Mary Anne*. Silently she cursed the storm that had changed her life.

With a heavy heart she watched her beloved Whitby pass by as the coach climbed out of the town to the road to Guisborough and beyond to Middlesbrough.

'It may be a long road home,' she whispered to herself, 'but one day I'll be back.'

Their arrival in Middlesbrough did nothing to lighten the depression she had felt since leaving Whitby. The journey had been cold, even the rugs

178

provided bringing no warmth to her. Her body was chilled and chilled it remained. The other passengers had been dour and the intermittent conversation at the start of the journey petered out into a silence broken only by the creak of timber and leather and the shouts of the coachman, urging his team to greater efforts. Luke had tried to instil some cheer into his sister but, when she made little response, had respected her desire to be left alone with her thoughts.

The weather deteriorated into a clinging dampness accompanied by low, unmoving, grey clouds which spread smoke from the works by the river across the town.

There was activity as soon as the coach pulled to a halt at the coaching inn. Knowing no one among the bustling people, Lydia wished she was back in the town she knew and loved. There at least she would have had a roof over her head; here she did not know where she would rest for even one night. She looked forlorn, standing beside their two bags which had been handed down to Luke from the top of the coach.

'I'll see if there are any rooms for the night here,' said her brother, starting towards the door to the inn.

At that moment a young man hurried out of the building. In his haste, his eyes on the team being released from their harness, he failed to notice the bags. He crashed into them, stumbled and automatically reached out for support. His hands grasped Lydia's arms. She staggered backwards under the impetus but managed to keep to her feet. He struggled upright, his face

179

red with embarrassment as he relaxed his grip.

'I'm sorry, miss,' he gasped.

'No, no. It was my fault, I shouldn't have had the bags in the way,' returned Lydia as she shrugged her coat back into place.

'Sure, now, there's no reason for you not to have them there. I should have looked where I was going.' The rich Irish accent was so full of genuine apology that Lydia was drawn to make a gracious acceptance.

'You've just arrived on the coach, miss?' he asked in order to stay in the company of this pretty girl a few minutes longer.

'Yes. My brother has gone to see if we can get rooms for the night, then we'll look for more permanent lodgings tomorrow.'

'You are intending to stay in Middlesbrough?'

'Yes. My brother's work has brought him here.'

'Maybe I can help, or at least my landlady might know of somewhere.'

'It would be wonderful if she did. A recommendation is better than speculation. Ah, here's my brother.' She paused then added as Luke joined them, 'You *are* looking gloomy.'

'There's only one room available so we'll have to start enquiring, and I don't relish walking these streets on a day like this.'

'We may not have to,' said Lydia. 'This young man might be able to solve our problems.' She turned to the Irishman. 'I didn't catch your name?'

'Sean Casey, miss.'

'Very well, Sean Casey, meet my brother, Luke Middleton.'

180

'Sure and I'm pleased to meet you, Luke.' Sean held out his hand in a friendly fashion. Luke wondered how much of that was born of a desire to get to know his sister better.

Sean turned a mischievous gaze on Lydia. 'And you, miss?'

'Lydia.'

'It's delighted I am to meet two such charming people.'

Lydia smiled to herself as all the blarney of the Irish made itself evident. But she did not mind. Already the dismal day had taken a turn for the better. She quickly explained about Sean's offer to Luke.

'Then we are grateful to you, Sean,' he said.

'You'd better hold your thanks until we see if my landlady, Mrs Hartley, can help.' Luke and Lydia picked up their bags. 'Here, let me take yours,' Sean offered her, and would not take no for an answer.

Under his direction they made their way towards the Market Square.

'Lydia tells me your work has brought you here?' said Sean without disguising his curiosity, for he had judged that this young man would not be humping iron.

'We're from Whitby where I supervised the shipment of iron ore. The operation is not running smoothly at this end and my employer has sent me here to sort things out.'

'I hope you can.'

'It affects you?'

Sean gave a small laugh. 'Well, indirectly, yes. I'm a humper of pig iron when it returns from

181

the furnaces at Witton, twenty miles away.' He shot a glance at Lydia to see how she reacted to the information that he was merely a labourer, but saw that she did not hold that against him. He was pleased that there was no snobbery in her. 'When your men are bloody-minded – sorry for the expression, miss,' he read in her returned smile that there was no need for an apology, 'the amount of stone going to Witton slows and so the supply of pig iron is interrupted. It is at the moment, so some of us have been laid off temporarily.'

'That may be our good fortune,' put in Lydia, 'or we wouldn't have had your help.'

'It's an ill wind...'

'Sean,' put in Luke, his expression serious, 'I would prefer you to say nothing about the reason I am here. I want to make some first-hand observations for myself.'

'Sure now I understand. You can trust me. I won't breathe a word.'

Reaching West Street, Sean opened the door to the house and called out, 'It's just me, Mrs Hartley. I've brought someone with me.'

A door at the end of the passage opened and Lydia saw a plump, motherly figure appear wiping her hands on an apron.

'Mrs Hartley, I'd like you to meet Lydia and Luke Middleton. They've just arrived from Whitby and I think you might be able to help them.'

Nell had surveyed the newcomers quickly and thoroughly. She took to them at once, sensing that they were a cut above her usual lodgers and came from a good, respectable family.

'I'm pleased to meet you both. Come through here and tell me how I may help.'

Sean smiled at Lydia encouragingly, while she in turn was delighted with her first impressions of his landlady. This was enhanced when they went into the kitchen. Though he judged that Lydia had been used to servants, she immediately commented on the cosy homeliness of this room, and of the house.

'Sit down, my dears, and I'll make you a cup of tea,' offered Nell Hartley. 'You'll need it after a ride from Whitby on a day like this.' She bustled about getting cups and saucers and pouring water from the kettle, already boiling above the fire. At the same time she passed pleasantries, but once she had poured the tea and handed round some home-made biscuits, she sat down and asked, 'Now, how can I help?'

'Luke has been sent here by his employer in Whitby and he and his sister are looking for accommodation,' Sean explained. 'I bumped into them just after they arrived and thought you might be able to recommend somewhere.'

'Yes, I can.'

Even Sean was surprised by the immediate reply.

'I'm sorry I have no room here,' Nell went on. 'I'm full with Sean and his two friends, Seamus and Kevin, but I think Mrs Turnbull at number sixteen might be interested. She's been considering the idea of taking lodgers, and you two might be just the people she needs to help make up her

183

mind. When you've finished your tea, leave your bags here and I'll take you along to meet her.'

Lydia felt a huge sense of relief. She had liked this woman from the moment she had entered her house. Even if Mrs Turnbull decided against taking lodgers, she knew Mrs Hartley would not abandon them until they had found somewhere suitable.

If Mrs Turnbull had not already reached a decision her mind was made up when she saw brother and sister. It was not her place to pry into the past but she judged they were used to better things than lodgings in a two-up, two-down terraced house. Their clothes were of good quality, well cared for, and their manner was polite and friendly. Very different from some of the tales she had heard about lodgers, though Mrs Hartley had never had any trouble.

Once Mrs Turnbull agreed to have them, Mrs Hartley left them to discuss terms, telling them to collect their bags whenever they were ready.

When they returned to number ten Luke managed a quiet word with Sean while Lydia and Nell were discussing how Lydia could occupy herself while in Middlesbrough.

'Are you working tomorrow morning, Sean?' he asked.

'No. Like I told you, I've been temporarily laid off.'

'Well then, might I ask a favour of you?'

'Ask away.'

'What time would the unloading of the ship from Whitby begin? I know it was due to arrive yesterday, late afternoon.'

184

'Should be started by eight.'

'Will you show me where?'

'Certainly. A jetty near the rolling mill is used exclusively at the moment for the Whitby iron ships.'

'I'd like to be close by when the men are due to start unloading.'

'Right. Be here at half-past seven.'

At precisely that time the next day Luke was knocking on the door of number ten. It was opened by Sean who was shrugging himself into a three-quarter-length thick serge coat.

'Top of the morning to you,' he said brightly as he looked Luke up and down. 'Glad to see you've put something warm on. It can blow cold off the river even on the warmest day.'

'I'm used to it at Whitby though here you are more exposed, lacking the cliffs which shelter the river at home.'

Sean grabbed a cap. 'Right, I'm ready. Let's away.'

They walked to the Market Square and crossed to North Street. Already people were about their daily business. Men heading for work greeted fellow workers and teamed up in twos and threes, some merging into larger groups. Joking banter passed between them, betting tips were exchanged in good faith, last night's activities were remembered and legs were pulled.

Luke and Sean were swept along by the flow and absorbed the atmosphere of jollity and friendliness. Luke's curiosity was raised when he noted that few greetings were made by Sean, whereupon he learned that the Irishman and his friends had been in Middlesbrough little more than two weeks.

After passing the Bolckow and Vaughan Ironworks fewer people were about. Luke caught snippets of conversation and judged that he was among Whitby men here. He noted that the atmosphere had changed. There was a lack of cheer; the pace here was slower as if they had no enthusiasm for the work to which they were going.

He remarked on this to Sean and added, 'Is there a place from which I can observe what is going on without drawing attention to myself?'

'I know a spot. When Mr Langton, our works manager, told me about the trouble at this jetty I was curious so I scouted around to see what was happening for myself.'

'You know Mr Langton?'

Sean grinned at the incredulity on Luke's face. 'Sure now, why wouldn't I?'

'Well, to be on such confidential terms...'

'With the Works Manager?' Sean finished for him. 'Well, I'll tell you this and tell you no more: when you've done a man a good turn you do tend to get a bit closer, no matter what your station in life. And I promise you, I'll not always be humping iron.'

'I'm sure you won't. But how...'

'Ask no more, Luke, and you'll hear no lies.' Sean did not want to be bragging about his own heroics. 'This way.' He took a narrow path running beside the river and turned Luke back to the quest in hand. He halted at a point from which

186

they could discreetly observe the ship, the jetty and the workers. 'This do?'

'Perfect.' Luke settled himself to watch.

It did not take him long to size up the situation. There was some work going on but in general the men were making a pretence of it. Ironstone was certainly being loaded into railway trucks but at a rate which meant the ship would not be cleared today. The captain was talking in an agitated fashion with a group of men. Voices were raised and Sean, catching the odd word, judged that the captain was pleading with the men to get on with the work quickly so he could clear the Tees on the evening tide. He appeared to be receiving no cooperation. The group drifted away from him and joined others who sat doing nothing or were playing toss the penny.

Having taken all this in Luke cast around for sight of Jos Sigsworth, the man whom Mr Martin had put in charge of the Whitby team unloading the ore.

'Seen what you want to see?' asked Sean.

'Aye, but not what I'd like to see. That bunch wants a stick of dynamite up them. And where's the man in charge? I want to see what happens when he comes. You go if you want to. Thanks for bringing me.'

Sean gave a grin and shook his head. 'I'll stay. I can see there's going to be fun when you try to get that lot back to work.'

'Try?' Luke raised an eyebrow. 'I won't be try-ing. I'll do it.'

They settled themselves more comfortably. Five minutes later Luke grabbed Sean's arm and indicated a man approaching the jetty at a leisurely pace, pausing now and then to gaze across the river. 'The overseer?' said Sean.

'Aye, Jos Sigsworth.'

They watched him near the jetty. He stopped to have a word with some of the men but there was nothing to indicate that he was attempting to get more of them to join those working slowly between ship and train. No orders were shouted, no persuasive powers used. The men just went on doing what they were doing. Meanwhile Sigsworth went to a hut which Luke presumed he used as some sort of office. He reappeared a few moments later carrying a chair, placing it in a position where he was in the sun and from which he could see the activity or lack of it shown by his so-called workforce.

'Right, let's go,' snapped Luke, his voice filled with irritation at what he had seen.

Chapter Eight

A tap on the door drew James Langton's attention. He looked up from the plans he had been studying and then jumped quickly to his feet.

'Mr Vaughan, a pleasure to see you, sir,' he said, coming from behind his desk to greet one of the owners of the ironworks.

'And you, James,' said Vaughan pleasantly. He was a man of medium build with no outstanding features and no immediate presence. But those who knew him, and James had come to know him well since their first meeting in Carlisle, were aware that he was a man of ingenuity and keen ambition which had brought him success in the iron trade and a partnership in the most important venture on the south bank of the River Tees. But he wasn't a man who had ridden roughshod over others to achieve his aim. He was a man with tact, one who could handle his workers and draw the best out of them. Because of these attributes he was liked by everyone.

'Sit down, James. There's something we must discuss.' Almost immediately Vaughan changed his mind. 'No, don't sit down, we can discuss the situation as we go.'

James knew better than to query what was on his employer's mind. He fell into step with him and they headed for the river.

'What's happening about our shipments of ore from Whitby?' asked Vaughan.

'I've had word from Mr Martin that he will send someone to look into the matter.'

'No one's come yet?'

'No, sir.'

'Then we'll have to see if we can do something about it ourselves. These supplies must come through quicker.'

'Yes, sir. But this is a Whitby operation, remember. We agreed that Mr Martin could employ his own workforce to unload the ships.'

'Yes, I was part of those negotiations. It's a pity we ever agreed. We'd have had more control if we'd been the direct employers as we are with the

189

coal imports. However, what's done is done. Let's see what the trouble is, why the men aren't working to full capacity. We must try to sort it out ourselves without waiting for someone to come from Whitby.'

'Yes, sir.' Though James knew Mr Vaughan had a gift for handling men, he doubted whether it would extend to those under someone else's jurisdiction and who, in his opinion, were taking advantage of a weak overseer.

'We need the flow of ore to Witton to be continuous and if Martin can't supply us as was agreed, then we'll have to find someone who can. A pity because I like Martin, a good, honest, straightforward man. I believe he's being let down by his workers.'

As Luke and Sean walked purposefully towards Jos Sigsworth they drew only a cursory glance from some of the men. A few shot them a second glance but then doubt clouded their minds. A vaguely familiar face? Couldn't be. Luke Middleton would be in Whitby.

They reached the overseer to find him with his eyes shut, even this early in the day.

Sigsworth had become familiar with the men's go-slow attitude and accepted that he could do nothing about it. Not that he wanted to, he liked the way things were and was happy to let the situation go on to his advantage. And there was nothing the Bolckow and Vaughan officials could do about it. This was purely a Whitby operation, and Whitby and Mr Martin were far enough away.

So it came as a violent shock when a voice boomed in his ear, 'Sigsworth, on your feet!'

He almost fell off his chair as he jerked upright. His eyes widened and anger flared at this untimely disturbance. It faded quickly when he recognised the man before him. 'Luke Middleton!' Caught out in an embarrassing and compromising situation, he struggled to his feet, losing his hat and knocking over the chair as he did so.

'What the hell's going on here?' Luke's voice thundered across the open space, resounding off ship and train so that no man listening could miss that note of authority.

Sigsworth, trying to pull himself together, muttered something inaudible.

'Speak up man, I want an explanation.' Luke swung round, sweeping out one arm to encompass the sorry scene. 'All of you, over here. And that includes you men unloading ore with all the speed of dead lice.' The penetrating voice demanded obedience, and received it. The men moved closer. 'Some of you may recognise me. Those of you who don't will know me now. I'm Luke Middleton, sent by Mr Martin to get this operation moving properly again.'

In those few moments Sigsworth got over his shock. He sensed Luke's presence spelt trouble he did not want, so hit back quickly. 'You've no right to stick your nose in here,' he barked, eyes flaring with fury.

'Haven't I?' countered Luke. 'Read this.' He pulled a sealed envelope from his pocket and thrust it at Sigsworth.

191

He took it suspiciously, hesitated, then tore it open. Silence had descended over the whole scene. Tension hung over the men. They waited expectantly as Sigsworth read the letter.

The heat of the exchange reached Mr Vaughan and James Langton who were within earshot of the jetty.

'What's going on?' wondered Mr Vaughan, at the sight of the workforce gathered in a group around three central figures, one of whom had his eyes fixed on a piece of paper.

After a few more steps, Vaughan stopped and put a restraining hand on James's arm. 'Wait, let's see what's happening.' He paused then added, 'Who's that young man holding centre stage?'

'Don't know him,' replied James. 'The man reading the paper is the overseer of this gang. The one to the young man's left is a new employee of yours from Ireland – Sean Casey. He, along with several others, is laid off until we get more ore moving through. What he's doing here I couldn't...' He let the words trail away when Vaughan raised his hand for silence.

'Let's listen.'

Sigsworth, face draining quickly of colour, looked up slowly from the letter.

'I know the contents,' said Luke firmly before Sigsworth could mouth a protest. 'See that you are on this ship when it leaves for Whitby on the evening tide.'

The impact of what was happening hit the overseer hard but it brought rebellion to the surface.

'It won't be unloaded in time,' he sneered.

'It will.' There was a note of assurance in Luke's tone which would have wilted any man's resistance. But Sigsworth thought he would have his men's support. They had enjoyed an easy time under him.

An atmosphere of uncertainty had settled over them. Unsure what was happening, they looked askance at the man who had been their boss.

Sigsworth held up the piece of paper for all to see. 'This recalls me to Whitby, takes this job from me and leaves this upstart in charge. You've heard him. Thinks this ship will be ready to leave this evening. That means very hard graft. What do you have to say about that? Will you...'

Luke intervened. He wasn't going to permit Sigsworth to preach dissent and rally the men to his side. 'Before you make up your minds, consider this – anyone who doesn't want to work had better be on this ship too when it sails. And that will mean you have no job, no wages, nothing for your families in Whitby but hardship. If you stay here I can promise you hard work but you will earn money. The ore ships from Whitby must be turned round quickly. Iron ore is vital to the life of the Bolckow and Vaughan Ironworks. If you fail, or slow up delivery, then the workers here suffer. Consider your fellow workers. The quicker you deal with the ore ships, the better for all. And particularly yourselves, because I'm going to alter the wage structure. You'll now be paid piece rates for the quantity of ore you move.'

A buzz of interest went round the men.

'That will mean we're dependent on the shipments from Whitby and on the weather,' someone shouted. It brought a chorus of agreement from the crowd.

'It will,' agreed Luke, 'but that money will be on top of the wage you are already being paid which is not related to the amount of ironstone you move.'

This sounded an advantageous move and brought excited exchanges among the men.

'Does that include the rise we were promised three months ago?' someone shouted.

'You got that at the time promised,' returned Luke.

A ripple of denial ran through the crowd.

'I know it was paid. I checked the calculations with Mr Martin. The money was sent in its usual sealed container to Mr Sigsworth, and I know it arrived because the receipt for the unopened box came back to Whitby.'

'We got no rise.' The statement was repeated, and agreement ran through the men like a fire sweeping through dry tinder. Immediately the truth dawned on them.

'Sigsworth pocketed it!'

'Aye, must have done.'

'Bloody hook!'

There was ugliness in their attitude as these statements swept from mouth to mouth.

'Let's have him!' someone shouted. The hostility was echoed throughout the gathering.

Luke saw the makings of a lynch mob if things ran out of hand. 'Quiet! Quiet!' he yelled, holding his hands high in a gesture for calm.

'The bastard!' The crowd started to surge forward.

Luke held his ground in front of a quivering Sigsworth, who was suffering horrid visions of being torn limb from limb. Sean came to Luke's shoulder.

'Stop! Don't do this.' Luke's yell carried not only authority but the threat of what could happen if they ignored him.

There was a roar of disapproval but the men in the front had seen a determination to maintain law and order on the faces of Luke and Sean. They had also seen the two men's clenched fists and knew they would be the first to feel them. They stopped and the whole mob came to a halt behind them.

'That's sensible,' Luke approved. 'If any man steps out of line on this he'll be dismissed immediately. I don't like using threats but occasionally they are necessary. It appears Sigsworth has cheated you out of the pay rise that was sent to you, but there's nothing to be gained by using violence against him.'

'He told us it hadn't come!'

'Aye, so after a month we organised a go-slow policy. He said he had repeatedly asked for the rise but Mr Martin had taken no notice.'

'We heard nothing of this in Whitby. Thought everything was all right until just over a week ago when Mr Martin received a letter from the manager of the ironworks, asking us to investigate the slow delivery of ore. That's how I come to be here. Now, let's get this matter settled and get that ore moving. What I have told you about payment stands. My report will go to Mr Martin and I'm sure he will pay you the back money you have missed. Does that satisfy you?'

There was only a moment's hesitation while this sank in and then a murmur of approval was like music to Luke's ears.

He breathed more easily. 'Right then, let's get that ore unloaded.' The enthusiasm in his voice brought the men to life. They scattered to set about their work eagerly, streaming away to shift the ore so the ship could sail on the evening tide and take the man who had cheated them to his just rewards.

'Well done, Luke,' said Sean. 'You handled a nasty situation well.'

He nodded. 'Thanks. It was touch and go. I was pleased to have you beside me. Your presence helped when that mob got ugly. Want a job?'

'Job?' Sean was puzzled. What could he do here? Another pair of hands humping ironstone? Not much different from what he was doing already.

Before he answered, Luke called to two of the workmen, 'Keep your eye on Sigsworth until I'm ready to deal with him.' He knew the overseer daren't try anything now or he would feel the wrath of the men he had cheated. Luke turned back to Sean. 'You've been laid off, you haven't a job, so I'm offering you one – permanently, or at least as far as I can see for a long time ahead.'

'But you know nothing about me, except that I'm humping pig iron when it gets back from Witton.'

'Someone who took pity on two strangers and

found them lodgings can't be bad. And from what I saw then and this morning, you have a nimble brain and I don't think you would shirk responsibility.'

Sean smiled. 'Thank you for your trust. I'll decide when you tell me what...'

Luke saw Sean look beyond him and turned to see what had drawn his attention. Two men were walking quickly towards them. They were well-dressed, men of obvious substance and authority. Luke speculated quickly but came to no conclusion as to who they might be or what they were doing here. He was about to put a whispered question to Sean when the Irishman recognised James Langton. The other he did not know.

'Hello there, Sean. Didn't expect to see you here,' called James.

'I'm with Luke Middleton. Luke, this is James Langton.'

'Mr Langton? Manager of the ironworks?'

'Yes.'

'Then I have a letter for you from Mr Martin of Whitby.' Luke fished an envelope from his pocket and held it out.

'From what we have just seen I think this letter of introduction will be superfluous.' He shoved it into his pocket. 'I'll read it later. First I must introduce Mr Vaughan.'

'Holy Mother of God, the top brass himself,' muttered Sean under his breath, but there was sufficient strength in his words for them to be caught by the man himself.

Mr Vaughan grinned. 'I'm flattered that you invoke higher authority.' He held out his hand.

Sean felt privileged to shake the hand of the man who, with his partner, had brought industry and employment to the banks of the River Tees.

Vaughan shook hands with Luke. 'Pleased to meet you, young man. You handled that extremely well, and I appreciate the fact that you will have the ship cleared by this evening.'

'Thank you, sir, it's kind of you to say so. The situation was not quite what I expected when Mr Martin assigned me the job.'

'You have a way of handling men.'

'That's what Mr Martin tells me.'

'And I can confirm that, can't you, James?'

'I certainly can. You'll be an asset here.'

Mr Vaughan nodded his agreement. 'Will you accompany us to Mr Langton's office so that we can clarify the movement of ironstone from Whitby?'

At this request Sean said, 'I'll see you later, Luke, to discuss our little matter.'

Luke saw an expression of curiosity cross Mr Langton's face. 'Sir,' he said, 'I've offered Sean a job. If he'll take it, I would like him to be at this discussion.'

Mr Langton shot Mr Vaughan a look of enquiry. After all, it was he who had suggested this meeting.

'Very well,' Vaughan agreed.

James saw that Sean still seemed uncertain about Luke's proposal. 'You're not beholden to me, Sean. I'm sure Mr Middleton has offered you something better.'

'He doesn't know what I have in mind,' put in Luke.

198

'Then discuss it quickly and join us in my office.' He and Mr Vaughan left them.

First Luke spoke quietly to the two men guarding Sigsworth. 'Take him to his lodgings. Collect his belongings and return here. Don't let him out of your sight.'

As the men walked away with a very subdued Sigsworth between them, Luke turned to Sean. 'I can't always be at the jetty, so as well as a foreman on the site, whom I have yet to appoint, I need an assistant. I'm offering the post to you. Your first job will be to escort Sigsworth to Whitby, deliver him and a letter to Mr Martin. The letter will explain the situation here. You can confirm it, add any details requested and answer Mr Martin's questions. Will you take the job?'

'Sure, even the devil himself wouldn't stop me!'

The bargain was sealed with a firm handshake and the two new friends hurried after their superiors.

When they entered James Langton's office they were offered chairs.

'As you are here, I take it you have accepted Mr Middleton's offer, Sean?' said James.

'Too good to miss, sir. It gives me some authority which I will relish.'

'Good, I'm sure you'll do well.' He turned to Mr Vaughan. 'The meeting is all yours, sir.'

'I have no jurisdiction over you so all I can do is apprise you of our situation and ask what you can do or suggest to help. Especially you, Luke. I don't expect Sean to be familiar with the ironstone yields that pass through Whitby.

'They are vital to us, Luke. As you know, our best ore comes from Grosmont. It is important that that supply continues to supplement our own source near our furnaces at Witton. But the seams there are not yielding what we expected so we'll need more from Grosmont. It's important we build up stocks in case bad weather halts the supply. I'd like to make sure Mr Martin is aware of all this?'

'I understand, sir, and will do my best. Sean is escorting Sigsworth to Whitby, leaving on the ore ship this evening. I will be writing to Mr Martin informing him of what has happened here and will now add what you have just told me. If necessary I will go to Whitby after that but I'm sure Sean will be able to confirm and emphasise what I put in my letter.'

'You can trust me to give Mr Martin a full report,' he said. 'I'll impress upon him the urgency of an answer relating to the delivery of the ironstone. Hopefully I'll have his reply when I return on the next ore ship leaving Whitby, which I believe should be the day after tomorrow.'

'No doubt that Irish tongue of yours can be very persuasive,' commented Mr Vaughan.

Sean smiled. 'Ah, sure now, isn't that what it should do?'

Luke and Sean left the meeting. They were in good spirits as they headed back for the jetty.

Luke felt he had got the situation in hand and hoped that in a few minutes he would have it more firmly under his control. If his written

200

word, supported by Sean's testimony, convinced Mr Martin then the future looked bright.

Sean was grateful for the opportunity he had been given. With Luke's help he had thrown off the role of labourer and was determined not to let his chance slip. He was on the first step towards the future he had dreamed about, the one which would enable him to free Eileen from the dead end they had faced in Dublin. He hoped that, when she heard what he was doing, she would believe that coming to England had been the right decision.

When they neared the jetty they saw that the men were dealing with the cargo efficiently. Minds relieved of all doubt about what was happening to their pay, they seemed cheerful.

'All right, everyone, ease up a minute,' Luke shouted. 'I have a few words to say to you.'

The men stopped work and focused their attention on him. They had taken to the way he had handled Jos Sigsworth and solved their problem over pay. They saw here a man they judged knew what he wanted and would get it without exploiting them unfairly.

'I've appointed Sean Casey, here, as my assistant. What I want now is a site foreman. Someone you trust, from whom you will take orders without resentment. Someone you can work with, to whom you can go with any problems and be sure you'll get a fair hearing without any bias towards either you or the firm for whom you work. Our man must have the interests of both sides at heart. I don't know you personally so I want you to name someone.'

There was a moment's silence at the unexpected decision they had to make and at the responsibility that had been thrust upon them. Discussion broke out among them which was silenced as someone shouted, 'What about Bob Chase?'

There was a roar of approval.

'Seems unanimous,' called Luke. 'Where are you, Bob?' He scanned the crowd.

'Here!' someone shouted, and a tall, broad-shouldered man stepped forward.

Knowing he was coming under scrutiny, he walked towards Luke and Sean with a purposeful step. His eyes, strangely dark, were fixed on Luke as if he was trying to weigh up his new boss, though what he had seen of the way the young man had handled Sigsworth in a tricky situation had already impressed him.

Bob Chase looked like a man who would stand no nonsense. Apart from his sheer size, he was muscular without an ounce of fat on him. His hands were big; clenched they would present a formidable fist. Even here, in the open, he had a commanding presence which he must have kept subdued when Luke first arrived. Now, with responsibility thrust on him, it came to the fore. Luke's initial reaction was that he was pleased with the men's choice.

'Right, Bob, you are in charge on site. You must work harmoniously with the men, and of course with me and Sean. Bring any complaints or situations you can't handle to either of us. But the most important thing is that you keep the ironstone moving and turn the ships around as

202

quickly as possible. It is vital to the welfare of all of us. Fail, and Mr Vaughan and Mr Langton will look elsewhere for the ore.'

Bob nodded. 'We'll shift it.' He half turned to view the men. 'All right, stop gawping. Get on with it! Bend your backs! This ship has to sail this evening.'

Instantly the men were back at their task.

'Keep them at it, Bob. We'll be back later.'

'Right, sir.' He touched his forehead with the tip of his right index finger.

As he moved away Luke noticed Bob's eyes darting, taking in all the activity.

'I reckon we've got a good man there,' commented Sean quietly.

'My opinion too,' returned Luke. 'Right, back to West Street. You get ready to leave and I'll write the letters.'

Their immediate departure was halted by the return of the two men escorting Sigsworth.

'Get him on board and don't let him out of your sight until the ship's ready to sail,' ordered Luke. 'Then Sean will take responsibility. I've just appointed Bob Chase as foreman on site. Report to him and tell him what I've said.'

The two friends parted company in West Street. When Luke entered number sixteen alarm immediately crossed Lydia's face.

'Back so soon? I didn't expect to see you all day.'

He smiled. 'Wipe that worry away. Everything is all right.'

'No hostility?'

203

'Only from Jos Sigsworth.'

'So that's who was in charge?'

'Aye, but running things to suit himself.' He went on to acquaint her of the facts and how he had dealt with them.

'Well done, Luke.' She was proud of her brother, who had been so decisive.

'And what's more, I've engaged Sean Casey as my assistant. His first assignment is to escort Jos Sigsworth to Whitby and give my reports to Mr Martin. I must write them now.'

'Then he could deliver a letter from me to David?'

'I'm sure he would.'

Brother and sister set about composing very different letters which were safely in Sean's possession when he sailed on the evening tide.

As he watched the *Nina* head downriver Luke felt the satisfaction of a job well done. He was also pleased with his ability to step from the shadow of his sister and deal with a crisis in which she could play no part. He sensed the men too felt a touch of pride as well as relief. They gave a great cheer when the ship cast off and took the full flow of the river. He thanked them all, especially Bob who had organised his workforce so as to get the maximum effort from them in the shortest possible time.

'There'll be another ship in tomorrow,' Luke told them. 'Let's have her turned round quickly so that the jetty is clear for the return of the *Nina* the next day.'

'So she's gone! Now you might as well get her out

of your head, concentrate on your work and look for a new prospect who will be an asset to this business.'

Jonas Drayton eyed his son with smug satisfaction that his wishes had been obeyed. The threat of what could happen to David's inheritance if he persisted in pursuing Lydia Middleton had paid off.

'And you made sure I didn't see her leave.' Disgust coloured David's voice.

'One of us had to attend that meeting. I couldn't because of a request from Nathan Middleton to see him on a matter of some importance.'

'Aye, and you no doubt engineered both meetings to take place at the same time so I wouldn't be free to say my goodbyes to Lydia.'

'Poppycock!' snapped Jonas. His eyes narrowed with warning as he looked down at David seated behind his desk. 'Entertaining such thoughts about your own father should be beneath you. What your mother and I have done for you has always been for the best.' He placed his hands on the desk and leaned forward to peer hard at David. 'You'll not be above bedding a pretty girl, so consider bedding Isobel. It would go a long way to cementing the relationship between my company and Nathan's. I believe we could work on some profitable schemes together.'

'And what exactly might those be?'

'Oh, nothing concrete but with trade expanding who knows what might arise? To have someone who might be interested in joining us in deals we could not handle alone would be beneficial. So you consider that lass. Now I'm for out.' He turned quickly and left the office, leaving David pondering his words.

Jonas started down the corridor towards the outside door. He heard voices coming from the clerk's office and slowed his pace so that he could overhear what was being said. A puzzled frown crossed his face when he heard an unfamiliar Irish accent.

'I'd like to see Mr David Drayton, please.' Sean put the request to the clerk with an authority he thought befitted his new employment.

'Yes, sir. Who shall I say?'

'Mr Sean Casey. He won't know me. Tell him I have a personal letter to deliver.'

'I can see that he gets it.' The deep full-throated voice came from behind Sean.

As he turned to see who had spoken he caught a glimpse of the expression on the clerk's face. It told him that the man in the doorway was the man's employer and that he dare not go one inch against him.

Sean immediately realised why the clerk was in awe for he found himself disliking the man's overbearing manner and piercing eyes which spoke of a determination to get his own way.

Sean stiffened. He ignored the hand held out for the letter. 'Sorry, sir, my instructions were clear and I shall carry them out. This letter will be given to no one but Mr David Drayton.'

'I am his father. I will see that he gets it.'

'That is not for you to decide, sir.' Sean's tone was defiant.

Jonas's eyes darkened. 'Whipper-snapper!

These are my premises. I rule here. If I say so, I will deliver that letter.'

'Whatever you say, you will not.'

Anger reddened Jonas's face. His voice shook. 'Then get out of here!' he snapped. 'Or I'll have you horsewhipped.'

'Don't you threaten me, sir.' Sean's voice turned icy cold. 'I have nothing but contempt for a man who so blatantly ignores a lady's wishes.'

'Ah, so it is from a lady.' There was triumph in Jonas's voice. Sean's reaction was to curse himself for letting the information slip. 'My surmise was right. How you come to be delivering a letter from Lydia Middleton I neither know nor care.' His tone had gradually become more conciliatory. 'But I ask you not to let my son have it. That lady intends nothing but mischief and my son would be harmed if the letter reached him.'

Sean, who did not know the true relationship between Lydia Middleton and David Drayton, hesitated for a moment in the face of the older man's plea. He tussled with his thoughts. The man sounded reasonable enough now but his previous tone was probably more characteristic.

Sean's mind then went back to Lydia when she had presented the letter to him. He had read behind the look in her eyes a desire to put something right with the addressee. A lovers' tiff? A rift that needed healing? The clarification of a relationship? Whatever it was it was no concern of his. He had made a promise to her and would see that he carried it out.

'Sorry, sir, the letter remains with me. If you won't allow me to deliver it to your son then I

207

must return it to the sender. I have no more time to spare, I leave Whitby shortly.' Sean brushed past Drayton, hoping that his final statement had fooled him.

He lingered outside, using the movement of people going about their daily business to conceal his presence. He was sure that Mr Drayton had been dressed to leave the building when he had been halted by Sean's exchange with the clerk. He would nip back when the man left. But as the minutes ticked by Sean became more and more irritated. Jonas Drayton did not appear.

He cursed his own luck. The voyage had passed well so far. He had delivered Sigsworth to Mr Martin, given his report and received his new employer's gratitude. In the town he had found comfortable rooms at the Angel Inn as directed by Luke. All had gone smoothly until he had tried to deliver Lydia's letter. Now his determination strengthened. He would not be outdone. He'd fox old Drayton yet. But he could make no plan, only watch and seize his opportunity when it arose.

It did so half an hour later.

The clerk came out of the office and hurried away to his right, holding some papers he was obviously intent on delivering. Maybe, Sean surmised, he had been told that idling would not be tolerated and he should get back to the office as soon as possible. Sean could imagine Drayton checking his watch as if he knew exactly how long it should take his clerk to carry out the designated task.

Sean followed the man, keeping at a discreet

distance from which he could observe without being seen. He matched his pace to the clerk's, shadowed him across the bridge to the west side and then up Golden Lion Bank to a building in Flowergate. Sean waited close by the door.

A few minutes later the clerk came out with a quick step to find his path blocked. He was startled.

'Hold on,' said Sean, putting a detaining hand on the man's shoulder.

The man's instant scowl at being stopped vanished as he recognised Sean. 'You!' he gasped. Fearing the worst, he added disagreeably, 'What do you want?'

'Just a word and a favour,' returned Sean.

'I can't get mixed up in anything to do with that letter.'

'Ah, sure now, you have a sharp mind. That should help you look out for yourself.'

'Look out for myself? What do you mean?'

'You could make yourself a little money.'

The clerk licked his lips at the thought but then shook his head. 'No, no, I stand to lose more if old Drayton finds out I've delivered that letter to his son. I suppose that's what you want me to do?'

Sean gave a little smile and shook his head. 'No. All I want is for you to give him a message.'

The clerk still looked doubtful so Sean pulled a shilling from his pocket. He flicked it into the air so that its brightness and movement caught the clerk's eye. As it fell, Sean grabbed it.

'Now wouldn't that be better in your pocket?'

The clerk's eyes gleamed with greed. As Sean

started to return the coin to his own pocket the man said, 'Hold on a minute. You said a message?'

'Indeed I did.'

'You mean, not the letter?'

'Aye.'

'Nothing written down?'

'Not a single word.'

The clerk pursed his lips and rubbed his chin thoughtfully.

Sean sensed him weakening and pressed his point. 'All you have to do is to give a message from me to Mr David without his father knowing.'

'So there'd be no incriminating evidence?'

'None. Only me and Mr David would know and I don't think either of us is going to tell his father.' Sean flicked the coin temptingly in the air again.

The clerk watched it fall back into Sean's open palm and lie there gleaming as much as to say, I can be yours.

'All right,' he agreed.

'Now you're talking like a man.'

'Stop slopping around. I'm late already. What's the message?'

'Just tell Mr David that someone has an important letter for him from Middlesbrough. If he wants it, tell him to meet me at the Angel between seven and eight tonight.'

'Right.' The clerk grabbed the coin and made to start off.

Sean's strong fingers clutched the front of his coat and pulled him close. The man cringed from

210

the frightening expression that Sean had adopted.

'There's one more thing. Breathe a word of this to anyone and you'll feel my fist. And, after I've finished with you, all the wailing banshees of auld Ireland will haunt you for the rest of your life.'

The man's eyes widened. 'Your secret will be safe with me!'

'See that it is and see that you deliver the message correctly.' Sean thrust the clerk away from him and the man scuttled off as quickly as his thin legs could carry him.

Chapter Nine

Sean seated himself so that he had a view of the door to the snug and waited patiently for David Drayton. The small room was cosy with its own bar. Illumination came from two oil lamps hanging from the ceiling and four set in wall brackets. A fire burned brightly in the iron grate and banished all thoughts of the cold damp evening outside. Fog had rolled in from the sea and hung over the river, thickening as the darkness intensified.

The buzz of conversation from the well-dressed drinkers at the other five tables rose and fell and was occasionally pierced by laughter or amicable disagreements.

Sean grew uneasy as the deep ticking of the grandfather clock beside the door reminded him that the time he had stipulated was fast running out. Had the clerk failed him? If not, was David Drayton ignoring the message? Or was he not prepared to come out on a cold foggy night when a comfortable chair in front of a roaring fire would be more appropriate? Had the word 'Middlesbrough' no pull on him? That must surely indicate that the message was from Lydia. Sean wondered what sort of a relationship they had.

His attention was held by the sentinel clock. Its tick and the movement of the hands, drawing ever nearer the hour of eight, were hypnotic. Staring at them, he picked up his tankard and raised it to his lips. He started. Its emptiness drew his attention away from the mesmerising clock. He cursed to himself and called to the barman to bring him another.

As the man placed a full tankard in front of him, Sean was aware that someone had come through the door and had stopped to survey the room. He was good-looking, or at least Sean reckoned women would see him that way. He had a self-assurance to him which Sean thought would be more in evidence in the company of men. A shy streak might come out when the ladies were present, but it would be slight and might well add to his attraction. If this was the man to whom he had to deliver Lydia's note, Sean could see why she might be attracted to him and want to keep in touch.

'Who's that?' he whispered in the barman's ear as he stooped to retrieve the empty glass.

The man glanced over his shoulder. 'Mr

Drayton,' he replied.

'Mr David?'

'Aye.'

'Please ask him to join me.'

'Yes, sir.'

The barman crossed the room to David and inclined his head in Sean's direction as he delivered the message. David nodded, thanked the barman, and came to Sean.

He rose from his chair. 'Mr David Drayton?'

'Yes. You have the advantage of me.'

Sean gave a friendly smile. 'Sean Casey.' He offered his hand. They exchanged a handshake and sat down.

'You must have got my message from your clerk?' observed Sean.

'I wouldn't be here if I hadn't,' David replied a little haughtily, and then added in a mystified tone, 'What is this all about?'

'I'm sorry to have acted so mysteriously but after my heated exchange with your father, I had to take precautions.'

David frowned. 'My father? You've had altercations with my father?'

'Yes. I have a letter which I was asked to deliver to you personally. I came to your office. Your father said he would give you the letter but I refused to let him have it and he told me in no uncertain terms to leave. Hence the need to resort to subterfuge.'

'This becomes more puzzling by the minute.'

Their conversation ceased as the barman placed a bottle of brandy and two glasses on the table.

'I took the liberty of ordering when the barman pointed you out. I hope you'll take a glass?'

'I'd like nothing better,' returned Sean, though he couldn't remember when he had last tasted brandy.

David poured, allowing the heavy aroma to linger between them. 'Well?' he said. 'The rest of your story.'

'There is little more except to hand you the letter which I think will explain everything.' Sean drew the envelope from his pocket and handed it over. He realised instantly from David's brightening eyes that he had recognised the writing and knew who had sent it.

'Please excuse me,' he said, breaking the seal.

Sean nodded, took his glass and leaned back in his chair, his mind taken up with thoughts of Lydia and her possible relationship with this man.

Dear David,

I was sorry you were not at the coach to say goodbye and wish me well. I missed you then as I shall do in Middlesbrough.

What the future holds for Luke and me in this new town I do not know. One day we may return to Whitby, and hopefully under happier circumstances than those in which we left.

I am sorry that recently we have had our disagreements. Maybe one day the cause of those will be overcome and our relationship be what it once was before misfortune changed it. I will dwell on this no longer nor expand on what happened between us. I will not hold it against

214

someone who I feel has always been a very dear friend to me and, at times, perhaps more than that.

However, if during our time apart you find someone else, I will understand. I hope you will reciprocate the feeling.

Please keep writing to me with news of yourself and of what is happening in Whitby – still my hometown and dear to my heart.

My fondest regards,
    Lydia

David sat staring at the letter, no longer reading words. He chastised himself for not being at the coach and cursed his father for putting obstacles in his way. Deliberately, he believed. Why hadn't he defied Jonas? But if he had, he and Lydia would have faced a life of hardship and possible poverty which could well have strained their love. If only she could see that his way offered a chance that his father would relent and their love could blossom in the sort of surroundings they had known all their lives. But she gave no indication of such understanding. The touch of hope in her letter had faded before the final words. She had never mentioned love, merely sent fond regards. She had even suggested he might find someone else.

David's mind was in a tumult. Someone else? He frowned. Maybe she had done that, even in this short time. Maybe this Irishman...

He looked up slowly. 'Tell me, Mr Casey, how do you come to be the carrier of Miss Middleton's letter?'

Sean quickly related the circumstances in which he and Lydia had met. David listened carefully and realised that this man had charm, which was emphasised by his smooth Irish brogue. And he had been kind. He had put himself out to help a lady in distress; not everyone would have done that. Maybe there had been an immediate mutual attraction and Sean Casey had made the most of it.

As he was speaking Sean hoped for some hint of the relationship between this man and Lydia, but obtained nothing from David's response when he merely asked, 'When do you return to Middlesbrough?'

'Tomorrow on the *Nina*, with another cargo of ironstone. We sail at ten in the morning.'

'You are turning her round fast.'

'The ironstone is needed as quickly as possible.'

'You'll take a letter for me?'

'If that is what you want.'

'I'll come to the ship.' David stood up, paused and then sank slowly on to the chair again. He leaned forward and fixed his gaze firmly on Sean. 'Miss Middleton, is she well?'

'When I left she was.'

'Her journey had not been too uncomfortable?'

'She never mentioned it to me. When we met she was too concerned about where they were going to stay.'

'And you said that her lodgings are comfortable?'

'That's what I said.'

'Describe them to me.'

Sean gave him a description of Mrs Turnbull's

216

terraced house.

David pursed his lips. 'Hmm, not what she has been used to. Luke is with her?'

'Of course.'

David hesitated a moment and then stood up. 'Thank you. I'll be on the quay tomorrow morning.'

Sean nodded and watched him go. He had gleaned a little and now surmised that the relationship between Lydia and David Drayton had been deeper than friendship but that something had happened to mar it.

He signalled to the barman who came to him. 'Tell me about Mr Drayton.'

The man quickly imparted what he knew which led Sean to ask about the Middleton family. The barman was only too ready to talk of the recent tragedy and when he had finished left Sean contemplating Lydia's background and the life she must have been used to once, so different from the circumstances in which she now found herself.

As he walked home David too thought of Lydia and what had been said. He drew some comfort from his conclusion that there was nothing between her and Sean Casey, but then doubt began to sow its seeds. Wasn't there such a thing as love at first sight? Had they instantly experienced a rapport between them? How could he tell? Casey had not been forthcoming and his words had been delivered without any inflection that would betray his feelings towards Lydia.

As soon as he reached home David cast all such

217

troubling thoughts aside to compose his letter.

Few words were exchanged on the quay from which the *Nina* would be leaving. Such as were spoken were curt, non-committal, and David sent no verbal message to Lydia. Sean put the letter safely in his pocket along with two for Luke from Mr Martin.

David thanked him and left. Sean went on board and from the rail watched all the activity prior to sailing, noting the efficient way in which the final loading was carried out. Mr Martin, who had been encouraging his men, went to have a word with the captain and then came to Sean.

'Tell Luke I would like him to stay in Middlesbrough certainly well into next year to see that everything runs smoothly. Maybe he might even like to be there permanently? Tell him so, but that I'll understand if Whitby has too great a pull on him.'

The *Nina* made a good voyage, using the breeze to her best advantage on a calm sea, grey as pewter.

Once the vessel was tied up at the jetty close to the rolling mill, Sean was quickly ashore. He threw a brief greeting to Bob Chase who was already marshalling his men to carry out the unloading.

Luke, who was standing at the end of the jetty, greeted Sean with a warm smile and a firm handshake.

'Everything work out?'

'Ah, sure now, and why shouldn't it? Mr Martin

218

was pleased with the results you achieved so quickly. He would like you to stay on here, certainly well into next year and maybe even permanently.' Seeing no reaction from Luke, Sean went on, 'He'll deal with Sigsworth. He approved of my appointment, too, saying the onus was on you if I turned out badly.'

'See you don't,' laughed Luke, then added seriously, 'What about the supplies of ironstone?'

'Mr Martin will give it some thought and let you know.'

'Good,' he said, satisfied with all the messages and with the way in which Sean appeared to have handled the responsibility thrust upon him.

He handed over the two envelopes from Mr Martin and, realising that Luke must be curious about the third, said, 'For your sister.'

'Then you'd better be off and deliver it.'

Sean went straight to West Street where he found Lydia, anxious to learn all she could from Mrs Turnbull about the practical side of housekeeping, helping with some baking.

'Away with thee, lass, and read your letter. You've been on edge all morning.'

An excited Lydia took the letter and impulsively kissed Sean on the cheek. 'Thank you,' she cried, and scurried away out of the kitchen and upstairs to her bedroom.

Mrs Turnbull made no comment but smiled to herself when she saw Sean touch the place on his cheek where Lydia's lips had been.

Lydia's hands trembled a little as she slit the envelope open. What reaction would her words have elicited from David? She sat on the side of her bed to read the letter.

Dear Lydia

Thank you for your letter. I was pleased to receive it and to know that you had arrived safely in Middlesbrough. I am thankful you have found suitable lodgings there.

I regret that I was not at the coach at the start of your journey, business matters got in the way.

Your Father more like, she thought. And you hadn't spunk enough to sneak away. She gave a little wriggle of annoyance and continued to read.

I am sorry that you refer to me only as a very dear friend but draw some consolation from the fact that you say at times you felt I was more than that, though I had hoped that your feelings matched mine for you. You hold out hope for the future yet spike that with the thought that I may find someone else and that you would under-stand if I did. And you expressed a hope I would reciprocate such an attitude. Does that mean you think you will find someone else? Or maybe you have already done so, even in the short time since you left Whitby.

Lydia paused. She was hurt by his formal, cold attitude. She had hoped for something different, that he would take the lead to repair what had gone wrong between them. Instead he was sus-picious she might have found a new love. He must

220

be thinking of Sean, that a friendly gesture had blossomed into something else. Ah, well, let him think what he liked. She turned back to the letter.

So that our friendship is not lost and that something else may follow from it, I shall do as you request, so here is my first attempt to bridge the gap between Whitby and Middlesbrough.
I am well and the business keeps me occupied. Its future success can mean so much to me. There is a shortage of ships in Whitby. Your uncle is looking for new investments. My father thinks a closer relationship between the two firms might be advantageous to both. They have met two or three times but there have been no definite proposals yet.
I believe your uncle and his family are well. I ran into Isobel when I was in town yesterday and she is concerned for you. I said if ever I had any news of you, I would let her know.
So please continue to write. Communication can keep us close and maybe help you to see why I chose the path I did. I think the best way to pass letters between us is by the ironstone ships. I am sure the captains would oblige and they could keep the letters from you until I collect them.

Lydia gave a little smirk. So your father doesn't know, she thought.

I look forward to hearing from you again. I hope there is no one else.
I am your devoted,
David

Lydia sat, not knowing how to react. The letter had not been the declaration of passionate love which would surmount his father's objections that she'd longed for. 'Devoted' was the strongest word he had used.

'Oh, David,' she whispered, 'our whole lives could pass us by before your father relents. I understand your concern for me – or is it for yourself? That could destroy our relationship. In fact, I can feel it happening, even so soon.' She pulled herself up sharp.

Yes, it may be happening but she must not allow it to sever all communication between them. She needed information out of Whitby and David could provide it innocently. The desire for revenge against her uncle still lay deep within her, crying out to be fulfilled. And already she had some information on which she could build. Already she had an unwitting spy. She must continue communicating with him.

The following Sunday morning Sarah vacated her pew before the priest had reached the sacristy after saying Mass. Concerned because she was alone, Kevin followed her before any of the others were ready to leave. Outside, he saw she was already hurrying away. He hesitated a moment then, chiding himself for doing so, ran after her.

'Miss Langton,' he called.

She stopped and turned.

'Miss Langton,' he gasped when he reached her, 'your father is not with you. Nothing wrong, I hope?'

She smiled. 'Nothing. But thank you for your concern. He came to early Mass as he wanted to visit a sick friend this morning.'

'Oh, good.' Kevin spluttered as he went on, 'I mean, good about your father, not good about the sickness.'

Sarah's merry laughter caused his head to spin. 'I knew what you meant, Kevin, and I'm grateful for your enquiry. It was thoughtful of you.'

Kevin, a shade embarrassed by her words, managed to say, 'You are alone, may I escort you home?'

Sarah inclined her head in gracious acknowledgement. 'I will be glad of your company.'

'You were in a hurry. I don't want to slow you down.'

'You won't. It was just that I did not want to be delayed by conversation outside the church.'

'Maybe you would rather be on your own?' suggested Kevin shyly.

'Kevin!' There was a note of reproach in her voice. 'That's not true. Someone who helped save my life will always be welcome company to me.'

'Thank you, Miss Langton.'

'And I prefer Sarah to Miss Langton.'

'Very well,' he returned, pleased to be on more intimate terms.

They fell into step, Kevin matching her pace which she slowed to a Sunday morning stroll while enjoying the sun and fresh autumnal air.

'Are you settling here in Middlesbrough?'

'Yes.'

'And the work?'

He gave a shrug of his shoulders. 'We were laid

off for a few days, but now the flow of ironstone is back to normal so is the pig iron and we are back to full-time work.'

'Father tells me that it is due to a man sent from Whitby, Luke Middleton, and that he has employed Sean as his assistant. Quick promotion for him.'

'It is that, but that's what Sean wants. He's a dreamer.'

'Will he realise his dream?'

'Who knows? But give him his due, he'll try.'

'Because of a girl?'

Kevin gave a half smile. 'He's always been one for the girls, but recently he has been going steady with a Dublin girl, Eileen Nolan. Maybe it's because of her he wants to fulfil his dream and escape from poverty.'

'And you? Where do your ambitions lie?'

He spread his hands in a gesture of uncertainty.

'Oh, come, Kevin, I'm sure you have some. The work you are doing is obviously different from what you have been used to.'

'To be sure it's different from digging docks. I don't know which I'd say I preferred except that humping iron has brought me into contact with a charming young lady.'

Sarah made no comment on this. Instead she said, shooting him a searching look, 'And neither iron nor clay is really what you're used to.' The words were issued as a challenge. She saw him start and then become embarrassed like a naughty schoolboy caught out in some misdemeanour.

'What do you mean?' he asked warily.

'You weren't brought up to manual work. Oh, I've no doubt you could stand alongside any man and do it,' she added hastily as she saw the protests rising on his lips. 'But you are not what you outwardly portray.'

Kevin did not answer. Should he deny Sarah's statement? If he did he might wreck a relationship he would prefer to cultivate. And would she believe any denial? He felt sure the answer would be no for she struck him as a young woman who knew when she was right.

'What makes you say that?' he asked tentatively.

'A feeling I had from our first encounter in Liverpool. Then, when you and Sean came to dinner, he was hesitant at table, watching Father and me before he made a move. But you weren't. You knew exactly how to behave. Sometimes you let your guard slip. Sean and Seamus don't because they don't have one. They are what they are all the time while you are not.' She had been watching him intently while she was speaking but he had avoided her gaze until now when she continued, 'I would say you have had a better upbringing. So why are you here, doing rough work, when you could be doing better things?'

Kevin gave a wan smile and a shrug of resignation. He felt unmasked and knew it was no use trying to cover up the truth. He nodded. 'You are a shrewd young lady. It's true that I'm not from the same background as Sean and Seamus. They're Dubliners through and through, while I only assumed that background after I met Seamus. He and I have been together for five years.'

225

'But why?'

He hesitated, wondering where to begin and how much to reveal. But he liked Sarah, who was a good listener, and found her easy to talk to. His story unfolded.

'You're right in what you say. My people have land, a large estate about ten miles outside Dublin. I have an elder brother who loves the estate and enjoys managing it as Father has trained him to. I was the second son and really had no role there, or not in the way I would have liked. Father and my brother did everything and I was merely a lackey, carrying out their orders. I had no incentive, no objective towards which to direct my own talents.'

'And you have now?' There was criticism in Sarah's tone.

'Ah, well, no, I must admit I haven't, but I still nurse the ambition that one day, some time in the future'

'Why wait until then?'

'Because...' His voice trailed away.

'Because?' she prompted, sensing that he had ceased to speak not because he was reluctant to reveal what had happened, but because his thoughts had drifted back to the past.

'Well,' he continued, 'when I realised that a future on the estate would bring me little but comfortable inertia and that there was a whole wide world apart from the Irish countryside, I decided to leave home. I must say my father was understanding. While he did not want to see me go, he gave me his blessing and some money, and said goodbye.

'I lived in Dublin for a while, not knowing what I wanted to do or where I really wanted to be. Adventure beckoned – America, Australia – but unlike many who sought new lives in those places they were too far away for my liking. It was then that I realised my roots were in Ireland, that I did not want to go far from the country of my birth. Adventure came to me in a strange way. I'd explored Dublin thoroughly, seen the seamier side of the city, met snobs who thought themselves above everyone else, experienced the ruthlessness of many who had money and were not beyond exploiting the lower classes to gain more.

'I saw that spill over outside a factory. The workers were angry there had been a cut in their pay, and were calling for the owners and making threats. The owners appeared, accompanied by a bunch of thugs, supposedly bodyguards. In reality they were there to make the trouble erupt into violence so that the bosses could teach their employees a lesson.

'They picked on a small wiry man towards the front of the workers. He was obviously the worse for drink which led to his shouting obscenities he would never have uttered sober. His yells inflamed the mob so he was immediately singled out as a ring leader. Four of the so-called bodyguards made a sudden rush and barged their way unceremoniously through the crowd to get him. They dragged him to the front. People were incensed by their actions and began to retaliate. The remainder of the bully boys moved in and scuffles and fights broke out. Meanwhile the man who had been hauled to the front was being beaten about the head and body and, though he tried to fight his assailants off, he was no match for them. He fell to the ground and they started kicking him with their heavy, steel-capped boots.' Kevin's voice faltered at the recollection.

'It was then you intervened to save Seamus,' said Sarah.

Kevin nodded. 'You guessed?'

'I think anyone would who had met the pair of you. What happened next?'

'I got him away.' Kevin did not want to enlarge on the action he had taken. 'I escorted him back to my lodgings, got a doctor and nursed him for two weeks, by which time he was up and about again.'

'And you've been together ever since?'

'Yes. I got to know him well in those two weeks. He isn't the wild man he appeared that day, drink had got the better of his tongue, but he will stick up for what he thinks is right. I found him to be a big-hearted man who would do anything for anyone he took to. He was extremely grateful for what I did for him that day, and we stayed together. I could see that he needed my help. Drink was his demon but I managed to get him to take less. He likes his beer but I feel he is now in control which is why I don't hang around him all the time. This isn't to say the relationship has been all one-sided. He's done me many a good turn.'

'I dare say he has,' commented Sarah. 'Does he know your background?'

'Yes, and so does Sean, but I swore them to

secrecy. It made for a better relationship amongst ourselves, but also did not damage our standing with the people we worked alongside.'

'And you were prepared to sacrifice your own prospects to see that Seamus was all right?'

Kevin shrugged his shoulders as if to say, I don't see it as a sacrifice. 'One day, maybe, I'll get around to shaping my life differently.'

'I think you should start thinking about that now,' said Sarah wisely.

'But I can't desert him,' Kevin protested.

'There would be no need. I take it that you believe he could move no further than labouring?'

Kevin gave a sad shake of his head. 'I don't think he could, and I believe he knows it. He sees labouring as his role in life and therefore looks upon it as important, which of course it is because where would we be without the likes of him? And he's happy in what he does, asks no more from life.'

'Then if he's happy, there's no need for you to confine yourself,' said Sarah. 'Are you any good with figures? Any good at letter writing?'

'Sure now, didn't my father see that I had the best education he could provide?'

'Good. Then I'll give away a little information which won't be officially revealed until next week when an advertisement will be placed in the local newspaper. Or maybe it need never appear.'

'You are being very mysterious,' said Kevin, his interest aroused.

'My father is finding the paperwork he must deal with too much for him. There are constant meetings with Mr Bolckow and Mr Vaughan, as well as negotiations with the ironstone suppliers and several other affairs he must attend to. He is spending less and less time around the rolling mill and having to leave more and more to Eric Gilmore, whom I believe is not the ideal assistant. I know Father would like to reorganise things so as to spend less time in the office and this would be the first move. Interested, Kevin?'

She had seen the light of anticipation brighten his eyes so it came as no surprise when he said, 'Of course I would.' But before she could say more he added, 'But I can't desert Seamus.'

'You wouldn't need to. You are both still working in the same place. In fact, from your office you would be looking across to where the pig iron is unloaded. You'd both still be in the same lodgings, so you'd be able to keep a closer eye on him there. Besides, you've said you don't have to be with him all the time now that he has his drink problem under control. I think it would be a good move for both of you, and I'll bet Seamus would want you to do it.'

Kevin smiled. 'You're a persuasive young lady.'

She laughed, delighted that he had taken to her suggestion. 'Then I'll tell Father what I've told you and have no doubt that tomorrow he'll want to meet you. See you convince him. Don't let me down.'

'I could never do that to the sweetest person I've met outside Ireland.'

Sarah laughed and, mimicking his Irish accent, said, 'Away wi' you. I bet you tell that to all the young ladies you meet.'

Kevin laughed with her. Then he became serious. 'But there's only one to whom I mean it.' His eyes were locked on hers and she knew who that was.

'Harper!' Gilmore's voice barked across the open space.

Kevin straightened up from shifting pig iron. He exchanged a glance with Seamus.

'Over here, and quick about it!'

'What's that bastard want?' muttered Seamus.

'I'll soon know,' returned Kevin. He peeled off his leather gloves, tossed them to Seamus, and wiped his sweating hands down his rough trousers. He headed for Gilmore who was standing outside the door to the offices.

He glared at Kevin. 'Mr Langton wants you. Get in there quick, and see you're straight back on the job when he's finished with you.'

Kevin said nothing but brushed past him and entered the building. He knocked on Mr Langton's door and went in.

James was sitting behind his desk, elbows resting on the arms of his chair and hands steepled in front of his chin in pensive fashion.

'Sit down, Kevin.' He slowly lowered his hands to the desk, all the time his eyes fixed firmly on his employee. 'My daughter has told me what she learned about you yesterday. I make no comment on that for I am sure any appraisal would only embarrass you and I do not want that.'

'Thank you, sir,' replied Kevin, relieved.

'You should not be in a dead-end job humping iron, you are worthy of a better position with better prospects. I have a job you might be interested in. It would mean taking responsibility for practically all the paperwork here. At the moment a lot of it is being done by Gilmore but he really should be spending more time outside, particularly in the rolling mill. Between you and me, he uses it as a chance to take things easy and doesn't keep on top of things. Are you interested?'

'Yes, sir,' replied Kevin.

'Good. You can start tomorrow, eight o'clock. I'll show you what's what and then you can devise your own system and organisation.'

'Very good, sir, and thank you for this opportunity.'

James nodded. 'Give Gilmore a call. I told him to wait outside until I'd seen you. And you come back with him.'

Gilmore didn't like being summoned by a mere labourer, someone he regarded as beneath him, but he had no time to make an issue of it. Mr Langton wanted him. He disliked it even further when Kevin accompanied him back into the office.

'Eric,' said James Langton, leaning back in his chair. 'I've decided all the paperwork is getting in the way of your duties outside and in the rolling mill, so in future you'll do none of it. Harper will be taking all that over. He'll be my assistant inside the office, you'll be my assistant outside.'

Gilmore seethed but dare not voice his feelings. This whippersnapper of an Irishman hadn't been here five minutes and he was in Langton's good books. He'd sneaked a job Gilmore had found

232

convenient for taking things easy when he liked, especially when Mr Langton was engaged in meetings and negotiations. Now that easy time was gone and Gilmore didn't like it. He bit back the torrent of harsh words which would have jeopardised his job and merely said, 'Yes, sir.'

'So Harper is off your gang as from now.'

'Yes, sir.'

'That is all.'

Once outside the office block, he gave a snort of contempt. 'Still living off the past, Harper?'

'I didn't ask for the job,' replied Kevin coldly. 'Mr Langton offered it to me.'

Gilmore sneered. 'No doubt you did a bit of crawling.'

'It's no concern of yours, Gilmore. Think what you like, no doubt you'll get it wrong.'

'That other bastard Irishman escaped me, and now you. Ah, well, I've still got the little runt.' There was a note of menace in his laughter which seemed to hang in the air as he headed for the rolling mill.

When Kevin rejoined Seamus he refused to take back his gloves. 'You keep them, Seamus, I don't need them any more.'

'Why?' Seamus looked astonished. 'What's happened?' He was alarmed by Kevin's serious expression.

'I no longer have this job.'

'What? Kicked you out, have they? That bastard Gilmore been telling lies about you? I'll get him.' The words poured out so fast that Kevin could not interrupt. 'I'll see Mr Langton. He can't do this to you, to us. Maybe Sean will give us a job, or at least put in a good word for us with Middleton.'

Kevin raised his hands to quieten Seamus. 'Hold on, hold on. It's nothing like that.'

'Then what is it? Why don't you need these gloves?'

'Mr Langton's offered me a different job, handling all his paperwork. Assistant in his office.'

For a moment Seamus looked astounded then, comprehending, his face broadened into a grin of delight. 'Good for you.' He slapped Kevin on the arm. 'That's one in the eye for bloody Gilmore.'

'That's as maybe, but you'd better look out, there'll be only you on whom to vent his dislike now. Maybe I'd better turn this offer down?'

'Y'd better not. Sure, isn't it right you shouldn't be labouring alongside me anymore? Never should have been.'

'But, Seamus, you and I...'

'You've done enough for me. I'm all right now, and you know it. So don't feel bad about this. Besides, you'll be around. We'll still be in the same lodgings.' Doubt came into his eyes as he added, 'We will, won't we?'

'Of course. Where else would I go? Mrs Hartley's is good enough for me.'

'Well, there you are, so best o' luck in your new job.'

'Thanks, Seamus. You watch out for yourself. Don't let Gilmore rile you.'

Seamus made no comment on that but winked and turned back to his job.

Kevin walked away with a heavy feeling he'd

234

deserted a friend. Since the day outside the factory in Dublin they had shared much together without a single harsh word passing between them. They had taken life in their stride even in the toughest of times. Seamus realised that Kevin had come from a better background but never queried it and took the attitude that if his friend wanted to tell him about it he would do so in his own good time.

He was grateful to Kevin for weaning him off his hard drinking, subtly, without criticism. Seamus still loved his beer and stout but, under Kevin's eye, had come to know his limits and keep within them.

Now he was pleased for Kevin, but, as he bent his back to the pig iron, his heart was heavy at the feeling of suddenly being alone.

Chapter Ten

'Had a good day, Father?' Sarah asked, turning from the small table where she had just poured him his usual measure of whisky.

This was a routine only occasionally broken. Recognising his opening and closing of the front door she would break off whatever she was doing and prepare his drink.

She knew that these moments at the end of a day's work were precious to him. They had been started by her mother to help him relax and dismiss the cares of responsibility. They had talked about the trivialities of the day, exchanged local news and gossip, indulging in the pleasure of being together, or sharing a silence which only true lovers know how to do.

When her mother had died, Sarah had resolved to keep up the tradition. Though she knew she could never step into her mother's shoes and take over the togetherness her parents had shared, she brought a different bond of love, that between daughter and father.

'Yes,' James replied, kissing her with fatherly affection on the cheek. He stretched, easing the tension of the day from him, and thanked her as he took his glass and went to his favourite chair. He sat down, drew a deep breath and sank back into its soft luxury. 'Highly satisfactory.' He gave a little nod as if agreeing with himself.

'Kevin settled in?'

'Oh, yes,' he replied with enthusiasm. 'He did the very first day. Eased my burden greatly by giving me more time to see to things I was beginning to neglect.' He took another sip of his whisky. 'You know, it was a good day when we met up with those Irishmen even though the circumstances were fraught. Kevin you know about, and Sean is doing well with Luke Middleton. He tells me the young man from Whitby has a real way with the men, gets the best out of them without any antagonism. He's certainly organised the turnaround of the ironstone ships from Whitby to our benefit.' He pursed his lips thoughtfully. 'Maybe we should invite him to dinner, meet him socially. It could help things.'

236

'A good idea, Father. Give me a date and I'll alert Mrs Jepson.' Sarah knew that their cook would be only too delighted to provide something more than the usual meal for two.

'What about next Tuesday?'

'Very well.'

'By the way, Luke Middleton has a sister. We'll ask her too, then you won't be burdened with men's talk all evening.'

Sarah smiled at his consideration for since her mother's death he was always trying to ease what he considered her lonely life, though she never complained.

By the following Tuesday Sarah and Mrs Jepson had devised a simple but mouth-watering menu. Sarah had had difficulties in trying to keep the cook from over-elaboration. 'Maybe another time,' she had said to soothe Mrs Jepson's disappointment that her range of kitchen skills was not to be fully exploited. 'Maybe Christmas.'

The evening was crisp, a hint of the first frost in the air. It sharpened Lydia's and Luke's appetites and made them pleased to enter the warmth of the house in Queen's Terrace. Sarah and her father were pleasant hosts, sweeping away any doubts they had had about this visit.

James greeted Luke with a hearty handshake. 'Pleased you could come. And you, my dear,' he added, turning his welcoming smile on Lydia.

'Thank you, it is most kind of you to invite us.' Her reply was soft but sincere. She turned her eyes to the young woman beside him. 'You must be Sarah? I have so looked forward to meeting

237

you ever since Kevin Harper told me about you.'

The flush which came to Sarah's face told Lydia the admiration was not one-sided.

'Indeed,' said Sarah, as the maid took the coats from the guests. 'All good, I hope.'

'Nothing but, Miss Langton,' replied Lydia.

'Sarah, please. I hope there will be no formalities between us.' She had felt an instantaneous liking for Lydia. Although the girl was a stranger, Sarah felt she had known her all her life.

Lydia held herself with the confidence that comes from mixing with many people, obviously someone who had enjoyed an active social life. Sarah was curious. She knew from her father that the Middletons had come from Whitby and wondered what sort of life Lydia had led there.

'Thank you for your kind welcome. I had heard about you, Mr Langton, but did not know that you had such a charming daughter.'

James gave a proud smile but said teasingly, 'She's a bossy-two-shoes really.'

'I'm sure she isn't,' chided Lydia.

'If I am, I'll boss you all to go into the drawing room,' said Sarah. 'There's no need to stand here when we can be more comfortable.'

They entered the room and Lydia, who was chatting to Sarah, pulled up sharp and let her remaining words go unspoken. Sarah glanced quickly at her new-found friend, fearing there was something wrong.

'Oh, a piano!' gasped Lydia. There was no mistaking the ecstasy in her expression as she gazed at the highly polished black grand piano

238

that stood in one corner of the large room.

'You play?' asked Sarah.

'She certainly does,' replied Luke when his sister seemed to have lost her tongue.

Lydia started. 'May I look?' she asked hopefully.

'Of course,' replied James.

There was an air of excitement about her as she crossed the room. Her fingers tingled, anticipating the feel of the keys. She stopped in front of the instrument, admiring it for a few moments before allowing her hands to caress the smooth wood lovingly.

'Open it.' Sarah was beside her. The words, delivered softly, enticed Lydia.

She hesitated only a moment then slowly raised the lid to reveal the contrast between black and white. She ran her fingers lightly across the keys.

'You must play for us later, my dear. Come now and have a glass of Madeira.' James innocently broke the spell which had lured Lydia into another world.

Slowly she lowered the lid and glanced at Sarah. 'You play, of course?' she said.

'Not very well,' came the reply. 'The piano was my mother's. She played extremely well. Taught me.'

'Sarah could have been her equal,' put in James, 'but I'm afraid she did not get all the practice she should have done. You see, it was too easy for her to persuade her mother to play. She so loved to do that.'

'And I loved to listen,' added Sarah with a reminiscent smile.

239

'I've tried to encourage my daughter to spare more time for it now, but I think the lack of someone competent with whom to share the joy holds her back. Maybe you...' He left the implication hanging in the air.

The meal passed off pleasantly with a growing familiarity between hosts and guests.

James admired the serious intellect behind Luke's easy conversation. Inevitably talk turned to their work.

'Shipping the ironstone from Whitby to your jetty, then by rail to Witton and back again as pig iron for the rolling mill, must be a costly operation?' he observed.

'No doubt about it,' agreed James. 'What we really need is to find ironstone in a more convenient situation.'

'On your doorstep.'

'Exactly. Cut out the shipping costs.'

'That would be a big blow to Mr Martin.'

'Progress in one trade inevitably harms another,' James commented, then added, 'It may never happen, and we'll go on as we are for as long as it is viable.'

'Now that's enough work talk,' chided Sarah firmly. 'This is a relaxing social occasion. We must make that a priority for our guests.'

'You have made it so already,' said Lydia. From the way she'd conducted herself all evening, Sarah deducted that this young woman and her brother had left a similar world behind. She wondered why?

Throughout the remainder of the meal Sarah subtly drew from them the information she

240

wanted. In imparting the story of their life in Whitby, Lydia was careful to avoid the facts surrounding her father's death or her subsequent desire for revenge.

With dinner over everyone felt a pleasing sense of contentment. James drained his glass, leaned back in his chair and said, 'Shall we relax in the drawing room with some coffee or tea? And then maybe Lydia will play for us.'

'Are you sure you want me to?' Although the desire to play was strong, she felt she had to put the question. She was not setting herself up as an equal to Mrs Langton and wanted to avoid causing Mr Langton painful memories.

'It would be better if the piano were played more often,' he replied.

Lydia knew this was directed at his daughter, but also guessed that Sarah had refrained from playing out of respect for her father's feelings. Maybe she could help them both.

Lydia, accompanied by Sarah, went straight to the piano while the two men sat down. Sarah raised the lid, Lydia made herself comfortable on the piano-stool, flexed her fingers, paused for a moment with her fingers held above the keys, then filled the room with notes of sweetness.

Lydia was entranced. To her it seemed there was only the piano and herself in the room and they were as one. The others were bewitched by the flow of the notes which drew them into a different world.

Two maids came in with trays of coffee and tea. Hearing the music, they opened the door quietly, glided across the floor without a sound, placed the trays on a table and left as silently.

The coffee and tea remained untouched.

Lydia went from one piece to another. No one spoke to break the flow or mar the spell. The music went on and on. No one wanted it to stop, but then Lydia started. She suddenly realised how the music had taken her over and that she was monopolising the evening. She swung round on the stool, blushing as she uttered her apologies. 'Oh, I'm sorry I've gone on so, but I was lost... I shouldn't have allowed myself to get carried away.' Her words came out in a rush.

'Don't apologise, my dear. That was enchanting,' said James. 'You held us under the magic of your touch.' He glanced at Luke. 'You were right, she certainly can play.'

He smiled, proud of his sister.

'Splendid, splendid!' cried Sarah, jumping up and giving Lydia a hug. 'I loved it so, I could listen to you all night.'

'I would love to play all night,' laughed Lydia, giving Sarah's hand a squeeze of appreciation.

'You must miss your piano?'

'It was the one piece of furniture I regretted having to part with. It nearly broke my heart.'

'Then your heart shall be properly mended,' said James. 'Please come and play here whenever you want.'

'But I couldn't impose,' said Lydia as she and Sarah sat down beside each other on the sofa.

'Of course you could.'

'And I will be pleased to see you at any time,' added Sarah.

'Your kindness overwhelms me, but I'm afraid

my time will be taken up. I will have to find a paying occupation.'

'From what you have told us of your life in Whitby, to do so will be foreign to you,' said James. 'I have a suggestion to make. A genteel occupation for you.'

As he paused, Lydia looked curiously at him. 'Mr Langton, you have the advantage of me.'

He smiled. 'I don't want you to take up this idea merely because I have suggested it, nor to regard it as charity for there is an ulterior motive behind it. Using that piano, you can give music lessons.'

For a moment everyone was speechless. The sense of this proposal hit Sarah first. 'Father, that's a splendid idea. You must accept, Lydia, you must!'

'But, Mr Langton, I cannot accept such a generous offer. It would be an imposition. And remember, you'd have strangers coming into this house.'

'They would only be strangers at first. You would get to know them, and no doubt Sarah too. And the power of vetting would be in your hands. With Sarah's assistance, if you like.'

'It will work, Lydia, I know it will. I just know it!' Sarah was passionate about the idea.

'Before you make up your mind, I must impose one condition.'

James's serious expression brought a sharp glance of surprise from Sarah. What was he going to say that might wreck what she saw as a chance of close friendship with this talented girl?

'I would like you to encourage Sarah to practise

243

more and improve her playing.'

'Nothing will give me greater pleasure.'

'Good, then it's settled. I will leave all the arrangements to you and Sarah.'

'Mr Langton, you are too kind to someone who is a stranger.'

'From what I have observed this evening and in my dealings with Luke, I can no longer regard you as such.'

The following morning as Lydia hurried to Queen's Terrace she recalled those words with delight and satisfaction. She had taken to Mr Langton and his daughter. With his kind and gentle manner she had seen in him something of her father, while in Sarah she had seen the friend she had craved ever since her direct ties with Whitby had been broken. She was looking forward to planning this piano venture with Sarah and getting to know her better.

The maid who admitted her directed Lydia to the drawing room as she had been instructed.

After expressing their delight at seeing each other again, and recalling the previous evening, they quickly fell to making plans to publicise the lessons which Lydia was prepared to undertake. Sarah thought she knew of several people who might be interested in having their daughter learn the piano and it was agreed that she should mention the project by word of mouth.

'And we must not forget you,' pointed out Lydia. 'I must fulfil your father's wishes. Come, let me hear you play.'

With Lydia's ability in mind, Sarah was shy

about her own playing and a little hesitant in her fingering. Lydia watched her carefully and when Sarah had finished a piece by Chopin she announced, 'There is nothing to stop you becoming a good pianist. You need to brush up on some basic aspects, practise and play often. If I am the means of you doing so then I will be satisfied with what I have achieved.'

'You really think I can be good?'

'Certainly.'

Sarah was pleased. She had always dreamed of emulating her mother.

'I believe you have not played as much as you would have liked because you thought it might remind your father of the past,' Lydia went on.

Sarah nodded.

'Well, with his kind suggestion that I give piano lessons here, he has cleared the way for you. You must not miss this chance, I am sure it will please him.'

'You are right. I should no longer be afraid of hurting him by playing the piano.'

So the plans were made and within the week Sarah had mustered enough pupils for Lydia to take two a day, four days a week.

Through her visits to Queen's Terrace a strong bond grew up between the two young women and they began to share the thoughts that only people in such close acquaintanceship can exchange.

Yet Sarah felt she was not getting to know the whole person. But do you ever? she wondered. There was something about life in Whitby that Lydia was holding back. Why she got this feeling

Sarah was unsure, for Lydia appeared to be perfectly open.

'Couldn't Luke have taken over the business after your father died?' asked Sarah when Lydia had finished telling her about her life as a merchant's daughter.

'That was Father's intention but alas the debts were too great for the business to survive. Everything had to go, even my beloved piano. If there had been half a chance of keeping the firm alive, I would have encouraged Luke to take it. I would have helped him and I'm sure we could have made a success of it.'

'Help? You mean in a practical way?'

'Yes. My father intended it, so why not? I'd been around his office and knew his ship and the way he traded. I think it came about because I wanted to be different from other girls who were content to follow in their mother's footsteps. After mine died I was more or less in a man's world.'

'Would you like to go back to that world?'

'Tomorrow if I could. It was more exciting than sewing, tea parties and gossip. Who knows? Some day I might be able to do it.' A wistful look had come over Lydia's face, but Sarah could not know that behind it lay a burning desire for revenge.

Observing the regularity of Lydia's visits with letters to the masters of the ironstone ships, Sean made it his business to be around at those times. His rich Irish brogue thickened in an assiduous display of charm and Lydia found herself looking

246

forward to the exchanges which passed between them.

One day when he suggested that the following Sunday they might take a walk in the country, Lydia, not wanting to appear too forward, held back her answer.

Fearing she was on the point of refusing, Sean hastily decided, for the sake of decorum, to add, 'We can ask Sarah and Kevin to come along too.'

She readily agreed.

That was the start of regular outings for the four friends. Enjoyable as they were, they raised a problem in Sarah's mind. According to Kevin, Sean had a girl in Dublin and she wondered if she should warn Lydia of this.

One day with the piano lessons finished Sarah and Lydia were enjoying a cup of tea when Sarah casually remarked, 'You seem to enjoy Sean's company?'

'I must admit I do,' replied Lydia, stirring her tea thoughtfully.

'Was there no one in Whitby?'

Lydia hesitated.

'Ah, I can tell that there was,' said Sarah. 'Do you still feel affection for him?'

'Yes and no,' replied Lydia evasively.

'And which is the stronger, the yes or the no?'

Lydia shrugged her shoulders. 'I don't know.'

'Has being with Sean confused you?'

Again she shrugged her shoulders. 'Maybe.'

'Did you love this person?'

'Yes.'

'Do you still?'

'That's where the confusion arises.' Lydia went

247

on to tell Sarah about David. 'So you see, I felt let down. I thought he would marry me in spite of my changed circumstances.'

'Does he still love you?'

'He says so and that he took the course of action he did to ensure our eventual marriage.'

'And he may be right,' Sarah pointed out. 'What do you know of Sean?'

'He has all the charm and glib tongue of an Irishman and can certainly weave a silver thread around a girl's mind. Beyond that I know very little. He has told me virtually nothing about himself.'

Sarah wondered how much she should divulge. Should she reveal what Kevin had told her? But she did not know how deep the relationship in Dublin was. Sean had never even mentioned the girl. Sarah decided that the best course, at this stage, was to say nothing and leave things as they were unless a situation arose where she deemed it imperative to interfere.

She smiled. 'Well then, I shall enlighten you on one aspect.' She went on to tell her friend about the accident off Liverpool and how Sean had rescued her and her father.

'I don't think Luke knows about that. Sean helped us to find somewhere to stay when we arrived in Middlesbrough, then showed Luke the way to the jetty where the ships unloaded the ironstone. Luke took to him and offered him a job as his assistant.'

'And he's very capable from what I hear. The next time you come for the evening you must bring him along and I'll invite Kevin too.'

Sean's conscience pricked him. He had been neglectful of Eileen – only four letters since leaving Ireland. He glanced at the clock. He just had time to pen a brief note before his appointment with Lydia. He wrote:

My dear Eileen,

Thank you for your letter. I am sorry I have not written more regularly. You are right to rebuke me. As I explained, things happened here so fast that I was reeling with the shock of my good fortune and, not wanting to waste it, everything else got set aside. I know you will understand that this can only be for our good and will help to fulfil the dream I have for our future together.

With more responsibility thrust upon me I can't see that I will be able to come to Dublin for some time so be patient, love.

You ask about Kevin and Seamus. They are well. Kevin is revelling in his role as assistant to the rolling mill manager, but poor Seamus takes some stick from his supervisor, Mr Gilmore, who did not like being ordered to take us on by the manager when we first came here. Now Kevin and I have escaped his clutches, he has only the one scapegoat. Seamus is being careful about retaliating and away from work Kevin keeps an eye on him, so that his hard drinking does not return.

I must close now, but first I must answer your words – 'Don't forget me.' How could I forget the feel of your warmth against me, the temptation I could not resist? No one could ever compare to my blue-eyed colleen.

Soon we will be together.

Love,
Sean

In the brisk air of a December Saturday morning he quickly walked the few yards to number sixteen West Street.

His knock was answered by Mrs Turnbull. 'Ah, good morning, Sean. Lass is ready and waiting.' She called over her shoulder, 'Lydia, he's here.'

Immediately Lydia appeared, dressed in a warm top coat, sealskin hat and matching gloves.

'Good morning, Sean,' she said, obviously pleased to see him.

'And to you,' he greeted her, eyes twinkling merrily. 'What's it to be this morning? Window shopping?'

They made their way along Sussex Street, pausing every now and then to look in shop windows while carrying on their light teasing banter. On the way Sean posted his letter.

Eric Gilmore knocked on the door of Mr Langton's office in response to a summons by the manager. James looked up from some papers he was studying as the burly man entered.

'Gilmore, some serious allegations have been made about your attitude and behaviour towards the men.'

'Sir?' answered Gilmore, putting on a puzzled expression.

250

'There's no use denying what I have to say though I will give you an opportunity to answer these charges. I have already investigated the allegations, privately and unknown to you. I have more than one witness as to your behaviour towards certain of your men, and one in particular. From what I have learned your treatment of Seamus O'Leary is unwarranted. You try to cover your vindictiveness by mistreating and bullying others, though not to the same degree as you bully O'Leary. What have you to say?'

'But that's rubbish, sir,' protested Gilmore gruffly.

'I told you it was no use denying these charges,' returned James coldly. 'Can you justify your actions?'

'He's a poor worker, needs bullying to get the best out of him.'

'Not from what I have observed. He does his share.'

'But he's crafty and needs watching, otherwise he'd slack.'

'Again, not what I've noticed. He's never late and looks for no more time off than anyone else.'

Gilmore's lips tightened. His temper was beginning to fray. 'Who are you going to believe? I think you've already made your mind up that I'm in the wrong and he's right.'

'O'Leary has made no charges against you.'

'Damned Irishmen,' muttered Gilmore to himself, but said loudly, 'I've always got good results out of my men, haven't I?'

'Yes.'

'Then let me do it my way.'

251

'Not unless you stop hounding O'Leary.'

'You're mollycoddling the little runt! I know how best to handle him.'

'No, you don't,' returned James, eyes boring into the man who stood before him. 'I'll not have intimidation and bullying on this site.'

Gilmore's face reddened as his anger boiled to the surface. 'You've favoured those damned Irishmen ever since they came here, gave Harper my job and now you're listening to that runt O'Leary. No doubt he's egged others on to talk against me.'

'That's not true and you know it,' James replied, his voice level.

'I bloody well don't!'

'If that's your attitude, you're fired. Get out and don't let me see you around here again.'

Gilmore set his lips tight. For a moment he glared down at the manager then he hissed, 'Someone will pay for this, and don't you forget it.' He banged his fist on the desk. 'Damn you, Langton! You and that bastard O'Leary have just spoilt my kids' Christmas!' He turned and stormed out of the room, slamming the door behind him.

If he'd thought the mention of his children and Christmas would make his superior reconsider his decision he was mistaken. James Langton had carried out a thorough investigation not only into the man's working practices but also his home background. He had found out that Eric Gilmore kept his wife short of money, and, in spite of her efforts to protect her children, ill-treated them. In reality Christmas would mean nothing to a man like him. James hoped that the money he was proposing to send secretly to Mrs Gilmore to help her over this period would be kept to herself and not end up being poured down Gilmore's throat.

Outside the manager's office Gilmore strode with angry strides towards the men unloading pig iron. They could sense trouble even before he reached them. They stopped work and watched him approach, his fury plainly visible.

He went straight to Seamus. 'You little runt,' he snarled. 'Lose me my job, would you?'

The fire in his eyes warned Seamus what was coming. As Gilmore's huge fist swung, the Irishman ducked. The blow flashed close to his head and Gilmore, even more enraged, threw himself forward. Seamus skipped lightly out of the way. Gilmore staggered under the momentum of his own weight. He saved himself from falling and turned quickly, hoping to gain an advantage over the smaller man. As he did so he caught a glimpse of Mr Langton coming out of his office. He knew he would be in even greater trouble if he persisted. The constable might be called. Rage burned in him as he hissed, 'I'll get you, O'Leary. As sure as you're a bloody Irishman, I'll get you,' and stormed away.

An uneasy silence settled over the men as they watched him go.

The Saturday evening before Christmas, still three days away, was sharp with frost, but as yet there was no snow. It didn't even threaten for the sky was clear and brightly lit with stars.

Lydia, Luke, Kevin and Sean were thankful for such a fine night for it made their walk to Queen's Terrace much more pleasant.

Lydia revelled in her escort of three young men as they weaved their way through the crowds flocking around the market stalls and filling the streets with their usual Saturday-night forays.

Noise from the pubs penetrated the shouts of the stall holders and the protests of irritated customers waiting to be served. But the four friends were not worried by the din. Laughter was on their lips and their hearts were light in anticipation of pleasant company, good food and an enjoyable evening with Sarah and her father.

After a welcoming drink in the drawing room there followed a sumptuous meal with which Mrs Jepson had excelled herself. Conversation flowed smoothly with descriptions of the life the Langtons had led before they moved to Middlesbrough, the lighter side of Whitby, and general praise for the beauty of the Irish countryside which could never be marred even by the desecration wrought by famine. Tall tales interspersed the serious, and laughter flowed as friendships deepened. The merriment continued into the drawing room where, after a few minutes' relaxation, Lydia and Sarah were called upon to play the piano.

Sweet notes filled the room as each of them played their own particular favourites and the occasional Irish air for the pleasure of the Irish guests. The magic of the season crept into the room as note blended with note, enticed from the keys by delicate fingers. The piano came alive. It became one of them, bringing happiness and tranquillity, and transported both mind and imagination to other climes.

Luke felt the pull of home as he had known it in Whitby. How many Christmases there Lydia had played happily like this and their future had seemed bright.

Sean was drawn to remember Christmases spent with Eileen, when even his dreams of a new life for them both could hardly better the love she gave him as a Christmas present. But the music also made him query his feelings now. Shouldn't he have sent for her when he received promotion? Was he betraying her with his weak excuses? His eyes settled on Lydia at the piano. He knew of her genteel past as the daughter of a merchant. Maybe this woman of talent and refinement would be a more fitting mate if he could bear to break his promises to Eileen.

The lilting notes transported Kevin back to a country house in Ireland. He had not realised how much he had missed such civilised entertainment until now. The music and the convivial atmosphere brought an urgent desire to be home again. And how he longed for Sarah to see his home, and meet his mother and father. Maybe one day...

Their thoughts were interrupted by a loud hammering on the front door. Lydia stopped playing and looked at Sarah. The rest of them exchanged uneasy glances.

They heard a maid hurry across the hall, the front door opened and there was an urgent exchange of conversation. All eyes were on the

255

drawing-room door in anticipation of the maid's appearance. James was already on his feet when, after a barely audible knock, she burst in.

She was flustered, hardly able to get her breath as she announced, 'I'm sorry, sir, but Mrs Hartley said it was urgent. She's in a terrible state.'

Before anything else could be said the men's landlady was pushing past her, breathing hard from her exertions, face contorted with distress. 'I'm sorry to barge in, Mr Langton, sir, but it's a matter of grave importance.'

'What is it?' James spoke quietly to calm her as he moved to take her arm and lead her to a chair. 'Sit down and tell us in your own good time, Nell.'

Sarah and Lydia came over to lend their support.

'Oh, sir!' She looked up with tear-filled eyes. 'It's Seamus ... he's dead.' This wasn't the way she had planned to break the shocking news. It wasn't the way she had rehearsed it as she'd rushed through the streets to Queen's Terrace. But now the words were out, stark with their chilling news.

'What?' Everyone gazed at her in disbelief. Kevin and Sean exchanged glances of horror. This couldn't be true. Their friend couldn't be dead. He had been at Mrs Hartley's before they left and in very good humour, asking them to thank Mr Langton for the invitation he had refused four days ago. Although Kevin had tried to persuade his friend to accept Seamus would not, saying he had other things planned for that evening. But Kevin knew the real reason: he did not want to find himself in a situation in which he would feel out of place. Now Kevin wished he had been more persuasive. If he had, Seamus would still be alive.

'What happened?' asked Luke, posing the question they all wanted to ask but seemed incapable of voicing in their shock and distress.

'He was found in an alley beside the Iron Smelter, badly beaten. Jim came looking for Kevin and Sean, and told me. I knew where you were so I came straight away.'

'Did he tell you any more?' pressed Kevin.

'He said there'd been trouble earlier. Seamus was having a quiet drink when Eric Gilmore and his cronies came in.'

'I knew it!' Kevin exploded. He struck his fist into his palm. 'Why wasn't I there?'

Sarah moved quickly to his side. She laid a hand on his arm. 'You weren't to know what would happen.'

'Go on, Nell,' prompted James.

'My brother said that Gilmore acknowledged Seamus in a friendly sort of way and bought him a drink, asking him to let bygones be bygones. Seamus said he held no grudges and hoped Gilmore didn't either. For ten minutes all seemed well but then Gilmore offered Seamus another drink which he refused, saying he'd had enough. Gilmore then took offence. His cronies crowded Seamus and forced him to take two more pints.'

Kevin's lips tightened in distress. Seamus had conquered his hard drinking. Knew when he had

had enough. But bullies like Gilmore wouldn't be ignored.

'Jim tried to calm the situation but Gilmore took no notice. He started accusing Seamus of costing him his job. Seamus denied it and Gilmore threw a punch at him. His cronies closed in but Jim had anticipated this and signalled to a couple of his friends who always stand by on a Saturday night in case of trouble. They moved in and, in no gentle fashion, removed Gilmore and his cronies from the pub. My brother advised Seamus to stay where he was, in fact all night if he wanted. Seamus was there for about half an hour and then Jim noticed he had gone. An hour later he was found in the alley.' Her terrible story told, Nell Hartley seemed close to fainting.

Lydia, kneeling beside her, put a comforting arm round her and offered words of solace. Sarah quickly organised a cup of tea.

'I must go,' said James, starting for the door.

'Wait, sir.' Kevin's voice was firm. 'There is nothing you can do. Sean and I will go, he was our friend.'

'I'll come too,' offered Luke.

'It would help us more if you and Lydia would see Nell home when she is ready.'

'Very well, but if you need any further assistance let me know.'

The two friends spoke little as they hurried through the town. People still went gladly about their Saturday night revelry. Though the news of the Irishman's death had swept quickly through the town, many chose to ignore it. As far as they were concerned it was just another street brawl.

'Morbid vultures,' hissed Kevin with contempt when they reached the Iron Smelter and saw folk still hanging around the end of the alley, heads together, tongues wagging under pretext of having inside knowledge of what had happened. They pushed their way through and entered the pub.

When Jim saw them he motioned them to come through to the private quarters. With the door closed, shutting out the noise which rose from the bar as if nothing had happened, he said, 'I'm very sorry about this.'

'Your sister told us what had happened,' said Sean, seeing Kevin was too shaken to speak.

'I thought she would know where you were.'

'Gilmore? Did they get the bastard?' There was venom in Kevin's voice when he spoke.

Jim shook his head. 'Nobody saw the killing so we can't be certain it was him.'

'Can't be certain?' Kevin's voice was filled with derision. 'It was him all right.'

'After what happened in here, my finger would point at him,' said Jim firmly, 'but I couldn't prove it and nor can anyone else.'

'And so the authorities will do nothing,' snapped Kevin. 'Well, I can.'

'Steady on, don't land yourself in trouble. Seamus wouldn't want that,' insisted Sean.

'So I just let him lie there, cold, without doing anything?'

'Gilmore will never admit it,' Sean pointed out.

'He won't,' agreed Kevin, 'but maybe one of his

259

cronies will talk. Who are they, Jim?'

'I'm not saying. I don't want you confronting them.'

Kevin's lips tightened. He glared at Jim. 'If you won't tell me, I'll find out from someone else. There are always those who'll talk if the price is right.'

'Kevin, forget it!' Sean insisted.

Kevin's eyes flared with annoyance. 'I thought you'd understand. I thought you'd want to do something. We can't let Seamus's murderers go unpunished.' He turned his burning gaze on Jim. 'The names?'

Jim hesitated, moistened his lips while he weighed up what he should do, then nodded. 'All right. I want to see those bastards dealt with as much as you do, but I don't want you taking the law into your own hands. That will only cause more trouble and grief.'

'Jim, I only want the truth. If they did it, or Gilmore, I want to know so the authorities can be told.'

Jim nodded. 'Very well. He has three main friends, all of them present tonight. Jack Jardine, Fred Sykes and Matt Forbes.'

'And where do I find them?'

Jim shrugged his shoulders. 'Who knows? Used to live around here, then in Stockton. Then I heard of them moving to Yarm. Anywhere where there was work, though they always looked for the easy jobs. Came down here from Newcastle I believe, so, if they were involved in what happened in the alley, they could easily have gone back north and that'll be like looking for a needle

260

in a haystack. Forget them. Gilmore's the man you want. He was the ringleader.'

Kevin nodded grimly. 'Maybe you are right. The law can deal with them after I've found Gilmore.'

'Not tonight,' put in Sean. 'In your state of mind you'd only do something rash.'

'Maybe that's what's needed.' Kevin started to walk away.

Sean grabbed his arm. 'Leave it for now. Remember you said you'd go back and report to Mr Langton? Do that and nothing else. I'll come with you.'

'No! You'd better go home to Nell. She was so upset.'

'Lydia and Luke are with her.'

'I know, but they may want to get back to Mrs Turnbull who will no doubt have heard the news.'

Reluctantly Sean agreed, but only on condition that Kevin promised not to pursue Gilmore that night.

Kevin hurried to Queen's Terrace, his thoughts full of revenge. If he did not seek it he would never rest easy with himself.

Reaching the Langtons, he quickly acquainted them with the situation and his theories as to who might have perpetrated the crime.

Sarah became more and more alarmed as she listened for she recognised that a desire to avenge his friend's death burned deep within Kevin. If he fulfilled that, other lives too would be ruined and she did not want that. She did not want him committing another crime as heinous as that

261

which had happened in a lonely alley beside the Iron Smelter. Kevin was carving out a decent career for himself at the rolling mill. Her father had told her that he foresaw a time when Kevin could take over his job, or else take advantage of the growth in trade along the river. Nothing must mar his future. She must do all she could to soothe his anger.

James was quick to advise a cautious approach. 'If there were no witnesses it's going to be difficult to prove who did it,' he warned.

'I know, sir, but there are ways and means.'

'And are you prepared to circumvent the law?' Kevin shrugged his shoulders.

'If that is the only way.'

'No!' cried Sarah. 'You might end up like Seamus.'

He gave a wry smile. 'I can look after myself.'

'Seamus would have said that,' said Sarah, her face grave, on the brink of shedding tears.

'The odds will be stacked against you,' warned James. 'There's more than one man involved, remember.'

'I know, but Gilmore won't have gone far. He's married, remember.'

'I don't think that would stop him leaving and staying away until things cool down here.'

'Even so, I can pay his house a visit. If he isn't there Mrs Gilmore may know where he is.'

'Be careful, young man. Don't get yourself into a situation you may later regret. Go home and sleep on it.' James looked hard at him. 'I want a promise that you will, and I want to see you at work Monday morning at the usual time.' He saw

Kevin hesitate. 'Do you promise?' he demanded.

Kevin nodded. 'Very well, sir.'

'Good.' James received this with a sense of relief, for he judged Kevin to be a man of his word. He did not see that the Irishman had crossed his fingers.

'Good night, sir.'

'Good night, my boy.' James diplomatically stayed in his chair while Sarah accompanied Kevin to the front door.

She grasped him by the arms and looked up into his eyes pleadingly. 'Please don't do anything rash. I saw your crossed fingers when you made that promise to Father.'

He gave a wry smile but that did not soften the fierce anger she saw burning in him. She pressed on, 'Don't take the law into your own hands. There'll be investigations, enquiries, and you'll end up on the wrong side of the law.'

These words had the opposite effect from what she'd intended. They fanned his need for revenge and it showed. 'Gilmore must be made to pay. We know he was behind this.'

'You can't be certain. Someone else may have done it. Even if it was Gilmore, you'll never prove it. Never!'

He wanted no more of this attitude. All his friends were adopting it. Well, so be it. He'd go it alone.

She tightened her grip on his arms. 'Don't, Kevin. Please! Don't seek revenge.' She stretched up and kissed him on the cheek.

He felt her hands relax their hold. He hesitated, wanting to declare his love even though he may go against her wishes. Impulsively his arms came around her and pulled her hard against him. His lips fastened hungrily on hers with a passion born of fury. His kiss was hard and long as he held her tight. Sarah's heart pounded. This was the Kevin she wanted, the man she'd loved almost from the start. She responded and hoped her gentle kisses would show him that in their future together there was no place for revenge.

He suddenly released her, opened the door and stepped out into the frosty air. She shivered and watched him stride down the street. He did not look back but was lost to the night.

Chapter Eleven

On Monday morning, from records in his office, Kevin was able to learn Gilmore's address. He kept this information to himself, and throughout the day gave James no indication that he still harboured a thirst for revenge.

He played that side of things down when James tentatively broached the subject of Seamus's murder, for he judged he was being tested.

'I'm pleased,' the manger concluded. 'Sarah thinks a lot of you and I wouldn't want her to be hurt.'

'I think a lot of her. Admiration and respect go hand in hand and I would not want to do anything that would upset her.'

Nevertheless, early the following morning

Kevin made his way to the Gilmores' house. It was one of a row west of the Market Place, the bricks already showing traces of grime spewed from the chimneys of the rolling mill. It was an area of the town that even in this early stage of its existence was beginning to look rundown. It had an atmosphere that spoke of poverty, of people who didn't care how they looked and had no pride in their homes.

It came, therefore, as no surprise to Kevin when, in answer to his knock, the door was opened by a woman whose hair hung lank and untidy, her face smudged as if she had wiped a sooty hand down her cheek. Her eyes were blank, her shoulders drooped. She held a young child whose face and hair were equally dirty. Her dress, marked where the bairn had dropped its food, hung like a sack, down-at-heel shoes splitting at the seams. Yet Kevin detected in the high cheekbones, the set of her mouth and delicate nose that, given encouragement and the will and money to better herself, she could have turned heads. Maybe she had one day but unfortunately the wrong man's.

'Mrs Gilmore?'

'Aye.' She looked at him suspiciously.

'I'm Kevin Harper. I would like a word with your husband.'

'He ain't here.'

'Do you know where he is?'

'I ain't seen him for two days. Went out saying he had some business to see to, but didn't tell me what or where. Now, if that's all, please be on your way.'

Kevin saw her glance quickly along the street in both directions. Automatically he did the same and saw that already there were several nosy neighbours scrutinising him.

'I'd like to talk to you a bit longer if you don't mind,' he said.

Her first instinct was to shut the door in his face, but she'd been raised to be more polite than that in her old life before she'd married Eric Gilmore.

'Then you'd better step inside, Mr Harper, out of sight of that gawking lot. Though what interpretation they'll put on this visit, I think you can guess.'

'Then I'll make it brief so they can't think the worst of you.' She stepped aside to let him in and then closed the door.

She led the way to the kitchen, which was a scene of chaos. Dirty pots were piled in the stone sink. The table was still littered with food and a poor fire struggled against the ashes in the grate.

'Do you know when your husband will be back?'

'Never do. I have to take him as he comes.'

'Does he often go off like this?'

'Not when he's in work, but now... Don't know why he got the sack. Never told me but I did hear him ranting on about "some little runt called Seamus", as he put it.' She was about to go on when she pulled up sharp and stared with widening eyes at Kevin. 'The murdered man I heard about was called Seamus too... You don't think...'

Kevin nodded.

'Oh, my God.' Mrs Gilmore slumped on a

chair. 'And you...'

'I am the murdered man's close friend. I know your husband believed that Seamus got him the sack.'

'And now you think my husband did him in?'

'Well...' Kevin felt a little embarrassed. 'I have no proof.'

'Eric wouldn't,' she protested.

'We can't always predict how people will react in anger.'

'But Eric wouldn't! He's loud-mouthed and a bully and wears that bloody bowler hat 'cos he thinks it gives him authority and power. He ill treats me and the bairns ... but murder?' Her voice rose. 'No, he wouldn't!' Tears started to stream down her face.

Kevin realised that she didn't want to believe it possible even though she feared it might be so. In spite of Gilmore's rough ways and lack of affection, she still loved him.

'I'm sorry, Mrs Gilmore, if I have distressed you. I'll be off.'

She gulped. 'Please, Mr Harper, leave this alone.'

'Maybe I can't.'

'Think what will happen to me and the bairns. Look around you. You can judge he gives me little enough as it is but I do my best.'

'Then he's a brute for not giving you more. Except, I suspect, his fists.'

She flinched. 'He'll find more work. He's not afraid of it. He'll still keep most of his money for himself, expecting me to work miracles on a pittance, but I do know he helps his ageing

267

mother.' She saw the questions springing to Kevin's lips. 'Before you ask, I'll not tell you where she lives except it's not in Middlesbrough. Now, please go.'

He nodded and said, 'I'm sorry to have taken up your time.'

He went down the passage to the front door. As he did so he heard her call out, 'Please, leave it, Mr Harper. No good will come of this. You'll only bring misery on me, his bairns and his mother.'

Her words were still ringing in his ears as he walked down the street.

The following morning, the wind drove glowering clouds across the river and over the salt marshes. It swirled through the graveyard, emphasising the chill of the loss the mourners were feeling. Kevin was filled with grief as he watched Seamus's coffin lowered into the ground.

Sarah slid her hand into his and gripped tightly as she felt the tension in his body. The coffin reached the bottom, the ropes were retrieved and the priest said the necessary prayers. It was all a blur to Kevin. He was picturing the friend he had known. Seamus had had eyes which could dance with merriment, and a way with words, ever-appreciative of the effort his friend had made to rescue him from the oblivion of drink. Kevin cursed himself now. He had saved Seamus from one set of thugs only to allow him to fall victim to a different gang. The desire for revenge which had abated with Mrs Gilmore's final words welled up inside him again.

He splashed the coffin with holy water from a pewter bowl held by a server and turned to depart with Sarah by his side. There were few mourners, but who in Middlesbrough had really known his friend? He appreciated the kindness of those who had come to pay their last respects and drew strength from Sarah and Sean's presence. Then his eyes settled on a lone figure, holding a child in her arms, standing a little distance away.

Their eyes met for a brief second and in that moment her words returned to him. Like Seamus, Mrs Gilmore was an innocent. If he acted against her husband he would shatter her life too.

Christmas came and went, not as cheerfully as it might have done but they all recognised that life must go on. As Kevin said, 'Seamus would not want us to mourn, but rather give thanks for his life and remember him in happier days.'

The bond between Kevin and Sarah had deepened and, when it was known that Gilmore was back in Middlesbrough, she was fearful of what might happen. She was not certain that her pleas to Kevin to forget all thoughts of revenge had been successful.

The news that Gilmore was back did indeed revive Kevin's thoughts of vengeance but it also brought back memories of his interview with Mrs Gilmore and for a few days a battle raged in his mind over which course of action he should take. He did not want to risk losing Sarah's good opinion.

Until one day, on his way to work, he saw Gilmore at the gates to the rolling mill yards. Kevin's step faltered. Hatred for the man left him feeling breathless. His body tensed. Why should this man, whom he felt sure was a murderer, be alive while Seamus was cold in his grave? Oh, why was there no evidence to prove it?

Gilmore glanced round and met Kevin's cold-eyed gaze. Kevin received a shock then. He'd expected to see the Gilmore of old, all bullying bombast and foul-mouthed aggression. But this man cringed before him, and he was bare-headed, the customary bowler hat gone. Whatever had happened since Gilmore had been sacked, and wherever he had been, it had had a sobering effect. Then doubt sprang to Kevin's mind. Was this act put on for some reason or other?

'Gilmore.' Kevin's voice was curt, his eyes challenging the other man to tell the truth. 'What are you doing here?'

'I hoped to see you, sir.' The last word came out a touch reluctantly as if he did not relish thus addressing a man who had once been under his thumb.

'Me?'

'Yes. I hoped you might be able to help me.'

'And why should I do that even if I could?'

'I can't give you a reason. Wouldn't blame you if you told me to get the hell out of here. But I hoped you might help me get a job. Oh, not my old one – I couldn't expect that.'

'You certainly couldn't,' snapped Kevin.

'I'll do anything, anything at all.'

Kevin had been studying the man closely. All

the old bravado was missing, the desire to throw his authority around gone. His eyes no longer roved about as if seeking out some fault for which he could inflict punishment. This man had been shaken to the core by something. Could it be the murder of Seamus?

'Do you deserve my help after the way you treated three Irishmen on their arrival? Do you deserve it after Seamus's murder?'

'You think I did that, don't you?' Gilmore's voice was calm. There was no immediate denial, no words of protest. 'My wife Kate told me you did.'

'I'll not deny it.' Kevin's eyes narrowed. He leaned slightly forward. 'And let me tell you this. If I'd found you that night, I'd have given you the same treatment as Seamus got.'

'And you would have punished the wrong man, brought endless misery on my wife and bairns, and likely ended up on the gallows yourself with the real perpetrators still alive.'

He answered in such a matter-of-fact way that Kevin found himself reluctantly accepting this as the truth. He reeled under the impact of what might have happened if he'd carried out his threat of revenge. His mind was in turmoil. Then he realised that Gilmore was still speaking.

'I'll not deny I was close to it, believing that Seamus lost me my job. I'll not deny that I and three cronies roughed him up in the Iron Smelter, but he was all right when we left and we didn't linger outside. Someone else must have thought he was ripe for the picking after we'd put too much liquor in him.'

271

'Then you are almost as bad as the murderers,' snapped Kevin.

'Maybe that's the way you see it, but we weren't the killers.'

'Then why did you leave Middlesbrough?'

'Because I knew what some people would think, and I didn't want Kate and the bairns to be involved in the trouble that would follow. I hoped that while I was away the real culprits would be found. Maybe I was wrong to go, but I'll tell you what, Mr Harper, it's had a sobering effect on me. I'm a different man nowadays. So please, for the sake of my wife and kids, try and get me a job.'

Kevin hesitated. Though it hurt him to admit it, he was sure now that Gilmore was telling the truth. It would be easy to deny him his request for his old cruelty to Seamus, but would there be any satisfaction in that? Would he not always suffer himself from the knowledge that he had helped deprive Kate Gilmore and her children of a better chance in life?

'All right, I'll see what I can do,' he growled.

Gilmore's eyes lit up. 'Thank you, Mr Harper. I'll not let you down.'

'I don't know whether I'll be able to persuade Mr Langton, mind. However, I'll do my best. But, and this is a big but, I want a promise from you that most of your wage will go to Mrs Gilmore to help her keep a better home for your children. I think she could do that, given the money and the chance.'

'My Kate's a good woman. I know I've not been right to her.'

272

'Then you promise that you'll treat her better?'
'Aye.'
'Right. Be here this time tomorrow and hopefully I'll have some good news for you.'

'Sir, there's a marked change in the man.' Kevin made his point forcefully as he faced a doubtful James Langton.

James's eyes were fixed unseeingly on an envelope on his desk. He did not reply immediately. He had listened carefully to Kevin's account of his meeting with Gilmore. At first mention of the name he had shaken his head in disbelief that Kevin had even considered talking to the man, but he let him have his say.

Now he looked up slowly until his gaze met Kevin's. 'You really think a leopard can change its spots?'

'In this case, yes. I believe what he told me, and I truly think that Seamus's murder has shaken him to the core.'

'I don't know. I don't want a disruptive presence among my workers.'

'He won't be. I think he's had a terrible shock, and I believe his wife has greatly influenced his reform. I haven't mentioned this to anyone but, in an effort to trace him, I went to see her.'

'You did what?' James was taken aback by this admission. 'That was a risky thing to do when you didn't know the woman.'

'Maybe but I'm glad I did.' He went on to relate his interview with Kate.

Once again James listened patiently. When Kevin had finished, he was satisfied.

'All right,' he said, 'we'll take Gilmore back. You said you had an assurance that he would treat his wife right? Make him understand that if we hear anything to the contrary, or if he causes any upset here, he will be dismissed immediately.'

Later that morning Kevin was called into James's office.

'Ah, Kevin, about this evening, I have been instructed to attend a meeting with Mr Bolckow and Mr Vaughan.'

'Very well, sir. I'll change my plans.'

James chuckled. 'Don't look so disappointed, my boy. The invitation for you to dine with Sarah and me still stands, but I won't be there. In fact, I want you to tell her I won't be home until late.'

'Yes, sir.' Kevin visibly brightened. 'I'll do that, sir.'

'Well, it's no good cancelling the whole evening. After all, our cook will have started her preparations. Besides,' added James with a twinkle in his eye, 'I wouldn't want to disappoint Sarah.'

'Er ... yes, sir. No, indeed,' spluttered Kevin.

'Ah, away wi' y' now,' laughed James, mimicking Kevin's accent. 'And wouldn't y' know I'd be wanting y' to give my daughter a pleasant evening?'

When the maid admitted Kevin to the house on Queen's Terrace he heard the gentle sounds of the piano. 'Don't bother,' he said as the maid started towards the drawing-room door to announce his arrival.

'Very good, sir,' she said with a half smile before hurrying away to the kitchen to inform the cook that Miss Sarah's young man had arrived. The servants had come to regard Kevin as such and tacitly approved, hoping that nothing would upset the relationship.

He opened the door quietly and saw Sarah engrossed in her playing. Even with his small knowledge of music he could tell how much she had improved since Lydia had been instructing her. He stood quietly inside the door until she had finished the piece. As the last note faded away he started to clap.

Startled, Sarah looked up quickly. 'Kevin! I didn't hear you arrive.' She was swiftly on her feet and coming towards him, her face showing her pleasure at seeing him. 'You're here before Father.' She kissed him on the cheek.

'I know,' he returned, hands coming to her waist so that she could not move away. 'He told me to tell you he had received notice to attend a meeting at Mr Bolckow's and would probably be late.'

She looked up at him. A twinkle had come into her eyes. 'And?' she prompted when he paused.

Kevin's mouth twitched. 'Your father said he did not want to spoil your evening and that I was to give you a pleasant time.'

She reached up and kissed him on the lips. 'Just being with you does that,' she whispered.

Their eyes met with that intensity which only comes between two people deeply in love. She slid her arms around his neck, he pulled her to him, and they kissed passionately.

275

A few minutes later Sarah reluctantly broke away, saying, 'I must inform Cook that Father won't be dining with us this evening.' She let her outstretched fingers trail through his before they parted enough for her to pull the bell-cord.

She gave the message to the maid, and as the door closed again Kevin said, 'I saw Gilmore today.'

Alarm crossed Sarah's face. She had dreaded such an announcement, knowing it might reignite Kevin's desire for revenge.

'Where?' she asked.

'At the works.'

'What on earth was he doing there?'

'Looking for a job.' Kevin went on to explain his encounter and its outcome.

When he had finished Sarah was suffused with relief. 'Oh, I'm so glad that your wish to avenge Seamus has burnt itself out.'

'When I was convinced he was telling the truth I realised that taking revenge would only cause misery to many people, especially you.'

She came and put her arms around him. 'I am so relieved, Kevin.'

'If I had done anything, my heart, soul and mind would have been tainted forever.'

'Thank goodness you were true to your real self. The one I love so dearly.' She kissed him in joy and relief that there was no hatred left in his heart now, only love for her.

Lydia laid out the letters on the small table in her bedroom. She had carefully numbered them on the envelopes as she had received them. They had come regularly once a week until winter storms interrupted the delivery of ironstone from Whitby. Then they had been spasmodic until the new year brought the first signs of spring.

Her flow of letters to David in Whitby had followed the same course. She expressed her feelings for him in terms which, though vague, were calculated to engender hope in the recipient. And they'd had the effect she desired. Interpreting them in his own way he was pleased with their tone and pandered to her constant requests for the latest news of Whitby.

Now, as she fingered the envelopes, she dwelt on visions of a time when she would achieve her fondest desire and wreak revenge on her uncle. But what she needed first was a ship and for that she would need financial backing. Maybe that would come from the names she had noted in David's letters, people who had been friendly with her father about whom she had elicited information. She knew who was doing well, who might have cash to spare, who might be interested in investing in a new enterprise. And Lydia had noted that a fast-growing town beside the Tees, built on the back of the iron trade, offered other possibilities for trading which in turn could give her the chance to outwit and ruin her uncle. But she needed something more than speculation to attract investors to her, she needed to be able to offer them something concrete, something from which they could anticipate a return. But what?

When the answer came three days later it almost caught her unawares.

Luke arrived home early in a state of agitation.

'What's wrong?' she asked.

'I'm summoned to Mr Bolckow's this evening.'

'Mr Bolckow's?' Lydia gasped. 'Whatever for?'

Her brother shrugged his shoulders. 'I don't know. No reason was given, I was just told to be there at six.'

'But you don't work for him.'

'No, but indirectly I am of importance in seeing that the supplies from Whitby are dealt with efficiently. And that's what worries me. I know Mr Bolckow would like to see another ship engaged in the trade. That suggestion has been put to Mr Martin but I've received word, via the ship that arrived this morning, that Mr Martin is seriously ill and therefore nothing can be done about another vessel at the moment. I'm wondering if Mr Bolckow has heard this.' He paused, frowning, then as he realised the time said with a touch of irritation, 'Lydia, I can't stand here gossiping. I must get ready.'

He left her pondering on what he had said. Another ship? Could she do something about that? If so, it would be her opportunity to re-enter the old family trade. Her mind spun with endless possibilities. By the time Luke re-appeared her thoughts had calmed with the recollection of David's letters. Could she capitalise on this knowledge? The glimmer of a plan began to form in her mind.

'Luke, you do look smart, you'll impress Mr Bolckow no end,' she said when he came into the room.

'I've got to. We don't want to lose the ironstone trade.'

'You won't,' she said with conviction.

'Don't be too sure,' he said with a half laugh.

'But I am.' Lydia's voice filled with excitement as she went on, 'If Mr Bolckow is worried about another ship then tell him we'll get one.'

'Us?' Luke was astonished at her unexpected suggestion.

'Yes, why not?'

'We haven't the capital.'

'We'll get it.'

'How? Nobody would back us when we were in Whitby.'

'Because we had nothing definite to offer them. People were suspicious. They thought their money might go the way Father's did. But now we have something to offer: definite shipments of ironstone from Whitby. A ready market. It's an investment that can't lose. Mr Bolckow needs all the stone he can get. We can add to that supplied by Mr Martin.'

Luke appeared doubtful but Lydia knew he was impressed by her suggestion.

'And, don't you see, if we are able to do this, we will have the means of expanding further, taking us into an area in which we can directly challenge Uncle Nathan!'

Luke stiffened. 'You still harbour the idea of revenge? I thought that living here in Middlesbrough, among new friends, you had forgotten.'

'No! Never!' Her eyes widened. 'Don't tell me you have?'

His lips tightened. 'Well, no, but I don't want to

279

jeopardise my future here.'

'You'd be risking nothing. You'd keep this job. I'd see to the business side of our new venture.'

'You?'

'Why not? I knew as much about Father's business as you did. He encouraged us both to take an interest in it. Hoped we would run it together after he died. Well, that was not to be but here is an opportunity to get back into trading and recreate his dream. You'd be here to help me, Luke. We must try it, for his sake.'

'This needs some careful thinking about,' replied her brother, trying to inject caution into her enthusiasm. He held up his hand to stifle the words of persuasion. 'I haven't said I'm against it, and I would like to see Uncle Nathan pay in some way, but we can't be certain that he caused Father's death.'

'As near as can be,' rapped Lydia.

'But revenge can ruin lives.'

'Or bring satisfaction.'

Luke shrugged his shoulders. 'I must be off, I don't want to be late for this meeting. We'll talk about it again.' He started for the door.

'Luke.' The sharpness in her voice stopped him. 'Don't miss a golden opportunity. If it's a question of a ship, tell Mr Bolckow I'll see that he gets one. You needn't say that you will be directly involved. It wouldn't do for him to think you are trying to steal Mr Martin's trade. I will merely be supplementing it.'

Her words were uppermost in his mind as he walked to the house on the corner of Cleveland Street and Lower Gosforth Street. Lydia was a determined young woman when she got the bit between her teeth. But there were possibilities in what she suggested. And with this scheme they would return to the trade they knew. Maybe if she got involved in this venture her desire for revenge would ease, something he devoutly wished would happen. They had a new life here in Middlesbrough, with new chances to succeed. And the meeting with Mr Bolckow could be one of them.

Luke had passed this house several times but had taken little notice of it. Now, summoned there, he observed it with different eyes and interest.

He knew it served as the home of both Mr Bolckow and Mr Vaughan as well as being used for their offices. For those reasons it was large. It stood three stories high, each of the upper floors having six sash windows. Stone columns supported the lintel above the centrally placed door which was painted a rich dark green, showing off the highly polished brass knocker.

As Luke waited to be admitted he wondered why he had been summoned here. He had got the ironstone deliveries running smoothly. There had been no more disruptions and the ships were turned round quickly. The only interruptions had been due to winter storms which had held up some of the sailings. He knew, through Mr Langton, that these delays had been of concern to Mr Bolckow for the constant flow of ore was essential to the continuous production of pig iron at the Witton works to keep the rolling mill at Middlesbrough busy enough to meet demand.

But there was nothing he could do about the weather, that was in God's hands.

The small fox's head on the right-hand doorpost he judged to be the bell-pull. That he was right was proved a few moments later when the door was opened by a butler.

Luke was determined not to show any nervousness at being called here by a man people held in awe. 'Mr Middleton to see Mr Bolckow.'

The expression on the butler's face became a shade more respectful. 'Please step inside, sir. You are expected.'

Luke found himself in a lofty hall, the sheer scale of which he had never before experienced. He had lived in a fine house in Whitby, but nothing like this. There was money to spare here and it confirmed everything he had heard about Mr Bolckow being an astute businessman.

'Can I take your coat and hat, sir?' Luke was startled out of his reverie. Once the butler had disposed of the garments in a small cloakroom, he said, 'Please follow me, sir.' He led the way across the hall to a door at the far right-hand corner. He knocked, paused, then opened it. 'Mr Middleton, sir,' he announced, and stood to one side to allow Luke to enter the room.

'Ah, Luke.' Mr Bolckow rose from his chair and came forward with hand extended. He smiled but his eyes were openly appraising his visitor. 'You don't mind me calling you Luke?'

'No, sir,' he replied, awed nevertheless at being in the presence of the man who controlled the iron trade on the Tees.

Since coming to Middlesbrough Luke had

282

learned that Mr Bolckow had made his money from speculative dealings in the corn trade while living in Newcastle, having gone to live there at the invitation of a friend in 1827. He had met Mr Vaughan when the two men were courting sisters. Mr Bolckow was looking for a new investment, and Mr Vaughan, who was at the time a manager of an ironworks at Walker, persuaded him to invest in the iron industry. The two men subsequently became partners and in looking for a suitable site for their enterprise had become friendly with Joseph Pease, a partner in the Owners of the Middlesbrough Estate.

Though Middlesbrough was then a settlement of only a few houses, Mr Pease had seen the potential of its situation on the River Tees. He encouraged Bolckow and Vaughan to move there by offering them cheap land. The two men jumped at the chance to achieve their ambition and in 1841 their rolling mill commenced operations. The blast furnaces at Witton followed and continued success seemed assured. But a crisis in the supply of ironstone was now threatening to disrupt their venture. Luke knew this was the likely reason for his being invited here, along with Mr Vaughan and James Langton.

'You have already met Mr Vaughan, I believe,' Mr Bolckow continued. 'He has told me about the way you handled the tricky situation with the Whitby men. Very commendable, and we are highly appreciative of the way you have kept the ironstone flowing ever since. And, of course, you know Mr Langton.'

283

Both men gave Luke a pleasant 'Good evening' and he responded.

'Sit down, my boy.' Mr Bolckow indicated a vacant chair, one of four which had been drawn up around a small table on which stood a decanter of wine and four glasses, only one of which was empty. 'A glass of Madeira?'

'Thank you, sir,' replied Luke, aware that the other two men had their eye on him, though in the friendliest of ways.

Mr Bolckow poured the wine and handed the glass to Luke. 'No doubt you are wondering what this is all about?' he said as he resumed his chair. 'Well, I'll come straight to the point. We are gravely concerned about our ability to keep sufficient iron coming through to the rolling mills. As you know, that depends on the supplies near our blast furnaces being supplemented from the mines of North Yorkshire. The shipments from Whitby have been adequate until recently. You solved part of our problem there but we do need to increase our capacity. I believe it was mentioned to you, and that you were going to communicate with Mr Martin?'

'Yes, sir, that is correct.'

'Well, we are in need of his answer. If he can't do anything, let him say so and we'll have to look to another supplier to supplement his deliveries.'

'Sir, there has been a shortage of available ships in Whitby. I know that was of grave concern to Mr Martin. He wanted to do all he could to help you. I know he has been trying throughout the winter but I am sorry to say, sir, he has been unsuccessful. And just today I have had further word from him which is a grave setback.'

He had the undivided attention of the other three.

'And what might that be?' Mr Bolckow's expression was serious.

'Mr Martin has been ill these last three weeks. The news is not good. His condition is serious. As a result he is unable to give his full attention to solving your problem.'

The three men exchanged glances of concern.

Mr Bolckow frowned. 'This is indeed bad news. I am sorry that Mr Martin is ill and hope his recovery will be soon and permanent. Please communicate these sentiments to him.'

'I will, sir, and I know he will appreciate your kindness.'

'Is there no one else who can take over the role of negotiating for another ship?' asked Mr Langton.

'No, sir. No one else in the Martin family is engaged in the business and his manager would not have the necessary connections to negotiate outside Whitby, which I know is what Mr Martin intended to do.'

'Then we are going to have to find someone else who can guarantee another ship,' put in Mr Vaughan. 'The existing supplies through Mr Martin's firm will continue, I suppose?'

Luke nodded. 'Certainly, sir. Mr Martin's manager is quite capable of arranging that.'

'Luke, you know the merchants in Whitby, how do you see the situation?' asked Mr Langton.

'The word is that there is a shortage of ships in the port for this sort of work. I believe that has come about because of increased shipments to the Tyne. So the situation is difficult.'

'Could we bribe one away from that trade?'

'I doubt it, sir. I've had word from two of the captains that there are rumours persisting in Whitby that your venture into the iron industry is failing.'

Mr Bolckow's face darkened. 'Rubbish! Who starts these rumours?'

'Hold on, Henry. You must admit things are a bit precarious at Witton because the supply of ironstone in its vicinity did not come up to expectations. Such facts do get out,' pointed out Mr Vaughan.

'And if I may say so, sir,' said Mr Langton, 'they are blown up out of all proportion and so affect traders' outlook. If things sound uncertain they become wary.'

'So what's the answer?' asked Mr Bolckow.

'Find a ship elsewhere, sir.'

'How do we do that? Can you do it?'

'Maybe yes, maybe no,' replied Luke.

'What sort of an answer is that?' snapped Mr Bolckow.

'Well, sir, I could try but the real negotiator would be my sister.'

Mr Bolckow stiffened. His swift glance at Mr Vaughan was not lost on Luke. He knew which word had instantly sprung to Mr Bolckow's mind. Female? A female dabbling in a man's world?

'Surely not?' he said.

'Let's hear him out,' returned Mr Vaughan, intrigued by this unexpected development.

'Very well, young man. Explain.'

Luke went on to tell them of Lydia's background and the experience she had gained from her father's business. He also gave brief details of the collapse of his father's business and the reason they had come to Middlesbrough. 'So you see, sir, she has experience, she knows people in the trade, and with her feminine charm would be much more persuasive than I.'

'And it sounds as though she knows the predicament we are in?'

'Yes, sir. I told her the latest news about Mr Martin and she realised it could be a blow to your enterprise. She is anxious to be back into trading and suggested that she might help.'

'Well, I must say, it's unusual to receive an offer like this. But we should not spurn any attempt to relieve our desperate need for more ironstone.' Mr Bolckow paused momentarily. The others sensed that he was making a decision and awaited his words. 'Can you bring your sister here tomorrow evening?'

'Yes, sir.'

'Very well. We'll all meet here at six.' He glanced at Vaughan and Langton and received their nods of agreement. 'James, why not bring Sarah? Mrs Vaughan and Mrs Bolckow will enjoy entertaining her while we discuss business with Miss Middleton. Besides Sarah's company throughout dinner will make the occasion less formidable for Luke's sister.'

His invitation left everyone with the hope that the next evening would be profitable as well as enjoyable.

Chapter Twelve

When Luke reached the house in West Street he found that Mrs Turnbull had gone to bed but Lydia, anxious to know the outcome of his visit, was awaiting his arrival.

'I wouldn't have slept, wanting to know what happened,' she explained when he expressed his surprise that she had not retired.

'It was a pleasant evening,' he declared, shrugging himself slowly out of his coat.

'And?' she replied irritably.

'Give me time to sit down.' He kept up his teasing. 'It was an enjoyable walk...'

'Luke! Tell me!'

'Mr Vaughan sends his regards...'

She stamped her foot. 'Stop it.'

'So does Mr Langton...'

Her mouth tightened with exasperation and her eyes flared with annoyance. Luke knew it was time to stop teasing.

'You are invited to meet Mr Bolckow tomorrow evening.'

There was a split second when the announcement didn't seem to have registered. Then the full meaning of Luke's statement struck home. Her eyes widened. She flung her arms around his neck. 'You did it? You told them?'

'Yes.'

'And they want to see me?' She needed his

original statement verifying to prove she wasn't dreaming.

'That's what I said.'

'Oh, Luke, you're wonderful!' She gave him an extra hug, then pushed him into a chair. 'Now tell me all about it?'

He explained what had gone on and gave her the views of the three men. 'And I told them that, apart from your business knowledge, your feminine charm would be an asset, but I think Mr Bolckow wants to judge that for himself.'

'What about Mr Vaughan and Mr Langton?'

'Well, Mr Langton knows and likes you, so that will be in your favour, but of course he doesn't know how much influence you can bring to bear in getting another ship. Mr Vaughan is just as much at a loss about you as Mr Bolckow and those two are very close so you will have to impress them both.'

'I will!'

When Lydia came down the following evening she was arrayed in her best dress, pale grey silk with a motif of roses, the skirt flared from the waist. The wide neckline plunged from the shoulders to reveal a jet necklace. The sleeves puffed from the shoulders and came tight to her wrists. Her hair was held by a broad red ribbon matching the rose print. She carried a pale grey woollen shawl ready to drape around her shoulders against the chill air.

'You'll certainly catch their attention,' said Luke with undisguised admiration.

Mrs Turnbull was equally fulsome with her

praise and her mind swept back to her own young days before she came to Middlesbrough. Though Lydia and Luke had not disclosed the reason for their visit to Mr Bolckow's, Mrs Turnbull knew it must be something special, for people from this area of town never usually got to dine with the owners of the ironworks.

Even though she knew Sarah would be present, Lydia had butterflies in her stomach as she and Luke waited at the door of Mr Bolckow's residence. From her brother's description of his visit the previous evening she was prepared for the size and elegance of the entrance hall. The furniture was of the very best, not too much, not too little, each piece able to stand on its own merits. It was the same when they entered the drawing room. Lydia assessed it at a glance. That was all the time she was able to spare for her entrance had brought Mr Bolckow and Mr Vaughan to their feet. Mr Bolckow, smiling broadly, came forward to welcome her.

'Miss Middleton, I am pleased to see you. Your brother told me a lot about you yesterday evening and I have so looked forward to meeting you.'

'It is my pleasure too,' replied Lydia softly, her eyes appraising the man who took her proffered hand and bowed as he did so.

'Come, meet the others.' Mr Bolckow led her further into the room. 'Mrs Bolckow, my wife, and her sister, Mrs Vaughan.'

Lydia counteracted the assessment these ladies were making of her with expressions of delight at meeting them, exuding a charm she knew would win their acceptance. Something that was essential if she was to win the men over to her ideas.

A moment or two later, when she was introduced to Mr Vaughan, she turned her charm to flattery with a touch of flirtation. She knew immediately that she had the two gentlemen under her spell.

She was under no illusion that this alone would win their support. Luke had described them as hard-headed businessmen. He had said they were kind, charming, able to share a joke. But when it came to considering investment ventures, they would need to be convinced of any scheme's merits.

Wine was poured and handed round. The sisters engaged Luke with queries about Whitby while their husbands were extolling the charm of the neighbouring countryside, conversations which established contact and enabled initial assessments to be made.

Five minutes later Sarah and her father arrived and merged easily with the company. Lydia managed a brief word with her friend before Mrs Bolckow whisked Sarah away to meet Mrs Vaughan. In that brief exchange Lydia gleaned that Sarah knew the reason for this invitation and hoped that it would lead to a return to the life Lydia had once known.

The dinner passed off with the most pleasing rapport between everyone. The sisters got on well with Sarah and Lydia, and enjoyed the younger company. Mr Bolckow was pleased to have his wife's approval of Lydia. It would make things easier, for he too had fallen under the spell of the pretty young woman.

He was pleased that he had decided not to meet Lydia in a purely business atmosphere. Relaxing around a dinner table, sharing a meal, had given him a chance to study at his leisure the young lady who had claimed she could solve his problem of bringing more ore to the Tees.

As they left the dining room Mr Bolckow managed to have a quiet word with Mr Vaughan while Lydia was engaged in conversation with his wife and the others had their attention on Sarah. 'Well, John, what do you think?'

'If her business sense is as pronounced as her charm then she'll not fail us.'

'My sentiments too. Well, we'll soon find out.' He crossed the hall to Lydia. 'Miss Middleton, this has been a most pleasant and interesting evening so far, now we come to the more serious aspect of it. If you'll come to my study, we'll join the gentlemen.' He inclined his head in the direction of the other three who were parting from Sarah and turned briefly to his wife. 'We'll be with you as soon as we can.'

She gave him a smile, and Lydia saw that it carried not only love but admiration.

'Very well, dear.' She turned away to join her sister who had taken charge of Sarah and was about to enter the drawing room.

When Lydia walked into the panelled study she found five chairs had been placed around a low circular table on which stood an assortment of glasses, decanters of whisky, brandy and wine, and small dishes of sweetmeats.

Mr Bolckow escorted her to a chair and, as the others settled down, poured them the drink of their choice.

Lydia began to feel a fluttering in her stomach. With the serious business of the evening looming, she found she had tensed and apprehension began to gnaw at her. She faced four men and, though she expected Luke to back her ideas, she still had to convince him, and even more so the others, that they would work, and that she was capable of carrying them out.

She took a grip on herself. She must show no doubt, no weakness, she must sound convincingly at home in a man's world.

'Well, Miss Middleton, I expect you know our position from your brother or you wouldn't be here. You apparently suggested that you might be able to help us.'

'Mr Bolckow, the word is not might but can. I CAN help you.'

The words were out almost before she knew it, but her voice was firm and she drew strength from that.

Mr Bolckow raised his eyebrows. Lydia was aware of him exchanging a quick glance with his partner, but it was so quick she was not able to interpret it.

'Well, young lady, I must say you are brimming over with confidence, but can you bring that confidence to fruition to the benefit of us all? Let us hear what you have to say.'

Lydia sat upright, her eyes fixed firmly on Mr Bolckow at first, but as she spoke she let them take in everyone with a glance that made each listener in turn feel he was the really important one.

'Well, gentlemen, let me first sum up the situation so that there is no misunderstanding on either side. You want Mr Martin's shipments of ironstone supplemented so that your furnaces at Witton can supply the required amount of pig iron to meet the orders you already have and attract more.'

'Exactly,' admitted Mr Bolckow.

'Agreed,' said Mr Vaughan.

Mr Langton nodded.

She continued. 'Mr Martin has been unable to fulfil your request for two reasons. The poor man is ill, and there is a shortage of suitable ships in Whitby.' She gave a brief pause to emphasise what she was about to say next. 'And you do not know where to look for one.'

'That's not strictly true, young lady,' Mr Bolckow's voice was curt. He did not like his business acumen being questioned. 'We are not devoid of contacts who could tell us where to look. Last night your brother was invited to bring us up to date regarding Mr Martin's dealings. His information led us to agree to look elsewhere for another ship. It was then that he mentioned what you had said. We were surprised to say the least, but he sang your praises as a determined young woman who knows what she wants and can get it because she has contacts. So we agreed to listen to you before pursuing other avenues.'

Lydia groaned inwardly. She hoped Luke hadn't piled on his praise too thickly and that, whatever he had said, she could live up to it. She met his glance and received an encouraging nod.

'Please go on,' prompted Mr Bolckow.

'You do not mind where this ship comes from?' She put what sounded to be a silly question but she needed a moment to re-order her thoughts after Mr Bolckow's interruption.

'A ship is a ship, Miss Middleton. It carries goods and that's all that matters,' Mr Vaughan pointed out.

'As long as it can navigate the Tees and tie up at our jetty,' Mr Langton added practically.

'Of course.' Lydia inclined her head in acknow-ledgement of these facts. 'To buy a ship takes money.'

'Ah,' said Mr Vaughan, 'and you can't supply it?'

'I never said I could, sir. I merely stated that I could get you a ship.'

Mr Bolckow eyed her suspiciously. 'Are you expecting Mr Vaughan and me to finance the enterprise?'

'No,' Lydia was quick to reply, hoping her sharpness would eliminate any doubts the men might have. 'I did not suppose you would but I was hoping you might take some shares in the ship.'

'Young lady,' Mr Bolckow's countenance was stern, 'you should not surmise any such thing in business. Neither I nor Mr Vaughan is interested in shipping as an investment. We are industri-alists, iron our principal interest. The trade has a great future and our enterprise on the Tees must succeed. It will if we can increase our supply of ironstone. That is the only reason we are interested in ships.'

Lydia cast a quick glance round the others to

see if she had any support. Mr Vaughan showed agreement with his partner. Luke wore a worried frown. Mr Langton was impassive.

She moistened her lips and recovered her poise. 'Sir, it is precisely because you need the iron-stone that you should invest in something that would guarantee your means of supply. I am not suggesting that you and Mr Vaughan finance the whole enterprise on your own – I intend to seek out other investors as well. If it was known that you and your partner had taken shares in a ship, I am certain I could persuade others to do so as well. With your names involved I am sure there would be no problem.'

Mr Bolckow was silent. He stared at his hands, face wreathed in thought, and shook his head slowly.

Lydia's heart sank. Further words of per-suasion sprang to her lips but she did not express them. She saw concentration in Mr Bolckow's eyes and knew better than to break it.

He looked up slowly and met her gaze. He saw hope there. He realised how much success meant to her. He sympathised, recalling similar moments in his own career, then pulled himself up sharp. He chastised himself, Silly old fool, falling for a pretty face. But am I? he questioned himself. Didn't she make sense?

He ran his hand across his forehead and said, 'Miss Middleton, if – and I must stress *if* – we agree and you succeed in interesting other people, where will you find a ship? Haven't we been already told there are none available in Whitby?'

'There are other ports, Mr Bolckow. My father

296

had several connections with shipbuilders in Hull and Newcastle.'

Mr Bolckow made no comment but glanced at his partner, seeking his opinion.

Mr Vaughan did not give it immediately. Instead he asked, 'Miss Middleton, the question I am about to ask implies no disrespect to you. I admire your acumen and vision, but do you think people will be prepared to deal with a woman? Won't they have doubts about your being able to cope in a man's world?'

For a moment Lydia bristled but quickly realising that he meant no affront to her capabilities, replied in a steady voice, 'Mr Vaughan, I am capable of putting my proposals as clearly as any man.'

'I am sure you are, but will people listen to them?'

'If they don't then they are not worth dealing with, poor narrow-sighted fools. It will be their loss. I am sure that this venture, if you and Mr Bolckow back it, will not fail. And let me remind you that I will have the counsel of my very capable brother readily available at all times.'

'Would he be deeply involved in this?' asked Mr Langton. 'None of us has any direct authority over him but I know Mr Bolckow and Mr Vaughan will be very much in agreement when I say I would not like to see him leave the job he is handling so successfully. And his authority will be needed all the more if there are further deliveries to oversee.'

'Mr Langton, I would not wish to relinquish my present job. I see it as vital to the smooth running of Mr Bolckow's and Mr Vaughan's ironworks. Another ship will mean I will need more men and overseeing them will be more demanding, but if my sister needs advice I will give it to the best of my ability.'

'Behind those words I detect a great faith in her capabilities,' commented Mr Vaughan.

'Indeed, sir, I have. And I know my father saw her as a prospective equal partner in his business whenever we took it over. Alas, that was not to be. But the tragedy of his death and the loss of his concern has not diminished Lydia's enthusiasm, nor the ability she will bring to the venture she is proposing.'

'Ably put, young man, but it is only natural that you should sing her praises,' said Mr Bolckow. There was a tone of dismissal in his voice that indicated he was not yet fully convinced.

'Sir, I have seen more of Miss Middleton than either you or Mr Vaughan since she became friendly with my daughter,' said Mr Langton. 'I have seen the enthusiasm and thoroughness she brings to everything she does, weighing up possibilities and situations very carefully before venturing to the next stage.'

Luke saw that the two men were puzzled. 'May I explain?' he put in. 'Mr Langton is referring chiefly to the piano lessons she is currently giving after he kindly gave her the opportunity.'

Mr Langton took up the explanation, readily expounding Lydia's virtues.

Mr Bolckow glanced at Mr Vaughan and received a look of agreement to his unspoken question.

'Young lady,' he said, 'you have sat quietly through these praises from Mr Langton and your brother, showing admirable modesty. Your replies to our questions have impressed us.' He paused momentarily as if finally weighing up his thoughts. 'Very well, we'll ask you to go ahead with your proposals.'

A broad smile of satisfaction appeared on Lydia's face. Her eyes carried a new brightness, behind it triumph and satisfaction at her success. 'Thank you, Mr Bolckow. You will not regret it.'

'I hope not. When do you propose to start?'

'Right here and now,' she replied, catching them all unawares with this unexpected statement. 'By persuading you to take shares in the ship.'

'One that doesn't yet exist?' Mr Bolckow threw up his arms in horror. He had never dealt with anything so risky before. There had always been something tangible in which to make an investment but here there was nothing, a ship which existed only in the mind of this slip of a lass.

'Ah, but it does, sir. Somewhere there is a ship just right for us. I can find it but cannot obtain it without financial backing.'

Mr Bolckow smiled to himself. He liked the confidence of this young woman. 'Very well, I'll take an eighth share in whatever ship you find.'

'Thank you. That is a good start.'

'Then you'd better put me down for the same,' put in Mr Vaughan.

'Thank you. That makes it a very good start.'

'I cannot match those two proposals,' said Mr

299

Langton, 'but I'll certainly take a sixteenth.'

'Thank you, Mr Langton. That makes it an excellent start.' She reached for her glass and raised it. 'Gentlemen, my thanks to you. And may I propose a toast to the new company – Tees Shipping.'

As they raised their glasses, Mr Bolckow said, 'A name already? That shows confidence. To your success and our mutual benefit.'

As they walked back to West Street, Lydia felt the warm glow of satisfaction that comes with the attainment of a desire. Her smile was wide as she held up three pieces of paper, memoranda of the shares the three investors had taken in the ship.

'Those, Luke, are our passport back to what should rightfully be ours.'

She had found a way back into her father's world. With this initial ship, which she was confident of finding, she could resurrect the firm of Tristram Middleton, albeit under a different name and in a different location. She would challenge those people in Whitby who had shown no trust in either her or Luke after their father had died, and she would build herself a position from which to destroy her uncle. Then her father could rest easier in his grave.

'We've done it, Luke, we've done it!' She gripped his hand and he felt her sense of triumph. 'Now we have the chance to do what Father hoped we would do, and more. We'll have power!'

Her tone and choice of words disturbed him. He frowned.

'Don't look so worried, Luke. You should be pleased. This is a great day. One we never expected to see so soon after coming to Middlesbrough.'

'You certainly did well,' he agreed, but in the gaze he turned upon her there was concern. 'But how far do you want to go?'

'All the way. To the ultimate,' she replied, eyes sparkling with a vision of the future.

'And the ultimate is?'

'Uncle Nathan's downfall!'

'Lydia, don't get carried away with this idea. Don't use other people to attain it. It could destroy you and hurt others. I don't want to see my dear sister consumed by a burning passion for revenge.'

'I won't, Luke, really I won't. But I want your support.'

'You shall have it,' he promised. 'But remember, as much as I want to see Uncle Nathan pay if he was responsible for Father's death, we still need definite proof and that will be hard to find.'

'Proof? We don't need proof. We *know* it. We *feel* it. That's good enough for me.'

Lydia began to lay her plans and by the following morning had a scheme to raise the remaining capital. She seized on a chance offered innocently by her brother.

'I'll be sending Sean to Whitby after the weekend to appraise the situation regarding the Grosmont ore. He'll be able to deliver your letter to David personally. That is, if you still want to correspond with him?'

301

'Of course I do. I get all sorts of valuable information from him about trading conditions in Whitby.' The revelation was out before she realised it.

'You what?' Luke was astounded.

'Oh, just the usual gossip from around the port.'

But her brother had read the real implications. 'You've been gathering information to use once you had reached a position in which you could exploit it. You've had something like this in mind ever since we left Whitby, Lydia, you've *used* David.'

'No, I haven't,' she protested. 'I just wanted to keep up with our home town.' Exasperated by her own slip, she changed the subject. 'I'll go with Sean. I'd like to see David, and I can make enquiries about raising the rest of the capital in Whitby.'

'Who'll be likely to help us there after we were refused help when Father died?'

'We have notes of agreement from our three existing investors. They'll help swing things our way.'

'They could,' Luke agreed. 'But there's one other thing. Uncle Nathan will hear about your visit and he'll wonder what is going on after the accusations we made. He won't like you recreating Father's firm in Whitby, even if it is under a different name.'

'We won't operate from Whitby. We'll register the ship in Middlesbrough and our name won't appear on the documentation.'

'I can see it might be possible to do that but

he'll hear about you trying to raise money in Whitby.'

'He won't even hear that.'

Luke was puzzled. 'What's going on in that pretty little head of yours?'

Lydia smiled. 'I think Sean could be very useful to us here.'

'Sean?'

'Yes. Why not? He has the Irish gift of persuasion.'

Luke was taken aback by this suggestion but his active mind was fast seeing possibilities in her proposal.

'Supposing he doesn't want to help?'

'Oh, he will. Just leave him to me.'

'Lydia, be sure you make him a genuine offer and give him a proper explanation. Remember, I don't agree with using people for your own ends.'

'I won't, dear brother.' She gave him a reassuring kiss on the cheek.

Lydia arrived early to give her piano lessons at the Langtons' that same afternoon.

Sarah sensed the excitement still gripping her friend when she was shown into the drawing room.

'I'm so pleased everything went well for you last night,' she said.

'Now I've the chance I've dreamed of much sooner than expected,' replied Lydia.

Sarah reached out and grasped her hands. 'I'm delighted that you've got what you want.' Worry clouded her face. 'But it's a man's world, isn't it?'

'Aren't we just as capable?'

Sarah looked doubtful and said without a great deal of conviction, 'I suppose so, if we are given the chance.'

'And this is *my* chance. I'm going to succeed.'

'You're a very determined young woman.'

'And why not?'

Sarah felt herself being caught up in Lydia's enthusiasm. 'Yes, why not? So have you a ship in mind, or do you know where you might find one?'

'Not yet. I need to be assured of the capital first.'

'Where are you going to raise that?'

'I made a start last night. Mr Bolckow, Mr Vaughan and your father have all taken shares.'

'Father told me. I'm surprised he did, I've never regarded him as a speculator. Who else will you approach?'

'Whoever might be interested.'

'Try Kevin.'

'Kevin?' Lydia was puzzled by this suggestion, and the tone of her voice betrayed the fact that she believed he would not have money to invest. She knew that Sarah and Kevin were seeing more of each other and for that, of course, must have Mr Langton's approval. But for her friend to suggest that someone who had come to England as a labourer might be a possible investor...

'Kevin isn't quite what you imagine,' replied Sarah. 'What I tell you must be kept strictly to yourself. I do not want him to think I betrayed his trust.' She went on to reveal his background. 'So, you see, he may well have money he might be interested in investing.'

Lydia had listened carefully. 'I didn't know any of this. There's nothing I'd like better than to have people like him included in this venture. I'll ask him.'

'No, please don't, I'll do it. Then it won't look as if I've told you anything about his life.'

'Very well,' Lydia agreed. 'And then if he's interested I'll give him more details.'

'I suppose this will mean the end of our piano lessons?' said Sarah. There was no mistaking the regret in her voice.

'Of course not. Obviously there will be other things which will need my attention but I want to keep up the lessons. They help me relax. Besides, I don't want to lose the pleasure of seeing you.'

'That need not happen if you gave them up.'

'I know, but they mean we'll enjoy each other's company frequently, and that I value.'

'So do I. I'll ask Kevin for you, and if there is anything else I can do, please say.'

When Luke left for work the next morning Lydia accompanied him as far as number ten. His knock was answered by Sean who'd expected him, for Luke's timing was impeccable every morning.

'Top o' the morning to you.' No matter what the weather, Sean's greeting, accompanied by a smile, was always the same. The words were out before he realised that Lydia was with her brother. He turned his smile on her and added with an exaggerated bow, 'And top o' the morning to you too, fair lady.'

Lydia, amused by his effusive greeting,

responded with a merry laugh.

'Ah, miss, that laughter is music to my ears. It will accompany me for the rest of the day and keep me sane while this brother of yours nags and nags me.'

'Enough of your flattery, you dummy,' admonished Luke with a friendly grin.

Sean raised his eyebrows. 'Flattery, is it?' He assumed a hurt expression. 'And who do you think keeps the ore ships moving?' He turned to Lydia. 'Now, miss, you don't think I'm a dummy, do you?'

'Not at all. You certainly won't act the dummy when my brother tells you he wants you to go to Whitby next week, will you?'

'Sure I won't, miss.'

'Good. And you won't act the dummy when he asks you to escort a young lady on the voyage?'

'Ah, sure now, I will not. It will be my pleasure and will greatly relieve the monotony of the voyage.'

'And would you mind if that young lady were me?'

'Not at all. It would double the pleasure.'

'Then that is settled.'

'Whatever the time of sailing I'll be there, awaiting your fair presence, and you can rest assured that your safety will be my foremost concern.'

'Thank you, kind sir.'

Luke saw more effusive words springing to Sean's lips so intervened quickly. 'An end to this backchat or we'll get no work done today.'

Sean sprang to attention and saluted. 'Sorry,

sir. We shall end this delightful conversation now.' He turned to Lydia. 'I look forward to the voyage when we may converse without being interrupted by this clod of a fellow.' He bowed to her. As he straightened up he caught her eye and winked.

In a flash he was after Luke who had started along West Street towards the Market Place. Sean sensed Lydia's eyes on him and his ears registered the light laughter which floated along behind him. He wondered what the voyage might bring.

The following morning when Lydia reached the Langtons' the maid ushered her in quickly out of the rain. She shrugged herself out of her cape and handed it to the maid along with her bonnet and umbrella. When Sarah hurried into the hall to greet her friend, Lydia sensed she had something to tell her.

'I've news,' she cried, taking Lydia's arm and hurrying her into the drawing room. When she had closed the door she could hold back no longer. 'Father and I persuaded Kevin to take a share in your ship.'

Lydia's face broke into a broad smile. She grasped her friend and hugged her. 'That's wonderful!' she cried excitedly. 'I just know this is going to succeed, I feel it in my bones.'

'But there's more.' Sarah's eyes sparkled.

'More?'

'Yes. Kevin said he would have to go to Ireland to see his family and arrange for the transfer of some of his funds. And guess what? He's asked me to accompany him and meet his people.'

307

'Splendid,' cried Lydia, swept along by her friend's enthusiasm.

'Father approved.'

'When do you go?'

'This coming weekend.'

'Meeting his family... Does this mean what I think it might mean?'

'Who knows?' laughed Sarah. 'I wouldn't say no.'

As she snuggled closer to Kevin in the coach as it rumbled towards Dublin, Sarah looked back on her visit to Ireland with satisfaction.

Though she had approached the meeting with nervousness and apprehension this was soon swept away by the family's warm and friendly greeting. Throughout their three-day stay she had been thoroughly spoilt. Kevin's mother, having taken to her immediately, was pleased and relieved that her son had found such a charming and modest girl, and one with a practical head on her shoulders. His father fussed around her, delighted that his son had brought a pretty girl to their home. She had felt at ease immediately with his brother and sister who involved her in their own pastimes and pleasures.

'Enjoy yourself?' asked Kevin.

'Never more.'

'And I know my family loved you, but who couldn't?'

'Flatterer.' She smiled.

'We have a hotel in Dublin for the night and sail in the morning. This evening, I want to try to find a girl.'

Sarah was taken aback by this statement but then she saw the twinkle in his eye and knew he had phrased it in such a way as to tease her.

'And why might that be?' she returned, countering his tease with a feigned haughtiness.

Kevin changed to a more serious tone. 'She's Eileen Nolan. Sean's girl.'

'I didn't know he had one. I thought he was making eyes at Lydia.'

'Well now, that might just be the case and that's why I want to see Eileen. Sean always had an eye for the girls but Eileen was permanent, if you get my meaning. Sean was always a dreamer and he said he was going to make his fortune and whisk her away to a land of riches. Well, he's made progress since coming to Middlesbrough, but he might just get carried away by Lydia's scheme and forget Eileen.'

'But is it right to interfere?'

'It might be wrong not to do so. People might get hurt if I don't. Eileen's a nice lass. Sean has promised her so much that I should hate to see her let down. He did promise to send for her as soon as he saw what prospects there were in England. Well, he's had time to do that but he's shown no sign of sending for her so far.'

'Maybe he has a reason.'

'Maybe, but if that reason's Lydia, I think he's wrong.'

'She's nice enough,' protested Sarah, quick in defence of her friend.

'I'm not saying she isn't,' returned Kevin quickly. 'I've nothing against her. I like her. It's Sean I'm bothered about. I don't think Lydia is

309

right for him whereas Eileen is another matter.'

Sarah shrugged. 'You know her, I don't. But be careful. Don't play matchmaker.'

'I don't like to see people lose the happiness they once had. And Sean and Eileen are right for each other.'

'Can I come with you to find her?'

'If you wish, but we will not be in the best part of Dublin. It's respectable but on the edge of poverty, not far from the dereliction and destitution of an area called the Liberties.'

Sarah saw what he meant when they made their way through streets lined on either side by identical houses, some shabby with refuse stacked outside, others boarded up. Alongside those were others where an attempt had been made to wrest some decency from the poverty around them. Sarah felt eyes watching them every step of the way. Men lounged on street corners, children in rags raced past them, and from behind curtains at unwashed windows faces peered out. She was thankful when they turned a corner where the houses showed signs of being better cared for, though some of these were beginning to verge on the shabby. At least many of them showed attempts to keep windows and curtains clean.

Kevin glanced at the numbers until he came to the one he was looking for. He rapped hard on the door and then, as they waited, gave Sarah a faint smile.

When the door was opened Sarah saw immediately why Sean had been attracted to this girl. Not only was she pretty but there was a jaunty air about her. She was the sort who would never let life or the knocks it dealt her get her down. Though her dress showed signs of wear she wore it as if it was new and designed to make the best of her figure.

'Kevin!' Her face lit up and her blue eyes danced with pleasure.

'Eileen, it's good to see you.'

'Sean? Is he here in Dublin?' Her voice was filled with eager anticipation.

Kevin shook his head. 'No, I'm sorry, he's not.'

'He's all right?' Eileen's eagerness changed swiftly to concern.

'Yes. May we come in?'

She was flustered by her own seemingly inhospitable behaviour. 'Of course, I'm so sorry. Come in, come in.'

'This is Sarah.' Kevin made the introduction as they stepped inside.

The two young women exchanged polite greetings. Kevin noted that Eileen was appraising Sarah's clothes and by her automatic gesture of smoothing her skirt he knew she felt shabby alongside the visitor.

'Sean? Tell me about him,' she pressed, eager for first-hand news as she indicated for them to sit down. 'His letters say that he is doing well and that he will come for me before long, but he never names a date so I can tie things up here. Not that that would take long. I'd walk out now if he said so.'

'He is doing well for himself, better than he expected when he left Ireland.' Kevin went on to give Eileen an explanation of what had happened to them since they had last seen her, his narrative only faltering when he told her of Seamus's death.

'Then why hasn't Sean come for me or even sent for me?' she asked when Kevin had finished. 'Has he found someone else?'

Kevin hesitated.

'He has!' Eileen's voice soared with fury at the thought that she might have lost Sean.

'There isn't and there is,' replied Kevin. 'He is very friendly with the sister of the man who gave him employment as his assistant and took him away from labouring. I think Sean believes that he should be friendly with her.'

'Maybe,' said Eileen, 'but friendship can sometimes develop into more. Is she keen on him?' She looked to Sarah for an answer, judging that a woman would recognise this more readily than a man.

'I know she likes him, is smitten by his charm, but she has a young man in Whitby where she came from.'

'He's not in Middlesbrough, Sean is.' Eileen's mind had been racing, trying to find ways of counteracting Sean's interest in this other girl. She immediately voiced the best of these ideas. 'I think I'd better come to Middlesbrough. Can I travel with you?'

Both Kevin and Sarah were surprised by the swiftness of this decision.

'Of course,' he replied, 'but haven't you things to see to here?'

'They don't matter. All I need are a few personal belongings. I could pack them now.'

'Then come with us to our hotel. We'll all be

312

together to sail in the morning,' suggested Sarah.

'But I couldn't afford...'

'I'm sure you could fix it, Kevin.'

'You get your things and come with us,' he said kindly. 'I'll take care of the expense.'

'But I couldn't let you...'

Sarah, realising that Eileen knew nothing of his background, said, 'Kevin, you'd better explain.'

He nodded and went on to do so.

Eileen listened with interest and, when he had finished, said, 'I always thought there was something different about you, Kevin Harper, but I couldn't put my finger on it. You're a lovely man, so you are, particularly for what you did for Seamus. Take care of him, miss.'

'Sarah, please.'

Eileen saw friendship in Sarah's eyes and was pleased to have that comfort as she set sail for England and her reunion with Sean.

Chapter Thirteen

'You mind and look after my sister, Sean,' Luke ordered as they stood at the foot of the gangway of the *Nina*, bound for Whitby. In five minutes the ropes would be cast off and the ship would be free of the jetty. Backs would bend to oars as she was towed into midstream and taken downriver until her sails could catch the breeze in safety.

'Sure now, she'll come to no harm with me,' replied Sean. He glanced at Lydia. 'These ore ships offer no comfort for passengers but the captain has made his cabin, such as it is, available to you.'

'Thanks, Sean, but more than likely we'll spend the time on deck this fine day.'

'Be sure you keep well wrapped up,' advised Luke. 'See she does, Sean.'

'Brother, stop fretting,' said Lydia, an edge to her voice which showed she was irritated by the fuss. She was thankful that, almost at the same moment, a cry of 'All aboard!' put a stop to any more talk. She kissed Luke quickly and hurried up the gangway.

Sean exchanged a handshake with Luke. 'I'll confirm that the Goathland mines are still able to meet our needs.'

'Good, and clarify the situation with Mr Martin. Give him my best regards and my hope that his prolonged illness has turned the corner.'

'I will,' Sean took long strides up the gangway. 'Best of luck,' Luke called after them.

There was an element of backchat in their conversation and observations as the ship proceeded downriver.

With the sea in sight, Sean said tentatively, 'Are you a good sailor?'

'Yes. Occasionally, if my father was going to London on his ship, Luke and I would go too. We loved it.'

Sean looked surprised. 'Your father's ship?' he queried as if he had not heard her correctly.

'Yes, he was a merchant in Whitby. You did not know?'

314

'No.' Sean did not want to disclose the snippets of information he had picked up on his previous visit to Whitby. He hoped his denial would lead Lydia into revealing more.

'Luke has never said anything about our background?'

'No. I thought he had come here as an employee of Mr Martin.'

'So he did. Father had him gaining experience in all manner of trading so that his knowledge would be wide when he and I took over the business, but sadly with Father's death that was not to be. There were debts.'

'I'm sorry about that.' Sean expressed his commiserations then added with a touch of doubt, '*You* were going to be actively engaged in the business?'

'Yes. Why not? I was close to my father. I'd seen how he organised everything, met the people he dealt with. I knew what had to be done. So, as I say, why not?'

Sean shrugged his shoulders. He had no argument against what she had said except that it was a man's world, but he certainly wasn't going to voice that opinion after sensing the determination of this interesting and attractive young woman. He agreed, 'Why not? Though I've never thought of a charming female running or helping to run a business.'

'Well, you see one here who is going to prove it can be done.'

Sean saw the fire of ambition in her eyes. He also read desire and resolve.

'You want the old life back?'

315

'Oh, yes, and I'll get it.'

There was a ruthlessness in her tone that was foreign to Sean's easygoing nature. It made him think. She had dreams of the future, just as he had. But had he been wrong in his approach? Should he have had the same attitude as her?

'Do you want to help me?'

The question, torn away by the wind as the ship met the first waves, caught him by surprise. Even so it echoed the thoughts he had just been entertaining.

'What do you mean?'

'Let's go to the cabin for a few minutes, then I won't have to compete with the sound of the wind in the rigging.'

Sean nodded and escorted her below deck. The cabin was small, containing two chairs and a table on which there were some charts. The bunk was neatly made with bedclothes ready for the captain's use whenever longer voyages were incurred.

Sean looked at Lydia questioningly after he had closed the door.

'My visit to Whitby is not just for pleasure,' she announced.

'I thought you must be going to see the friend to whom you write and to whom I delivered a letter on my first visit.'

'David.'

'Yes.' Sean hesitated a brief moment and then put the question. 'You had an understanding with him before you left Whitby?'

Lydia tensed. What right had he to ask such a probing question? Sharp words sprang to her lips but she suppressed them. She had need of him and should not alienate him. Rebuke him and all cooperation could be lost.

'We'd known each other all our lives. People took it for granted that we would marry,' she answered quietly.

'And will you?'

Lydia paused before answering, 'I'm not sure.' She gave a wistful shake of the head as she remembered her last days in Whitby. 'Things were confused when we left. David did not come up to my expectations then.'

'You don't see him in the same light nowadays?'

'His attitude hurt me, but you can't wipe out a lifetime's feelings.'

'But other things happen. You meet other people.' He stepped towards her. His eyes held hers. A tension, sparked by attraction, rose between them. He reached out to rest his hands on her shoulders. She did not pull away. She felt pleasure in the contact. Since their first meeting she had grown used to his company, enjoyed his Irish sense of humour and revelled in the attention he gave her. There were times when she had wondered if her feelings ran deeper. But always thoughts of David, and the wish that he had defied his father, intervened. But now they did not. She was lost in a welter of emotions as Sean drew her close and his lips met hers gently. His hands moved slowly to her waist and held her tight. Her fingers slid round his neck, caressing it sensuously, and her lips moved in a passionate response.

These moments sealed Lydia's conviction that

Sean would meet the request she was about to make.

As their lips parted, Sean felt a sudden pang of guilt. Eileen! She thrust herself into his thoughts, but he tried to ignore the memories as Lydia brushed his lips temptingly again. Then, as he was about to take her to him, she spun out of his arms with a teasing, coy look that brought longing to his eyes. He reached out for her.

'No, Sean, we have serious things to discuss.'

He recognised that this was no prohibition of a future embrace but whatever she had in mind had to come first. To step over the present boundary could sour everything between them.

'Serious?'

'Yes. I have business to attend to in Whitby but I need your help.'

'My help?'

'Yes. Will you give it?'

'Anything for you.'

Lydia smiled gratefully. 'Thanks, Sean. You'll not regret it. You'll be suitably rewarded, especially if I achieve what I want. No, not if but when.'

She sat down and he did likewise. His curiosity was roused by her reference to the future and what it might mean.

'What I have to tell you must be kept strictly confidential. I want you to promise me that it will?' She cocked an eyebrow at him, turning the statement into a question.

'It will go no further than this cabin,' he replied. 'By the Holy Mother of God, my lips will stay sealed.'

She nodded and continued. 'As you know, Mr Bolckow is concerned about the supplies of ore. You know the details so I won't go into them. I met him a few nights ago because I had indicated that I could find another ship to deliver additional supplies. That needs financing. Mr Bolckow, Mr Vaughan and Mr Langton have taken shares but I need more investors.'

'I'm afraid I have no money for that purpose,' put in Sean.

'That's not what I want of you. Because of the loss of my father's ship and the subsequent collapse of his business on his death, my standing and Luke's are not high in Whitby. We could find no one to back us to revive his business.'

'And you are here to try again?'

'Not me, you.' Lydia was very clear about this.

'Me?'

'Yes. I want you to be the person looking for investors in Tees Shipping, a new company which you propose to run from the Tees with the immediate prospect of shipping ironstone but expansion into other trading in mind. You must not mention me or Luke. If you do, the whole enterprise would be suspect.'

Sean was beginning to appreciate the role he would have to adopt. 'I will need briefing about who to approach. I surmise you have that all worked out?'

'Yes. That was one of the purposes of my corresponding with David. I kept in touch with commercial life in Whitby.'

Sean made no comment but suspected that Lydia had had this move planned for some time

319

and had probably worked towards it ever since she'd arrived in Middlesbrough. He was surprised to realise that he found that just a touch alarming, but he dismissed the thought immediately. There was really nothing in what Lydia had said to justify that feeling, and those thoughts were already being supplanted by speculation of his own. Maybe he could use this situation to further his dreams.

'I'm sure you can do this, Sean. Your Irish charm will work wonders.'

His ready smile in response held a promise that he would work his magic in whatever capacity it was needed.

She took three envelopes from her handbag. 'And these will help to persuade those you approach.'

'What are they?'

'They are proof that Mr Bolckow, Mr Vaughan and Mr Langton have taken shares in the ship as yet to be purchased. Their names, especially those of Bolckow and Vaughan with their reputation in the iron industry, should lend weight to your argument that the proposition is a sound one.'

He took the envelopes from her.

'They are precious. Be careful with them,' she warned.

'They will never leave my person. Now, you must tell me as much as you can about the people you want me to see and about the commercial life in Whitby.'

The next hour was spent on this briefing. At the end Lydia made the following stipulations. 'You must not approach David and his father, nor Nathan Middleton and his family.'

'A relation?'

'My uncle.'

'I would have thought he would have been the first person on your list.'

'There are personal reasons why I don't wish that. There's no need for you to know what they are. Heed my words, Sean, do not approach those I have mentioned. They will no doubt get wind of you and what you are seeking. If they approach you, you must make some excuse for not entertaining them. That is vital to my scheme.'

'Do your present investors know of this stipulation?'

'No. Only you, Luke and I know. That is how it must stay. If it doesn't there could be serious consequences.' She saw other questions coming to his mind and quickly interposed. 'Ask no more about that side of the business. It is a private matter and there is no reason for it to intrude on the straightforward matters I wish you to deal with.'

'Very good,' Sean readily agreed, for the icy tone which had come into her voice when her uncle was mentioned had not been lost on him. It had raised his curiosity. Maybe he should find out more. And why hadn't David to be approached? This whole affair was growing more intriguing by the minute. His astute brain was already wondering if the embrace of about an hour ago was genuine or had it been employed to trick him into agreeing to help her? Well, he had done so, so he was committed. No matter, he'd play along. And be ready to turn any opportunities to his own advantage.

'Good.' Lydia still had not relaxed. Concerned that every aspect of her plan must be dealt with, she went on. 'In Whitby we do not know each other except as acquaintances who happened to take the same ship from Middlesbrough. The only person likely to make an association is Mr Martin and he is ill so will not see me there.'

'What about David Drayton? Remember, I carried a letter to him from you. If he sees us, even separately, he may draw conclusions which would not be far from the truth. He's bound to hear I'm trying to raise interest in a ship sailing out of the Tees.'

'Leave that to me. If by any chance he does question you, deny that I know anything about it.'

Seamus nodded and asked, 'When do we return?'

'You, when you have done all you can. Luke knows about this and is expecting you to be away a few days. We must not leave together. I will spend four days here, leaving on the fifth. That should give you plenty of time to raise the necessary interest.'

'And you would like to know of my progress before you leave?'

'Most certainly. In fact, every day.' She paused thoughtfully. 'I will be staying at the Angel Inn. It will be best if you stay at the White Horse on Church Street.'

'Not together? Not even in the same inn?' He

looked disappointed.

She gave a wry smile and shook her head slowly, her eyes intent on his.

Did he read in them a promise beyond this refusal? He decided to test her. 'Not even discreet contact at either?'

'Well, who knows?' She let the words convey a subtle suggestion, but what followed was said in deadly seriousness. 'But nothing must get in the way of the success of this venture, Sean. It means a lot to me that I get this ship. More than I can tell you – much more.'

The sharpness in her voice, the tension in her body, emphasised her words and Sean read there an obsession born in the past. It made him wonder if there was more to this young woman than he had seen.

'Very well,' he acquiesced. 'When do we meet for my first report? And where?'

'Let's say the day after tomorrow. I'll be on the west pier at three o'clock. If it is raining I will send an envelope to you at the White Horse by two. It will contain an address at which you can meet me, again at three o'clock.'

'Very well. You seem to have covered most things except two – do I mention a specific ship, and have you a list of the people you think might be interested?'

'You can indicate that you are close to making a deal for the ship, but it is a matter of getting enough interest in the rest of the shares. If necessary you can mention the name Slater, a small but reliable firm who build sound ships on the Tyne.' As she was speaking she opened her

323

handbag and withdrew two slips of paper. She handed one to Sean. 'That is the list you want – I have put the names in the most likely order of interest.' She paused while he gave the paper a quick glance then went on, 'Remember five-sixteenths have already gone and three more are spoken for. One for me, one for Luke and one for you.'

Sean's expression was a picture. 'Me?'

'Yes.' She smiled encouragingly. 'To keep you interested? To make you work harder to get others to invest? As payment for your work? Describe it how you will, I think you deserve a sixteenth.'

'But I have no capital,' replied Sean, still bewildered.

'Neither have I. Neither has Luke. We lost everything on Father's death.'

'Then how...?'

'My dear Sean,' she began, as she held out the second sheet of paper, 'unknown to them the rest of the shareholders will have paid for the three-sixteenths we cannot finance. You'll see my calculations on that paper, the cost of the ship, the fitting out, crew's wages and so on, plus the fact that there will be three shares which cannot be paid for.'

It began to dawn on Sean what a dangerous game she was playing. This was a most unequal venture with some investors financing Luke, Lydia and him as well as themselves.

'See the figure you must quote? Commit it to memory, Lydia instructed. 'I want those calculations back.'

I'll bet you do, thought Sean. It wouldn't do for this sheet of paper to get into the wrong hands. He memorised the figure and returned the paper to her.

'Don't let me down, Sean. This is dearer than life to me. If I control that ship, I can fulfil a dream.'

He noted that a coldness had crept into her voice which almost carried a threat. But to whom? Certainly not him. There was no cause. Besides, she had taken him a long way into her confidence. He wondered what lay behind all her schemes. Such thoughts were forgotten in a host of more pleasant speculations as she stepped closer to him.

'Business is over, Sean. There are other things in life.' She cupped his face in her hands and kissed him passionately.

Sean thanked the captain for a safe voyage. He raised his hat and called his goodbyes to Lydia who was coming along the deck. Neither showed any trace of the emotion they had felt on the voyage.

When he stepped ashore, Sean tossed a coin above the heads of a crowd of urchins who clamoured to take his bag.

The coin spun temptingly. Cries of excitement rent the air. Youngster jostled youngster as they all leaped up with arms outstretched, grabbing at the tantalising coin. One arm seemed to stretch above the others. One urchin seemed to hang in the air longer. His fingers closed round the money.

'It's mine! It's mine!'

The cry brought groans from the others who immediately turned their attention to Lydia who had started down the gangway.

'Where to, mister?' The sharp query came from a tall, skinny boy who looked as if a good feed would do him no harm.

'The White Horse on Church Street,' replied Sean.

'Follow me.' The boy started off.

His pace was brisk as he threaded his way through the frantic activity on the quayside. He kept up the same pace when they moved into the more residential area away from the river.

Sean called a halt.

The boy looked anxious.

'Your name?'

'Tim, sir,' he replied. His eyes showed a fear of reprimand, though he could not think what he had done.

'Very well, Tim. What's your hurry? Eager to get this job done and find another? Maybe carrying a housewife's shopping, a basket for the fishmonger, planks for a carpenter ... or maybe picking pockets?' Sean had seen all these activities taking place after they had left the quay.

'Not the last, sir. I never do that. It's dishonest.' Shock that he should be thought capable of picking pockets showed on Tim's face.

Sean nodded. 'Right, I believe you.'

'I do any other job, sir. Why not? I have to make an honest penny as quickly as possible or my income falls.' Confidence had returned to Tim's voice.

Sean smiled. 'An honest penny, eh? Sure now, that's commendable. I'm here on business and don't know Whitby. I don't want to waste time looking for various offices, so will you show me around?'

'Yes, sir,' replied Tim, his eyes bright at the prospect of an assured income for a few days.

'Right, on your way.'

With urchins crowding round her, Lydia could not move from the bottom of the gangway.

'Stop!' she shouted. Her command was piercing.

The urchins gradually stopped pushing when they realised it was going to get them nowhere and that this lady demanded respect. Their shouts subsided into quiet murmurs of 'Miss ... miss...' until they too died away to leave only expectant expressions on dirty faces.

'That's better,' called Lydia, placing her two bags on the ground. She straightened and cast her eyes over the group. She almost fell into the trap of hiring them all thanks to the woebegone faces and pleading eyes. But, realising that this was all a part of the tricks of the trade, whenever passengers disembarked, she stopped herself. She cast her gaze over them then said, 'You, and you.'

The rest moaned and turned away, trying to ignore the triumphant shouts of the chosen two.

'To the Angel,' Lydia ordered.

The two boys picked up her bags and started off, mocking the unlucky ones.

Lydia was welcomed by the landlord of the Angel and found herself allocated a most comfortable room. The bed looked inviting after her voyage so she slipped out of her dress and lay down. In her mind she started to make plans for the next four days. There was no business to attend to apart from meeting Sean at the allotted times. To all outward appearances this was a visit to see her old friends. Lydia dozed and fell into a deep sleep.

Sean settled himself in his room and then went downstairs to partake of the landlord's recommended ale, a hunk of cheese and some home-made bread, layered with butter from a local farm. He had much on which to ponder.

The voyage had revealed sides to Lydia he had never suspected. Apart from the sweet, endearing female he knew as Luke's sister, there was also a person who was comfortable among people like the Langtons, an accomplished pianist, someone who had been used to a comfortable life in very different circumstances from those in which she was living in Middlesbrough.

Now he had learned that a deeply ambitious woman lay below the surface. A capable one who had learned about ships and trading by being acutely observant of her father and his business. And he had detected a devoted daughter who had been stunned by his death. And that death, he had come to think, was linked to her desire to make a success of this investment in which he had become involved. For her father's sake? To resurrect the firm he appeared to have lost? Sean felt somehow there was more than that behind her desire to succeed.

But what else could there be? Why was she so particular that her uncle should not be approached to take shares in the ship? Was there some sinister reason behind the stipulation that she had emphasised should be strictly observed? Was there anything in this that he could turn to his own advantage? If there was would it be straightforward or would he be dabbling in things best left alone?

He had progressed since coming to Middlesbrough, he should be careful not to destroy his achievements. They were such that he could build on them, especially the share Lydia had promised him. But were they a sop to entice him into a web of intrigue being spun around him? And was part of that web the endearing things she had said during their passionate loving in the captain's cabin, or did she really mean them? Even here he felt himself being drawn into a quagmire of his own making. Hadn't he used his charm to persuade her to allow him to be her escort in Middlesbrough? Had that resulted in the advances she had made on board ship? Were they made for her own ends or was she really attracted to him? And where did his own feelings lie? With Lydia or with the girl he had left behind in Dublin?

Lydia came awake slowly. The moment of wondering where she was was replaced by realisation which brought her wide awake. She swung from the bed, felt the pain of hunger and, after refreshing herself and dressing, went downstairs to the dining room. She chose a table which occupied one corner of the room and gave her a view of the door and the rest of the tables.

She ordered broth to be followed by game pie with potatoes, accompanied by wine.

When the soup was brought Lydia was deep in thought and, for a moment, not fully aware that she was being served.

In that moment the maid spoke. 'Why, it's Miss Lydia.'

Startled at hearing her name, Lydia looked up to see a girl who used to be in her father's employ, 'Maggie,' she said.

'Hello, miss. It's nice to see you again.'

'And you, Maggie. I'm pleased you found another job.'

'It's all right, miss. Brings in the pennies but it's not as pleasant as when I worked for you.'

Lydia smiled. 'It's good of you to say so.'

'Miss?' Maggie hesitated. 'Do you mind if I ask you something?' Her face went red.

'Of course not. What is it?'

'Well, seeing you here, I wondered if you were coming back to live in Whitby?'

Lydia gave her a sympathetic smile. 'No, I'm afraid not. Well, not for some time. I've just come on a short visit to see some friends.'

'If ever you do, please think of me.'

'Of course I will, but you may be snapped up by some nice young man before then.'

Maggie blushed even deeper. 'Don't think that'll happen, miss.' Before Lydia could comment further Maggie scurried away.

While they had been talking Lydia's view of the door had been obscured but now she was aware of two people sitting down at a table further along the room. The man had his back to her and blocked her sight of his female companion, but Lydia could tell he was making a fuss of her. As he sat down he half turned and gave Lydia a view of his friend.

'David! Isobel!' she gasped. She stared as if to convince herself that the man who had said he loved her was wining and dining her cousin. Lydia felt her heart thump a little. Was she jealous? She stiffened and chided herself for thinking such a thing. No. Hadn't she set down in writing that she would not blame him if he found someone else? But ... her cousin! Really! Lydia stamped her foot in irritation at herself. She picked up her spoon and started on her soup. She must occupy her mind with something else. But her eyes, in spite of her effort to keep them fixed on what she was doing, kept straying to a particular table where the serving girl was taking their order.

As the girl moved away Isobel looked beyond her companion to see who else was dining at the Angel. Her eyes rested on Lydia. For one moment she stared in disbelief then she jumped to her feet, saying something to David as she did so, and hurried across the dining room.

'Lydia! This is a surprise.' She leaned forward and kissed her cousin on the cheek. 'What are you doing here? When did you arrive?'

'Just a few hours ago. A short visit to see my beloved Whitby.'

David thought he had caught the word 'Lydia' when Isobel had left the table but wasn't sure.

But as he turned in his chair to let his gaze follow Isobel it was confirmed. He jumped to his feet and joined the cousins.

'I don't believe it. What brings you back?' he asked.

'Just arrived on a short visit, nothing special.' Lydia smiled to herself for David was blushing like a naughty boy caught in some misdemeanour.

'She was pining for Whitby,' trilled Isobel, her eyes sparkling with laughter and pleasure at seeing her cousin. 'You are just starting your meal. Come and have it with us.'

'I don't want to intrude.'

'You won't be. Will she, David?'

'No, of course not. I'll arrange it.' He turned away and a moment later was in earnest conversation with one of the servers.

Once they were settled Lydia immediately asked about her uncle and aunt.

After what she had said when she and Luke were turned out of their home by Nathan, Isobel knew it was only a courtesy enquiry.

'They are very well, thank you.'

'And Cousin Christopher?'

'He is in good health too and will be thrilled to know I have seen you.'

'And your mother and father?' Lydia queried of David.

'The same,' he replied stiffly, knowing that Lydia had no liking for them either.

'I do not send my regards to them nor to my uncle so neither of you need tell them you have seen me.'

332

There was a moment of silence.

'Very well, Lydia,' said Isobel. 'Now we have those enquiries out of the way we can talk without rancour about ourselves. You know, I do miss you so.'

'And I you,' Lydia returned, letting her eyes stray to David and wondering how he'd interpret her look. Would he take it as a reproach for his attitude when she'd left Whitby?

'Tell us how you are getting on in Middlesbrough. What's it like? How is Luke? Does he like his job?'

Isobel rattled out these questions as the meal proceeded and Lydia answered without giving any information away about the recent scheme she had instigated.

Their talk moved to what had been happening in Whitby since she had gone to Middlesbrough. Though she knew some of the gossip from David's letters Lydia made no reference to receiving them.

Gradually she steered the conversation to the commercial life of the port. 'Anything new or exciting happening?'

Isobel chuckled, 'You always were one to take an interest in your father's business.'

Lydia shrugged her shoulders. 'That's the way I'm made.'

'Things are very much the same as when you left,' put in David. She felt that he said it with a little more haste than was necessary. Was he trying to hide something?

'I'm not sure about that, David,' said Isobel. 'Your father and mine have had several meetings but I don't know what they were about.'

Lydia was alert to this snippet. 'Really?' She registered her surprise. 'I thought Uncle was very much a loner.'

'He is but...'

'I don't think there's been any real progress,' put in David. 'Father hasn't said anything to me.'

Though she would have liked to probe further, to test if David was covering something up, Lydia thought better of it and asked for news of the Chambers family who had become noted for their marine paintings, one of whom had depicted one of her father's ships at sea.

The rest of the evening passed amiably and a relaxed atmosphere transcended recent tensions as friendly childhood days were recalled.

When Isobel and David were leaving, Lydia managed to whisper to her cousin, 'Come to tea, three o'clock tomorrow.'

Isobel squeezed her hand in acknowledgement.

With that little intrigue over, she smiled to herself when David seized his moment to say in an urgent, don't-deny-me tone, 'I must see you. Tomorrow, ten o'clock?' She read his relief as she pressed his elbow, conveying her acceptance.

The timepieces of Whitby were showing the hour of ten when David strode into the Angel the next morning to find Lydia waiting for him.

'Good morning, my love.' He deliberately used the endearment as he swept his hat from his head and bowed to her. He hoped that it would counteract the term he had used when addressing Isobel the previous evening.

334

'Good morning,' returned Lydia in a tone into which he could read nothing. But her heart had given a little flutter when she saw him and she realised she still held a deep affection for him.

'I see you are anticipating a walk?' he said, noting her three-quarter-length, waist-fitting coat over a full-skirted dress. Their colours of brown and beige complemented each other and were brightened by red velvet trimmings. Her bonnet was small, worn to the back of her head, revealing hair flowing neatly from a centre parting. A red ribbon, tied under the chin, secured the bonnet to her head. 'And might I say how charming you look.'

Lydia smiled. The same David, attentive, observant, oozing charm to match his handsome, neat appearance. 'That's a new coat since I saw you, David.' She admired his redingote-style overcoat with its astrakhan collar. His trousers were striped in muted colours and his hat grey to match his coat.

'You are observant and have a good memory. It gives me pleasure that you remember.' His eyes were searching for her reaction but Lydia gave nothing away.

'Shall we walk?' he said, and offered his arm.

She took it and they left the hubbub of the inn.

'You've escaped your father's eye,' she said, and immediately regretted the touch of sarcasm in her voice.

'Things have changed, Lydia,' he replied, a slightly hurt note in his tone.

'I'm sorry, David. I shouldn't have said what I did.' She felt contrite. 'How have they changed?'

'I have much more authority within the firm.'

'I am pleased to hear that.'

'I insisted that if Father expected me to take the interest he was demanding then it should be with more responsibility.'

'Good. And does that include courting Isobel?' Lydia could not resist the question.

David ignored it. Instead he suggested that they walk on the East Cliff. 'It's more private,' he added.

'And we need privacy, do we?'

'I would like it.'

'Very well, the East Cliff it is.' Lydia felt a little flutter inside. This had always been one of their favourite walks.

They left Baxtergate and crossed the bridge to the east side. The streets were thronged with folk going about their daily business but David was expert at guiding her among them. It brought back memories to Lydia.

They reached the one hundred and ninety-nine steps leading up to the ancient parish church and climbed them steadily, pausing now and then to look back over the red roofs of the houses which climbed the cliffside as if they were reaching for the sky and freedom from the crowded conditions below. At the top they turned along the path among the graves, memorials to lives dictated by the sea. Beyond the cemetery the path took them to the cliff edge, dominated by the ruins of the ancient abbey, home to Benedictine monks in Norman times. Lydia, as she had always done when walking beside it, imagined them singing their office and finding peace in their communication with God.

But this path also brought back personal memories of the day when David had first told her he loved her. Then the future seemed to be mapped out for them, their marriage certain. But the death of her father and David's reaction had stunned her and changed all that. Was he now wanting to make amends for his treatment of her, or was there another reason for his wanting to see her this morning? Was he going to tell her that Isobel was now the girl in his life, the girl he would marry? He still had not answered the question she had put before they decided to come to the East Cliff.

She paused and looked out over a tranquil sea. The waves hardly broke at the foot of the cliffs. The breeze was slight but it held a sharp nip and she turned up the collar of her coat for extra warmth around her neck. She breathed deep, feeling a sense of well-being as the cool sea air filled her lungs.

'I miss this, David,' she said wistfully. 'So different from the grime and smoke pumped out by the ironworks.' She sighed. 'But that's where Luke's job is.'

'Maybe you'll return here one day.'

'Who knows what life holds?' She shook off the nostalgic feeling. There was something she had to know. 'You didn't answer my question about Isobel?'

He tightened his lips as if reluctant to answer. Eventually he did. 'The answer is no, but I have been seeing her quite a lot lately.'

'Why, if you are not courting her? You seemed

337

on intimate terms yesterday evening before you knew I was there.'

'We're very good friends.'

'Does Isobel see it as just that?'

'I don't know.'

'David! You don't know?' Lydia frowned at him.

'As far as I am concerned our two families have always been linked by the ties of friendship.'

Suspicion was instantly roused in Lydia's mind. 'What are you telling me, David? Friendship between two members of merchant families such as yours and Isobel's often means someone somewhere is wanting to take advantage of a marriage.'

David looked embarrassed. Lydia saw it and knew she had struck home.

'That's it! Your father again. I can see him behind this.' Her voice had risen, her eyes blazed angrily. 'I was all right for you until I had nothing, no firm and no trade to bring as my dowry. Now it's Isobel he wants for you because my uncle has a thriving business. I thought you said things had changed?'

'They have! They have!'

'Oh, yes, you may be right about having more authority but you're still dictated to by him for his own ends. David, be a man and leave him.'

'I can't. My whole future is with the business. Leave and I have nothing and never will. I'll be cut off forever. That's no future for us.'

'Then you see a future with Isobel?' she cried.

'No! I'm only complying with his wish to be friendly, no more. Father would like a closer relationship between the two firms. Isobel means no more to me than that.'

'And when this deal between your parents, whatever it is, is completed, your relationship with Isobel will end?'

'Yes.'

Lydia looked disgusted. 'You're using her to meet your father's demands.'

'No, that's not the way of it. You know that your cousins and I have always been friendly, even when you were here.'

'But now I'm not in Whitby, has something stronger developed between you and Isobel?'

'No, Lydia, no. You are the one I think about. You are the reason I am trying to win my father's favour so that he will be more easily persuaded that I should marry you, the girl I love.'

'Will he ever agree, I wonder?' There was a contemptuous note in her voice.

'Just give me a chance to work this out my way. Everything will be all right eventually and I will be able to give you the life you deserve.' As he was speaking he took hold of her shoulders and eased her closer.

She did not pull away. Realising that she had not resisted, she knew she still felt something for him, that she wanted to believe him and that their future lay together.

'Lydia, it's you I love. I always have, even since schooldays. You know that. The future will be right for us...'

'So long as I bring something to satisfy your father,' she broke in.

'I want only you,' said David. His eyes never left

hers as he pulled her close and let his arms slide to her waist. His lips came down to her willing upturned mouth. They met hers with a ferocity born of passion as if he was determined to convince her of his love for her.

Lydia strove to let his kiss banish the confusion from her mind, where images of her father, her uncle and David's father were obliterated by Sean's smile and the words he had said to her in the small world of a ship's cabin.

Their lips parted. 'I love you.' His words were whispered but each was clear and filled with devotion.

Then their lips met again and Lydia longed for her own feelings to match what he had just expressed. Maybe Sean's success would bring her riches enough to surmount Jonas's opposition. It was on the tip of her tongue to tell him she was involved with Mr Bolckow but she held back, remembering that this venture must be kept a secret so that she could manipulate it as a tool for her revenge.

Thoughts of what had happened on the cliff were still occupying Lydia's mind when she awaited the arrival of her cousin that same afternoon.

She had asked that Isobel be shown to her room on arrival and that tea should be served ten minutes later.

Affectionate greetings were exchanged on Isobel's arrival, and after she had shed her outdoor clothes they fell into an animated conversation filled with local gossip.

The flow was halted when the maid, neat in her

black dress and white apron, brought them tea with fresh scones and home-made cakes.

Lydia seized her chance to ask her cousin, 'Do you and David see much of each other?'

'We have lately,' replied Isobel.

'You like him?'

'Like is probably the right word.' Isobel's lips were touched with a small smile. 'Are you wondering where you stand with him?'

Lydia shrugged her shoulders, trying to convey the impression that she didn't care.

'Oh, come now, cousin,' said Isobel. 'You were sweet on him until you went to Middlesbrough. Now you're wondering if I'm stepping in.'

Lydia gave a grunt. 'Things changed when Father died. Because I was left with nothing, his father forbade talk of marriage and pressured David to forget me. David should have stood up to him. However, that's the way things are. I thought when I saw you two together yesterday evening...'

'David's very attentive, kind, considerate, fun to be with. I enjoy his company. We have some pleasant times together but I don't feel any more for him than friendship.' She gave a thoughtful little pause. 'You know, Lydia, there are times when I think I am being used. No, not by David. That both of us are being used.'

'How do you mean?'

'That our relationship is being encouraged.'

'By both sets of parents?'

'Yes, but more as if the fathers are behind it.'

'A business alliance through a family union?' suggested Lydia.

341

'If that is so then David would have to know about it,' Isobel pointed out.

'Maybe he does and is a willing partner.'

'But he has never mentioned marriage.'

'Maybe he will. Maybe the time is not yet right. It might be if your fathers initiate a business partnership.'

Isobel looked thoughtful. 'I suppose you could be right.'

'Then pressure will be brought to bear on you and David.'

Isobel showed anxiety.

Lydia, keen as she was to know what her cousin's answer would be, suppressed that desire and instead fished for information she thought more vital to her at this moment, but quickly realised that Isobel knew nothing of any use to her.

Although there were many questions teeming in Lydia's mind to which she would dearly love answers, she deemed it unwise to press further. Besides, she doubted her cousin would have the details. She would have to find other ways to elicit the information she desired.

Chapter Fourteen

Sean had had a contented night's sleep but when he awoke his mind was filled with the events of yesterday and the questions which had been raised in his mind. He decided that his enquiries might go further than strictly required by Lydia.

After enjoying a hearty breakfast he went outside to find Tim waiting for him.

'I've a number of people I want to see. I want you to take me to them.' Sean held out a piece of paper.

Tim ignored it. His head drooped. 'Can't read,' he muttered.

Sean cursed himself for overlooking that possibility and embarrassing the boy. 'Sorry about that,' he said.

Tim, worried that he might lose the chance of earning, looked up quickly. 'Read 'em out, sir. I've a good memory.'

Sean seized on this suggestion to get him out of what had become an awkward situation. 'Right, listen carefully.' He looked at the sheet of paper. 'Mr Wesley of Wesley and Harcourt.'

'Grape Lane,' put in Tim quickly to impress his employer.

'Correct,' replied Sean, and continued, 'Mr Brewster of Baxtergate. Mr Wright, Cliff Street.'

'Which Wright?' interposed Tim.

'Ah, yes. L.'

Tim nodded.

'Mr Medd, Church Street. Mr Parker of Parker and Parsons, Market Place. Mr Brook, Old Market Place. Mr J. Murray, Flowergate. And Mr B. Webster, also of Baxtergate.'

'Got them,' replied Tim brightly.

'Good. Now, I don't mind which order we visit the rest but I must call on Mr Wesley first,' Sean said, in order to follow Lydia's instruction that this gentleman must be his first contact.

'Right, sir, follow me.'

Tim started off from the White Horse along Church Street in the direction of Bridge Street. Whitby's population was already about its daily business. Shops were open and shopkeepers were shouting their wares to attract custom. Dock workers hurried to the ships they were to unload; others had already bent their backs and flexed their muscles to fill the holds with produce bound for London. Boats were tying up, bringing bustle to the quay, so that their night's catch could be brought quickly to young women eager to earn a penny or two gutting fish.

Before they reached the bridge Tim stopped at the corner of Grape Lane.

'Yonder,' he pointed at the second door on the left, 'Wesley and Harcourt.' Sean nodded. 'Ask for Mr Wesley. He's just gone in.'

Sean raised his eyebrows at this information. 'Know your merchants, do you?'

'Aye, I keep my eyes and ears open.' The boy gave a knowing little smile.

'Wait here for me.'

'I'll see you come out even if you don't see me.'

No doubt you will, thought Sean as he walked to the door to the offices owned by Messrs Wesley and Harcourt.

When he reached it, Sean hesitated. He felt a little flutter of nervousness. This was something new to him. He had rehearsed in his mind how he would go about the approach he would make, but now his boldness seemed to have vanished. He was on the threshold of a new chance to advance himself, another step on the road to his dreams. Lydia had... He cut off that thought. No!

344

This was a move towards fulfilling the promises he had made to Eileen. But if that became known to Lydia would it stall the chance she had given him? He drew in a deep breath and put his own problems firmly to the back of his mind.

He opened the door and entered a small room with a counter. A clerk looked up from the ledger in which he was writing, pinched the spectacles from his nose and came to attend to Sean. He was a thin man with slightly hunched shoulders. He blinked as he said, 'Good day, sir. What can I do for you?'

'I would like to see Mr Wesley,' said Sean, firmly but politely.

'May I ask your reason?'

'Please tell him that Mr Sean Casey wishes to discuss matters concerning Tees Shipping, a firm actively engaged in trading in the North East.'

'Yes, sir.'

The clerk disappeared through a door behind him to re-emerge a few moments later. 'Would you like to come this way, sir?' He raised one end of the counter to allow Sean to pass through. He then opened a door and announced, 'Mr Casey, sir.'

The office was a large square room with two mahogany desks set aslant across each corner of the room and facing the door, with a long window set in the middle of the wall opposite Sean. On one desk was a neat arrangement of papers, pens, pencils and notebooks. The other was completely empty.

'Good day, sir,' said Sean, as he crossed the room towards the man coming from behind his

345

desk to greet him. 'It is kind of you to see me.'

'And good day to you.' The man's smile was cheery, broadening what was already a round chubby face. There was a bright and friendly air in his pale blue eyes, but Sean felt their assessment of him and knew that their charm probably hid the workings of a shrewd mind.

'Tees Shipping? I've not heard of them,' said Mr Wesley as he indicated a chair to Sean.

'We are based at Middlesbrough and see great prospects in the development of trade on the river.'

Mr Wesley nodded thoughtfully as he returned to his seat behind the desk.

'How might that interest me?'

'Well, sir, the name of your firm came to us as one interested in maritime investments. If your partner is due in later today, maybe it would be best if I returned then.'

'Ah. Your informant has somewhat misguided you. I am the sole owner of the firm. There is no Mr Harcourt now. I need not go into detail, sufficient to say that he had to move to the south of England. So, Mr Casey, I am the one to make all decisions. And, yes, it is true I am interested in sound investments. But you'll have to convince me.'

An hour later the two men shook hands over a deal and Sean had in his possession a note that Mr Wesley would take three-sixteenths share in the new vessel.

'I suppose you are making this offer to other merchants in Whitby?' said Mr Wesley.

'Yes, sir, the sooner all the shares have been

taken, the sooner we can start trading.'

'Oh, I think you'll find receptive minds in Whitby, Nathan Middleton would certainly be interested, but I warn you, he'll cast a very probing eye over the enterprise.'

'And his brother?'

'Ah, sadly, no. He died and his firm no longer exists.'

Sean put on a look of surprise. 'Oh, dear, my informant is certainly not up to date.' He made a little grimace. 'And no family to carry on?'

'Well, there was a son and a daughter. I've no doubt they would have done well but they could get no backing because their father had left the firm in deep debt and the bankers feared they might do the same.' Mr Wesley shook his head sorrowfully. 'Real tragedy. Tristram's ship was lost with all hands and that broke him. There were those who said he had committed suicide but, if that had been the case, his children would not have received the insurance money.'

'So they were able to pay off his debts?'

'Aye, but had to sell everything to make up the balance. They were left penniless. And to pile on the agony, Mr Nathan turned his nephew and niece out of the house in which they were living.'

'But could he do that?' queried Sean.

'Apparently the house belonged to him and he wanted it.' Mr Wesley shrugged his shoulders. 'And that was it. A great pity. Mr Tristram was a much kinder man than his brother, liked by everyone. So now you know the type of man you have to deal with if you go to Mr Nathan Middleton.'

'Well, thank you for that, sir. Maybe I won't have to approach Mr Middleton,' said Sean, rising from his chair. 'And thank you for your time. I am certain you won't regret investing with Tees Shipping.'

'I hope not, Mr Casey. I trust you will make sure I am satisfied with the investment I have made.'

The two men shook hands and Sean left the office. He was pleased with himself. His patter and charm had worked. He had persuaded Mr Wesley to take three-sixteenths, better than he had expected. If he could do it once he could do it again. His confidence was high. But he had also gained some new knowledge regarding Lydia's father and what had caused her to leave Whitby. In the light of what he had seen of her yesterday that knowledge was worth considering, even investigating.

When he stepped outside Tim was nowhere to be seen but within a matter of moments he was by Sean's side.

He saw two other possible investors that morning, one of whom took a sixteenth share while the other showed no interest whatsoever.

He saw one possible client in the afternoon who was willing to take another sixteenth. Sean then decided that Tim should show him something of Whitby, during which he located the place appointed to meet Lydia the next day.

As they walked on the west pier, Sean put a question to his guide. 'Do you know Mr Middleton?'

'There's two,' returned Tim quickly, then

corrected himself. 'Nay, one, t'other's dead.'

'Oh,' said Sean in feigned ignorance.

'Aye. Mr Tristram died. It's Mr Nathan...' Tim cocked an eyebrow at Sean. 'But he ain't on the list you read out.'

'I know. But I've had his name mentioned to me.'

Tim gave a grunt. 'Wouldn't recommend seeing him meself,' he growled. 'Nasty man. Gave me a clip round my lughole rather than pay me for an errand I ran for him. Said I'd been too slow – I hadn't, it was an excuse so he didn't have to pay.'

'Was his brother like that?'

'Nay, not him. Always free with his pennies. Pity it wasn't Mr Nathan that drowned.'

'What happened?'

'Fell off the end of this pier. Though there are those who said he jumped 'cos he'd lost his ship.'

'Do you know where he fell?'

'Aye. Near the lighthouse at the end of the pier.'

When they reached the spot Sean looked it over carefully. He realised that losing one's footing here could prove fatal, but the situation set his mind exploring other possibilities for Mr Tristram Middleton's death and he tried to link them with what he knew of Lydia.

Even as he lay in bed that night they kept drifting back into his mind. Supposition followed supposition with little to commend them, but Sean let them come and go, taking the view that sometimes the unlikely proves to be the truth.

The following morning Tim was waiting for him

outside the White Horse. He remembered there were four names remaining on the list and led Sean to the first of them in Baxtergate.

By one o'clock Sean could look back on a satisfactory morning. He had found two more interested parties, each willing to take a sixteenth share in the ship. Only one more to dispose of but, with two refusals, he had exhausted the names he had been given. Maybe Lydia would make another suggestion when he saw her in two hours. He paid Tim, bringing an extra wide smile to the youngster's face when he doubled the money he'd promised. Then Sean returned to the White Horse, where he dined on bread and cheese and apple pie washed down with a pint of the landlord's best ale.

With his hunger assuaged, and having the satisfaction of knowing he had almost achieved his task, he was in a state of well-being as he strolled across the bridge. Oblivious to the flow of people, he paused a moment to survey the activities along the river banks and wondered what part in all of this Lydia was preparing to play. He had come to the conclusion that there was more in her mind than merely shipping ironstone from Whitby to Middlesbrough. She had seen her father trade on a much broader horizon. Was she set on emulating him? Or was there something more to it than that? She would rival her uncle for whom he knew she had no love, having been turned out of her home. But was she intent on developing that rivalry for more sinister purposes? Was there a link here to her father's death?

Sean continued his stroll. He turned into Saint Ann's Snaith, unaware that he had caught the eye of David Drayton who was nearing the bottom of Golden Lion Bank.

David's footsteps faltered, suspicion flooding into his mind at the sight of the man from Middlesbrough who had brought him that first letter from Lydia. What was he doing here? Was there some connection with Lydia's presence or was it mere coincidence? His lips tightened as he recalled the questions which had come to his mind when the letter had been delivered. He had wondered then if she had a liking for the man she had entrusted with the letter. Now they were both in Whitby at the same time. Yesterday Lydia's kisses had allayed any doubt he had of her love for him, but now... David took a watch from his waistcoat pocket and glanced at it. He gave a nod of satisfaction. He had time.

He diverted from his intended path and turned into St Ann's Snaith. He could make out Sean a short distance ahead and matched his pace.

They went down Haggersgate with high buildings rising on both sides, imparting a claustrophobic feeling. This was relieved as they emerged on to the Promenade.

David hesitated. Was this just a pleasure stroll? Was the Irishman on an errand which would mean nothing? He was about to turn back when he noticed Sean quicken his pace. It was much more purposeful now, as if he had suddenly realised he was late for an appointment. David decided he would continue his shadowing.

When Sean walked beyond the projection

known as Scotch Head it was obvious that he was making for the west pier. David modified his pace. In the more open space and with fewer people around it was easy to see Sean. A few moments later David drew up sharply. A lady was standing at the side of the pier looking over the waves rolling on to the beach. She turned. Lydia!

David stiffened and his lips tightened into a grim line when he saw her smile, take Sean's arm and fall into step beside him as they strolled towards the end of the pier. He watched them for a few moments. They were in earnest conversation. They stopped. She kissed him!

Fury almost overwhelmed him. He half started forward, but thought better of making a public display of his disappointment. He swung round and walked briskly back the way he had come, anger in every step.

'I hope I haven't kept you waiting,' said Sean when he reached Lydia. 'I got carried away by the sights of Whitby.'

She shrugged. 'I've been here only a few minutes. I was enjoying the sea air, and it also gave me time to think.' She took his arm and he matched his stride to hers as she turned along the pier. 'Well?' she asked eagerly. 'How have you got on?'

'All shares taken except one-sixteenth,' he replied, a note of satisfaction in his voice.

'What?' Lydia stopped and stared at him with a touch of disbelief.

'It's true,' he proclaimed. 'A spot of Irish charm worked wonders.'

'That's marvellous.' She pushed herself on to her toes and gave him a quick kiss, her joy temporarily overcoming the dictates against such a display in public.

Sean's hands came to her waist. He held her close, eyes dancing with pleasure. For a moment she hesitated then slipped free from him but, still holding his arm, continued their stroll.

'Tell me who?'

Sean related in detail what had happened, leaving out the details he had gleaned for his own purposes.

'So, if you have anyone else in mind who I can approach, I'm sure I'll be able to dispose of the final share. What about your uncle? Surely he...'

'I told you, not my uncle.' Her voice was sharp. He could even detect hatred there. Did that link up with what he had learned?

'Mr Drayton then?'

'Nor him.' Her voice still held that sharp edge.

Was there some connection between the two men that roused this feeling in her? Sean was anxious to know more but he could not question her, for he knew from her demeanour that he would receive no answers.

'There's no need for you to try to sell the remaining sixteenth. It slipped my mind to tell you that it is likely that Kevin will invest with us.'

'Kevin?' Sean feigned surprise.

'Yes. When Sarah's father was interested she thought Kevin might be too.'

'Then it's as well I didn't sell the remaining share otherwise Kevin would have been disappointed. But are you sure he can raise the

353

money? After all, he is just...'

'...not what you think,' broke in Lydia. 'His family in Ireland are quite well off.'

Sean raised his eyebrows. 'You know?'

'Yes, there's no need to keep his secret from me.'

'So what now? Do I return to Middlesbrough tomorrow, or do we return together?'

'Not together. You go tomorrow. I have other things to see to here.'

Other things? Sean's curiosity was roused. He would dearly love to know what they were but his chances of finding out would be curtailed by leaving unless...

'Do we celebrate this evening?' he asked hopefully.

'No.'

This was obviously the person in control speaking, the person who was running the enterprise. Sean felt he had been put in his place. He sensed she held a secret she did not want him to know about, and that it had its roots in Whitby.

Throughout the rest of the afternoon, David could not concentrate on what he was doing. His actions were automatic. He contributed nothing to the meeting of a committee set up to encourage expansion of trade through Whitby. His mind was too preoccupied with what he had witnessed on the west pier, and whether he should disclose this knowledge immediately on seeing Lydia that evening.

His attention was sharpened only after the meeting closed and members sat around chatting

354

in general terms while finishing their drinks.

'Anyone been approached to invest in Tees Shipping?' someone asked.

Two members indicated that they had.

'Seemed a very sound investment with Mr Bolckow and Mr Vaughan backing it,' commented one of them.

'Likeable young Irishman,' added the other. 'He certainly had the gift of the gab, but he was sound enough with his facts and figures.'

David's mind was brought sharply to what was being said.

'Neither I nor my father was approached,' he put in casually.

'The Irishman...' The speaker hesitated slightly as if trying to think of a name. 'Er ... Sean Casey was looking specifically for investors in a ship which he was proposing would move ironstone from Whitby to Middlesbrough. All the shares must have been taken before he got to you. Bad luck, David.'

He gave a nod, accepting the explanation. 'But Martin is doing that.'

'Seems Bolckow and Vaughan need more.'

'I've never heard of Tees Shipping,' said David. 'Has it been trading long?'

'Newly founded as far as I could gather but there must be potential for the two iron men to invest.'

The conversation drifted but the facts were turning over in David's mind. They were still doing so when he returned home to prepare to meet Lydia for dinner at the Angel. He did not like what he had heard and seen and was now determined to tackle her.

'You are looking exquisite, my dear.' David was his usual polite and charming self when he arrived at the Angel.

But Lydia saw a difference in his eyes. Usually tranquil on such occasions, this evening they were tinged with a sharp expression as if they were searching. For what?

'A new dress?' he noted.

'Purchased today, especially for your visit,' returned Lydia, her voice smooth.

'I'm flattered.' He ran his eyes over the light blue twilled silk with wide borders of dark blue velvet. The square neckline came to the top of her breasts and the puff sleeves were tight to her wrists. She wore a jet necklace and carried a white shawl. 'You've had a pleasant day?' he asked.

'I enjoyed seeing Whitby again and visited Mrs Harrington.'

'She would be pleased to see you,' he said as he escorted her into the dining room.

'Yes. I was glad to find her in good health.'

They were shown to a table already set for a meal. He remained standing until he saw she was seated comfortably.

'You saw Isobel again?' he asked as he sat down.

'Yes, we had tea together.'

'Here?'

'Where else? You know I would not step over my uncle's threshold, and especially now that he has moved into the house I still regard as mine.'

'He has the law on his side,' David reminded her.

Lydia frowned. She knew he was right. 'The idea of him in that house which Father thought so much of galls me.' The venom in her voice was not lost on David. He had hoped her time in Middlesbrough would have eased her hatred, but it appeared not to have done so. And her return to Whitby, even for just a visit, had apparently only heightened the way she felt.

'And you'd do anything to get it back?'

'Of course!' The words came out sharply and before she could stifle them. She chastised herself. She must be careful not to give too much away.

'Have you something in mind?'

Lydia eyed him cautiously. He was probing too much. She merely shrugged her shoulders, and was thankful that the serving-girl came for their order.

During the meal conversation drifted between Whitby and Middlesbrough until David's enquiries about Luke and his work enabled him to mention Sean in a casual way.

'The Irishman who delivered your first letter to me after you had gone to Middlesbrough...' He halted as if searching for a name.

'Sean Casey,' Lydia automatically prompted.

'That's him. I hear he's in Whitby raising interest in a ship.'

'Is he?' She feigned surprise.

David fixed his eyes on her. He needed to observe her reaction to what he was going to say next. 'You know he's in Whitby.'

357

Lydia tensed. 'What do you mean?'

'Exactly what I said. I saw you with him on the west pier.'

'Oh.' There was casual regret in the way she uttered the word, and David read the same in her expression.

'Then you don't deny it?' The edge to his voice was sharpened by her relaxed attitude, as if she didn't care that he knew. 'How could you after what we said to each other yesterday?' His eyes bore hurt and anger.

'It's not what you think, David.'

Unable to detect whether her outward sincerity was real or assumed, he gave a contemptuous sneer. 'That's what I expected you to say.'

She placed her knife and fork on her plate and leaned forward, resting her arms on the table. She adopted a purposefully no-nonsense attitude. 'From what you saw, and I presume you are including the kiss I gave him, you could not begin to understand what it was all about.'

'I conclude from what I saw that you have feelings for this man,' he said coldly.

'Not in the way you mean. I like him. He has done a good job for me, and for that I am grateful and respect him.'

'Job?' He gave another little laugh of disbelief. 'What are you dreaming up now to exonerate yourself?'

Lydia stiffened at the disbelief in his voice. 'Hear me out. If you still don't believe me or don't like what you hear then I'll walk away, out of your life for good.'

David read determination in her delivery. He

358

knew that in moments of crisis Lydia was her own woman. She would stand or fall by her decisions, or by the things she had caused to happen. There was nothing he could do but listen to her or their relationship, which he had thought strong again, would be destroyed forever. He nodded. 'Convince me that what I saw meant nothing.'

'It was a spur-of-the-moment reaction. I was pleased to hear what he had achieved for me.'

'Achieved for you? Was I not here in Whitby? Could I not have done whatever it was?' There was still anger in his voice.

'No, you couldn't. What Sean did will in the end benefit you and me, David.'

'Me?' He was puzzled. How could he be involved in whatever had gone on, or was still going on, between Sean Casey and the woman he loved?

'Yes. Now hear me out. I needed to get people interested in investing in a new ship.' She went on to tell him how this had come about. 'When Luke and I needed to raise capital after Father's death no one would back us. You can't have forgotten that? Now, if I had come to Whitby to try to raise capital for a new ship, I believe I would still have been regarded with suspicion. So I had to have someone else to do it – Sean Casey. When you saw us on the pier he was making his report to me, and highly satisfactory it was. He had disposed of all the shares in the first ship to be owned by Tees Shipping.'

David had concentrated on her every word. They all sounded so convincing. But there was one thing left unexplained. 'You said that what you were doing would be for my benefit also, but

Casey didn't approach me.'

'I told him not to.' She did not proceed to enlighten him on this but said, 'Don't you see, David? If what I am doing is a success your father can have no objection to our marriage.'

His eyes brightened with the realisation of what lay behind her scheme. 'But why not come forward now?'

'Two reasons. The enterprise might fail, and I don't want that humiliation again. If it was known in Whitby that I was involved in Tees Shipping, my uncle would know and he would not be pleased that I was in opposition to him. He would take every precaution to offset any harm I might do him. Try to see that we did not succeed.' At the mention of her uncle her voice had grown cold. 'I do not want you to mention what I have told you to anyone. It must be kept a strict secret between us.' Her tone left him no doubt that she was serious.

'You have my oath,' he said, a solemn promise in his voice which was matched in his eyes. He picked up his glass and raised it to her. 'May you succeed for the sake of our future together.'

Chapter Fifteen

Sean stood at the rail as the *Nina* was manoeuvred downriver on the noon tide towards the sea. Sailors went about their allotted tasks under the watchful eye of the captain with an efficiency he admired.

As his gaze scanned Whitby's east side, he had a pleasurable sense of achievement at having completed Lydia's task to her satisfaction. Not only that, he was pleased he had gained some new knowledge about her, though it disturbed him.

He liked Lydia. In the light of what had happened in the captain's cabin on their voyage to Whitby he had thought they might even enjoy a deeper relationship. But from her attitude towards him in Whitby he had begun to wonder if that interlude had been only a means of persuading him to help her. What he had learned since only strengthened that view. It had shocked him. Was Lydia a manipulator, using people for her own ends? He had known there was toughness behind that ladylike exterior, but now he wondered if it was tinged with ruthlessness and a determination to get her own way at any cost.

His gaze settled on Burgess Pier and the smoke rising from the kipper houses situated at its head. A figure moved along the pier. His eyes narrowed as he stared into the distance. Lydia! Was she there on purpose to see him sail? As a lover saying goodbye? Or to make sure that he had left Whitby? He let his gaze settle on her, travelling over the water as if it was not there. She must have felt his eyes upon her. She lifted her arm and gave a small wave of her hand. He raised his and then doffed his hat in return. He bowed his farewell and when he looked up again could sense the amused smile on her lips, though she was too far away for him to see it clearly.

With the wish that he could came the return of his former troubled thoughts. As the ship met the first undulations of the sea and sails were unfurled to take advantage of the freshening breeze, away from the shelter of the cliffs, he wished he had someone he could confide in, someone with whom he could talk through his thoughts.

Luke? But he would support his sister. Maybe he was even involved in what Sean judged to be Lydia's schemes. Kevin? He would be a sympathetic listener, maybe even offer advice, but that would be tempered by his feelings for Sarah who was very friendly with Lydia. Kevin would not want to upset his sweetheart. But he was still the most likely to listen and offer advice about what Sean surmised and what he had gleaned from Drayton's clerk.

After his meeting with Lydia on the west pier, Sean had made his way to Drayton's office where he had kept watch for the clerk he remembered from his last visit.

He emerged finally and Sean followed him at a discreet distance. When the man held brief conversations with three separate people, and there seemed to be no urgency about his movements, Sean judged he was not about Drayton's business.

As they neared the Black Bull at the corner of the market place, Sean quickened his step and caught him by the arm. Startled, he reacted with annoyance that was soon replaced by alarm.

'You! What the devil...?'

'In there.' Sean propelled him towards the inn.

'I want to talk.'

'No more messages. I won't do it.' There was alarm in his voice and in his eyes. He tried to shake off Sean's grip.

'No messages,' rapped Sean. 'I just want some information, if you have it. We'll do it over some ale in a quiet corner.'

By then they were at the Black Bull and Sean shoved him inside.

Sean took in the scene with a quick glance. Tobacco smoke hung against the blackened ceiling like thin cloud awaiting a breeze. Several men lounged against the bar which ran the length of one wall. After calling for two pints of the best ale, Sean indicated a vacant alcove.

'Well, good to see you again, Mr...' he said heartily.

'Potter,' the man said automatically. He turned to go but Sean caught hold of him. Potter could do nothing but slide into one of the seats. Sean, his eyes never leaving the clerk, settled on the opposite side of the small table.

'I know nothing, Mr Casey,' muttered Potter, trying to wriggle out of any questioning which might land him into trouble.

'You remember my name. You must have a retentive memory.'

'Well, sir, there was something that made our previous meeting memorable.'

'And this one could be just as memorable, maybe even more so.'

The conversation was halted for a moment as a barman brought two tankards of ale and placed them on the table between them.

Sean raised his. 'Here's hoping your memory continues to be good.'

Potter gave a sly grin. 'Who knows?'

'You move around Whitby carrying messages for your employer. You overhear things outside and in the office. I think you may remember the time I want to know about.'

Potter screwed up his face doubtfully. 'Well, I don't know about that...'

Sean slid his hand into his pocket and drew out a shilling. He placed it on the table where no one could see it except Potter.

'What time are you talking about, sir?'

'The time of Mr Tristram Middleton's death.'

'Mmm.' Potter feigned deep thought.

'He lost a ship, I believe,' put in Sean.

'Aye, he did, with all hands.'

'It broke him?'

'In more ways than one.'

'What's that mean?'

'The debt he faced. I have it on good authority from a man who worked for Mr Tristram that the ship was not insured.'

Sean raised one eyebrow.

'I heard Mr Drayton...' Potter let the words hang in the air and glanced greedily at the coin. Sean slid it across the table and claw-like fingers closed over it. '...say that Mr Tristram had made some bad investments with the money he should have used for insurance.'

'So was there no one who could help him? Not even his own brother?'

Potter gave a grunt. 'Never got on, those two. Mr Nathan's a shrewd businessman but not liked. Why, he even turned his niece and nephew out of their house 'cos he wanted it.'

So it was true. Sean noted the confirmation he had received.

'And they had to sell everything to add to the insurance Mr Tristram had on his life so they could pay off the debts he had incurred.'

'Then his death was fortuitous if you care to look at it like that?'

'Aye, I suppose so.'

'Slipped off the pier, I hear.'

'Well, now, there's some that say so but...' Once more Potter let his words remain unspoken.

Sean read his intent and slipped another shilling across the table where a hand quickly removed it from sight. '...there are those that believe he fell on purpose but made it look like an accident so that the insurance money would help his children.'

Sean nodded his understanding of this theory.

'Mind you,' Potter put in quickly, 'them's only rumours. Whoever paid the insurance must have been satisfied that it was an accident.'

'One more question.' Sean leaned over the table and put it quietly. 'Did Mr Tristram approach his brother for help?'

'Aye.'

'That's the truth?'

Potter gave a little grin. 'Oh, I know with certainty.'

'How?'

'We clerks exchange news. Keep our ears open for items we might turn to our own advantage.'

'Like now.'

'If you see it that way.'

Another coin slid across the table.

'Mr Nathan's clerk saw Mr Tristram visit his brother the day after the ship was lost. Told me they had a terrible row, loud enough at the finish for him to hear. Mr Nathan refused to help his brother, called him names he didn't deserve and told him to get out in a voice that held hatred. The clerk saw him leave, said he looked a broken man. Not long after, Mr Tristram was seen to fall from the pier.'

Sean pursed his lips thoughtfully. 'And Tristram's children?'

Potter rose to the prompt, comforted by the three coins in his pocket. 'They visited their uncle. There were more harsh words, especially from Miss Lydia who accused her uncle of causing her father's death by refusing to help him. He laughed at her, but she persisted in her accusation and swore that one day she would get her revenge.'

Sean was gripped by this information.

It returned to his mind now as the *Nina* left the river and took to the sea.

He went over it again and again, trying to connect it with events he had witnessed since meeting Lydia. She and Luke had come to Middlesbrough with nothing. He had a job so they were not poverty-stricken but there was little she could use towards achieving revenge until the formation of Tees Shipping had come about. Now she had something she might be able to use against her uncle. But to compete with him would take time and even then what could she do? Unless she was able to turn circumstances to her advantage...

Sean was troubled. He had met a charming, likeable young woman, but he had also seen a hard, calculating side appear, one which could easily take over if her obsession became too much to control. If it did it could spell disaster for her and Sean did not want to see Lydia destroy herself.

It was early evening, the sky filling with low clouds scudding before a freshening breeze, when the *Nina* docked at Middlesbrough. Though its cargo would be unloaded the next morning, Luke was there to see that there had been no snags in Whitby or on the voyage. When Sean came down the gangway the two friends greeted each other with a warm handshake.

'Thought you might be away for a few days,' commented Luke as they walked away from the jetty, their shoulders hunched against the wind.

'So you must have known about the proposition Lydia was going to put to me?' returned Sean.

'Yes.'

'Therefore you must have approved of keeping her name and yours from being mentioned?'

'Yes. And I suppose she gave you a good enough reason?'

'Indeed.'

'And told you who you should and shouldn't approach?'

'Yes,' replied Sean and, with pride in his voice,

went on to give Luke the names of those who had taken shares in the new enterprise.

'You did well. And you got no reaction from anyone else?'

'No. But it will soon get around that Tees Shipping is venturing into the iron trade. Are you expecting rivals?'

Luke was cautious. 'I think Mr Bolckow and Mr Vaughan will be glad of anybody entering the trade so long as it means more ore for them.' He quickly changed the direction of the conversation. 'When will Lydia be back? I thought she might have come with you.'

'She'll leave tomorrow. She thought it best we weren't seen together.'

Luke nodded. 'Very wise.'

'I suppose you know she offered me a share in the new vessel? And that Kevin is interested too.'

'Yes.' Luke smiled. 'I know all about Kevin. He's in Ireland now arranging his money. Took Sarah with him to meet his family.'

Sean raised an eyebrow. 'Looks as though those two...'

'Yes. Sarah was very kind to him after Seamus was killed, and it seemed to bring them closer.'

'What happens now that Lydia has sold all the shares in the ship? She mentioned a shipbuilding firm, Slater's, does it really exist?'

'Oh, yes, it certainly does. And Lydia made sure they had a ship available. They have one nearing completion. Confident that she would raise sufficient investment, she's already negotiated to buy it.'

Lydia watched the mud flats and salt marshes slide past as the *Amanda* made her way up the Tees towards the jetty close to the Bolckow and Vaughan works. She saw potential in this desolate landscape, an expansion of the industry which these two men had established. Ship more ore, produce more pig iron, process it for all manner of goods, and prosperity could line the banks of the river. There was money to be made here. She would make sure that more ore was shipped from Whitby.

Her eyes narrowed with a vision of others following her lead to take advantage of the demand for ore, and if she knew her uncle he would be one of them. Then she would be able to exploit him. How? That did not occupy her at the moment. She would take advantage of the situation as it developed.

Luke and Sean were at the jetty when the ship docked. She came down the gangway with a quick step and an air of achievement. Sean watched her with desire, Luke with brotherly admiration.

'Sean will have told you of his success?' she said, excitement in every word.

'Yes, he has. He did well to gain support so quickly.'

She offered no further praise, merely nodded and gave Sean a half smile as Luke turned away to have a word with the captain.

'Did you have a good voyage?' asked Sean.

'Yes.'

'Better than the one to Whitby?'

'Neither better nor worse,' she replied, without

a sign that she knew what he was hinting at.

'Mine was the poorer for being on my own,' he replied.

Again she ignored the inference. Instead, seeing Luke return to them, she turned in his direction.

'We have a lot to talk about, I'm sure Sean is capable of seeing to things here.' She linked arms with her brother as if she was taking possession of him.

Luke raised his eyebrows and shrugged his shoulders at Sean as if to say, I can't refuse my sister.

Sean said nothing. He watched them walk away, wondering at Lydia's coldness. It was as if nothing had ever happened between them. In fact, it had looked that way from the moment they had arrived in Whitby. Had she merely used him? Got what she wanted from him and was now casting him aside? Maybe he was making too harsh a judgement. He did not want to be too hard; after all, there were many qualities he admired in her. Maybe the cold, ruthless streak he had witnessed was foreign to her real nature and had only been brought about by the death of her father and harsh treatment from her uncle.

'So the whole visit was successful?' said Luke.

'Yes, far better than expected,' Lydia went on to tell him all that had happened. 'David has promised to keep me in touch with developments in Whitby.'

'No doubt he couldn't refuse you,' said Luke with a grin.

'I made sure of it. And I made him promise that

370

no one should know that you and I are behind Tees Shipping.' Excitement charged her voice as she went on, 'Luke, I feel it in my bones that this is going to be our opportunity to hit Uncle Nathan hard and let Father rest easy in his grave.' Before he could comment she went on, 'I must go to Newcastle and get that ship underway.'

'A crew?'

'That's one reason why I stayed an extra day in Whitby. I saw Captain Anderson, persuaded him to raise a crew to take over the ... we must have a name for her, Luke.'

'How about the *Ironmaster?*'

Lydia looked thoughtful as she pondered the suggestion. 'A good strong-sounding name. Why not? She'll lend strength to our cause.'

'Captain Anderson will take over the *Ironmaster* when she arrives in Whitby, having been brought there by a crew from the shipyard.'

'You had it all worked out.'

'Anticipation gets you on,' returned Lydia.

'Also Captain Anderson knows that our names should never be mentioned in connection with this scheme. He understands that he is employed by Tees Shipping, and, as far as anyone else is concerned, was hired by the gentleman raising the finance – Sean Casey.'

Lydia left the next morning by train for Darlington, where she would change to another for Newcastle. She'd had time to savour this turnaround in her fortunes and was determined that they would never go into decline again.

371

'Eileen, you'll stay with me and my Father.' Sarah made this announcement as their train approached Middlesbrough station.

'But I couldn't impose on you any more than I already have.'

'Nonsense. It's the best solution.'

'But your father...'

She was cut short by Kevin whose knowing smile confirmed his words. 'Don't worry, Sarah can twist him round her little finger.'

'It's a useful asset,' agreed Sarah, a twinkle in her eye.

'In any case, you'll like James,' said Kevin. 'He's a kind man and I know he'll take to you. You'll get on well.'

'Then it's settled,' said Sarah.

'When will I get to see Sean?' asked Eileen.

'If he's back from Whitby, I'll bring him this evening,' promised Kevin.

'Whitby? What has he been doing there?'

'Luke sent him to cheek on the supply of ironstone. He left the day before we did, so he should be back by now.'

'I'll arrange a meal for this evening. Kevin. Don't tell him Eileen is here, let it be a surprise.'

'Good idea.'

'And tell Luke and Lydia to come as well.'

'I'll do that, if she's back.'

'Where has she been?' asked Eileen tartly. 'Whitby, no doubt.'

Kevin, annoyed with himself for letting those words slip out, could only answer, 'Yes, she went to see friends.'

'I suppose they travelled on the same ship?'

372

'Yes. But I don't think that means anything.' Sensing Eileen's jealousy, Sarah tried to sound reassuring.

'I hope not.'

'Sure it's good to see you, Sarah,' said Sean when she greeted him in the hall after the maid had answered his knock on the front door. 'Kevin tells me you had a grand time in Ireland, short though it was.'

'We did,' replied Sarah.

Kevin gave her a wink as he came over. 'Lydia and Luke will be along shortly.' He kissed her on the cheek and whispered in her ear, 'Thought it best to bring him on his own.'

The maid took their coats.

'Father's in the drawing room,' said Sarah and led the way to the door. She opened it and stepped inside followed by Kevin and Sean. Sean closed the door behind him. When he turned round to greet Mr Langton he froze and stared in open-mouthed amazement.

'Hello, Sean.' Eileen's voice was soft but the words were delivered with an unmistakable depth of feeling for the man she addressed.

'Eileen! What? How?' He looked round to find faces smiling at his bewilderment.

She came to him, slotted her arm through his and kissed him on the cheek. 'Arrived today. Kevin and Sarah visited me on their way back and persuaded me to come with them. Not that I took much persuading. So here I am, and thanks to Sarah and Mr Langton more than comfortable.'

'And you are here to stay?' queried Sean, still bemused.

'If you want me to?'

Her query was made lightly but he knew what she was really saying. For one moment thoughts of Lydia loomed in his mind but then were dismissed. Here was the girl who had shared his life in Dublin, who had brought a sparkle to it even in the harshest times and in the face of public criticism. How could he ever have thought of abandoning her for someone else? If he had, his position would have been precarious, not knowing what Lydia really wanted from life. No, here was a girl who knew him, his ways and his dreams, who would give him a devoted and secure marriage. When this last word sprang to mind it jolted him. But in the situation they were now in, among such friends, there were only two options – to part or to marry.

'Of course I want you to. I said I would come for you when things were better. Well, they are decidedly better. Kevin and Sarah have just beaten me to it.' He swung her round and kissed her unashamedly with a fervour that spoke of the old Sean she had known in Dublin. She knew then she had nothing to fear from any rival.

Half an hour later when Lydia and Luke arrived, they found a stranger in the house. Lydia hid her surprise when Eileen was introduced as Sean's sweetheart from Dublin, for he had never mentioned having a close relationship with anyone.

His fears about Lydia's reaction were allayed by

the look she gave him. He knew their liaison on the way to Whitby would never be disclosed by her. For that he was thankful, but he also realised it was proof that she'd had no interest in him other than to use him for her own purposes.

'So, we are celebrating Eileen and Sean's reunion,' Lydia commented when she had been told how this had come about. 'Well, we have something else we can celebrate. I returned from Newcastle yesterday evening. The *Ironmaster*, our new ship, will have sailed for Whitby today. The day after tomorrow should see her bring the first of what I hope will be many cargoes of ironstone for the Bolckow and Vaughan works. And that should mean good profits for those with shares in the ship.'

A buzz of excitement passed through the small gathering.

In a quiet moment, as James Langton charged glasses for a toast, Sean explained to Eileen what lay behind Lydia's statement. 'I have a share in that ship,' he concluded, though he made no reference as to how that had come about.

'Then you are on the way to the future you always dreamed of,' whispered Eileen.

'For you,' he returned.

'You're a fine man, Sean Casey.' There was love in the pressure of her hand on his.

With the *Ironmaster* fully loaded, Captain Anderson prepared to sail from Whitby.

A new ship in the port, built elsewhere, always raised interest locally. Captains between voyages studied the craft; sailors out of a job wished they

375

had been chosen by Captain Anderson to crew her; shipbuilders cast a critical eye over her construction, wondering why, if the ship was to sail from Whitby, they had not been given the work of building her; while merchants were more interested in her cargo and whether they could embark in the same trade. Among them was Nathan Middleton.

He drew on his cigar. 'Another ore ship?' There was scepticism in his tone as he spoke to Aidan Wesley. 'Not Edgar Martin's, surely? He has two already, would have thought that enough for the trade.'

'No. New firm. Tees Shipping. Good prospects.'

Nathan, noting the keen edge to Aidan's tone, eyed him with curiosity. 'You sound enthusiastic. I'm surprised to see you here. Didn't know you had any interest in ships.'

'Ships themselves – not much. But they're part of the life of this port and in that respect I'm interested in what they do and the money they bring to boost Whitby's economy. That's of prime interest to us all.'

'True,' agreed Nathan. 'So why are you sounding so keen on this particular vessel?'

'Haven't you shares in her?'

'No.' Nathan looked mystified.

'You weren't approached?'

'No.'

'Young Irishman. Smart young fellow. Mind, he had a persuasive tongue but there was a genuine knowledge of the situation behind it. Seems there's a growing demand for ore along the Tees,

376

more than Martin can supply, so this Irishman was looking for investors in a new enterprise with the names of Bolckow and Vaughan also involved. Know them, do you?'

Nathan gave a little nod. 'I've heard of them.'

'Well,' continued Aidan, 'with their interest I thought the investment must be sound. I'm surprised you weren't approached.'

Nathan made no comment and a few moments later he said goodbye to Aidan. With his thoughts still on what he had just heard, he headed for his office. He'd make some enquiries about the demand for ironstone. Maybe a switch in his trading pattern would be profitable. If he was to have a closer working relationship with Jonas Drayton, he should also tell him what he had heard about the possibilities opening up in the iron trade.

Chapter Sixteen

My Dearest Lydia

I write again so soon in order to keep you abreast of events in Whitby, especially in connection with your venture.

The port is buzzing with excitement after three voyages by the *Ironmaster* alongside those of Mr Martin's ships. Rumours abound as to the quantity of ore needed along the Tees.

Your uncle has shown great interest and is annoyed that he was not invited to take shares in the ship. Father told him that all the shares may have been snapped up before the Irishman had a chance to approach him. This only heightened his interest. Your uncle is talking about switching his ships to the ironstone trade, and is trying to persuade Father that it will be a better investment than anything else they were discussing.

But Father won't consider doing that. He's being rather crafty. He sees that if your uncle did so the Middleton wine trade with Spain would be there for the taking. Of course, he cannot put that in hand until your uncle moves into the iron ore trade.

These are exciting times in Whitby. I wish you were here to share them. With your venture meeting such success it may be that you will soon be able to declare that to my father and so seal our future together.

I look forward to that day and until then, and beyond, my love is always yours.

David

Lydia read that letter with glee. Though she was reassured by David's declaration of his love, she was more excited to learn that her uncle was on the brink of moving into the ironstone trade. Make that final move and his trading would be in close proximity with hers, enabling her to watch and hopefully, before too long, make a calculated move against him.

Buoyed up by these thoughts and with the need to discuss the situation with her brother she persuaded him that as the day was warm and fine they should spend the afternoon together in the

Eston Hills six miles south of Middlesbrough.

'It'll do you both good to get out into the countryside and the fresh air. You'll be away from all this grime and smoke and be able to hear something other than the din from the rolling mill,' said Nell when Lydia announced what they were proposing to do. 'I'll pack you a picnic – a few sandwiches and a piece of that homemade fruit cake you like. Then you needn't be thinking you'll have to be back by a certain time to eat.'

'You are so kind.' Lydia gave her a hug. 'And you're right, it will be good to get away from all this noise and smoke. I wonder how you stick it.'

'It's where I've lived for ten years, I'd miss it if I left, but you're different. When you returned from Whitby I could tell that you wished you could have stayed. I think you'll go back some day.'

Lydia smiled. 'I believe I will. Maybe one day soon.'

Luke passed a packet to his sister and started to open a similar one himself.

They had found a small outcrop of stones on the hillside and settled themselves on the flattest. The sun shone on their backs. The air was clear and they had enjoyed its purity after the smoke that hovered over Middlesbrough. From where they were sitting they could see the chimneys of the works spewing out smoke which hung in a dense cloud over the houses and buildings. People, dependent on it for their livelihoods, grumbled about it but knew they must tolerate it.

No smoke, no money. No money, no opportunities.

'This is wonderful,' commented Luke, looking over the hillside and drawing fresh air into his lungs. 'I'm glad you persuaded me to come.'

'Well, you haven't been outside Middlesbrough for months. It's time you did. Wouldn't you like to escape all that?' She waved in the direction of the smoke and grime.

'Who wouldn't?' he replied. 'But it was necessary to come here. We needed a living.'

'I know, Luke, and I'm proud of what you have done. But now we have a new chance.'

'You mean Tees Shipping?'

'Yes.'

'But I thought you didn't want our names mentioned in connection with it?'

'That's right, but only until the right moment, when our trading is successful and we will be in a position to avenge Father. That could be sooner than you think. Here, read this.' She handed him the letter from David.

He read it quickly and, with the implications dawning on him, again more slowly. He looked up and handed it back to Lydia.

'Well?' she said.

'I can't believe that Uncle Nathan will concentrate wholly on the ironstone trade.'

'Why else do you think I told Captain Anderson to extol its prospects every time he was in Whitby?'

'You did what?' Luke sat up in astonishment.

'I merely suggested that he might spread the word there were great chances for profits in the ironstone trade as more and more stone is wanted.'

'But you don't know the capacity of the furnaces at Witton, nor if there will be any demand for the quantity they can turn out. Besides, it's a costly operation. At any time Mr Bolckow may decide it is too expensive to ship ore in from Whitby.'

'Where else can he get it?'

'True, he doesn't appear to have another source.'

'Then it's got to be shipped in.'

'But if it proves too expensive he may decide to close down the whole operation.'

'You're being gloomy.'

'No, only practical.'

'Well,' snapped Lydia, irritated by Luke's pessimism, 'that's not likely, in my opinion. Besides, what's more important to us is the fact that Uncle is prepared to invest heavily in the trade.' Her voice was harsh now, eyes narrowed as she dwelt on the vision conjured up by her next statement. 'And that will give us the opportunity to sink him.'

'Lydia!'

'Don't look so shocked, Luke. You have always known that is what I desire. You can't desert Father now!'

'As much as I would like to see Uncle pay in some way, I can't help wondering what Father would have wanted.'

'Revenge!' she cried, passion in her voice.

'Would he? I'm not so sure. Wouldn't he just have got on with life as we have done?'

'He didn't get a chance because of Uncle Nathan.'

'He did have a choice, but he chose...'

'A way to help us,' cut in Lydia sharply. 'Don't ever forget that, Luke.'

'You don't know for certain that it was a deliberate act on his part.'

'I believe it,' she cried. 'Surely you do?'

Luke shook his head. 'Lydia, I don't like what this thirst for revenge is doing to you. It is changing you, making you into two people. There is dear likeable Lydia, the side you show to your friends and the sister I've always known. Then I see someone I don't like, a cold calculating person who is prepared to use people to achieve what she wants.'

'Use people?' She tossed her head. 'I don't do that.'

'You mean, you don't want to believe that.'

'Tell me, how do I?'

'David. You were disgusted that he would not forsake his position in his father's firm yet you played up to him so that he would supply you with information. I wonder whether you reciprocate the love he expresses in that recent letter?'

He waited for her to tell him but instead she prompted, 'And?'

'Captain Anderson. You got him to spread the word that more ironstone is wanted, and that information has only a thin foundation in truth. Sean, by some means, you persuaded to interest people in investing in the *Ironmaster*. As for the investors, your main aim was not to make money

382

for them but to finance a company you could use as a means of revenge.' He paused and looked hard at her. 'Lydia, don't destroy the sister I know.'

She smiled at him, the smile he had always known, the smile filled with warmth and love. 'Luke, don't worry, that sister will always be here. The other woman you think you see will step back the moment I achieve my aim.'

'Very well,' he said, with a resigned shrug of his shoulders. 'If you say so. But be careful, don't antagonise anyone who might be able to hurt you.' With that veiled implication he let the matter drop, and they turned their attention to enjoying the rest of the day.

They took up the packages they had left untouched when Lydia had produced the letter from David, and sat in the warm sunshine enjoying the picnic.

'Yon must be the blast furnaces at Witton.' Luke pointed towards smoke rising in the distance across the river to the northwest.

Lydia acknowledged this and added a question. 'Then why did Mr Bolckow and Mr Vaughan build the rolling mill at Middlesbrough?'

'That was established first when they were importing pig iron from Scotland. When the price of that rose they needed to find another source. They decided to build their own blast furnaces and make their own pig iron.'

'Why at Witton?'

'The proximity of coal in the Durham coalfields and an expected source of ironstone nearby.'

383

'And that didn't materialise?'

'The coal did but the ironstone didn't. Well, not in the quantity they had hoped, so they had to import Grosmont ironstone through Whitby.'

'And that's the situation now, the costly enterprise you talk about?'

'Aye. And it worries Mr Bolckow and Vaughan.'

They lapsed into silence, each surveying the scene before them. The slope of the hills gave way to green fields and grazing cattle, and beyond the river with its huge bend taking it southwards, and just to the east of that the new town of Middlesbrough between the river and the railway.

Street upon street of identical houses crowded together to house the workers of the rolling mill, the pottery and the coal staithes, as near to their workplaces as possible. Lydia could make out the towering chimneys of the rolling mill belching their smoke, creating grime which settled over land and buildings alike and polluted the air. But where it was there was money. Wages to be gained, money to make existence palatable if handled right. But there were those who couldn't, who had little pride in their homes and surroundings, and already sections of the new town were getting a bad reputation for their squalor and unruliness.

Lydia had witnessed it all. She wanted to escape back to her beloved Whitby where she could breathe fresher air and feel the tang of the sea in her lungs. Yet she knew there were other people who would not exchange this busy, grimy town. They enjoyed being part of the rapid growth of an infant industrial centre and did not know that there was every possibility their livelihoods could disappear and the town stagnate if the cost of producing iron could not be reduced.

'Let's walk a way.' Luke's suggestion, breaking into her thoughts, startled her.

He jumped to his feet and held out his hand to Lydia. She took it and he pulled her from the ground. She stretched, then smoothed her dress.

'Which way?' she asked.

He glanced from left to right. 'This.' He started to the right.

Their gaze continually roved across the landscape, speculating on this landmark or that. They aired their knowledge of the plants and grasses they saw and negotiated the occasional outcrop of rock or jumble of stones.

Lydia's foot caught on some stones half hidden in the grass. She stumbled and fell. Luke was beside her in an instant and stooped to help her up. His left arm came round her shoulders, his right gave her support, but at that moment he froze, making no effort to take her weight.

She glanced up at him. He was staring at the ground beside her, where the stones and rocks she had dislodged had scattered. 'What is it, Luke?'

He said nothing but helped her to her feet and then crouched lower, picking up stones and examining them. He discarded some, placed others to one side.

Surprised by his actions, struck by the intense concentration on his face, and sensing the tension which gripped him, Lydia put her question again.

He did not answer directly but said almost to himself, 'I don't believe it! I don't...'

'What?' Lydia's tone was sharp.

When he looked up at her, she saw fire in his eyes.

'Lydia, this is ironstone!'

For a split second this announcement did not register, then as he repeated 'ironstone' the implications struck her.

'What? It can't be.'

'It is, I'll swear it. Look.' He pulled her down to crouch beside him, picking up one of the pieces of stone he had set aside. 'Look, the stones in this pile are different from those in the other. These have a green cast. They're like the stones we're bringing from Grosmont. Ironstone, here, right on the doorstep of the works.' His voice rose with excitement. 'Think what this means, Lydia!'

She already had. 'But there might not be any more,' she added by way of a caution and hoped she was right.

'And there might be,' he countered, springing to his feet. 'We must look around.'

He started off, stopping every few yards to examine more stones. Lydia made a pretence of similarly looking but her mind was on what it would mean if there was a huge supply of ironstone here. No more needed from Grosmont, no more shipments from Whitby. Announce a find now and Whitby ship owners, ready to invest in the ironstone trade, would retreat from doing so. Among them her uncle.

And her chance of revenge would be lost!

'Come on, let's go this way,' Luke called and waved for his sister to follow him. She could do no other. When she caught him up he said, 'There's a depression yonder, I'd like to look there.'

Still locked in her own thoughts, she said nothing.

Luke paused on the rim of a hollow and surveyed it. It had the look of a small quarry to which grass was beginning to return and, in some parts, cling precariously to patches of soil between layers of rock.

'Over here,' he said, and started down the slope. In a few moments he was examining the places from which rocks had been taken. Stones lay scattered around. Lydia saw his eyes brighten with excitement. The greenish cast was unmistakable. Luke started to scrape at an area of exposed rock on the side of the quarry.

'Yes!' he yelled. 'Yes!' He swung round to face his sister. 'What a find!'

'Don't get excited too soon,' she warned him. 'You can't be sure how much there is.'

'I know, but I reckon we've stumbled on to something big. Mr Vaughan will instigate a proper exploration as soon as I tell him. Come on, Lydia.' He grasped her hand. 'We must get back.'

She resisted. 'Wait, Luke! Wait! Think what this means.'

'Wait? Why?' He was astonished by his sister's reaction and the desperation which clouded her face.

'Think, Luke. This will alter everything.'

'I know it will,' he broke in. 'It will lower the cost of transporting the iron ore and make Mr Bolckow's and Mr Vaughan's production less costly.'

'No, I don't mean that,' returned Lydia irritably.

'What then?' he demanded.

'It will set back our chances of avenging Father's death.'

'What?' Luke was astonished at this connection.

'I showed you the letter from David. Uncle Nathan is seriously considering switching everything to the iron trade.'

'If what we've found reveals big deposits then Uncle had better think again.'

'Exactly. But if we say nothing about this until he is fully committed, this revelation will ruin him.'

Luke shook his head. 'He'd switch back to his contacts in the Spanish wine trade.'

'Not if we'd cornered his market there.'

Luke stared at her, taking in the implication behind her statement. 'You mean, we take his wine trade, knowing he's let it go in favour of the iron trade, then reveal what we have found today?'

'Exactly. Uncle will face ruin.'

'But we can't keep this to ourselves. It could affect many more people. Supposing, because of the expense, Mr Bolckow decides to close down the works? What happens to all the workers? This find could prevent all that, save them hardship, keep them from... You're using people for your own ends again.'

'It won't come to that,' protested Lydia.

'How can you be sure? No, Lydia, we can't do this. We can't play with so many lives.'

'We won't be. Uncle is on the point of investing. As soon as his ship has made one voyage we will tell Mr Vaughan of our find.' Luke looked doubtful. 'Just keep this knowledge between us for a little while.' She saw doubt in his eyes. 'You want Uncle to suffer for what he did, don't you?' He did not speak. 'Don't you?' she pressed.

He gave a little nod. 'Yes,' he said quietly. 'But not at the expense of other people.'

'Then just give me time,' she said. 'Everything will be all right.'

He bit his lip, still reluctant to agree.

'Please, Luke. For me?'

He met his sister's pleading gaze. They had been so close all their lives, especially since their mother had died. He had never refused her anything, never opposed anything she proposed, he had always been there to help and support her. He could not refuse her this wish.

'All right. But if people's jobs are threatened, livelihoods put at risk, then we must reveal what we have found today.'

'Very well.'

'And I ask you again: be careful, don't destroy yourself nor anyone dear to you.'

'I won't. All I want is for Uncle Nathan to know that Father has been avenged.'

'...and your uncle is finally committing himself to

389

the iron trade. Father tried to make him see that he should not put everything into it, but he was adamant.'

Lydia reread the paragraph in the letter she had received from David the day after she and Luke had discovered the iron ore. Excitement gripped her. Things were beginning to fall into place. Now she must make her next move quickly. She left the house and sought out Sean.

'I want you to do another job for Tees Shipping,' she said with an engaging smile.

'Very well,' he replied. 'I'm only too willing if it will raise the dividend on my shares.'

'Oh, it will that, if you are successful. I want you to go to London and contact an agent who represents the most important wine-producing family in Spain. I know that their usual shipper can no longer oblige and want you to get that trade for Tees Shipping.'

'But I know nothing about wine,' Sean pointed out.

'You don't need to. All I want you to do is to make sure we get the contract to ship their wine to England. You negotiated the sale of the shares in the *Ironmaster* successfully. Now I want you to make sure it is our ship which fills the void left by my uncle's switch to the iron trade.'

The statement was out before Lydia could halt it. However, Sean showed no sign of realising what she had said. Did it matter if he had? He knew nothing of her strained relationship with Uncle Nathan.

But Sean had noticed and noted. Was there a link here with what he had learned in Whitby?

How did she know of her uncle's dealings in sufficient detail to be able to step in and take up the trade he was abandoning? David Drayton? Was she using him? Was there some ulterior motive in her actions? And what of the *Ironmaster*? Surely Mr Bolckow wouldn't allow the ship to be diverted to another trade? But did he know? If not, why had Lydia acted on her own?

Questions whirled in Sean's mind but he had no answers. He needed an ally, someone who would listen to the facts and his suppositions and help him draw conclusions.

'All right, I can see that, but if the question of wine comes up, and it's likely to if I'm dealing with an expert, I'd be stumped to sound authoritative. It would be safer if I had someone with me who had some knowledge of wine.'

Lydia looked thoughtful for a moment. 'Maybe you are right. I want no queries. The agent must see that we know how to handle the product and that we have some understanding of the types of wine. Kevin could help. He displayed some knowledge when we dined at the Langtons'.'

'Very well.' Sean breathed more easily. The suggestion had come from Lydia, but he had his ally.

'See him today. You must leave for London tomorrow. I cannot afford to miss this opportunity.'

That sounded personal, as if this enterprise was for her benefit alone. What had she in mind?

Sean had marshalled his thoughts by the time he and Kevin boarded the train for London. He was going to have ample time to recruit an ally.

As they proceeded south, Kevin listened intently while Sean acquainted him with what he knew of Lydia, and what he had gleaned in Whitby. He voiced his suspicions and theories.

'There it is, Kevin. Throughout all this Lydia seems to be using people for her own ends, though I think that only becomes apparent when you look beneath the surface, and I believe it is not in her true nature. But have we the right to interfere?'

Kevin gave a little shake of his head. 'Tricky. We have all found Lydia to be a genuine person so far, kind, considerate, friendly. From what you learned in Whitby, and supposing the account of a row with her uncle after her father's death is true, her actions could be aimed at revenge.'

'Is there anything we can do?'

'If we don't, we'll have to live with the consequences. I know how thin the line can be between survival and utter destruction. My obsession with revenging Seamus's murder nearly led me to commit a heinous crime myself which would have affected many others. Lydia may never resort to what I was planning to do but she will still have to live with her actions for the rest of her life. If she is seeking revenge other people will be hurt, maybe even destroyed by what she does.'

When Jonas Drayton entered his son's office, David knew immediately that his father had something important on his mind and that whatever it was had exciting implications. He did not speak but leaned back in his chair and waited for his father to disclose whatever it was. Jonas sat down opposite his son.

'David, now Nathan Middleton has committed everything he has to the ironstone trade, I think we should seize the opportunity to acquire his Spanish wine trade. I want you to go to London and seal an agreement with the Zabaleta Wine Company's agent to take over Middleton's shipments.'

David already knew that his father had set his mind on this move and there was no question of not agreeing to carry out his request. Besides it would be a great asset to the business to have this trade. 'Very well, Father. I'll go tomorrow.'

'May I ask who has obtained the contract to take over the shipments formerly handled by Mr Nathan Middleton's company?' It was a disappointed David who put the question in the office of the agent for the Zabaleta Wine Company. He had arrived in London full of confidence that he would return to Whitby with a solid addition to the Drayton business. But he'd been too late.

'Certainly, Mr Drayton. The two Irishmen gave no indication that the deal should be kept secret. The contract has gone to Tees Shipping. Their negotiators were pleasant, made us a good offer, and I was convinced our future prospects would be good with them.'

David was hardly hearing the final words. Tees Shipping? Lydia! She had used the knowledge he had disclosed in his letters to snatch this par-

393

ticular trade from under his nose. She knew that his father was interested in taking it, yet she had not done the honourable thing and held back. Two Irishmen? One must surely be Sean Casey whom he had met in Whitby. The other? He did not know. If Casey was negotiator for Lydia, how close were they? Close in business? Or was there more to the relationship?

'I'm sorry we have missed having the pleasure of dealing with the Zabaleta Wine Company,' said David regretfully. 'As a matter of interest, can you tell me where the two Irishmen are staying?'

'Yes, but I can assure you they will not think of selling you their rights.'

'I did not have that in mind. I was merely interested in their trading activities and thought it might be advantageous to both our companies to see if there is any area in which we might work for our mutual benefit.'

Though such a thing was farthest from David's mind, his assertion produced a result.

'That is a commendable attitude,' replied the agent, 'particularly as they have just beaten you to the contract. The Irishmen are staying at the Mitre Tavern in Fleet Street.'

David rose from his chair. 'Many thanks.' He extended his hand. 'Maybe we can do business some time in the future.'

The agent shook hands. 'There is always that possibility.'

David had many things to occupy his thoughts as he walked to Fleet Street. There was much he needed to find out.

He had no trouble in locating the two Irishmen, for they were enjoying a celebratory meal in the tavern's dining room.

Sean's cheerful smile, as he exchanged a quip with Kevin, changed to more than a casual surprise when he saw David approaching them.

'Good day, gentlemen,' he said pleasantly when he reached their table.

'Good day to you,' returned Sean. He glanced at Kevin. 'This is Mr David Drayton from Whitby. Mr Drayton – Kevin Harper, a colleague and good friend of mine.'

The two men exchanged pleasantries, Kevin trying to sum up the man who had figured in some of the things Sean had told him about Lydia. His quick assessment was favourable. There was something about David Drayton that spoke of a man of integrity, an impression which was swiftly confirmed.

'You do not seem surprised to see us,' commented Sean, 'which can only mean one thing. That you knew we were here.'

David gave a slight bow in acceptance of Sean's perspicacity. 'That is true.'

'And that means you want to speak with us.'

'Yes, I need some questions answering.'

'Then please join us. As you see, we have only just started our meal.' Sean looked across the room, and saw a waiter watching them in anticipation of being of service now that the two Irishmen, who had tipped him handsomely for one of the better tables, had been joined by a third man. Sean raised his hand. In a flash the waiter was at the table. 'Please set a place for this gentleman and serve him with what he wants.'

'Yes, sir.'

Kevin made room for David beside him. His place was soon set with cutlery and a glass, and he quickly made his choice of food.

'Because you came here to find us you must have got the information from the agent of the Zabaleta Wine Company.'

'Yes, and was surprised to learn that two Irishmen representing Tees Shipping had forestalled me on a deal my father particularly wanted to secure. I assumed one of the Irishmen must be you, Mr Casey, for not long ago you were in Whitby looking for investors in a ship to be owned by that same company. Of the other Irishman I had no knowledge.'

'I am sorry you were disappointed, Mr Drayton, and that you have had a wasted journey.'

'It may not be wasted,' replied David, then paused while the waiter poured some wine. 'But that will depend on the answers I get.'

'And whether I can give them.'

'That is right. But I have a feeling you can.' He cast a glance at Kevin which Sean interpreted as a question.

'You can talk freely in front of Kevin. He knows as much as I do. He has a share in the new ship and so Tees Shipping is of interest to him as well, though he knows no more than I have told him.'

'I suppose Miss Lydia Middleton is the reason you are here?' queried David. He noted a surprised reaction in Sean's eyes which was disguised almost as soon as it appeared. He gave a wry smile and went on, 'Oh, I know that she is behind Tees Shipping. She told me herself when she was in Whitby recently, at the same time as you, Mr Casey.'

'Were we?' Sean was cautious.

'I saw you together on the west pier.'

'Oh.'

'I thought then that you and Lydia were more than friends, but I saw her later and she convinced me otherwise.'

'Let me assure you that is the truth. I am a great admirer of hers, and at one time that admiration might have gone further, but I realised my heart was with an Irish girl and still is.'

'And that girl is now in Middlesbrough,' put in Kevin.

David nodded, pleased to have this news and to know that there had been no serious relationship between the Irishman and Lydia. He realised that if he was to have answers to queries about Lydia's behaviour he would have to reveal more of his own.

'I don't know whether Lydia ever told you about me,' he said, 'but we go back to childhood.' He went on to tell them about his father's opposition to his marriage to Lydia and the reasons for the course of action he had taken. 'Now Lydia tells me that she took the opportunity to form Tees Shipping in order to break down my father's opposition, but there is something about it all which troubles me. This venture into the wine trade seems a deliberate move to take over her uncle's contacts. Why? And how is she going to do that? She has only one ship and that is committed to the iron trade.'

'The answer to the second question is, we don't know,' said Kevin. 'She has disclosed nothing to us but was adamant that we get this trade.'

'As to why, all we can assume is that she wants to make things difficult for her uncle if his switch to the iron trade goes wrong,' suggested Sean.

'That would put her in a position to inflict further harm,' added Kevin.

'Why would she want to do that?' asked David cautiously.

Kevin gave a wry smile. 'You tell us, Mr Drayton. From what Sean learned in Whitby, there were some doubts about why, or even how, Miss Lydia's father died, and apparently there were family rows and threats resulting from that. You were in Whitby at the time, you must have heard talk.'

David nodded, and went on to confirm what Sean was told by Potter. 'And I do know how she hated her uncle after her father's death. It changed her in some ways, changes which I hope the passage of time will eliminate because the dear, sweet girl that I love is still there.'

'Exactly,' agreed Sean.

'We all like Lydia,' confirmed Kevin. 'Sarah won't hear a word against her.'

'And my Eileen, since she arrived from Dublin, has taken to her too.'

'This is all very well, but admiration gets us nowhere. We need to know what she is up to. And if she is bent on avenging her father, how she hopes to achieve it.' There was distress in

398

David's voice.

'I begin to see that she has used, and will go on using, people for her own ends,' pointed out Kevin.

'Then she needs to be stopped one way or another,' cried David.

'And we can't do that unless we know what she is doing and planning.'

Chapter Seventeen

Anxious to receive Sean's and Kevin's reports, Lydia hurried to the station. Coming on to the platform, she saw a handful of people awaiting the train's arrival. They stood or strolled, trying to hide their impatience, they read notices for the fourth time and glanced in the direction from which the train would come.

Was that a low rumble? She looked along the track. It must have been. Others were looking that way too. It grew louder and louder. The engine came in sight. Nearer and nearer. Excitement heightened amongst those on the platform. They watched with something akin to awe the iron monster breathing smoke as it hauled its carriages with ease into the station. The shattering noise was flung back by the walls. The engine's speed decreased. There was a hiss of steam. The clash of metal on metal rang out the full length of the train as the links between the carriages clattered against each other. Carriage

399

doors swung open. Passengers stepped on to the platform. Mothers tried to calm exuberant children, and men struggled with luggage. Lydia ran her gaze over them, trying to identify her men among the throng of people.

Sean! Kevin! They were there. She raised her hand and waved. Her excited anticipation of good news was suddenly changed to surprise. David! What on earth was he doing here with Sean and Kevin? She stood still and waited. Passengers stepped around her, but three men, smiling broadly, stopped in front of her.

'Ah, sure now, I wonder why the little lady is looking so surprised?' said Sean, putting on a serious expression which could not disguise the twinkle of mischief in his eyes. He glanced at David. 'Would you be knowing now, Davey?'

Lydia cocked an eyebrow at Sean. 'As if you didn't know.' She turned to David. 'This is pleasant but most unexpected.'

'For me too,' he replied, allowing his eyes to speak of his continued admiration for her. He kissed her on the cheek. 'I met these two gentlemen in London and decided I may as well accompany them to Middlesbrough and see you before returning to Whitby.'

The answer sounded a little too glib to her. She felt there was more to this than there appeared.

'It's nice to see you, David, but Sean and Kevin have important news for me. Can I see you later?'

He ignored her question. 'Indeed they have, and it does, or rather did, concern me.'

Lydia glanced queryingly at Sean and Kevin. What had gone on in London?

400

'If there is no one in the waiting room,' Sean indicated a door close to the station exit, 'shall we talk in there?'

'Very well,' Lydia agreed and led the way.

The room was empty. It was austere but boasted a large table in the centre and several chairs. The walls were painted a light brown and hung with prints of Middlesbrough Farm, the villages of Linthorpe and Marton and, appropriately, a drawing of the railway suspension bridge across the Tees. Kevin quickly arranged four chairs for them.

But Lydia had little time to note her surroundings. 'Well?' she said as she sat down. She looked directly at Sean for an explanation.

'Kevin and I completed your mission successfully,' he started.

'This is excellent news.' She smiled her thanks to them with a feeling of relief that David's presence did not spell doom to that prospect.

'Kevin and I were having a meal at the tavern where we were staying when David came in.'

'Not by chance, I may add,' he said. 'I was in London to secure the Zabaleta contract but was told that Tees Shipping, represented by two Irishmen, had beaten me to it. Knowing that you, Lydia, were running Tees Shipping and were hoping you would eventually impress my father with what you had achieved, I was curious. I obtained the address where these gentlemen were staying and sought them out.'

'And was your curiosity satisfied?' she asked.

'Yes and no. I accept that you beat me to your uncle's trade with Zabaleta and that I was defeated fairly. But I was curious as to how you were going to deal with it when you had only one ship, and that committed to the iron trade out of Whitby to Middlesbrough. These two gentlemen could not supply me with an answer. I believed they were not holding anything back from me but were genuinely not privy to your plans. So curiosity got the better of me and here I am.'

Lydia gave a little laugh. 'My plans? Well, they are mine and no one else's.'

'Lydia, we have completed a deal to ship Zabaleta's wine,' said Sean. 'We have to fulfil that agreement. Before Kevin and I left for London you said it was imperative that we secured the contract, and you assured us you had everything in hand. But, as David says, how are you going to do it with our only ship committed to moving ironstone?'

'Try to switch it and Mr Bolckow and Mr Vaughan will block the move,' Kevin pointed out. 'Together they hold more shares than you, and with ironstone shipments booming the other shareholders will rally to their side.'

'What you say is perfectly true,' she agreed calmly, 'but you will see, they will agree to my plan to put the *Ironmaster* to the Spanish wine trade.'

The three men were astonished by her air of certainty. They glanced at each other as if hoping that one of them could supply an answer.

Lydia gave a little chuckle. 'If you can hold your curiosity in check until tomorrow evening, I will hopefully enlighten you then.' Taking further control she went on, 'What I suggest is that you

402

get David a room at the Middlesbrough Hotel. While you are there book us a private room for a meeting at seven o'clock tomorrow evening. We will all be there plus Luke. I hope then that I shall be able to answer your questions.' She eyed them all in turn but no one said any more. She rose from her chair. 'Very well, gentlemen, there is no more to be said now.' She started for the door.

'Lydia.' David's voice pulled her up short. She turned slowly to face him. 'Will you dine with me this evening?'

She gave the sort of pause which made him wonder if he should have made the invitation, then smiled at his uneasiness. 'Certainly, David. I would love to.' The relief on his face amused her all the more. 'But don't think that wining and dining me will persuade me to tell you any more. That is for tomorrow evening.' She walked out of the room.

Lydia's steps were brisk. She was elated. Thank goodness David had not contacted Zabaleta's agent first. If he had, all her plans would have gone awry for she dare not hold back the secret she and Luke shared any longer.

Her mind was so set on the future that she was oblivious to the hustle and bustle along the streets leading to the Bolckow and Vaughan rolling mill. But as she neared it she became aware of the thunderous noise coming from the mill, of the tall chimneys belching smoke into the air, of the smell and the grime which filled the air. She thought of Whitby and longed for the tang of the sea air, the breeze fresh from the ocean filling her lungs, and the cry of the seagulls lazy in their flight. 'Soon, soon,' she whispered, filling herself with an urgent longing which would not be denied.

Reaching the jetty used by the ore ships, she saw Luke and waved. He immediately left Bob Chase, to whom he was talking, and came to her.

Before he reached her he could tell from her obvious excitement that she had good news.

'They've done it!' she cried.

Without breaking his step, he swept his arms round her waist and whirled her round.

'Then we are safe when we break the news to Mr Vaughan,' he cried, his faced wreathed in smiles. He too longed to be back in Whitby. This would give them the chance, for the *Ironmaster* could switch her port to Whitby and trade from there.

'And Uncle will face ruin!'

The triumphant note in his sister's voice alarmed him. His face became serious. 'Lydia, things are going well for us. We can use Tees Shipping to expand, free from the shackles of the iron trade. Don't let a vendetta ruin everything.'

'It won't,' she replied forcefully. 'When Uncle Nathan comes crashing down everything will be so much better.'

He knew it was no good arguing with her when she was in this sort of mood, besides he wanted his uncle to know that they held his future in the balance, but such drastic measures as his sister envisaged... He was not sure.

'Luke,' she went on, 'go now and arrange a meeting for us two with Mr Vaughan tomorrow morning. Don't give any hint as to what it is about but say it is important.'

He nodded. 'Very well. Where's Sean? I thought he might have been with you.'

'He and Kevin are taking David to the Middlesbrough Hotel.'

'You mean David Drayton? What's he doing here? And why with them?'

Lydia explained quickly. When she told him about the meeting tomorrow evening, she added, 'That makes it all the more essential that we see Mr Vaughan in the morning.'

'Lydia, come home to Whitby. I'm sure Tees Shipping will be proof enough for Father.' David put his plea as he strolled arm in arm with her towards the green fields of Linthorpe.

The evening was warm. Though the light was beginning to fade, the sun still held sway in the west.

'I can't, not yet. There are things I have to do first.'

'Do them from Whitby if you need to. Surely you want to get away from all this?' He glanced over his shoulder and with a nod of his head indicated the ugly consequences of industrialisation beside the river.

'Yes, I do, and I will as soon as I can.'

'That can't be soon enough for me.' He stopped and turned to her. His arms slid around her waist and he pulled her gently to him, all the while his eyes expressing a feeling she could not mistake. 'I love you, Lydia. I want to make you a home in Whitby.'

'You shall, my love, but not just yet.'

405

'What is holding you back? We can overcome Father's objections with what you have achieved.'

'There is more,' she said, 'as you will see tomorrow evening.'

'What more have you to offer?'

She laughed. 'I told you earlier today you would learn no more this evening. And you won't.' She pushed herself on to her toes and kissed him. 'Be patient, my love.'

She would have slipped from his arms but he held her. His lips met hers passionately. 'I love you, Lydia.'

She returned his kiss with equal fervour. 'That's a promise for the future,' she whispered.

'And the future can't come quickly enough for me. I hope this meeting will speed that up.'

'It probably will. But it depends on what happens tomorrow morning.'

'Tomorrow morning?'

'I thought that would arouse your curiosity.' She laughed. 'And don't look so expectant. I'm telling you no more, so don't raise the question when we dine this evening.'

Excitement gripped both Lydia and Luke the next day as at nine o'clock they approached the home of Mr John Vaughan.

'Mr Luke Middleton and his sister,' said Luke when the door was opened by a maid.

'You are expected, sir, miss. Please come in.'

They stepped inside and she closed the door.

'May I take your coats? Come this way, please.' She led the way to the large drawing room. 'I will tell Mr Vaughan that you have arrived. He will be with you in a minute.'

'Thank you,' said Luke.

'Should I take your bag, sir?'

'No, thank you. I will need it.'

The maid retreated and a few moments later the door opened and Mr Vaughan came in.

'Good day to you both.' He greeted them with a smile. 'Your request yesterday intrigued me, Luke, and I have been puzzling over it ever since, especially as you said it was so important. And it intrigued me all the more, Miss Lydia, when your brother said you would be here too. So let us sit down and you can tell me what this is all about.'

Lydia sat down but Luke remained standing for a moment.

'May I, sir?' He indicated that he would like to place the bag on the table.

'Certainly.'

Luke opened the bag. He took out a cloth and laid it on the table to protect the surface. Then one by one he took out four pieces of stone and placed them carefully on the cloth.

As he was doing so, Lydia kept her eyes on Mr Vaughan. She saw him lean forward and peer curiously at the stones. He reached out, picked one up and turned it over in his hand, examining it with care. When he looked up, she saw in his eyes the light of recognition mingled with excitement.

'You know what this is?' Before Luke could answer he replied to his own question. 'Of course you do. You've been handling it ever since you came to Middlesbrough and no doubt before that in Whitby. Where did you get it? You

407

wouldn't be bringing it to me if it was from one of your shipments.'

'In the Eston Hills.'

'What?' Mr Vaughan raised his eyebrows in surprise.

'Lydia and I went for a picnic there. We were walking the hillside when she tripped over a heap of stones hidden by the grass. Some were scattered. When I went to help her to her feet I noticed these. We looked further and found evidence of more. We came across a small quarry. It looked as though stone had once been taken from it for making roads. There was ironstone there.'

'This could be a find of great importance.' Mr Vaughan's voice was charged with emotion. 'If there is more, if it has indeed come from a big seam, then it could alter our whole operation along the Tees. Its close proximity to the works could save us a lot of money. I'll get a map, you must show me where you found it.'

He hurried from the room and when he returned a few minutes later was accompanied by Mr Bolckow.

'I'm sorry to disturb you, Henry, but this is a matter of supreme importance,' he was saying as the two men came into the room.

Mr Bolckow exchanged greetings with Luke and Lydia. As he did so he saw the stones on the table. For a moment he stared at them then said, 'Ironstone.'

'Yes,' said Mr Vaughan. 'Miss Lydia and Luke found it in the Eston Hills. They are about to show me where.'

Luke removed his bag and, as Mr Vaughan unrolled his map and spread it on the table, Lydia placed a stone on each corner of the paper to hold it flat.

'Show us,' directed Mr Vaughan.

They examined the map.

'This is approximately where we had our picnic.' Luke indicated an area and Lydia agreed.

'We walked this way.' She traced a route with her forefinger.

'We hadn't gone too far before you fell.'

'Maybe about here.'

'And then a little further on and a little higher up the slope we found the quarry,' Luke glanced at the two men who had been following their story with intense interest. 'I don't think we can be more precise than that.'

'Never mind,' said Mr Vaughan. 'What you have shown us is very interesting.'

'It could be of enormous significance,' said Mr Bolckow as he and his partner sat down. 'Is it anywhere near where you have been looking, John?'

'Not too far away. That is one reason why, though I am excited by this news, I am also a little cautious. It doesn't do to get carried away and then be disappointed.' He turned to Luke and Lydia to offer an explanation. 'Before you arrived in Middlesbrough I had investigated the possible existence of ironstone inland from the Skinningrove mines, which had come into our hands, and from other workings along the coast, but without success. It has been a case of trial and error, a little knowledge and a certain amount of luck, but all three never led to anything worthwhile. This may be just another of those times but let us hope it isn't.'

'You'll investigate right away?' queried Mr Bolckow.

'Immediately, Henry, if these two young people will accompany me to the Eston Hills.'

'We are at your service, sir,' said Luke.

'Good.'

'Will you take Mr Marley?' asked Mr Bolckow.

'Yes. It will save time if he is with us.' Mr Vaughan rose from his chair and went to the bell-pull beside the fireplace. 'Mr Marley is a mining engineer,' he explained to Luke and Lydia as he returned to his seat. 'He has been involved with my earlier investigations. We were due to make some more, but your find will direct us to a place where we know there is definite evidence of ironstone.'

The door opened and a maid came in. 'You rang, sir?'

'Yes. Tell James to bring round the carriage. We will fetch a gentleman from the town and then take a trip into the Eston Hills.'

Once in the hills, Lydia and Luke soon found the spot where they had had their picnic. From there the direction of their walk was easily traced.

Mr Vaughan and Mr Marley paused every now and again to pick up and examine stones. Lydia could sense their mounting excitement.

'You say there was a quarry, Mr Middleton,' called Mr Marley. 'Let's go to it now.'

Luke led the way and in a few minutes they

were looking into the depression. Mr Marley paused, surveyed the scene for a moment and then hurried to one of the areas where stone had been exposed. He examined it, and removed more soil. After a few anxious minutes, he called to Mr Vaughan, 'This is better than we have found elsewhere. I think we ought to move westward.'

The eagerness in his voice caused the others to follow him and within a few minutes they were staring in wide-eyed amazement at a huge piece of solid rock lying bare before them.

'Unbelievable,' gasped Mr Vaughan.

'If this outcrop continues we have made a discovery of enormous impact,' cried Mr Marley. 'This way.'

Their explorations over the next hour gave them all the proof they needed, and it came without their having to do any boring for the ground was pitted by numerous rabbit and fox holes which made it easy for them to follow the line of the ironstone.

At the final moment, when any doubt about the extent of the stone was gone, Mr Vaughan's exuberance was allowed to boil over. 'Ironstone! Here! So close to our works!' His eyes were bright with a vision of the future. 'It will transform Middlesbrough and the river. And it's all because of you two.' He grasped Luke's hand and shook it vigorously. Turning to Lydia, he embraced her and kissed her on the cheek. His laughter was infectious as he shook Mr Marley's hand, and congratulations rang across the hills from a small group of excited people who barely

411

recognised the truth behind John Vaughan's next words.

'The eighth of June 1850 will be a day etched on our minds forever!'

They all cheered.

'What happens now?' asked Lydia as some sort of calm settled on them.

'I have to obtain leases on the land. I will do that this afternoon, after we have returned to Middlesbrough and I have informed Mr Bolckow. I ask you all to keep this quiet until I have done so. I will not try to deceive the owners, but, with the quantity of ironstone still undetermined, I will secure advantageous terms. Then we start quarrying. So much appears to lie near the surface. We'll soon have a tramway laid down to take the stone by trucks to the railway where it will be transported to our furnaces at Witton Park.'

'So this find means that shipments of ironstone from Whitby will cease?' queried Luke.

Mr Vaughan tightened his lips. 'If the ironstone here is in the quantities we need, then I am afraid it will.' He shook his head sadly. 'It will cost you your job, Luke.' He added as a further thought struck him, 'And it will mean the end of Tees Shipping.'

'It won't do that, Mr Vaughan,' replied Lydia quickly with a note of determination in her voice. 'I have made provisions should this ever happen. The *Ironmaster* can be switched to other trading as soon as she is no longer wanted for the ironstone. But that will depend on none of our investors wishing to withdraw.'

Mr Vaughan recognised his obligation and her

412

determination to succeed. 'I am sure that no one will want to withdraw. Certainly I will continue with my investment, and I am sure Mr Bolckow will also. After all, we owe you a huge debt for what you have found. And, I might add, I am sure he will agree that you deserve a royalty on the ironstone we extract. Say a penny a ton?'

'Sir, you are more than generous,' replied Luke.

'What sort of timetable do you envisage?' asked Lydia.

'Ah, a young woman with an eye to the future,' said Mr Vaughan with a smile. He rubbed his chin thoughtfully. 'Let me see. If there is no trouble over the leases, and I expect none, then I can start making arrangements to open a new quarry. Mr Marley will have to do some more investigating as to best place to start, there'll be men to engage for the work, the rails and trucks to be made for the tramway... If everything goes smoothly, the end of August or beginning of September should see the first ore being moved.'

'Will we know before then if the shipping of ore from Whitby is likely to cease?'

'We should know that once we have seen what the first quarrying yields. Middle of August, would you say, Mr Marley?'

'Yes, sir. I suspect the young lady is anxious to know so that she can make provision for the future of the ship she mentioned.' He glanced at Lydia and saw her nod of assent. 'I should be able to give you some idea in, say, a month or six weeks' time.'

'I would appreciate that, Mr Marley. Can we definitely say a month?'

He looked thoughtful for a moment. 'Very well,' he agreed.

When Lydia and Luke entered the room at the Middlesbrough Hotel which Sean had booked for her proposed meeting, she could sense an atmosphere of expectancy. She smiled to herself. She knew how she had built up their curiosity with her mysterious hinting. Now she was going to burst it like a bubble.

She didn't even sit down at the chair they had arranged for her but drew herself up straight and announced, 'I am sorry, everyone, but I have nothing to tell you.'

There was an immediate outcry. 'What do you mean?' called Sean.

'What are we doing here?'

'You promised a disclosure.'

'Did you know this, Luke?'

'Only this morning,' he replied.

'What's going on, Lydia?' asked David.

'It's simple, I have nothing to tell you.'

'What about the agreement with Zabaleta?'

'We'll fulfil it.'

'I thought you were going to tell us how?'

'I will tell you in a month's time.'

'A month!'

'There will still be plenty of time to make the shipment after that. We won't lose anything, and nor will Zabaleta.'

'What will be different then?' asked Sean. He was beginning to suspect further intrigue to add to the suspicions which had been aroused in Whitby.

414

'Probably nothing,' replied Lydia. To stop any more questioning she added quickly, 'Sean, book this room for a month's time. All of you, be here then. I'd like you to be here too, David, even though it means coming from Whitby.'

She turned quickly and hurried from the room. Luke followed, not wanting to come under questioning from the others.

Chapter Eighteen

My Dear Lydia,

The pleasure of seeing you in Middlesbrough was only marred by the fact that you did not see fit to confide in me who one day hopes be your husband. I console myself with the belief that it concerns your need to ensure Tees Shipping is a success in order to impress my father.

I am worried that, having obtained the agreement with the Zabaleta Wine Company, you will not be able to meet that agreement.

I hope you know what you are doing!

Since I got back to Whitby I have learned from Isobel that your uncle is so enthusiastic about the iron trade he has secured a loan on his house in order to invest in another ship. It seems that he is throwing everything into this enterprise. In fact, he has tried to persuade Father to do so as well but he is resisting all your uncle's blandishments.

Father was disappointed that I was beaten to the Zabaleta trade and wonders who is behind

Tees Shipping. He is going to get a shock when he finds out, but surely he can have nothing but admiration for what you have done. Don't ruin it all by over-reaching yourself. Be careful.

I will continue to write until I see you again in a little under a month.

Love,

David

Lydia was elated when she finished reading the letter. Uncle Nathan was getting himself into a financial position of which she might be able to take advantage. She re-read a paragraph. The words hit her forcibly. The house! If her uncle had used it to secure a loan then the bank would hold the deeds. If they foreclosed when her uncle was in financial trouble the house could be sold on. She hoped against hope that the discovery of ore in the Eston Hills was not discovered until she was ready to make the disclosure.

The prime movers were reliable. She knew that Mr Vaughan and Mr Bolckow would say nothing until the moment suited them. Mr Marley, employed in a responsible position, would say nothing until his employers wanted him to. The people she feared might disclose their true activities were the quarry workers but, with their bosses placing no particular emphasis on what they were doing, and the fact that they had already been involved in unsuccessful trials, she calculated they would not realise the true significance of their work. She also reckoned that the same attitude would prevail among those who commented on the activity in the hills.

Nothing had come of previous attempts to find ironstone closer to the Bolckow and Vaughan works.

Nevertheless, she spent an uneasy month. She distracted herself with visits to Sarah and Eileen, found relaxation in their chatter, and delighted in playing the piano, especially accompanying Eileen whom they discovered had a good singing voice. These visits were an oasis among the worry and anxiety.

The friends assembled at the Middlesbrough Hotel at the appointed time, hoping that on this occasion there would be no further anticlimax.

'I have important news for you,' Lydia informed them. 'It will soon be public knowledge but until it is I would ask you to keep it to yourselves.'

The air became charged with a tension as she allowed her words to hang in the air.

'The day this knowledge is revealed to the world the *Ironmaster* will be on her way to Spain to take on board our first shipment of Zabaleta wine.'

'She can't be!' Kevin protested, though he could tell by her attitude and the firmness of her voice that Lydia meant every word she said. He exchanged a look of surprise with Sean. 'She's tied into iron trade.'

That brought a murmur of agreement from Sean who then added, 'What will Mr Bolckow and Mr Vaughan say about that?'

'They already know,' replied Lydia calmly.

'And they agreed?' Sean and Kevin exclaimed together.

417

'Yes.' She smiled at their surprise.

'But I thought the *Ironmaster* was busy supplying them with ironstone?' David was curious, as he had been since he missed the Zabaleta trade.

'That will soon be taken care of. In fact, it has been ever since the day Luke and I went on a picnic in the Eston Hills. Remember, Sean, you wouldn't come?'

'What has that day to do with the *Ironmaster* switching to the wine trade?' asked David.

'Because on that day we discovered ironstone in the Eston Hills.'

'What?' Gasps of amazement came from the three men.

'Is this true, Luke?' asked Sean.

'Yes.'

'But you never said anything about it when you got back. Surely you were excited?'

'Of course we were,' put in Lydia quickly, not wanting her brother to say too much. 'But we couldn't say anything until we had seen Mr Vaughan and he had investigated the extent of our find.'

Sean's thoughts had been tumbling, trying to grasp at something that had been said. It was true that Lydia and Luke had invited him and Eileen to accompany them to the Eston Hills but they'd had other plans. So that date was fixed firmly in his mind – two months ago. But large-scale activity in the hills had only begun a month ago. What had happened in the intervening time? He felt sure that Mr Vaughan would have investigated the find as soon as he was notified because a supply of ironstone on their doorstep would be an immense asset to the Bolckow and Vaughan enterprise. But it appeared that Lydia and Luke had delayed telling him of it. Why?

'This news is going to be a blow to those shipping iron out of Whitby,' commented David.

'They'll find other trade no doubt,' said Lydia dismissively.

'It is to be hoped so,' said David. 'If they've invested heavily they could be ruined.'

'Well, we needn't worry, we have the Zabaleta trade and it will give us a base to expand from. It may be more advantageous for Tees Shipping to trade out of Whitby and London, but that will need our shareholders' approval. If I have your agreement on that, I will return to Whitby tomorrow, Tuesday, with David in the *Ironmaster* and visit the other investors.' Lydia glanced round everyone and was pleased to receive their consent.

'Good. Then I can tell you that the announcement about the ironstone find in the Eston Hills will be made on Friday and quarrying will begin soon.'

'This is going to put me out of a job,' said Sean. 'After all, Luke employed me on Mr Martin's behalf and he'll no longer want men on the Tees.'

'I'll be in the same boat,' said Luke. 'But I think, with her ambitions to extend the operations of Tees Shipping, my sister will need my help.'

'Well said, brother,' replied Lydia. She turned her eyes to Sean. 'Of course there'll be work for you, Sean, operating out of Whitby. You showed your ability selling shares in the *Ironmaster* and capturing the wine trade. I'll be in need of a skilled negotiator with a smooth Irish tongue. What about you, Kevin? Will you come to Whitby?'

'I think not, Lydia, but thanks for the offer. I'm satisfied with my position with Mr Langton.'

'And no doubt influenced by the presence of Sarah?'

'Of course.' He bowed at the inference.

'Very well, everything is settled.' She rose from her chair, bringing an end to the meeting.

Sean and Kevin left with Luke.

David came over to Lydia. 'Why did you ask me to come from Whitby for this meeting? Nothing about it concerns me.'

She met his gaze and replied, 'But it does. You came from London with Sean and Kevin because your curiosity was aroused. I was not able to answer you then so, as I knew I would be giving an explanation now, I thought you ought to be here. And, more importantly, I wanted you to have further evidence of what I was doing and how others are reacting to it. What you have heard and seen should help to break down your father's opposition to our marriage, especially when he sees the *Ironmaster* sail into Whitby with that first consignment of wine.'

Luke parted from Sean and Kevin outside the Middlesbrough Hotel and made his way to the jetty which had become so much a part of his life and where he had proved to himself that he could stand alone. He thought of Lydia's manoeuvring to place herself in a position from which she could threaten their uncle. Would nothing satisfy her but to see Nathan beg for mercy? This could jeopardise her other desire, to build a firm that would fulfil their father's ambitions. Was she prepared to sacrifice that for the sake of revenge? He felt sure their father would not have wanted that. He had been too good a man. But how to save her from the path she seemed determined to tread?

'You're thoughtful, Sean,' observed Kevin as they walked towards the Market Place.

'There's something I don't like about all this,' he returned.

'If it's going to ease your mind then talk to me. You know I'm a good listener.'

Sean relayed how his suspicions about Lydia had grown since he and Kevin went to London.

His friend listened carefully and then said, 'You think that all her moves had but one thing behind them – to bring about revenge on her uncle because she thinks he caused her father's death?'

'Yes. But somehow that doesn't fit with the girl we know.'

'True,' agreed Kevin. 'But, you know, we can be affected by death in strange ways, especially if we have been close to a person. Sometimes we see events quite differently from other people and it's difficult to persuade us otherwise.'

'Then it's the impressions clouding Lydia's mind that we have to obliterate?'

'If we can, but we will have to be careful. We cannot interfere in what are really private matters,' Kevin cautioned.

'But we could make observations, suggestions?'

'Yes. It's just a matter of how we go about it.'

'Do you think we could approach Luke?'

'That might be a good idea,' Kevin agreed. 'If your ideas have any foundation he should know. He and Lydia are close. But we might meet a barrier there. He could be in agreement with what she is doing.'

'Well, let's go and see him.'

'I think it might be best to wait until Lydia has left for Whitby. She said she was going tomorrow with David.'

'But if she seeks her revenge when she is in Whitby, we'll be too late.'

'I don't think she will go that far yet. She said she wanted to get the shareholders' approval to switch to the wine trade and work out of Whitby and London. I believe she will wait to tackle her uncle until Friday when the announcement about the ironstone finds in the Eston Hills is made. Then she will disclose she is behind Tees Shipping, the firm that took his wine trade, leaving him nothing to fall back on.'

Lydia enjoyed the voyage to Whitby. It was as if she was no longer on a working vessel, plying its way to the old Yorkshire port for another cargo of ironstone. This vessel was taking her on the final step to achieving her heartfelt ambition. The thought of that elated her and she was in high spirits.

David was pleased with her mood, though he did not know the real reason for it. He found her tender, loving, excited, constantly talking of the future of Tees Shipping and what she was going to achieve.

On reaching Whitby he escorted her to the Angel Inn where she took a room for the night.

'Where from here?' he asked.

'I am going to go to see the people who hold shares in the *Ironmaster.*' She pre-empted his offer to escort her by adding firmly, 'There's no need for you to come. I want to do this alone.'

'Very well. Dinner this evening?'

'That would please me,' she replied.

'I'll be here at seven.'

'I look forward to that.' She kissed him on the cheek, sealing her statement.

After settling in her room and refreshing herself, Lydia strolled from the inn. She made her way to the bridge where, with the tide in, she took in the activity on the river. She breathed deep of the salt air, so different from the grimy atmosphere by the works beside the Tees. She listened to the mingled noises, the creak of ropes, the swish of water, the buzz of conversation, the shouts of sailors, and over it all the cry of the seagulls as they glided smoothly on the currents of sea air. This was her home and soon she would be here permanently, her uncle ruined, her father avenged.

She made her round of the shareholders who all expressed surprise when she revealed that she was behind the founding and running of Tees Shipping. She assured them that its future was safe, in spite of the fact that ironstone had been found local to the Bolckow and Vaughan works

423

and that shipments of ore from Whitby to the Tees would gradually come to an end. She told them it was vital that none of this information was made public until after Friday.

Delighted that they were all satisfied, she made her way to Chapman's Bank.

She had a feeling of satisfaction and achievement as she walked inside, anticipating the outcome of her interview with its owner, Mr George Chapman.

After making her request to see him, she was ushered into his office by one of his clerks. Mr Chapman was a small man whose rotund shape betrayed his liking for good food and wine. His round face bore a jovial expression as he rose from his desk to greet Lydia.

'Good day, my dear. I'm pleased to see you again. Are you back in Whitby permanently?'

'Not yet, Mr Chapman,' she replied. 'But I hope to be soon.'

'I was deeply sorry that I could not help at the time of your father's death.'

'Mr Chapman, think nothing of it. Luke and I understood your position perfectly.'

'And I must say, I admired the way in which you strove to clear your father's debts.'

'Thank you.' She withdrew her hand from his. 'You may be able to help me now.'

'If I can, I will. Please, do sit down.' He held a chair for her and, when she was seated, moved behind his desk. He leaned back in his chair and rested his hands on its arms. 'Now, what might I be able to do for you?'

'I believe you have the deeds to my uncle's

house, took them when he wanted to raise money to invest in the iron trade.'

Surprised, Mr Chapman raised an eyebrow. 'You seem pretty certain of your facts, young lady.'

'Oh, I am, Mr Chapman. I was only uncertain as to which bank my uncle was dealing with, but I knew that in my father's day he used your bank so thought it most likely the deal had been done with you. I see by your reaction that I was right.'

'In that case it will be no use denying it,' he replied. 'And I don't suppose it's any good asking where you got your information?'

Lydia gave a wry smile. 'No, it isn't, but let me hasten to assure you that it did not come from anyone within your bank. I don't want your suspicions to rest on anyone you employ, for that would be wrong.'

Mr Chapman pursed his lips and nodded. 'Well, I'm thankful for that, and also that you're being so forthright. Please go on. What interest is it of yours?'

'I would like to buy that house from you.'

'But first your uncle would have to default on his loan and I'm sure...'

'I am afraid, Mr Chapman, that it is entirely likely that will happen.'

'You amaze me, Miss Middleton. But tell me, in that unlikely event, how do you propose to fund your purchase?'

'Luke and I have shares in a ship. I will trade those for my uncle's house.'

Their eyes never left each other's face. They were both trying to read what lay behind those carefully blank expressions.

'A ship, Miss Middleton?' Mr Chapman spread his hands in a gesture that was dismissive, yet there was curiosity in his eyes. Lydia recognised that spark.

'Mr Chapman, please let me give you more details of this vessel and how I come to have shares in her.'

The banker could not refuse her request, nor did he want to. He was intrigued.

Lydia quickly informed him of the essential facts of her involvement with the *Ironmaster*, Mr Chapman listening carefully.

'Well, Miss Middleton, I must say your father would have been proud of the way you and your brother have picked yourselves up since you left Whitby.'

'Thank you, Mr Chapman. It is gratifying to hear you say so.'

'The vessel you talk of is in the iron trade?'

'Yes.'

'From what I hear that trade is bringing in a steady income.' He paused thoughtfully for a moment. 'This could be a good proposition for the bank.'

'And if for the bank, then for you. You *are* the bank are you not, Mr Chapman?'

He smiled. 'You are a shrewd young woman. Yes, I am interested.'

'If that is so, then I must be honest with you. I would not want you to think ill of me if your expectations of making steady money from the iron trade were dashed later this week.'

Mr Chapman was surprised. What was this

young woman up to, telling him that the ship would bring him a good return and then, almost in the same breath, saying the income from it could disappear? 'I'm listening,' he said brusquely.

'I will be taking the *Ironmaster* out of the iron-stone trade.'

'But...' He was bewildered.

'Ironstone has been discovered in the Eston Hills.' Lydia made her announcement sharply, cutting off his protests.

'What?' he gasped in surprise. 'If that is so then no more shipments will be needed from Whitby.'

'Correct,' she replied. 'I give you this inform-ation so that you will see my offer is a genuine one. I would not want to close a deal with you without your knowing this. You would have found out, and when you did would think I had purposely withheld information from you.'

'So you are offering me a ship without the steady income from the iron trade?' He started to shake his head.

'That is right,' she agreed, 'but I have in place another one which in the long run could prove more lucrative, for there will always be a demand for wine.'

'Wine?'

'Yes. I have made a deal with a Spanish wine company to be the sole shipper of their products for many years to come.'

'I repeat, you are a very shrewd young woman. You obviously had prior knowledge of the discovery of ironstone and acted upon it.'

Lydia smiled and offered quietly, 'Luke and I

discovered it.'

'You did what?'

'It's true, Mr Chapman. Of course it needed expert verification though Luke, who of course had been dealing with ironstone shipped out of Whitby, was pretty certain we had come across a big find. The official announcement will be made on Friday so I would ask you to say nothing about this until then. No use alarming the other shipowners making the voyage between here and Middlesbrough with ore. Besides, the trade won't cease just like that, its decline will be gradual.'

'I won't say a word.' He narrowed his eyes and cocked his head. 'But tell me, Miss Middleton, if this ship can bring in a good return, why do you want to exchange your shares in it for a house? Surely that does not make financial sense?'

'Well, Mr Chapman, from what I hear my uncle, being so heavily committed to the iron trade, could be in difficulties once news of the discovery of ironstone is made public.'

'He could.' Mr Chapman nodded his agreement. 'And it's more than likely he'll be unable to redeem the deeds.'

'My grandfather had that house built. It was my father's home, and mine and Luke's. If my uncle is not able to recover the deeds from you, the house could pass out of the Middleton family. I would not like that to happen. That is why I came to you with this offer.'

'It is noble to want to keep the house in the family and, though I say it again, your father would be proud of you.' He gave a little nod, accepting the unspoken thanks which showed on

428

her face. 'But tell me one more thing. It appears that you have been running Tees Shipping, and that is unusual in itself.'

Lydia broke in with a merry laugh, 'Because I am a woman?'

'Well, you must admit it is, though I must also say you have been running it successfully from what you have told me. But who will do that now?'

'Oh, I shall, with Luke. We will be moving back into Whitby and the ship will work from here and London. The other shareholders in Middlesbrough want us to run the company, and I have persuaded the Whitby shareholders to give their approval too. I must add that when we get a second ship Luke and I will have shares in it. In the meantime we will be paid a wage, to be approved by everyone.'

Mr Chapman's head nodded at each piece of information she delivered. 'Good, good. Then there is no more to be said. I will have the necessary documents drawn up for both parties. Shares for deeds.'

'May I collect them later today? I return to Middlesbrough tomorrow.'

'Certainly, I'll have them drawn up immediately.' He stood up and offered his hand.

Sean wore an anxious frown when he spoke to Kevin. 'Eileen saw that I was troubled by something and she was concerned it might be about our future. She pressed me to tell her what it was.'

'And you did?'

429

'Yes.'

'If you're worried because you told her, don't be. I was in the same boat, Sarah sensed something was wrong.'

'You told her?'

'Yes.'

There was a sense of relief in Sean as he asked, 'What now?'

'I suggest the four of us try to decide what to do next.'

Their meeting later that day only served to heighten their concern for Lydia, but they did decide to put their doubts to Luke before his sister returned from Whitby.

Expecting a pleasant social evening at the Langtons', Luke walked into the drawing room in a bouyant mood but his lively greetings faded when he saw his friends' serious expressions.

'Why so glum? What's the matter?' His gaze swept across them, seeking an answer.

Kevin, who had been elected spokesman, saw no reason not to come straight to the point. 'Luke, we are worried about Lydia.'

He put on a mystified expression. 'Why? There's nothing wrong, she's perfectly healthy.'

'It's not her health we are worried about.'

'Then what?' he queried, glancing swiftly round the solemn faces.

'We feel that behind all that is happening there is an ulterior motive.' Kevin went on to explain what they suspected and why.

Luke's mind was thrown into turmoil. He wanted to be loyal to his sister, but if other people had noticed that her actions could have a hidden motive... But even as these thoughts were churning in his mind he found himself defending her. 'But from what you say you have no evidence that she is intending anything but what is honourable. All you are doing is making suppositions and drawing the wrong conclusions.'

'We hope that is true,' said Sarah. 'But the things we have observed do cause us to wonder.'

'No need,' he replied sharply, hoping he sounded convincing.

'Luke, I have not known Lydia as long as the others,' put in Eileen, 'but I have come to like her a lot. I see her as a sweet considerate person as well as one with a good head for business. I would hate to see such a person pursue a course which could spoil her.'

'Not merely spoil, destroy,' Sean said to add weight to the argument.

'This is all ridiculous,' snapped Luke, 'and I would ask you all to wipe such ideas from your minds.'

'Can you deny that your sister would like to avenge your father's death? And what about you? Haven't you had such thoughts?' Kevin put the question so strongly that it forced Luke into an admission.

'Of course we have. It was only natural after what happened.'

'And we think that desire still burns in Lydia, maybe even in you both,' said Sean.

Luke saw concern in the Irishman who had befriended them when they first came to Middlesbrough.

431

'I think I can read in your expression that it does,' said Kevin.

Sarah saw protests rising to Luke's lips and pre-empted them. 'Revenge can be a very dangerous thing. If revenge is in Lydia's mind then we must stop her. Please listen to Kevin's story of how, in the same situation, he nearly embarked on a course which would have shattered the lives of many people, including me. He would also have destroyed himself.' She glanced across at Kevin.

He took up the story and related how his desire to avenge Seamus's murder had nearly led to his committing the same crime, and how he had been prevented from doing so. 'I had no proof, I was prepared to act on mere supposition. Then I realised the potentially devastating consequences of my actions.' As he spoke he saw that his words were having an effect on Luke, sensed that he had never been as strongly in favour of revenge as his sister. 'Think carefully about it, Luke. Only you among us know if we are anywhere near the truth. Only you can say whether we should take this matter further.'

The room fell silent as they awaited his response.

Luke avoided the eyes which were on him. He looked down at his hands resting on his knees. Ran his tongue over his lips.

'I know that you mean well and I thank you for your concern. I'll not deny that Father's death and our subsequent visit to my uncle left us with a desire for revenge. The loss of our home, turned out by our uncle because he felt it was rightly his, only heightened our feelings. More so Lydia's than mine perhaps. She was very close to Father so I admit the desire for revenge.'

'And Lydia's subsequent actions?' prompted Sean.

'I must agree with you. I have tried to reason with her but she would not listen. I believe her desire for revenge is overwhelming.'

'And she has come to use people for that end?' asked Sarah.

'I believe so.'

'But this isn't the real Lydia, not the friend I like and respect,' she added.

'I know,' said Luke with unmistakable sadness in his voice.

'Then we must do something to preserve that person. Make the real triumph over the false, for the path she is following can only lead to self-destruction.'

Chapter Nineteen

Lydia came down the gangway from the *Ironmaster* with a radiance which matched the bright sunshine and clear sky. It was in marked contrast to the drabness of the industrial landscape around her. Wasteland stretched downriver, dark smoke straggled into the air where it hung, hardly moving, in the absence of a breeze. Raucous shouts from the shore workers, waiting to unload the ironstone from Whitby, greeted the newly arrived sailors. Noise pounded out across the open ground from the rolling mills then reverberated from the warehouses, sheds, and buildings strung along the river. The clatter of metal on metal when buffer struck buffer, as trucks were positioned to be filled with ironstone, added to the unholy din.

Luke saw that his sister was oblivious to it all. There was triumph in her attitude, delight at something well done, and he knew that she had had a successful visit to Whitby.

'Luke! Thank you for being here.' She gave him a special hug which confirmed that she was well satisfied with what she had accomplished.

'It is good to have you back.' He stepped away but still held her at arm's length so that he could look into her face when he said, 'No doubt you persuaded our shareholders that going into the wine trade is an auspicious move?'

'Indeed I did,' she returned. Her smile broadened even more as she added tantalisingly, 'But there's more.' She twisted out of his hold and linked arms with him. 'Come, walk me to West Street and I'll tell you.'

'I should be here.'

'Bob's capable.'

Luke knew this was true. He glanced towards the group of men near the stern of the ship, saw Bob and indicated to him to take charge. Bob acknowledged the signal.

'Right,' said Luke. 'Now what have you to tell me apart from the fact that all our shareholders are happy?'

Brother and sister started away from the jetty.

'I paid Mr Chapman's bank a visit and saw Mr

434

Chapman himself.'

'What on earth for?' asked Luke mystified.

'I got him to take our shares in the *Ironmaster*.'

Luke stopped, his face clouded with disbelief. The laughter in Lydia's eyes did nothing to alleviate his bewilderment. 'You what?'

'I got him to take our shares in the *Ironmaster*.' She repeated the words a little more slowly and with emphasis.

'What do you mean? That we no longer have an interest in the ship?'

'Oh, we're still interested in her but we have no shares in her.'

'I don't understand.'

'Then take a look at this.' Lydia opened her handbag, drew out an envelope and handed it to her brother.

He took it carefully as if it contained something unsavoury.

Lydia laughed. 'Go on, open it.'

Luke turned back the unsealed flap and extracted some sheets of paper. He unfolded them and, as he read the first few lines, his eyes widened in astonishment. He looked up at Lydia with disbelief. 'These are the deeds to the house we used to live in.'

'Yes. And now they are ours!' The note of triumph in her voice was unmistakable.

'Mr Chapman exchanged these for shares in the *Ironmaster*? I don't believe it.'

'It's true. I persuaded him that Uncle Nathan was unlikely to redeem them. I hope you approve of what I have done?'

Luke was still bewildered but he managed to

give his consent and add, 'No doubt you did this by telling him of our discovery in the Eston Hills, so he would know Uncle Nathan faced a disastrous future and therefore he was better off taking our shares in the ship?'

'Exactly. And I told him, as I told all our shareholders, that our discovery should not be talked of until the news was officially released.'

'So does Uncle Nathan know that the house belongs to us?'

'Oh, no, not yet. That blow will fall when he learns that his investment in the iron trade is doomed.' Her voice was filled with elation as she savoured the anticipated confrontation and victory.

But Luke saw the coldness that had come into her eyes with that vision of her uncle subdued and beaten by her own burning desire for revenge. He recalled the warnings of his friends.

He did not speak.

Lydia frowned. 'Luke, you are pleased to have the house?'

'Of course.'

'Then what's the matter?'

Luke hesitated. He was about to voice his true thoughts, but at this moment considered it better not to. He passed off his lack of excitement by saying, 'If we have no shares in the *Ironmaster* we will have nothing on which to build the company you've always desired, and where are we going to obtain an income?'

'We will have something for discovering the ironstone, remember?' He nodded. 'As for the company – well, I was running it, as you well know. I have told Mr Chapman and the Whitby shareholders that you and I will continue to run it for a wage to be agreed.'

'What?' Luke was astonished by her audacity.

She smiled. 'I think I can persuade Mr Bolckow. He's a shrewd investor. He was satisfied with the job I was doing and I believe he'll want it left that way. Then, as we progress, we'll get another ship in which I'll make certain you and I have shares, and so it will go on from there.'

Luke saw the light of ambition in her eyes and with it a ruthless streak he had never noticed before. His sister was changing before his eyes but he knew it was no good pointing this out for she would only deny it. In her present frame of mind she would not be diverted from the course she had set. He could do nothing but fall back on the proposal made at the Langtons'.

'Sarah has invited us to visit this evening,' he informed her.

'Good. You and I can regard it as a celebration.'

The others were already there when she and Luke arrived. Lydia detected a slight uneasiness in the air but dismissed it as a false impression. However she found it confirmed when, after a query about her visit to Whitby, Luke deliberately brought the matter of their shares into the open.

'I think you should tell them that you and I no longer have shares in the *Ironmaster*.'

While Lydia shot him a withering look she noticed that the four friends exchanged glances of astonishment. 'It's only temporary.' She spoke quickly, trying to dismiss the information as of no concern.

'I think we should know more,' said Kevin.

There was no escape when the others backed him.

'It's a private matter. Chapman's Bank in Whitby will hold the shares.'

'That is not much of an explanation,' said Sean. 'Are you holding out on us? Keeping back something you know, like you did with the discovery you made in the Eston Hills?'

Lydia stiffened. 'What are you accusing me of?'

'Deliberately withholding vital information so you could turn it to your own advantage.'

She jumped to her feet. The words hammered in her mind. What did her friends know? And how? Had Luke...? He couldn't have. She glared at Sean. 'After what Luke and I have done for you, I thought you'd be a loyal friend. How can you suggest such things? Come, Luke, I have no need to sit here and listen to this rubbish.'

He did not move from his chair. 'I think you had better sit down and listen to what has to be said.'

She stood defiantly.

'Please, Lydia. It is for your own good.' Sarah's tone was soft but persuasive.

Lydia sat down slowly, still hostile. 'You have no proof of what you say,' she said, eyes fixed intently on Sean.

'I know the date you went for your picnic. You said that was the day you discovered the ironstone.' He presented his facts slowly and with deliberation so that she could not mistake what

438

he was saying. 'If you had revealed your find to Mr Vaughan then he would have investigated immediately because your news would have been of vital concern to him and Mr Bolckow. But he did not start his investigation until some time afterwards. There was quite a gap between discovery and investigation. The only conclusion we can draw is that you and Luke deliberately held back the information for your own purposes.'

He paused. When she did not react to his words, he continued. 'Within that time word spread about the need for more iron ore. More shipowners turned to the trade, among them your uncle who went into it heavily. I learned when I was in Whitby that you had had a serious falling out with him and were overheard threatening revenge. Therefore I could only conclude you had deliberately withheld the information about the ironstone to lure him into the trade. And I also noted that within that period you sent myself and Kevin to London to capture what had been your uncle's wine trade.'

Lydia drew herself up, eyes narrowed with anger. 'You are very clever with your theorising. I could deny it all but what would be the point? I can see by your faces that you believe this to be the truth. And I see that you have cornered Luke. So I'll ease your minds – you are right. And I'd do it all again to avenge my father's death!'

'I don't think you have any proof that your uncle caused that,' Kevin reminded her gently.

'One way or another he was to blame and deserves punishment. And now I'll tell you some-

439

thing else. You may as well know everything. I exchanged my shares and Luke's for the deeds to the house Uncle Nathan lives in. It was our home until he turned us out. Now I'll turn *him* out.'

'Please, Lydia, don't pursue revenge. Bitterness is eating into you and changing you,' cried Sarah. 'Stop before it's too late. I don't want to lose the good friend I know is still there inside you.'

'Heed her,' pressed Eileen. 'Kevin was burnt up by the desire for revenge when Seamus was murdered. Listen to him.'

Lydia started to rise from her chair. She had had enough. But when she met Kevin's gaze she knew she must listen.

He told her his story and concluded with a plea, 'I realised what my desire would lead to. Kill Gilmore and it would leave his wife and children in worse poverty than they already lived in. It would also destroy any chance of the life I wanted, even had I escaped the gallows. Would Sarah ever have recovered from the shock? Knowing her as I have come to do, I don't think so. And that would have devastated her father. The ripples would have gone on and on. Sean, Luke, you ... all would have been affected in some way, and that is not to mention my own family who would have borne the stigma of a murderer for a son. Please, Lydia, call a halt to your desire for revenge, now.'

For a moment no one spoke. They all thought that Kevin had made her see sense.

She rose slowly to her feet, looked at each one in turn, a touch of disdain in her eyes. So penetrating was her gaze, condemning them for interfering in what she saw as a personal matter, only Kevin could meet her eyes.

'There is a difference,' she said in a quiet but powerful voice, 'I won't be committing murder.'

'As good as,' he replied. 'You'll be destroying not only your uncle but his family as well. On top of that you'll take something from us, your friends. But more than anything else you'll be destroying yourself.'

She shook her head. 'I'll be doing that if I don't punish my uncle because then I will not have avenged Father's death and he will not rest easy in his grave.' She turned to her brother who had sat silently throughout the whole exchange. Close as she was to him, she sensed his changed attitude. 'You no longer support me.' Her mouth curled in disdain. 'Well, go your own way, but don't think you'll be welcome in what will be my house before long.'

There was sadness in his eyes as he looked at her. 'I am convinced by Kevin's argument. Don't do it, Lydia. Can't you see that even now it is beginning to take its toll? It has driven a wedge between you and me. You can abandon this scheme and bring us close again. But even if you don't, you will always have a brother's love.'

His words struck at her heart. She turned and walked from the room before they could overwhelm her.

As the door closed, Luke glanced helplessly round his friends. 'What more can we do?'

There was a moment's silence in which everyone tried desperately to find an answer.

'I don't want to lose the sister I love. She is still

there, I know. We must save her.' The plea was a cry for help.

'I think that now there is only one person who can do that.' The words came slowly from Sarah. Everyone looked at her, hoping that what she had in mind would solve their problem. 'David.'

'He will have to know Lydia's intentions and that might destroy their relationship completely,' warned Kevin.

'I have only met David on the two occasions he has been to Middlesbrough,' put in Eileen, 'but I would say that his love for her runs deep enough for him to want to save her from herself.' She looked to Luke for confirmation.

He nodded. 'I'm sure you are right.'

'Who's to tell him?' asked Sarah. 'You, Luke?'

He shook his head. 'I think Sean has the most persuasive tongue, but I'll be there to verify what he says.'

They all turned to Sean.

He did not hesitate. 'Sure now, I'll only be too glad to try. It could be advantageous to have Eileen with me. If David takes action he might find female company of help.'

'We must act immediately. Lydia will want to be in Whitby to confront her uncle when the announcement about the find in the Eston Hills is made tomorrow.'

'So she'll leave today?' queried Sarah.

'Sure to,' returned Kevin.

'I believe she'll use the *Ironmaster*,' said Luke.

'So how do we get there first?' asked Eileen.

'There's another vessel, the *Waverley*, unloading now. She'll sail on the same tide,' said Sean.

Luke snapped his fingers. 'Good, with all this worry I'd forgotten the *Waverley*. I know the captain well. He'll oblige me and cram on sail to beat the *Ironmaster*. Everyone in agreement?'

Everyone approved and Sarah reminded them, 'You must get on board without Lydia seeing you.'

'There's no time to lose then,' replied Sean.

Once the *Waverley* had cleared the mouth of the Tees, her master, Captain Merryweather, called for more sail to take advantage of the freshening wind. The canvas was run out, billowing with a sharp crack as the northeaster caught it. Ropes tightened, timbers creaked, and the sea, driven into curling foam by the cleaving bow, swished along the side to be left churning in a white wake.

On deck, the three friends, while anxious about the outcome of their mission, enjoyed the exhilarating sea air.

Eileen realised her former narrow views about remaining in Ireland were banished forever. She would go wherever Sean wanted. She hoped that would be to work in Whitby for Tees Shipping, but it would depend on today's outcome.

Sean saw the light of enjoyment in her face and slipped his arm round her waist to draw her to him. She snuggled close, content to be with the man she loved.

Luke glanced back towards the river and saw the *Ironmaster* meeting the sea. Thankfully they would beat her to Whitby. As he leaned on the rail and fixed his eyes on the coast, his mind was full of concern for his sister. They had shared many voyages along this seaway in their father's ship. Happy, pleasant days when they were so close they were almost able to read each other's thoughts. They had helped each other through trying times and had emerged with laughter on their lips and the promise of a bright future.

The future? Luke shuddered. Lydia seemed bent on destroying it now, oblivious to what she was doing, cocooned in the thought that once she had found revenge all would be well and life would revert to the way she had known it. She did not seem to realise that the past and present shaped the future and there was no going back. Nothing could ever be the same, but there was no need to mar the future by heaping more tragedies on those of the past.

As soon as the *Waverley* was at the dockside and the gangway was run out, the three friends were striding along the quay, leaving a trail of urchins lamenting that the new arrivals had no bags to carry.

They lost no time in reaching the Draytons' offices. They were putting their request to see David to the clerk when a door along the corridor opened. Jonas Drayton, dressed in outdoor coat and hat and carrying a walking cane, came towards them. He stopped.

'You!' His eyes fixed on Sean. 'I told you never to come here again. I thought you had heeded me but it seems you haven't.' His eyes swung to Luke. 'I'm surprised to find you with him, though why I should be I don't know. After all you're a nobody just like him.'

Luke drew himself up. His eyes narrowed and

his voice was hard. 'You wouldn't have said that once, Mr Drayton, when you thought my sister worthy of your son. Well, I'll tell you this, you're an arrogant old fool who isn't worth talking to. Now, out of our way. We are here to see David, not you!'

'You have no business with my son,' snapped Jonas. 'Get out of here.' His voice rose harshly.

'We will not be moving until we have seen David. You should let him listen, for it concerns his future.'

'Future be damned! You have nothing to say about that.'

'We have a lot to say about it, and we are going to say it, and you are not going to stop us.'

Jonas's lips tightened. How dare these whipper-snappers defy him? His body tensed so much that he started to shake. 'Out! Out!' he yelled. 'My son won't listen to you. I'll forbid him! He'll do as he's told.'

'I won't, Father.' The voice was quiet but the words were so full of defiance that they struck like an arrow from a bow. David had come quietly into the corridor to see what all the commotion was about. 'Now let them pass, Father. I will hear what they have to say.' He knew that their presence spoke of something important and that it must involve Lydia or why come to him? He put a restraining arm across his Father's chest and pushed him gently to one side. 'My office,' he said to Luke.

Eileen and Sean slid past Jonas and followed Luke. As they entered David's office they heard him say, 'No, Father, they have come to see me, not you, so you go about the business you were embarking on.'

A moment or two later he came into the office. 'I'm sorry about that,' he said as he closed the door. 'Please find yourselves seats.' He paused a moment as the three friends settled themselves, then went to his own chair behind the desk. 'A contingent from Middlesbrough. This must be important, especially as you all have such grave expressions.'

'I am afraid that we do not come on a very pleasant matter,' replied Luke.

'Lydia?' Unease clouded David's face and voice. 'Something's happened to her?' His eyes flashed across all three, trying to glean something quickly.

'No. Lydia is well and at this moment on board the *Ironmaster* heading for Whitby. In fact, she should be docking before long. When she arrives we have reason to believe she will immediately embark on a disastrous course. We need your help to stop her.' Luke looked to Sean to take over the explanation.

He did so in as few words as possible. He held David's full attention with what he disclosed. When Sean had finished David leaned back in his chair, staring at his friends in disbelief. 'This can't be true.' He shook his head. 'It's just not in her.'

'I agree,' put in Eileen, 'but I believe the shock of her father's death could have displaced some of her tender nature and turned it to hatred. It is now an obsession which must be exorcised by the only way she knows – revenge.'

'Don't forget, on top of Father's death, Uncle

446

Nathan turned us out of the house in which we had been brought up, a home which was very dear to Lydia,' said Luke.

'But it didn't affect you like that.'

'I must confess it did at first, but I managed to curb it. I had my work, that occupied my mind. Lydia had too much time to think.'

David did not reply. Eileen saw that he was tussling with his thoughts, trying to make sense of all that he had heard, attempting to reach a conclusion. She signalled with a slight shake of her head and movement of her fingers to Sean and Luke that they should say nothing.

David straightened. 'I love your sister, Luke. Where will she be?'

Tension drained from the room, leaving only the need for instant action.

'I believe she'll go straight to Uncle's office. There's nothing else for her to do.'

'Then we should be there.' David rose quickly from his chair. Ignoring his father, who was still standing in the corridor, he strode into the street followed by his three friends.

Lydia felt the pull of Whitby as the *Ironmaster* sailed between the piers and met the river's flow. This was home. This was where she belonged. This was where her future lay. This was where she would build a trading venture to match or even surpass that dreamed of by her father. This was where she would live, in the house she regarded as rightly hers. She was coming home.

She thanked the captain for a pleasant voyage and smiled at the disappointment on the faces of

447

the urchins who thronged the quay near the foot of the gangway. Though she did not know it this was the second time this afternoon they had been cheated of the chance of luggage.

She strode with a determined step, trying to conquer the flutter of unease she felt inside at the thought of confronting her uncle. She stilled it by looking forward to seeing him squirm, broken and begging, before her.

'I'm here to see my uncle,' she informed Nathan's clerk who recognised her immediately she walked in. He started to rise from his chair. 'There is no need to announce me, I know which room he uses.' With that Lydia was along the corridor. She did not hesitate but flung open the door and strode straight in, swinging it to with a determined push of her hand so that it shut with a bang.

Her uncle, startled and annoyed by this sudden intrusion, looked up sharply. His eyes widened in astonishment to see his niece, well-dressed and facing him with an air of confident authority. 'You! What do you want?'

'All in good time, Uncle. There is much to tell you and much I want you to know. May I sit down?'

He was still annoyed enough to dismiss her out of hand but, because of her attitude, curious to hear more.

'Well, get on with it, I can't give you much time,' he snapped.

'You'll give me all your time until I'm finished,' she said coolly, eyes fixing his, daring him to deny her.

'Now, see here, young lady...'

'No. You listen to me.' She was sitting ramrod straight on her chair, her body tense with defiance. He knew she would stand against any efforts to dismiss her lightly. He had to listen. As she was speaking she had opened her reticule without allowing her gaze to waver. She drew out an envelope and handed it to him.

'What's this?' he snapped.

'Open it, it's not sealed, and you'll see.'

He hesitated only a moment, took the envelope and withdrew some papers.

He looked down at the deeds and blanched 'How did *you* get these?' The words were hissed in dismay.

'They are mine, Uncle.' She delivered the information with an air of triumph, spiced with contempt.

'They can't be. They are lodged with the bank.'

She shook her head. 'No, I bought the property from Mr Chapman. The deeds belong to me now.'

'What?' Anger brought colour rising to Nathan's face as he jumped to his feet. 'We'll see about that!' He started to come out from behind his desk.

'Rushing off to the bank will do you no good,' Lydia returned calmly. Nathan stopped in mid-stride and glared down at her. 'Do sit down, Uncle, you'll give yourself apoplexy, huffing and puffing like that. Maybe that's what you gave Father when you wouldn't help him.' She waved her hand towards his chair. 'Do sit down. I have more to tell you.'

Reluctantly he returned to his seat. With those deeds she could regain the house, but what else was to come?

There was no time to talk, no time to make a plan of action, all knew they must reach the offices of Nathan Middleton as soon as possible. Breathing hard from their forced pace they entered the building.

'Is Miss Middleton here?' panted Sean.

'Aye.'

The four friends were relieved, but were they too late?

'She's with Mr Middleton, but I won't interrupt them. There've been raised voices already and I don't want the master's wrath coming down on me.'

'We'll see ourselves in,' replied Luke in a tone which would brook no objection. He started down the corridor but before he reached the door to Nathan's office Eileen, who was immediately behind him, grabbed his arm.

'Wait! Listen.'

Luke glanced questioningly at her.

She nodded meaningfully towards the door. 'Let Lydia derive some satisfaction from all she's done.'

David grasped her meaning and approved. 'We'll step in at the right moment.'

Not another word passed between them.

'Damn you, woman. What do you mean, the ironstone trade to Middlesbrough is doomed?' Nathan's voice rose with his demand.

'Exactly what I say.'

'How can it be? The blast furnaces and rolling mills aren't going to close down just like that.'

'They certainly aren't,' Lydia agreed comfortably.

'Well then, what nonsense are you talking? Is this an attempt to scare me?'

'It will when I tell you that ironstone has been found in the Eston Hills close to Middlesbrough. There'll be no need to ship ore from here.'

'I've heard nothing of this,' he said disdainfully.

'No, but you will. It is being announced today.'

'How do you know?' Nathan still sounded unconvinced.

'Because Luke and I found it.'

'You did what?'

'Luke recognised it. Investigations have been carried out and mining will soon begin on a large scale.' Lydia smiled with satisfaction. She could see her uncle was troubled by this news. Now was the moment to shatter him. 'When we made this discovery you were only thinking about joining the iron trade.' She paused, letting her words sink in.

'If I had known about the discovery I would never have committed myself so heavily to the trade.' The true meaning behind her statement made itself felt then. He stared at her in astonishment. 'You purposely withheld the information until I was engaged in the trade?'

She nodded. 'You surmise correctly, Uncle.'

'And I suppose you thought that would ruin me? Well, let me tell you, you have not calculated carefully enough. You see, I can switch back to a lucrative contract with a Spanish wine firm.' His triumph at having balked her scheme was evident.

She threw back her head and laughed.

'I'm afraid you can't,' she said, the note of triumph intensifying. 'You see, I now have the Zabaleta contract.'

'What did you say?' Though he put the question, it was only an automatic reaction to her statement. He knew it was true. Lydia wasn't going to make such an announcement unless there was substance behind it.

'I knew that contract was coming up for renewal. I made sure of it before revealing that there was iron ore in the Eston Hills.'

'So I didn't have the Zabaleta trade to fall back on?' he gasped.

'Exactly. You see, I am Tees Shipping!'

He stared at her incredulously.

'There's no need to go into detail about how that came about. Suffice it to say that as we talk my ship, the *Ironmaster*, which has just brought me to Whitby, is now on her way to pick up the first consignment of Zabaleta wine.

'You are in a precarious position, Uncle. Your commitment to the iron trade has left you in debt and I can outsmart you on any other contract you try to make.' She revelled in seeing him slump in his chair, his face ashen. 'Now you know how Father felt. Now you have to face the truth about what happened to him. Would you like to walk the same way to the end of the pier? It would be easy...'

Her words were cut short as the door burst

open. Startled, she swung round. Her eyes widened in disbelief on seeing her friends.

'Get out of here!' she hissed

'More of you come to gloat? This from Nathan in a tone of despair.

'No, Uncle, we haven't,' called Luke.

'Damn you, Luke! Don't you want him punished for what he did to Father?'

'You've no proof he did anything.' David's words came accusingly.

'Damn you too, David. You've no right to be here.'

'I have every right as the man who loves you and does not want to see you destroy yourself. As you will be doing if you pursue this vendetta any further. The consequences will spread far. Your aunt and cousins who think so much of you, and never agreed with their father turning you out of the house, will all suffer. And Luke will be devastated at losing his sister for whom he has a high regard as well as a brotherly love.'

'If he had he'd be standing beside me now,' screamed Lydia, trying to stem his words which were disturbing her.

But David did not let up. 'And there are all your friends – Sean and Eileen here, Sarah and Kevin in Middlesbrough, Mr Langton, Mr Bolckow and Mr Vaughan who admire your business acumen and proved it by asking you to continue with Tees Shipping. Do you want to destroy their trust in you? If that goes will they continue to have faith in your enterprises? Won't you feel your life is destroyed? And all because of your need for a revenge which isn't even worth bothering about.'

'How do you know it isn't? Do you know how I felt in here,' she pressed her heart, 'when I lost Father?'

'No, I don't. But I do know how I'll feel if I lose the girl I love.'

'You'll still have me and I'll be coming with a firm which your father will be proud of. There'll be no obstacle to our marriage.'

'You're right, there won't be if it is brought by the girl you were and still are. But if the girl I see before me now comes to me, having thrown away so much and destroyed other people's happiness, there won't be any marriage. I will not ask this girl to marry me as I asked the other.'

Lydia stared at him incredulously. She felt numb. Surely David couldn't mean it? Was this just a ruse to fool her into stopping her pursuit of revenge? He'd see things differently when she had taken possession of the house and witnessed the downfall of her uncle.

The house! Her house! To be living there again would mean so much. She and Luke. He would approve of her actions once he was there. He wouldn't be able to resist the memories of happy family times.

Family. The word spun in her mind. If she went through with this, what would her aunt and cousins think of her? The pleasant relations she had had with them would be tainted, maybe destroyed, forever.

She looked at her brother. She saw love in his eyes but sadness too. There was a distance growing between them lately and she realised that had hurt Luke. She glanced at Sean. There was pleading in his eyes for the return of the girl he had first met in Middlesbrough, two strangers in a strange town, drawn together but knowing there were others who would be hurt if they pursued a relationship. Was revenge the only relationship she was pursuing now? She looked at Eileen and saw a girl whose love for Sean had never been in doubt. If Lydia had pursued him what consequences would it have had for Eileen? Might she even have destroyed herself? Then wouldn't Lydia have been as guilty as the uncle she condemned?

Her whole world pressed in on her. Words thundered in her mind. Revenge! Father! Love! David!

'Lydia, please think...' Luke was speaking, the brother whom she'd thought would be standing by her at this moment, revelling in seeing their uncle brought down. Instead he had deserted her. '...the consequences could be catastrophic.'

The room was closing in. She must escape.

She turned sharply for the door. Eileen was in the way. She pushed the girl roughly aside and, flinging open the door, fled down the corridor.

David was the first to react. He ran after her. 'Lydia! Wait!'

But she did not hear. Her feet rapped sharply on the wooden floor. She reached the door, but before she could flee into the street a hand grabbed her arm. She twisted, trying to shake off the tightening grip. A hand closed round her other arm and brought her round to face her assailant. Her eyes were wild, furious at being stopped. Protests sprang to her lips.

'David! Let go!'

He held her tighter. She struggled fiercely.

'Revenge isn't the answer!' he cried.

'It is.' Anger replaced her fury. 'You won't stop me.'

'I must. For your sake. For ours. I love you.'

The others had come into the corridor but they saw it was best not to interfere.

She hesitated. 'If you do love me, you'll let me go.' Her voice softened. He saw she was taking control of herself. 'Please, David, let me go. Let me decide what to do next.'

Still he held her. Should he heed what she said? He stared at her, trying to discover what really lay behind her plea. Was she fit to be alone? If he let her go, would he lose her? But maybe he would if he forced her to stay. He concentrated his gaze on her, then, overwhelmed by his desire to save her, pulled her to him and kissed her. His undisguised passion cried out for her to realise that she would lose his unbounded love if she chose the wrong path now.

'Please, David.'

His grasp slackened. He let his arms fall by his side.

She looked at him gratefully. 'I must do what I think best.'

Her statement gave no indication of what she meant but he deemed it wisest to ask for no explanation. Instead he said, 'I love you. I want the girl I know to marry me.'

She said nothing but turned away and walked into the street.

456

David, still hoping she would make the right decision, watched from the doorway until she disappeared among the crowd.

He turned to find anxious faces studying him. He shrugged his shoulders. 'Lydia has to decide for herself to give this up. I can't force her.'

'But we don't know how she might react.' Luke, alarmed, started down the corridor, but David restrained him. 'Let her be. She won't do what you fear. The only way is to let her decide a course of action for herself.'

'And what do we do?' cried Luke, still anxious for his sister.

'Wait.' David turned him back to the office.

The brief interlude with David had been sufficient to stop the pounding in her head and clear her mind so that as she walked down the street, Lydia began to think more calmly. When she reached the bridge she stopped and looked down at the water flowing towards the sea. She watched it swirl and eddy and go on towards its destiny in the ocean's vastness. Where was her destiny? Would it be lost like the waters of the river if she took revenge?

Life went on around her, its daily routine unaffected by the drama in which she had been involved. One she had seen instigated by the loss of a ship far off in the English Channel. It was a drama that was still not concluded, and its conclusion lay in her hands.

Her eyes skirted the buildings to both sides of the river. Her gaze slid across the red roofs rising on the East Cliff. Beyond them, on the cliff top, lay her father. Could her answer lie with him? But all she heard was, 'Your future is in your hands.' Did that future lie here in Whitby, the place she loved? Would this port, pulsating with the commercial life on which it depended, be tarnished by the action she took? Would it ever mean the same to her again?

There was a future for her here. Tees Shipping could operate out of Whitby. Its ship – ships? – sailing the river, tying up at quays teeming with dockers unloading and loading cargoes, bringing wealth to her, to the shareholders, to Whitby. But would it mean the same if it was not shared with David and Luke, with Sean and Eileen?

She could savour her revenge and stand alone. She was strong enough. She needed no one. She wanted to drive her uncle to his final humiliation and watch him evicted from Saint Hilda's Terrace. But would she regret that when she subsequently faced life without the man she loved?

She glanced down at the waters again. She could end it all. Mesmerised, her hands tightened on the rail. She paused. A long pause. Her grip relaxed and she turned away to walk slowly from the bridge.

Her mind was still unfocused. It turned this way and that, so that she did not know the direction she was taking. But someone had been leading her by the hand for when she stopped she was before a row of houses. St Hilda's Terrace. She could see number twenty-one from where she stood.

Memories came flooding back with such

poignancy they brought tears to her eyes. Why should Uncle Nathan have it? Why shouldn't she step across the threshold once more, knowing that those memories could be translated into happy times again?

The house was hers. She had the deeds to prove it. All that was needed was to evict her uncle. She started to turn away, ready to retrace her steps to the office in Church Street and exact the final penalty.

Just at that moment she heard laughter and voices. She stopped and looked back. Isobel, Christopher and her aunt had just come out of the house. Their laughter rang with happiness and it seemed to her that the house approved. They would know nothing of the recent dramas that threatened their lives. If she took her revenge their future could be marred forever or even destroyed. And would the house know happiness then?

Before her aunt and cousins could reach the gate and turn in her direction, she hurried away.

David was anxious. The minutes had ticked away. The atmosphere in Nathan's office was taut. Maybe they were wrong in thinking that Lydia would return. But the drama could not be concluded anywhere else. Whatever she decided, she would have to face her uncle again. Unless... David had dismissed that thought once but now it had returned. He shouldn't have let her go.

As they waited, conversation was uneasy. Luke and Nathan were hostile to one another but held back from open confrontation.

David felt he should do something, but what? Where was Lydia? Finally he could bear the suspense no longer. He left without a word and paused outside. What good could he do? If he went in search of her he might be looking in the wrong place, and then if she returned he would not be there.

He paced up and down, ignoring the people who passed, searching for a sight of Lydia. A long fifteen minutes later his terrible musing on what might have happened was banished forever in a surge of relief.

'Lydia!' He was beside her instantly, taking her hands in his. 'Are you all right?' The words were inadequate, his eyes searching for a deeper answer.

She nodded in reply to the surface query, but he had seen in her eyes the answer he had longed for.

He grasped her shoulders and looked at her with all the love in his heart. 'I love you,' he whispered. 'Marry me?'

Unable to speak, she nodded again and there was joy behind her tears.

He kissed her and held her close, ignoring the glances of passers-by, some curious, some shocked and disapproving, others pleased at seeing romance.

'I must see my uncle,' she said.

He did not comment or enquire but kissed her again and led her by the hand to her uncle's office.

She looked around everyone and saw relief on their faces.

'I'm sorry. Can we take up as if this never happened?'

Luke gave his sister a hug. Sean's and Eileen's kisses told her that they too had already forgotten the Lydia they had not liked.

She dabbed tears from her eyes. 'Please, will you all leave me with my uncle?' They looked doubtful, fearing what she might do. 'Please,' she begged. 'Everything will be all right.'

When the door closed, leaving niece and uncle facing each other, there was a tense silence. Then they both spoke together. They stopped and Nathan gave a little bow.

'Uncle Nathan, I have carried hatred in my heart for you since Father died and you turned us out of the house. That made me seek revenge. I should never have allowed that to dominate my life, I see now I was wrong, though it will take some time still for me to forget the part I believe you played in his death. But I hope you can forgive any hurt I have caused you in return?'

He held up his hand, a signal to let him speak but also a gesture of forgiveness. 'You have done me less harm than I did you. I will regret to my dying day that I did not help Tristram when he came to me, but believe me, I had no idea what the outcome would be. If I was the cause of his heart attack then I am genuinely sorry. If you and Luke can find it in your hearts to forgive me, I ask no more.'

'That may take time.'

'I'll wait. When do you want to move into the house?'

'If I am to marry David, I shall not need it.'

461

'What about Luke? He'll want it.'

'I am sure he will agree with the decision I have made, and I have no doubt he will be able to look after himself.' She held up the deeds and dropped them on the desk. 'These are for my aunt and cousins. I have no doubt they were ignorant of your part in my father's death.'

'But I can't repay you.'

'They are yours. Just see that the house remains in the Middleton family.'

'Have no fear, it will.'

'That is some comfort.'

She started for the door but Nathan's words stopped her. 'Your father and grandfather would have been proud of you. You might like to know that I bought the family heirloom.'

'My piano!' Anger that he should possess it began to seethe inside her, despite her resolution to put this all behind her.

It faded when he added, 'You shall have it as my gift to you when you marry David.'

The publishers hope that this book has given you enjoyable reading. Large Print Books are especially designed to be as easy to see and hold as possible. If you wish a complete list of our books please ask at your local library or write directly to:

Magna Large Print Books
Magna House, Long Preston,
Skipton, North Yorkshire.
BD23 4ND

This Large Print Book for the partially sighted, who cannot read normal print, is published under the auspices of

THE ULVERSCROFT FOUNDATION